From

The Women's Press Ltd
34 Great Sutton Street, London EC1V 0DX

Wandsworth

BASEMENT STOCK

1 4
1 4 JUN 2000

27. JUL 0

- 9 AUG 2010

4.12.10

2 0 DEC 2010

WHL

West Hill Library
West Hill London SW18 1RZ
Telephone 020 8871 6386

THIS BOOK SHOULD BE RETURNED ON OR BEFORE
THE LATEST DATE SHOWN ON THIS LABEL.

L.211 (rev.3.2000.)

D0258369

Joan Barfoot is a Canadian writer and journalist who lives in London, Ontario. She is author of three previous novels, all published in Great Britain by The Women's Press: *Gaining Ground* (1980), *Dancing in the Dark* (1982) and *Duet For Three* (1986).

Joan Barfoot

Family News

The Women's Press

WANDSWORTH LIBRARY SERVICE

First published in Great Britain by
The Women's Press Limited 1990
A member of the Namara Group
34, Great Sutton Street, London EC1V 0DX

Copyright © Joan Barfoot 1989
Published in Canada by Macmillan of Canada 1989
A Division of Canada Publishing Corporation

All rights reserved.

British Library Cataloguing in Publication Data
Barfoot, Joan
   Family news.
   I. Title
   813.54 [F]

   ISBN 0–7043–4222–7

Printed and bound in Great Britain by
Cox & Wyman,
Reading, Berks

100632908

BURIED SISTERS

Two elderly sisters whose collection of newspapers almost filled their small home are in stable condition in hospital after a tunnel through the papers collapsed, trapping them for several hours Saturday.

Police said Eva Collins, 82, and her sister, Margaret Wentworth, 79, had thousands of papers dating back to the 1960s in the semi-detached home they shared on Roderland Road.

"They were piled nearly to the ceiling," according to Sergeant Alex Dungannon, who said the sisters had apparently devised a series of tunnels through which they could move on hands and knees to various rooms.

The women were headed from their living room to the kitchen Saturday when the passage they were using gave way, he said.

The collapse "sounded like an avalanche, like the whole house was coming down," said neighbor Tim Francis, who occupies the other side of the house. Francis rushed next door, but was unable to reach the women.

It took fire department and police officials several hours to rescue them, working through precarious piles of newspapers.

"There were tons of them," said Dungannon. "It may sound funny now, but it was a dangerous situation."

Neighbors said the sisters seemed friendly and normal when they encountered them outdoors, but they knew of no one who had been invited inside the home.

A hospital official said the women suffered a variety of injuries, none of them life-threatening. "They're both pretty tough, I guess," she said.

Well heavens, Susannah would have done a better job than *that* on such a story. Imagine!

Susannah would have gone to the house and described it herself. She would have hunted around for family members, talked to the neighborhood grocer, the pharmacist, certainly whoever delivered their newspapers, filling in the corners of the story: how often did the sisters go out, what did they talk about, did they seem to get along, how did they dress, were they thin or fat, friendly or gruff, what did they buy, what were their routines—Susannah could have built a life for them with words.

Then she might have found out what happened to them later. Even now she wonders, although the clipping is years old, and by now they're likely dead, of old age if nothing else.

At the time, though, some useful person would have cleared out the house—maybe a demolition crew, or Boy Scouts thrilled by such a paper treasure. In any case, everything the sisters had built—no doubt with great care, but obviously not enough care — would have vanished by the time they were released from hospital. What would it have meant to them to return to their house and see the true size of its rooms, forgotten shades of wallpaper and paint, the shapes of baseboards and windows? Would they be distressed by so much space and light and openness, which they might regard as emptiness?

How many years did they spend erecting internal walls with newsprint? Whose idea was it, and how did it begin? Maybe just the same careless way Susannah leaves things lying around, heaps of papers here and there, until the cleaning woman comes and does something about them. If Susannah had no cleaning woman, would she and Lizzie be resorting to tunnels through rubble by now?

You'd think somebody would have known. You'd think some family member, however distantly related, might have dropped by just once or twice in thirty years (although why Susannah would imagine that, given her own experience of families, must be only wishful thinking).

Perhaps the sisters found it sufficient to have their papers and each other. Rather pleasant, in a way, to share an obsession with a sister. To share anything with a sister, besides an ancient history.

Stories like this don't seem to come along any more. Younger generations (with the exception, apparently, of Lizzie) don't court death or entrapment by keeping too much information around for too long. Information isn't so precious now—maybe there's too much of it, really, exhausting amounts; madness to pile it up around the house. Even Lizzie has had the sense to keep only particular stories, not whole newspapers. Even so, she must have enough of these boxes and scrapbooks and envelopes of clippings to create a fire hazard; one she has apparently decided to shift from her own room into Susannah's office, where clippings now lie scattered across the floor, the windowsill, even the desk. Stray stories fall free, slipping under chairs or fluttering behind bookshelves. Susannah finds her attention caught by random headlines, and gets less work done than usual.

At least Lizzie has shown some judgment, a fine discrimination. These stories *are* interesting. Even in flat newspaper words they hint at astonishing worlds of sentiment and circumstance. At least if Lizzie was intent on collecting something, it didn't turn out to be silly or irrelevant, like rubber bands or string.

Still. Once when Lizzie was a baby, howling and howling in the middle of the night, a desperate Susannah almost threw her at a wall. "The point," Frannie said later, firmly, "is whether you did it or not, and you didn't." Recently, though, Susannah has sometimes felt brutality creeping back, a periodic urge to shout at Lizzie, or to shake her. For no good reason. Really, it would be too stupid to manage quite well, on the whole, for thirteen years, and then to fall apart in the adolescent stretch.

It's just that every change, every step of Lizzie's causes a tremor in this house. Crystal rattles on the shelves, and the sturdy wooden floors heave beneath Susannah's feet.

What it is is that rare emotion, fear, creeping up on her. It's not a feeling she's accustomed to, and in a way it's the fear itself that has started to be frightening.

Oh, but this home has very strong arms, after all. She was a child in a frame house in a windy maritime town, and it never felt solid enough. So like the smartest of the three little pigs, she has gone in as a grown-up for brick.

She has done a number of quite brave things, really, and there's no reason to suppose she won't again.

She left that town, having assessed it in a chilly sort of way for nineteen years and found it wanting. She came hundreds of miles to this city, all on her own, and has only occasionally found it wanting. She learned, in her first few years here, all the vices she'd been especially interested in: drinking, smoking up, and getting laid. In all the confusion she found Teddy and then managed to lose him (or he managed finally to shake her off his trail). Her heart was, if not broken, at least toughened, like the kind her mother used to bake, leathery brown-red things stuffed with onions and bread crumbs, for lunch. She bought this house, very smart if not necessarily courageous. But a sturdy brick house, nearly downtown — better these days than gold!

And then Lizzie, her bravest act (although she did not, of course, realize how brave. It doesn't matter, she would have done it anyway, so it still counts.)

Lizzie's thirteen years old, though. Surely Susannah's done something else that's huge, in thirteen years?

Well, she's brought up a child, hasn't she? No small matter.

Here she sits, on this overcast late-spring morning, in her sturdy valuable home, in her office with its uncurtained wood-framed windows and shelves of books, at her old oak desk, and what she's really doing is putting off work. This is nothing else than a sort of pre-partum depression: the gloom before the beginning. She's supposed to be doing the piece on Ida Lovender, that worthy and surprising *Aura* woman of the year, but she hasn't yet chosen the thread she will use to track her way through it, much less the words with which she will begin it. So she indulges in — what? self-pity, perhaps? Meanwhile her eye wanders, so that she is struck by what has struck her daughter.

Who would have dreamed that when Susannah started a four-year-old at clipping and pasting, it would lead to all this? She was a modern mother, in more ways than one; how could she have guessed, as she praised herself for this inspired bit of creative maternity, that Lizzie had such potential for intensity?

Lizzie's job was to look carefully through papers and magazines and cut around any stories with Susannah's name above them. Then she was to paste them (using not too much glue) into a special scrapbook. How sweet she looked then, her dark head bent over newspapers spread out on the floor, the tip of her tongue poking between her teeth and little lines forming between her eyes as she conscientiously sliced around the boundaries of her mother's work. At the time, though, Susannah's name was about all Lizzie could read. Later she began cutting more and keeping more; small stories often, the ones that got tucked away in awkward corners of a page just to fill a space, or odd ones that left a puzzled taste in the mind. By the time Susannah noticed that this was a larger business than she'd intended, there was no stopping the child. And no real reason to, anyway.

Kids don't read any more. They may not even care about stories or events. Shouldn't she be glad hers does?

Possibly Lizzie has leaned toward a certain type of story because she began by watching for her mother's pieces. Many of the stories Lizzie has kept are ones Susannah might have written, except that, as in the case of the two entombed sisters, she would have done a better job. Susannah, whose early ambition was to be a war correspondent (or, in the unlikely event there were no wars, a foreign correspondent), has instead made a career of a different sort of battle reportage: dispatches from the field of domestic flare-ups; rumors from the front lines of distress.

Anyway, it's all a war of one sort or another, with civilians almost always the most dreadfully wounded; like Ida Lovender, or even herself, although there's really no comparison between Ida's first family and her own. Entirely different categories of cruelty: the difference between visible and invisible scars.

Oh, no. No amount of self-pity, or mere desire to put off getting down to work, is going to put her in mind of those people. If they have no business in her life, they certainly have no business in her head, that's something she's been strict about (more or less). Let people like Frannie indulge in nostalgia: fond backward looks, periodic rosy glimpses of being a child, or angry ones. Let Teddy, too, pick over his memories, as he did for days when his parents died, as if that could make them mean something new and wonderful, or at any rate alive. For Frannie and Teddy, for most people, likely, nostalgia is harmless, but not for Susannah. If she were to set out these days on some trek into past events it would not be a matter of sentiment, but of checking her ability to remember, keeping tabs on the details of her history, making sure, really, that not too many brain cells are being lost.

Like Ida, she has made herself another family. Most families are small these days, after all. Some of this may have to do with economics, but surely also with desires.

Obviously she isn't doing well this morning; with her work, she means. She can hear Lizzie trotting around the house, getting ready for school. It might be better to go back to the kitchen for another coffee, wait till Lizzie has left before she gets down to business with the Lovender piece. Once she's figured out how to start it, she'll get it done in a day or so; savoring, meanwhile, the pleasure of breaking the news to *Aura*'s new editor, Bobbi Coxwell, about what her cover's going to look like.

"I look at this face in the mirror some mornings," Ida said, grinning, in the downtown coffee shop where they met two days ago, "and I think, I never would have had this life without this face. Such a lot I owe my first husband!" It seemed to Susannah a point of view that was both kind and vicious.

Ambivalence, though, has no place in this annual woman-of-the-year assignment. If Susannah had learned that Ida Lovender was a thief, a fraud, or merely a snotty white goddess descending daintily from her suburb to help people less fortunate than herself, she would still have had to find a way to look on the bright side.

A surprise, in a way, to find herself surprised. Like that cliche, when people learn how she makes her living: "You must meet such interesting people." Well yes, sometimes, but not all that often. Or she meets people in distressing circumstances, or when they are being someone they aren't, really. "What will you say?" Ida asked as they were saying goodbye at the end of their day. "How will you write this?"

"As well as I can. It'll be fine, don't worry." Susannah has years of experience in putting sincerity in her voice. Sometimes it's even sincere sincerity.

Ah, sometimes she finds herself fairly appalling; but funny.

Odd, what strikes people as funny. Ida laughed at the idea of her first husband, stopped in his tracks by the magazine cover, captured by his contribution to her success. But Susannah doubts Ida's children would appreciate her gratitude to him for her new and altogether improved life. "That's not funny, Mother," they might say in the same affronted tone Lizzie uses when she is unable to take the long view.

Kids haven't had enough years to find many events amusing. It takes time to stand back and laugh. Of course, a lot of grown-ups aren't easily amused, either. Years ago Susannah's father used to ask, "Isn't it time you stopped fooling around and settled down and had a family?" As if the life she had wasn't quite real and was certainly not important; as if she were just marking time in a frivolous sort of way before hunkering down to her destiny.

Her mother sighed, said, "We would so like grandchildren."

As if Elaine's sons named, peculiarly, Mark and Anthony, didn't count.

Okay, but did they laugh or even smile when, for reasons that had nothing (she thought) to do with them, she announced their prayers would be answered, their dreams fulfilled? Not at all; they fell apart.

No accounting, then, for what will tickle people.

She would have thought Lizzie might tickle them, but they'll never know.

When Lizzie was born, Susannah lay in her hospital bed, holding the baby in the crook of her arm, feeling triumphant and scared and also sad for one thing and another. "Poor little thing," she said, "what a silly, tiny family you're going to have. Just you and me, really." What must it be like to come into the world with no background, a whole history wiped out?

But they have managed. They have made a family. Frannie is a sort of honorary aunt, an auxiliary sister, and Lizzie has Teddy, too, of course, as an unpaternal kind of father. Anyway, family can be any damn thing Susannah wants it to be.

She sees, looking out the kitchen window, splashes of husky late dandelions she ought to be dealing with. When Lizzie was little, she picked dandelions for Susannah, arranging them in small vases here and there around the house. Now Susannah, no gardener herself, buys cut flowers, in this season daffodils and tulips, freesias for scent. There is no more reason to do without flowers than there is to do without food, both ways of taking care. There are storm clouds to the north, which is just as well. Rain will keep her at her desk. "Take your raincoat instead of a sweater," she says as Lizzie goes tearing by half-dressed, in white slacks and little child bra.

She can hardly blame Lizzie for that flash of irritation — she sounded just like her own mother then. Susannah can no longer remember her mother's voice, only certain words, and even that is eerie and awful, if happily rare.

"Sorry, honey." That didn't sound anything like her mother.

Really, Lizzie's a good kid. As it's turned out, they've done pretty well, and just the dangerous years to go.

In five more years, Lizzie will leave home and Susannah's family, not large to begin with, will undergo another of its periodic shiftings and shrinkings. But she'll be free again then: to work less, to travel, even, if she wants, to fly as high as Frannie, who got home Tuesday from a holiday in Paris and leaves tomorrow for Vancouver to cover a political convention. Frannie's family is small and odd, too. She was raised by her mother and her grandmother. A few years ago she tracked down the man she likes to call "my long and well-lost father," returning disappointed that he wasn't the glamorous figure she'd imagined. "At least I know now," she'd said, and it did seem that it was mainly her curiosity that had needed satisfaction.

Another case of futile nostalgia. And Susannah has no words on the subject of fathers.

What she should have are words on the subject of Ida Lovender. God, didn't it used to be easier to get her work done? Back in the days when she had a real job with real hours, do or die, first sentences were surely not so difficult to come up with, were they? That's another brave thing she did once, that she left off her list: she quit her job, before she had Lizzie. She was throwing out everything, starting again. She got heavier and heavier, but felt lighter and lighter.

How on earth did she dare? Who was the girl, and then the young woman, who set out so blindly on these new adventures (and occasionally horrors) every day? Not the growing-up Susannah, who was watchful and grumpy, and not the one she is now, either, the good-as-she-can-manage mother, the brisk writer-down of the events of other people. Someone else; but whoever, she's not so bad, is she? Not a bad person at all, if somewhat overindulged. Selfish, perhaps, but at least with the grace to know that.

In those days she really did believe, too, that words might alter: that describing a situation, a hardship, even a tragedy, could cause it to be repaired. She thought that with words, it should be possible to make people see, and feel, and then correct.

She must still believe that, in a way.

Maybe she just doesn't write well enough.

What words can she write that would make any difference to Ida Lovender? Except for making her briefly known, of course, those famous fifteen minutes of glory.

Cynical. The truth is, Susannah loves Lizzie and words. She loves to touch her daughter's shoulder, or her hair, and she loves to press her fingers down on keys and watch explaining words spring up. That's really no small success, is it, at the age of forty-three, to have two objects of love?

It's just that sustaining love requires some return. People don't simply toss it into a vacuum; or if they do, they shouldn't. There are plenty of returns from words: money, praise, occasional prizes, and more assignments. All very well. But the part that involves actual love is working and working over a piece until it says almost what she wants it to. Never perfect, of course (she imagines that doing something perfectly would be like dreaming her own death), but coming close, which is what will eventually happen with Ida Lovender. It's just a matter of getting down to it.

Remember when Lizzie was little? The sensuality of having a kid? That was a surprise, although perhaps it shouldn't have been. The intensity: not just when she was a baby, when Susannah might have expected delight (as well as terror) in such soft helplessness, but even more when Lizzie was old enough to wrap her arms casually and full-heartedly around Susannah, that compliment of joy and need. Love, really. An adult's embrace has so much history, and different sorts of need.

One of these years, Lizzie is going to be an adult, too, and the intent of her embraces may be different. There is more and more mystery about her these days. Those clippings, what on earth does she mean by them, and by setting them out so unavoidably in Susannah's view? What does she want?

They seem to indicate a taste for the weird. Quirky stories about quirky situations, quirky people; in some instances down-right morbid. Certainly Lizzie has curiosity, the greatest gift, and a willing imagination, and possibly even further virtues, such as empathy. That may all be true, but what really rises like steam from those pools of paper is some kind of yearning. As if Lizzie were a blind child, groping through those bits of lives for something huge.

When Susannah was Lizzie's age, her longings were enormous. She wanted, mainly, to be gone. All those rules and standards, apparently freestanding, nothing visible holding them up — she couldn't understand the reasons for them. Was she such a rational child, then?

It's hard to imagine that there might be children who don't want to leave their homes. Not just their homes, but the entire place that formed them. She can't quite picture not longing to become another person in another place — how could anyone resist?

Which is stupid, since now what she dreads is Lizzie longing to leave. Perhaps it doesn't happen, though, to children raised in the great rich variety of cities, where only space is missing. Where on earth would Lizzie run to?

She runs into stories, it seems: all these stories scattered across Susannah's office, terrible samplings of family grisliness. What does it mean?

Frannie, an altogether brisker person, impatient with even minor mysteries, would probably just ask. "What the hell is this all about?" she'd demand of Lizzie. Sometimes Frannie's bluntness gets her answers Susannah would not have dreamed of. Also, though, on occasion Frannie misses things by trying to go too swiftly to the heart of a matter.

They have been friends for almost twenty years. People need best friends; well, women do. Men, even if they need them, don't often seem to have them. Men have buddies, guys to hang out with. Isn't that odd? Their problem, though, not her concern.

Partly what she and Frannie have in common is a profession, but with such a difference in approach! Susannah, specializing in the domestic, has written much more terrible tales than Frannie. She has squatted outside a tent in a green ravine, sharing doughnut-shop coffees with a grimly cheerful, middle-aged woman who grinned and said that at any rate she had simplified herself to the essentials, which was comforting in its way because not so many people knew just what was essential. No, she had no husband, he had died. Yes, she had children, and even grand-children, she believed, but had no idea where they were. It seemed tragic to Susannah at the time. She couldn't imagine the abandonment involved, or even how the woman could survive the cold fall nights. She may have misunderstood, however.

In a public-housing development she walked through an obscenely graffitied lobby and rode an elevator, alone except for a tidy heap of human shit in one back corner, to the apartment of a mother of three children, who just a year before had lived in a large suburban house with her large suburban husband and a large suburban dog. Her husband had had large suburban fists, and finally she left, taking with her only her children and a set of silverware. Like finding her house was on fire, making quick choices, she grabbed what seemed important, and wound up with a trio of hungry teenagers and a felt-lined wooden box of Rogers sterling.

Once Susannah sat in the darkened living room of a woman whose sister and five nieces and nephews had been shot by her brother-in-law. A whole family dead. "My sister," the woman said over and over, shaking her head, showing Susannah the family photo album. "All the babies." Well, she was in shock. Susannah's job was not just to get a story, but the photo album, too, so that pictures of the dead and formerly smiling family could be lifted from it; also so no other newspaper could get its hands on it, a battle conducted so that readers could look at the pictures of dead folk over morning toast and coffee and enjoy a shiver of satisfaction that, unlike some unlucky others, they'd gotten through the night unscathed. Susannah did her soldier's job, but sent the album back to the woman by taxi. She didn't want to be looked at. What contempt she might see!

She did what was expected. A Nuremberg defense.

Frannie, on the other hand, moves in political circles, where tragedies are both more distant and more publicly compelling.

A national candidate who slips into scandal may be sad enough, but it's not the same as seeing a sister mourn a sister.

Susannah seems to have sisters much on her mind today. This will not do.

The question of the moment is, what is the difference between Ida Lovender's injuries — not the comforts of her life but her injuries — and those of a woman in, say, Lebanon, trapped in the crossfire?

Of course, Ida gets to be on the cover of a national women's magazine.

On paper, in the news release that will go out when she's officially named *Aura* woman of the year, Ida sounds serious and well-intentioned and tediously virtuous. The release says she was chosen because "she represents the commitment of ordinary women to causes affecting ordinary women." Forty-two, married to a physics professor, mother of four, including twins, cofounder of a shelter for abused women and "active lobbyist at all levels of government for improvements in welfare, health, and employment policies as they affect women."

Susannah detected Bobbi's hand in the choice and in the news release. "In other years," it said, "the award has generally gone to high-profile women whose activities tended to be on the national level. A few times, it's even gone to a woman known mainly for her spouse's achievements. This time, however, *Aura* has decided to honor one of the unsung heroines who has worked hard and quietly behind the scenes for concrete achievements on behalf of women in their communities." Trust Bobbi to attempt the unusual but express the result in cliché. "Unsung heroines," for God's sake.

No need, though, to have worried about having to portray unblemished goodness. When Ida rose to greet her in the coffee shop, Susannah's first thought was, "Jesus, that can't be her." Her second was that Bobbi was going to shit when she found out.

The woman moving toward her, hand outstretched, smiling, was grotesque: one side of her face purple and patched, skin puckered, the eye on that side squinting. The wound was too massive for a birthmark and too ingrained to be temporary. This was the face that was to appear on the cover of *Aura*, intended to sell thousands and thousands of copies? Good lord.

"It's all right," Ida said, "I'm used to it." Something odd flickered across the mobile side of her face. "Well, no, that's stupid, I'm not used to it. I just can't do anything about it."

Susannah prefers to resist as much as possible the idea that there are some things nothing can be done about; but of course there are circumstances in which it is dreadfully true.

"I'm off." Lizzie pauses in her morning rush to bend to kiss Susannah's cheek. More and more this will be the case: she will be off to new places.

"Have a good day. Are you walking or taking your bike?"

"Bike. I'm meeting Megan."

"Be careful, then." If Susannah had her real deep-down wish, she'd keep her daughter chained up safely in the backyard or her room. Too many dangers: speeding cars, young bodies found in freezers, awful stuff. "See you later." She will hope.

Lizzie has a tiny pink pimple under her nose. Two months ago she had her first period. It's a shame there's no appropriate ritual for the event, no custom corresponding to, say, a bat mitzvah or a debutante's coming-out party or, in another sort of society, a separation of the females from the males, in darkness, for a private initiation involving mutilation. Well, not *that*, of course, but something to mark the event. "That's terrific, honey," she'd told Lizzie, because she did want Lizzie to be pleased. Times, thank heaven, have changed, and Susannah has been careful to be as different as she can be from her mother. Still, Lizzie's period was another signal of tremblings ahead.

She doesn't imagine her own mother felt anything like that, anything ominous. She seemed only concerned with keeping it private, clearly a nasty secret. Well, it wasn't necessarily a joy, but surely such an ordinary matter! Whatever was the point of dealing with it in whispers and plain paper bags and supplies tucked into the backs of closets? Even Elaine didn't discuss it. Susannah was so proud of herself, she carried a packet of Midol to the dinner table, laying it beside her plate until her mother, with a sucked-in breath, whisked it away.

Susannah has intended Lizzie's whole life to be different, and it has been. Only, it means that sometimes Susannah has no way of knowing her, and she has nobody, really, to ask except Lizzie herself. She can do that, of course. Unlike herself, Lizzie isn't a very secretive child.

Back when she told Frannie she planned to have a baby, Frannie only shrugged. "It's up to you. Go for it, if you want to." (And this was before Susannah'd even told Teddy — how sure she was!) "I can see why, and it's terrific if you're sure. I have to tell you, though, don't count on me going halvsies. I may volunteer to help sometimes, but if I wanted kids, I'd have them myself. I don't think I'm suited to motherhood, though. Not being suited to motherhood runs in my family."

Susannah wasn't sure it ran in hers, either, but there it was, the idea, lodged in her head like a pebble. It grew into a vision, even crept into her dreams, so that she woke up feeling empty-armed because in her sleep she'd been holding something.

Perhaps when she called it a whim, Elaine wasn't far wrong. Except Susannah has metallic whims.

She thought it was because she hated to miss anything, and could imagine regrets when it was much too late. Her house seemed silent; she imagined footsteps and the sounds of voices, plates and spoons, children's music, reading books out loud. Well, crying, too, and yelling sometimes, not altogether happy sounds. She is no romantic, after all.

Mainly she is curious. She wants to know this, hear that, ask rude questions, grasp people by their lapels and insist, or sit politely beside them, seeking answers in a gentle voice. What is it she keeps hoping to find out? Anyway, she wanted to know about having a child, that was mainly it.

In the hospital, holding the tiny Lizzie, still damp, eyes tightly closed, tiny mouth pursed, sparse strands of dark hair curled across her scalp, Susannah was stricken by reality. This was no matter of asking a question, getting an answer, and going on to the next thing. To have made this creature who did not exist before and wouldn't have existed without Susannah's imagination and her will was so amazing her heart filled up. To have made this creature who might not continue to exist if Susannah made the smallest error—what could be more terrifying?

She hadn't quite expected that. Love, she supposed.

She also hadn't known precisely what being alone meant in these circumstances. Home from hospital with Lizzie, she kept watch in the night, Lizzie's crib in her room, a chair drawn up beside it. She leaned forward in the darkness to hear her daughter's breath.

So many fears. What if she dropped the baby, bathing her? What if she failed to feed her right, or poisoned her with some food that was off, or that her tiny system wasn't ready for? What if she stuck a clumsy finger through that soft pulsing bare spot on her head? She felt, really for the first time in her life, as if she might be stupid after all.

Just going to the supermarket or the bank became an expedition, and arranging day care and baby-sitters when she had an assignment was complicated and unnerving. How could she judge who to trust? Her beautiful, calm brick home was turned ass-over-teakettle by baby stuff, baby needs, baby time, a creature irritated by the sound of typing who might howl in the middle of a paragraph.

Even so, it was never precisely regret that she felt. More surprise at what she'd done.

None of that, of course, is in the story she's told Lizzie. For Lizzie, she's made it into something like magic, a matter of a desired child brought to life. Which is true enough; just not complete. The truest part may be that Susannah wanted everything and saw no reason not to have it.

It's an amazing thing, growing up in a generation in which everything seemed not only possible but necessary. Poor kids now (even Lizzie?) are much more frightened, and possibly duller, too, as a result. But when Susannah was young, there was that potent mix of rage and hope, sometimes confused with love but really a kind of faith that situations, possibilities, events could be changed for the better. That the nature of the beast itself could be improved. How sure and righteous and obnoxious they no doubt were, Susannah and the rest. But sweet, too. Expectant. Powerful with certainty.

It's the fashion now to sneer at all that, an entire decade of silly girls in transparent dresses sticking daisies into the barrels of guns, and young men like Teddy on the barricades of their own soaring voices. They thought they had discovered a new world, but it turned out only to be one that didn't survive. Maybe people sneer now because they're afraid of what was so apparent in those years. Or because they're mourning it; like making jokes at a funeral.

Susannah felt like a flower herself then, just opening up from the long maritime frost. And she still believes, although in a tougher way. Just like Teddy: still keeping steely hopes.

Lucky Teddy, who has maintained his outrage and also his hormones all this time, marching and demonstrating and carrying placards in the same staunch, unflinching, sweet, and hopeful way he did twenty years ago, and no doubt still pursuing women in the same spirit.

God, she's now old enough to remember herself as an adult twenty years ago!

And she can remember Teddy, too. How pleasingly circular it felt fourteen years ago, creating something with him, bringing her life neatly around on itself with him, after a separation of some years. Now he's forty-five and his body, like hers, is settling somewhat, and he has speckles of gray in his hair, which is even thinning a little, but that doesn't mean she can't see the lean jeaned youth making earnest, outraged speeches, stirring people in the open air, stirring her in small rooms. He was a furious young man, and arrogant, but what a beauty he was! She knew his bones in those days, was familiar with the mole in the center of his back and the precise fine texture of his long dark hair and the desperation with which he curled himself around her when his parents died. He was twenty-one, and she was busy learning everything she could. Tracing his skin was a new world to her, his body her absorbing map.

But he was hopeless, too. She was never the only one who

knew his bones and textures, although she was very likely the only one who'd seen him weep. A good deal of crockery bit the dust between the two of them, particularly at the end. She shivered, her own body out of her control, and thought that breaking any other addiction, even heroin, could not be any harder. She had said, "Nobody will ever hurt me like this again," and meant it as some sort of threat, although it was hardly menacing from his point of view.

She was dazed for a long time. It was true that she was unable to give herself away like that again, but of course that was no bad lesson. It just took some getting used to.

Lizzie has his eyes.

She also has Susannah's dark curly hair, and her wide mouth, sturdy bones, broad shoulders. It's not quite clear yet what else she may have of theirs.

Oh, Susannah has such hopes for her! It really would be heartbreak, to have a child the opposite of what you'd hoped.

Teddy, whose target when she knew him was a specific war, now opposes war, period. His concerns are absolute and global. She supposes that's one reason he still feels young to her: that he has clung to his purity of purpose. Well, he's welcome to that; it's his impatience with other matters that is irritating. He says, for instance, that her concerns, which have more to do with how people might live than with how they could die, are merely trivial, and he implies that women in general (while fervently pursuing them himself) are slightly mad. "You've got everything backwards," he likes to say. "What difference does that shit make when we could all be blown up?"

It makes a difference to people like Ida Lovender, she might point out. It makes a difference to anybody just trying to get through the day.

It's past time to start getting through her own day. It has begun to rain, just gently so far, and the house is otherwise silent. She has hours set aside, and a deadline to meet, money to make, a child to support, words to set down in just the right order and rhythm to create Ida Lovender on the pages of *Aura*. If anyone gets past the cover.

Thousands will, no doubt. People like their bit of gore.

It feels a long way from the kitchen back to her office. Well, she's dawdling, isn't she, pausing at the small mirror in the dining room to pull her long hair off her face and out of the way—it needs cutting, too, although the gray streaks look good. There are lines beside her mouth and around her eyes. She can pinch a good deal more than an inch at her hips—love handles? Not likely, not any more. Thank God for good bones. She will never entirely collapse as long as they're holding her up, keeping her straight, if not exactly firm.

God, she's forty-three years old. In twenty years, she'll be sixty-three. Teddy will be sixty-five, Frannie sixty, and Lizzie, Jesus, Lizzie will be thirty-three and may have children of her own. Imagine being a grandmother. Or, even odder, Teddy as a grandfather.

Susannah's other family has missed Lizzie's entire life, their only female grandchild, Elaine's sole niece. Susannah has missed her parents growing old and her nephews growing up and Elaine growing into middle age. Oh, she could be angry, she could be furious.

Her mother used to say (but does she still?), "It could have been worse. Worse things have happened to other people, after all." Enraging, that she wouldn't just let herself feel badly for herself. But it was true, too: whatever happens, something worse has happened to someone else. One event occurred to Ida Lovender, another to Susannah. Some people's children die. There's really no comparison.

Some people don't have sturdy brick homes, or comfortable possessions, or work they're good at, or children who by and large please them. Some people don't have the guts to attempt difficult things on their own. Some people have plans for the next twenty or thirty years.

Some people also know how to get down to work. Where is that first sentence, the one that will make the whole Lovender piece fall into place?

Ah, she can always find words. Settled in her office finally, of course she gets them shifted into place, building them one by one into a tidy structure, an Ida monument of sorts. By midafternoon it's solid, with only the cleaning up and decorating still to do. Almost what she'd hoped for, nearly satisfying.

Really, it's a reassuring sort of process, building words. Just the opposite of those poor old sisters building painstakingly over years a tidy (if narrowed) structure of their own, then being injured by the results in a messy tumbling of precarious paper walls onto frail bones.

Even so, though — even so, they had something that seems enviable. Susannah has today her piece on Ida Lovender, a home with spacious rooms, and a child arriving soon from school; but still, it would be nice to have a proper sister. She may have reached a certain age, with certain blessings, but she has never been able to get it into her head that not everything is possible.

LIZZIE'S STORY

An 18-year-old Toronto woman accused of drowning her newborn infant in a toilet in her parents' home has been charged with murder.

Police said the body of the minutes-old child, a boy, was found by the woman's mother, who reported the incident. Neither the young woman nor her mother had been aware of the pregnancy, police said.

The 18-year-old was not identified by police, who described her as a college student. She is to appear in court Tuesday.

Lizzie has lots of longer clippings, but sometimes her favorites are like this one, short and strange; kind of a tease, because they leave out the most interesting parts.

Like for one thing, how can somebody not know she's pregnant? Lizzie's a whole five years younger, and she'd know. So would her mother, who doesn't miss much. It's hard to imagine those people. Would they have not known or not seen on purpose?

But say that part's true, and nobody knew, what was it like? That girl, was she alone in the house so nobody heard her, or was she too scared to make a sound? How weird and awful, all that pain and then a baby coming out of nowhere. How did she know what to do? She'd have to cut the cord to make it separate, and even Lizzie, with all she knows, might have trouble there.

Then she must have pulled herself out of bed. What was in her head, going stumbling to the bathroom, just wanting to make it disappear? But it's not like a dead goldfish or a pet lizard she's gotten tired of, it wouldn't just flush away. She must have gotten down on her knees and held it under the water. Then what? Did she go back to bed?

Imagine her mother going into the bathroom, glancing into the toilet, and there's her grandchild floating. Face up or down? Lizzie sees a small, bloated, blank face, wisps of baby hair rising in the water from the scalp, a tiny penis above the surface like a flag.

What could they have told the police, or each other?

And where was that girl's father? Maybe he was the kind of man who drowns kittens, giving his daughter the idea. Maybe he told her once that it isn't cruel or hard if it's done right away.

Then there's the baby. Probably it wouldn't know enough to have nightmares about disappearing, the way Lizzie sometimes dreams about being left alone. The worst nightmares aren't the ones about being chased by something horrible and not being able to move. The worst are when something gruesome happens to her mother or Teddy. After the kind where something's been after her she wakes up scared, but after the other kind she gets an awful, hopeless, lost feeling. When she was little she used to have to get out of her own bed and crawl in with her mother.

It probably wouldn't have been like that for that baby, though. It would only have known about struggling to be born, so it might just have figured this was more of the same, kicking and waving its arms and legs to breathe and stay afloat, and before it figured out that this time it was different, it was over. So maybe it wasn't so terrible after all, quick like kittens, no lie.

It sure is strange, what people do.

She could ask her mother about this, except she's a little

annoyed with her mother right now. How could Lizzie have taken all that paper downstairs from her bedroom, spread it out across her mother's office (which in another house might be a family room, except this family is too tiny to need a special space for itself) and not get asked about it? Her mother hasn't said a word except maybe with a funny look or a raised eyebrow. Lots of things her mother will talk about; like, she'd probably talk about that girl killing her baby. But she has secrets, too, or at least things she doesn't say. Wouldn't anybody else ask, "What's with this mess, Lizzie? I didn't know you kept all these stories. Why did you, and what are you bringing them down here for, anyway?" That kind of thing.

Lizzie didn't have anything to do last Saturday. Megan was spending the weekend with her father's new family, Lizzie's mother was shopping, Teddy hadn't asked her over to stay, Frannie was in Europe, and it was raining. "You could get your room cleaned up," her mother suggested on her way out. As if Lizzie was a little kid.

So she did clean up her room, didn't she? Gathered up arm-loads of scrapbooks and boxes and brown envelopes and dumped them all downstairs. Doing it was like not being a little kid any more, like getting her period. Clearing out kid stuff: all the hours she's spent reading and cutting and glueing and setting aside, and mainly wondering. It's the only way she finds out about a lot of stuff, since her own family is so small and doesn't do anything very exciting. Not while Lizzie's been around, anyway.

She thought her mother would come home and they'd put away the groceries and then her mother would wander into her office at the front of the house, maybe to do some work, and see all those clippings. She'd start to look through some of them, because they really are interesting, and she'd say something like, "Gee, Lizzie, look at this one," or Lizzie might pick out one and hand it to her and wait to see what she said about it. Maybe if she chose just the right one, her mother might let something important slip. There are so many mysteries. Like, what's wrong with her mother's other family, that she doesn't talk about them?

Lizzie knows they're not dead, like Teddy's, and that her mother has a sister, but that's all. Her mother says, "I really don't want to discuss them. Maybe later sometime, when you and I are both much older." Like it's a joke, except she's not really kidding. Now Lizzie *is* older, though.

She can make them up. She can make up all kinds of things: like the bears she believed lived in her closet when she was just little, that would creep out and eat her if she let her eyes close (except maybe she didn't really believe that, because it was fun in a way, being scared); or like different stuff about the people in the clippings. She imagines those people in her mother's family are maybe murderers, or thieves, or crazy, locked up in a loony bin, banging themselves against walls. Something awful, but interesting, too.

Compared with Lizzie's little family, Megan's is enormous. She's got parents and aunts and uncles and cousins and grandparents and even two stepsisters — her life is so crammed with people, Lizzie's amazed she has room for a friend. Megan lives with her mother and visits her father, same as Lizzie. Her mother doesn't have lovers, though, like Lizzie's mother does sometimes, and her father has another wife and other kids. When Megan goes home from her father's, her mother always asks about the other family, how they get along, what they do, what sort of things they own. "It's awful," Megan says, lip trembling. "She hates it if I tell her Daddy's fine, she wants to hear bad things. It makes me mad."

"Maybe it's because they used to be married," Lizzie has suggested. It's the only reason she can think of that Megan's parents don't get along and Lizzie's do. Lizzie's mother and Teddy are even friends, sort of, even if it's not the same way she and Megan are friends, or her mother and Frannie. Actually what they talk about most is Lizzie, and sometimes it feels as if she *is* their friendship, so she's in charge of it somehow.

Lizzie doesn't have to tell tales, the way Megan does. Teddy hardly ever asks about her mother, except maybe how she is. Not what she's doing, though. Her mother knows things about Teddy, but not because she asks Lizzie. Sometimes Lizzie tells her things that are interesting or upsetting; like about people they meet out on the streets at night, or the time Lizzie dropped in at his place one afternoon and saw a naked woman coming out of his bathroom. That was really embarrassing, especially for Teddy. "But why did you go in the first place?" her mother asked.

Lizzie'd just meant to surprise him, for fun, but it was an awful mistake. "I think he was really mad," she told her mother later. She'd thought he'd be working in the middle of the afternoon and wouldn't mind her stopping in. Afterward she figured out that even though Teddy always says he likes surprises, he probably doesn't, unless they're his.

"He isn't mad," her mother said. "He thinks you're upset, though. He called a while ago, before you got home." Even so, Lizzie wasn't comfortable with him for a while. Like he has all these things going on when she's not there, not exactly secrets, but things he does.

Her mother makes jokes about Teddy's women, but sometimes when she laughs it sounds like a man Lizzie saw on television once who could whistle two notes at the same time. One was the tune, and the other was a couple of tones below, so you could hear it, but it was sort of off key. That's something like how Lizzie's mother laughs about Teddy.

Maybe she *is* a bit like Megan's mother after all, except it comes out differently.

Lizzie herself plans to get married some day. She wants somebody, a husband, who'd know her really well. Who is he, and where is he right now, at this very minute? Maybe he's putting on his jacket for school, just like her, picking up his books, going out his front door. Maybe he's thinking about her, too, only not knowing who she is, either. When will they meet and how will it happen and how will it feel to kiss, and the other thing, too? She hopes he doesn't have a mustache, although a beard wouldn't be so bad. He'll be slim, and he'll probably have dark hair. Blond would be okay, but not red hair. They'll know right away that they're in love, as soon as they see each other. That means it isn't anybody she knows yet.

She isn't going to be like her mother or Frannie or Teddy and have one after another so that nobody's very important. It's different lately, but men used to be around her house all the time, and then they'd just disappear. Her mother's steps would get light and she'd laugh a lot and hug and cuddle more. Sometimes late at night Lizzie'd hear them from her room upstairs, talking or laughing or whispering. Then sometimes when Frannie came over Lizzie'd hear her mother and her giggling, and sometimes her mother cried.

The last one was Peter, but he hasn't been around for ages. He used to send a dozen roses every month, with a card saying what anniversary it was of his and her mother's first date. Lizzie didn't think anybody could help loving somebody who did that. Also he was fun to talk to, maybe because he had kids of his own, and he was a photographer so he and her mother had plenty of things to say, and he was really good-looking, considering he was her mother's age.

Then her mother came home one day cross about something, and said, "Oh, Jesus, roses again?" and pretty soon after that Peter wasn't coming around any more.

Right now Frannie has a friend named Alan, who's an architect, and they come to dinner at Lizzie's house sometimes, but the funny thing is how Frannie and her mother laugh about him sometimes when he isn't there.

Teddy's just Teddy. He says, "God, I love women," as if Lizzie isn't one, or isn't going to be one. Women are there one night and then they're gone. Well, sometimes one lasts longer but finally she won't be around and if Lizzie asks, Teddy says something like, "Oh, I don't know what happened to her, really." As if he'd lost her on the street somewhere. He's not like her mother and Frannie though, he doesn't cry, or laugh either, about that sort of thing. Of course Lizzie isn't with him all the time and maybe just hasn't seen him sad.

"Your family's neat," Megan says. It is, too; only small.

Of all the stories Lizzie's heard, read, and collected in those boxes and scrapbooks and big brown envelopes, of all the stories that have caught her eye or her ear or her curiosity, her favorite is still the one about her own self. It makes her warm, and tiny as a baby again, curled in her mother's lap, head on her mother's shoulder, feet propped against her mother's knees. Hands where? Clasped to her own throat or her mother's.

She likes words like "clasped." They can make stories feel huge.

It *is* a big story, though. Her mother was brave and had so much love; Lizzie owes her mother her life, in a way even Megan doesn't understand. It's because of being chosen. It's hard to stay even a little angry when you know a story like that about yourself.

Megan is already waiting at the sidewalk in front of her house when Lizzie rolls up this morning. She lives five blocks from Lizzie, and they have another three blocks to go to school, so their races aren't quite fair, since Lizzie has farther to go. Even so, she wins sometimes, and does today, pumping hard, just making the green light at the only busy intersection, swerving around a confused kindergarten kid, not slowing because she can hear Megan's bike chain clanking right behind.

The trouble is getting to school all sweaty. And she has a pimple under her nose that appeared the same time her period did but didn't go away when it did. Megan's really pretty. She's got bright red hair and freckles and huge blue eyes and the sort of white skin that's like a piece of shiny pottery. Lizzie doesn't know about herself. People point out the bits and pieces that are like other people: Teddy's eyes, her mother's nose, that kind of thing. Maybe she has parts of other people, too, but how would she know?

She'll probably be tall, since both Teddy and her mother are, and her hair is dark like theirs, although they've both got gray bits. It's curly, like her mother's, too. Which parts of them was she supposed to get, though, and which parts maybe came out the wrong way around from what her mother had in mind?

Megan is hardly ever clumsy, even when they're racing their bikes, tearing right up to the racks and then bearing down hard on their brakes, skidding on their fat balding tires. They tell each other almost everything and walk through the halls at school with their arms around each other.

Are they like other pairs of girlfriends, though, one beautiful, one plain?

Lizzie's mother sometimes says, "Ah, you're a lovely kid," but that's more if Lizzie does something smart, not if she's just looking smart.

Maybe she is pretty, though. She used to be, she's almost sure. When she was little and went to demonstrations with Teddy, she had a sign he'd made for her to carry. It was a picture of herself coming out of the center of a flower, an iris she thinks, with small lettering underneath that said, "I need time to grow up." Television cameras sometimes pointed at her and later, back at Teddy's, she got to watch herself on the news and see herself from the outside, and honestly, she was cute.

Now she wouldn't be so happy, being on the news. Kids would probably make fun of her. Sometimes she still goes with Teddy, but now she tries not to stand out. Anyway the demonstrations were more fun when she was younger; it was great seeing grown-ups shouting and wearing costumes, clownish Uncle Sams and skeleton outfits with skull masks. Like Halloween, only noisier and without treats.

Sometimes it's hard to know what Teddy's mad about. Sometimes it seems like everything.

It's funny, the differences between his place and her house. His is all light and bright, as if it might fly off the building it's in, and it has big windows and white walls and white and yellow furniture and a lot of glass in the tabletops and picture frames. Her house is all brick and wood, solid and heavy. If they had voices, his place would be high and her mother's house low, which seems like the wrong way around. Anyway, sometimes when he's in a funny mood, Lizzie thinks it maybe should be darker, or closer to the ground.

One time he was in a funny mood was at her tenth birthday party. Sometimes he forgets he's been invited to something and doesn't show up, and sometimes he shows up but gets loud and silly. At that party, though, he just sat back watching, making Lizzie nervous, staring at her friends' faces and expressions and how they moved and sat. A couple of weeks later, at his place, she saw what he'd done with it. Sometimes she has trouble understanding just what Teddy's paintings are about, but that one felt kind of cruel, herself and her friends on a canvas, not quite done. A few months later he took her to the opening of a show he was having at a gallery and there was her party, all finished. From across the room it looked like some kind of joke about the Last Supper, with Lizzie as Jesus in a yellow cotton dress. She wanted to cry, maybe, but Teddy had his hand on her shoulder and was introducing her to people and pointing out the painting. He can't have meant it to hurt her, she knows that, and he was proud of it, so she couldn't spoil that. She'd like to know what it meant, though.

Someday she's going to be really famous and important. She doesn't know how yet, but when it happens Teddy can do another picture of her, except it won't be sly, like that one. It won't look quite like her, because that isn't the kind of thing Teddy does, but it'll show who she really is and how much he loves her. Newspapers and magazines will run photographs of it, and maybe that will make him really famous, too.

Maybe her mother will write about her and also about Teddy's picture of her. Then they'd all be together, in a way.

Years and years ago, long before Lizzie was born, her mother and Teddy were together. That's a kind of magic part about her story — they were together when they were young, and then they weren't for a long time, and then they were again, to make her. Her mother's told her the story over and over, since she was little. It's so true, it has real things she can touch. If she opens the top left-hand drawer of the oak cabinet in the dining room, she finds two golden-yellow candle stubs, which wouldn't be around if the story was made up. Her mother does keep bits from her past around the house, but they're never silly bits that don't mean anything.

There's the dress, too, hanging all by itself in the upstairs guest-room closet. Lizzie used to open that closet door and stare at it, and it made her mouth fall open with faith. She *believes*. It's a sort of miracle, so what does that make her?

Her mother is so powerful. Who else could have made exactly what she wanted with just herself and Teddy, a dinner, and a black velvet dress? Her mother says, "You can want something, but that's not enough. You have to want it really badly and then you have to *do* something about it." Usually her voice is sort of low and peaceful, but when she talks like that it gets a queer hard sound.

"Teddy argued," she says. "I had a hard time persuading him. It took a while, but I'd made up my mind." As if that was the whole entire explanation. But then, Lizzie could see it likely *was* the whole entire explanation.

When Lizzie's mother tells the story, it's not the way she usually talks. It has a stiff sound that's almost a humming, like there's more to it than words. "I was about to be thirty," it begins. "I expect that seems very old to you, but it isn't, really." But it is! When Lizzie's thirty, she'll be doing whatever great thing she ends up doing, and when she's forty-three, which is how old her mother is now, her life will probably feel like it's nearly over.

"You start thinking then about what you've done and what you still want to do. I didn't want to miss anything important. But time runs out, and everything won't always be safe or possible."

That puzzled Lizzie until she found out her mother was only talking about bodies: that having children could get dangerous. If she'd waited till now, say, Lizzie could be born without arms or legs, or as one of those kids with huge heads like pumpkins. They're supposed to be particularly loving, those kids, but love doesn't keep them alive, and it's hard to know if they have any dreams, never mind big ones.

"So I decided what I didn't have was you. A Lizzie. The more I thought about it, the more deprived I felt, and I started to feel quite desperate and frantic. So the only thing to do was figure out how to get you." They might, when Lizzie was little, be rocking together, as close as if they were still in one body.

"I started thinking about the right man for the job. I was looking for certain qualities, but when it came to the point, it couldn't have been anyone but Teddy. For one thing, he's good-looking. I'd have loved you if you were as ugly as the seven sins, Lizzie, but I did think you might as well have a good chance at everything, including beauty.

"Then, too, there was how we were back when we were together, and then when we were splitting up. We threw dishes and terrible words at each other, and it was awful, but at least we were passionate, and I did want a passionate child. Also it meant he'd seen me at my worst. That may not sound like much of a connection, but it's nothing to be sneezed at. Even now there aren't many people who've seen me at my worst, even you.

"But really it was his contrariness that clinched it. I thought one way to tempt him might be by appealing to his sense of the outrageous, the not-done. These days it's maybe not so strange, but then it was—unusual. I suppose we were pioneers in a way, you and I," her mother says, although most of the time, Lizzie can't see what difference it makes.

"I think he was surprised when I invited him to celebrate my birthday with me, but I told him it was the sort of occasion that involved assessments as well as celebrations and that I was asking him because he was a sort of symbol of my past. I think he was flattered. It must be either flattering or insulting, to be regarded more as a symbol than a human being. He sounded relieved." Her mother laughs then, as if she's made a joke, but right afterward her hands get tight and she looks excited.

"Oh, Lizzie, I lay awake nights, planning and imagining: planning for him and imagining you. Leaping into something absolutely new and unpredictable." But if she could do that for Lizzie, could she do it for something else? What if she gets desperate again?

To get ready, she'd cleaned the whole house—windows, door frames, books, floors, shelves. "I wanted everything perfect, I wanted all the odds for perfection to be in my favor." So she wanted Lizzie to be perfect too. "And I planned Teddy's sort of meal, not mine. Steaks for strength and protein, and marinated vegetables, cauliflower and carrots and broccoli and beans, because they'd look bright on my china." Also expensive wines, red and white, "But not too much, I didn't want him drunk. And I had just candles for light, because dimness makes a sort of vacuum, it makes the world outside less real. It was like a romantic novel, except there was nothing romantic about it. But I wanted everything just right, so you'd be right too, and maybe that is romantic, after all."

Lizzie isn't sure exactly what romantic means, when her mother says it.

She wore her hair in a braid down her back, tied with a black velvet ribbon. And the dress, the long black velvet with no back and not much front, just its softness and her skin—she probably looked amazing. Pictures of her when Lizzie was a baby show her slimmer than now, with wide, straight shoulders and long hair that was dark and waved down her back. She looked taller than she does now, maybe because she's not so thin any more, but that night in that velvet dress she must have been sort of royal-looking.

"Naturally Teddy was terrified when he saw me. Still, he told me I looked great and said how much better looking I was at thirty than I'd been at twenty, which was sweet of him, but also true because people generally do look better when they've been lived in for a while." Lizzie doesn't see how that's really possible, except she does have hopes of improvement, herself.

"We had dinner and the wine, and by the time we got to dessert we were talking about birthdays and age and our past: what we'd wanted back when we were together and how close we'd come or how far away we still were. Of course, I wanted to talk about what we could still do. I told him changes and choices were always still possible, the same as they were when we were twenty. It was odd, hearing myself say that, because there's something childlike about it, and Teddy's always been the more childlike one." Sometimes Lizzie's mother sounds as if she never really liked Teddy very much.

"It was late. The candles were almost burned down and there was a lot of smoke, from them and from our cigarettes. We were nicely drunk, just a little. I said, 'You know, Teddy, the one thing neither of us has gotten around to yet is a child.' Not you, Lizzie, just a child, because Teddy can get scared when he has to look at something too directly. Anyway he said he'd have maybe liked a child, but he was no good at settling down and it was too late.

"I told him that was ridiculous, he was only thirty-two and it was never too late, not for a man, not the way it is for a woman. I took a deep breath and said, finally, 'So I have a proposition for you, Teddy.' I was so scared. I hate that feeling of having my life in somebody else's hands.

"Well, wasn't he shocked! But I waited and let the idea sink in. Finally I started talking about what a child of ours might be like, how she'd combine the best of us, and most of all how interesting she'd be. He's such a sucker for what's interesting. He said, sort of joking, 'But what if she — or he, it might be a he, Susannah — what if it combines the worst of us instead of the best?'

"I said that couldn't happen. And I really didn't believe it could.

"Then he got serious. He said, 'A kid's not a hobby, you know. It's not something you can quit doing if you get fed up.' I knew that. I do get bored with things and give them up, but I think that's why I had a craving for attachment then. He also talked about how expensive a child is, but of course I wasn't poor. I told him I could afford it, that you wouldn't go naked or hungry or be left alone. That was just his way of making sure he wouldn't be held responsible in any way, of course. I told him it was up to him whether he had anything to do with the child, and the responsibility and all the other good things would be mine. One nice part of my idea was that it appealed to the selfishness in each of us."

Could Teddy not have wanted anything to do with Lizzie?

"Of course he was shocked, but I could see him warming up

to the idea. He was getting pictures in his head, the way he does; seeing a kind of love that might last him better than other kinds. At least, so I imagined."

But how many kinds of love are there, anyway, and why would one kind last better than others?

"It was my night for making first moves, although seduction has never been my strong suit. I was a bit tippy with one thing and another but I stood up from the table and walked around behind him and put my arms around his shoulders and leaned over so my chin rested on his head and started talking softly, on and on, about gentle things: rocking a sleeping baby, telling stories, and having someone to be silly with, because Teddy does like to be silly. I took his hand and stroked it down my velvet dress and pulled him to his feet and led him to the bedroom, and after that we didn't talk any more.

"It's interesting, you know," and no, Lizzie doesn't, how could she? "how different it was compared with the old days when we were so carried away by each other. This was just friendly, and I remember thinking how nice it was, to be starting a child in a friendly fashion. He stayed most of the night, but left when it was still dark. It must be hard to be the one who leaves, but he was wise to go. And then I slept quite happily, while you collected yourself inside."

Lizzie can see them making her, in her mother's big brass bed in her mother's darkened bedroom. The old white quilt with the pink-tulip stitching would be pushed aside, and the pale blue sheets would be a little rumpled by two bodies moving gently and quietly, in a friendly sort of way. Magic for sure, being brought to life on purpose. Nothing like being forced out of life on purpose.

Because of the story, Lizzie figured for a long time that when-ever a man and a woman went to bed together, the result was a child. "But how could you have been so sure?" she asked when she discovered differently.

"I don't know. I just was." Her mother grinned. "I have my moments."

"Bastard" is a hard word. They talked about it once when

Lizzie was little, just seven or eight, after her best friend Janice asked her about babies and where they come from. Since Lizzie knew, she told her, and that night her mother got a phone call. When she hung up she was so angry Lizzie was scared. "That was Janice's stupid mother. She says you told Janice all about sex, is that right?"

Unsure where the fault was, Lizzie nodded, but her mother surprised her and laughed. "Don't look so worried, you didn't do anything wrong. It's that woman, she's unbelievable."

"Why?"

"Oh, because she didn't want her innocent little girl to know anything. I expect she'd have been happier if you'd made something up. You should have heard the things my friends and I made up, Lizzie — I was a teenager before anyone told me. We decided husbands did something to their wives' belly buttons once a month, and then later babies came out of the same place. We had it all screwed up until somebody's older sister set us straight and that was almost worse because the truth sounded even weirder."

"Shouldn't I have told? She asked me."

"No, you weren't wrong. The trouble is, her mother doesn't want you and Janice to be friends any more."

"Why not?"

"Because she's an idiot. Anyway, nobody can stop you being friends with anyone you damn well feel like. But you won't be able to go to Janice's house any more, and she won't be allowed to come here. Aside from that, the two of you will have to work it out. Do you mind very much?"

"No," Lizzie lied, "Janice is stupid, too." And she must have been, or why would she have told her mother what Lizzie said? But Lizzie did mind. She and Janice told each other all kinds of secret things. Except Lizzie hadn't known Janice was telling other people, too.

Later she heard her mother on the phone with Frannie, angry again. "I could kill that woman. Do you know what she said? She told me to keep my bastard kid away from her daughter. She said Lizzie and I aren't fit to associate with decent people."

There was quiet and then, "I know it's funny in its way, Frannie, and *I* don't care, but it's hard on Lizzie. She didn't do anything wrong." Which was good to know.

Somebody else had already called her a bastard once, a boy who yelled it at her on the playground one recess. It sounded like something bad.

The morning after Janice's mother called, Lizzie asked her mother, "What's a bastard?" Right away she thought she'd made another mistake, because her mother's eyes went all narrow and sharp, and her lips got thin and even her skin went tight.

"Where did you hear that?"

Lizzie couldn't say she'd been listening when her mother talked to Frannie. "I don't know. I heard it someplace."

"Did somebody call you that?"

"Maybe. A long time ago. I was just wondering."

"Okay." Her mother looked at her for a minute. "Usually it's just a swear word, but what it means, technically, is somebody whose parents weren't married."

"Like you and Teddy?"

"Right."

But so what? Most kids' parents were married, or used to be, but why did it matter? Lots of kids lived with just their mothers, so what was the difference?

"What would you do," her mother asked, "if somebody called you a bastard now?" She kind of tripped over the word when she got to it.

"I guess if it's something bad, I'd hit him."

Her mother grinned. "Well, that's certainly one way of dealing with it, but then he might hit back and you might get hurt. There are other things you can do, you know, that might work better."

"Like what?"

"What you can do, I've found, is turn what somebody thinks is a bad thing into a good one. So if somebody who wants to be mean calls you a bastard, instead of letting it hurt, you can turn it around on him. You can say something like, 'Thank you, I'm so pleased my parents were smart enough not to be married. They're very clever people.' Or you could say, 'Yes, my parents went to a lot of trouble to have me. It's nice to be chosen.' You see, Lizzie, *you* define the word instead of letting the other person do it. That's a lot better than hitting people."

It made words seem so bendable, though, sort of double-jointed, like Janice's thumbs. How could her mother work with words if they didn't always mean the same thing?

Even though she loves it, sometimes Lizzie would rather not know her own story. Sometimes she wonders what it would be like to be somebody who doesn't know if she was started with love or hate or no particular feelings at all. Her mother may have made the story, but she doesn't seem to know how big it is. It might be nice if she said, "Listen, it's no big deal. I wanted you and I had you, but that doesn't have to mean anything to you." Instead she says, "You're only thirteen. The whole world is open to you."

But that's the trouble, all those choices. Teddy wants to be great and to save the earth from blowing up, and her mother writes, hoping, she says, for small improvements. In between there's everything else: save the hungry, save whales and seals, save water and land, save women, save the world. She was made so carefully, surely she must have some gift for saving something?

Teddy talks about having his heart in his work, and how that's the important thing, not fame. Except Lizzie doesn't think he'd turn down more fame if he had a chance at some. She thinks it's one reason he gets mad.

Who else besides great artists do hundreds and thousands and millions of people look up to? Some women used to get famous by having famous husbands or lovers, but her mother and Frannie disapprove of that sort of thing, and anyway Lizzie'd rather be something grand herself.

Maybe she could be a great doctor, doing lifesaving transplants, giving press conferences on television. Or she could make some important discovery, like Madame Curie or that guy who invented the vaccine for the disease that used to paralyze and kill kids. Her mother has told Lizzie that when she was young, she wasn't allowed to swim in certain places, and some class-mates got crippled just in a summer vacation. So to cure some-thing like that, or cancer maybe, would be big. Except it would take so *long*, and waiting is already hard enough.

Yesterday she read a story in the newspaper about a boy her age who won a big piano competition and would be giving concerts all over the world. Just thirteen years old, and he was already something, not wondering at all. But his mother, who was also his music teacher, said it was only to be expected, since he was raised in a house of music. What's Lizzie being raised in? A house of typing. That's no help.

Maybe she could be an actress, that can happen pretty fast, can't it? Of course she'd only take big important parts, the kind people go to see and when they leave they feel like different people. The applause! Eyes closed, smiling, she sees them bring-ing her flowers and reaching out to touch her. Why do famous people complain about that kind of thing?

A sharp, impatient voice is saying her name and sort of laugh-ing, too. "Lizzie? Lizzie, where are you? What are you smiling about?" When she opens her eyes, she's back here in class, and even Megan is looking at her, grinning.

Poor little toilet child, the only big thing it did was be born. And it was just as real, for a few minutes anyway, as those candle stubs and that black velvet dress. Maybe there should be some middle ground between Lizzie being wanted so much, even if it is awfully flattering, and that baby whose mother must have held it down so hard beneath the water.

Maybe Lizzie doesn't really have any big gifts. Maybe she just has some big dumb ideas. Anyway, sometimes she feels as if she's sort of drowning, too. One thing she'd never do, though, is cry in front of all these people; no matter what.

WAR STORIES

A Syracuse man who did his Christmas shopping for his 10-year-old son at an army surplus store was left brain-damaged Thursday, after a firearm he was testing discharged accidentally.

Roger Moyers, 35, was examining and wrapping his Christmas purchases when a Vietnam War-issue rifle went off, police said.

The bullet struck Moyers, an employee of an automotive parts factory, in the temple.

Moyers' gifts for his son, Roger Jr., also included two Second World War-era grenades and a flare pistol used in Korea. All the weapons were seized by police.

His wife, Cynthia, 32, said Moyers bought the weapons because their son "likes to play war" with his friends and enjoyed his first hunting trip with his father this fall.

"They weren't to be used," she said. "He just thought little Roger would enjoy owning the real thing."

And now little Roger will have a new view of "the real thing," won't he? Although, Teddy thinks, a brain-damaged father shouldn't be too surprising for the kid, since it doesn't look like Roger Sr. was shooting with a full magazine to start with.

Jesus, he loves stories like this. How sharp Lizzie is to know that and save them for him, presenting him with one that has especially struck her and waiting shyly for his reaction.

This one is so — American. Honest to God, how many countries can there be where a man could grow up and become a father with the idea that loaded weapons would make great gifts for his kid? Look what Santa brought; but oh, too bad, he's smashed up his head and now he isn't going to be the same guy at all any more.

Teddy pictures a cartoon of a man, wearing a flannel shirt and droopy trousers and steel-toed boots around the house, scratching his crotch with one hand and signing rifle-association petitions with the other. Demanding his God-given right not just to bear weapons, but to give them as presents to children as well.

Grenades could be tough to wrap so leave them, do the rifle first. Fiddle with it for a few minutes, caress the stock (but be careful of the barrel — sweat damages the finish). Hold it up and focus the sights — how about on the angel at the top of the Christmas tree? The angel's maybe a little yellow man. Lay the gun along the cheek, all cool and smooth — hunting deer or ducks is nothing compared to this, nothing at all. This rifle has been places, done things, who knows what it's touched and changed? The trigger seduces: just a small squeeze.

Moyers might have remembered that soldiers in Vietnam did complain throughout the war that their weapons were unstable and sometimes blew up in their faces. Just Roger Sr.'s bad luck to have bought a low-grade leftover, and Roger Jr.'s good luck that his father decided to try it out first.

Even after all these years, Teddy can feel that war in his gut, huge and terminal as a tumor. Roger Moyers blows out most of his brains by mistake, and Teddy has final visions. Bits of Roger Moyers head explode across his living room, and Teddy sees the earth burn, far beyond that one war into the final great one. Flames, a stunning, sky-filling conflagration, and screams and terror, panic and pain, and then a bone-deep, silent, sunless freeze, an icy stone sculpture. Jesus, how did it get like this?

Must be because there are too many assholes like Roger Moyers. To tell the truth, Teddy isn't sorry there's one less. Violence is a terrible thing, and it's exactly violence he opposes, but still, if it happens that way, by accident and through the guy's own fault, be grateful at least for the result: one less fool. Some people are just too stupid to love their children properly. If a kid was sitting naked in the snow or ran into the street in front of a bus, somebody'd snatch him up, but who cares that every kid could die any minute at the hands of some lunatic whose pride's been hurt? At what point, exactly, does love stop short of knowing that?

Those men who have the power to destroy, who do they love, only themselves? Don't they have kids, grandchildren, somebody small they need to protect? Teddy was angry long before Lizzie was born, but her existence has made him furious.

The war that was going on when he was young—even secondhand it was an outrage. It was, among a great many other things, both an insult to his sense of fairness and a focus for his rage. There was a kind of pleasure, if that's the word, in anger in a just cause. He discovered eloquence and power, an ability to sway people.

Those were awfully good years.

And when it was finally over, what? The same kind of evil people with their same evil and labyrinthine purposes, still willing to blow everyone up for their obscure and childish ends. No, not childish; children know better. Lizzie knows better. Those are the men who would blow up his child.

Susannah would point out that they are men. She never gets the main point, keeps getting sidetracked.

It's not that one side of the world is more righteous or more wicked than the other; only that one is more accessible. And having wrapped itself in some fancy coat of justice, reason, truth, also more hypocritical. Something better ought to be expected.

His own country a quiet collaborator. If it came to trial he, at least, would be able to prove himself virtuous.

He's always had words, at least in public, although he sometimes stumbles in private, where events are less clear. He prefers pictures, though, especially these days. These days hardly anybody listens, but a lot of people look, and maybe some will see what he does: various beautiful horrors.

He believes he does more with his work than, say, Susannah does with hers. Or he says more, even though she uses words.

Not that it's a competition; except sometimes over Lizzie, maybe.

He's pissed off right now anyway, specifically at Americans. His stitches are pulling, his whole head hurts—leave it to a Yank to be wearing one of those flashy, heavy-jeweled rings on the hand that ripped Teddy's skin. Okay, maybe it's just a small wound, but it wasn't fair. What was even less fair was how it got reported on TV, instant truth: scuffle breaks out at an unruly demonstration outside the U.S. consulate, American official knocked to the ground, five people arrested, charged with assault. Shit, that's not how it happened, but even the cameras made it look as if twenty people were ganging up on a couple of clean-cut diplomats.

If it was so one-sided, how come Teddy was the only one who needed stitches before the cops carted him to the station to charge him? "What the hell caused this, do you think?" he demanded, pointing out his bandage to the guy taking his fingerprints. "Do you think I did this to myself? *They* weren't hurt, *I* was, so why the hell are you charging me and not them?"

Teddy was so pissed off he forgot to give his phony name. He was supposed to say he was Louis Riel, a small way of slowing down the process; a minor means of harassment. In the heat of the moment, though, he forgot, so even though he got booked later than the others, thanks to the detour to the hospital, he ended up out on the street first and all alone.

It made him think: if Peace International didn't have a lawyer or a special fund, if he really was on his own, who could he have called for bail? Who would have come up with four hundred dollars for him? Well, his dealer, of course. Jenna will always protect an artistic investment. Or Susannah, even, she'd probably come through, if only to help the father of her child. Although calling her wouldn't have done much good, since when he did finally phone her after he watched the event on TV (assuming that since she was still a sort of reporter, she would keep a keen eye on these things), he only got to talk to her answering machine. If he'd had to depend on her, he'd still be drumming his fingers in jail.

It's not that he doesn't have friends, of course he has friends. It's just, how many would make bail for him?

Leo and Teresa, for sure. They wouldn't want him to miss this dinner tonight, and anyway four hundred bucks would be a drop in their petty cash bucket. Too bad he doesn't feel like good company. A blind date, at his age—what a weak moment! Still, he really is fond of Leo and Teresa, and he has a small feeling that he owes them: something simple, like his presence at dinner. They've got four of his paintings, two at home and two in Leo's law office, and what they were willing to pay kept Teddy in rent and food and booze and paint and freedom for practically a year. Sometimes Teddy even forgets the differences between them and him, and they just feel like good, small, thin, twin, pleasing people.

"I swear," Leo said, insisting on dinner, "this one's perfect. In her thirties, divorced, no hang-ups, no kids—I promise, she's absolutely right for you." An old friend of Teresa's, he said, recently rediscovered. "If it doesn't work out, nothing's lost, it's just a dinner."

It turns out, though, to be a dinner at the end of an unexpectedly brutal day.

And it's at Leo and Teresa's house, which always makes him remember who they really are. Or what they are, which is rich. It's as if during the day they do responsible, professional-type stuff, Leo in his law office and Teresa making her social worker rounds into truly godawful places, but at night when they go home and step through their door they start laughing, tear off their clothes, each other's clothes, and kneel on the floor, holding each other, howling with piggish pleasure till they fall into a carpet of cash, deep-piled to their knees, money trickling through the air like leaves. They might build money forts, tunnels through bills, all of it theirs, their own secret pleasure, greedy and corrupt. Finally they'd get tired or sober and stand and dress and go to the living room for a drink or the dining room for dinner, their private romp finished for the night.

None of that is true, it's only Teddy's picture sometimes. They're good people. He expects everybody has mean visions about friends sometimes.

He hated leaving home tonight, leaving the lights on behind him, locking the door, going down those dark stairs to the street. If he had to go out tonight, he'd have preferred his own streets, at least, not these dark avenues. Here are houses like the one where Lizzie and Susannah live, sturdy brick, neat yards, wooden fences or wire ones — a dark enclave of security and safety. A hoax, this: nothing's ever safe. These are the homes of people who hedge as many bets as possible; but watch them crumble and collapse as thoroughly and finally as anything else, come Teddy's vision.

Anyway, the colors are wrong. These streets may have greens that his don't, but he has all the rest. His colors are artificial, of course: brilliant neon in the night. Downtown, living in what used to be a factory where clothes were stitched to supply the stores below, the colors and lights can't be natural, and maybe the life isn't, either, but it's no monochrome, dulled the way it must be behind all these locked and silent residential barricades.

People on these streets stay inside after dark. Well, that's not entirely true, but night doesn't come naturally to them, they're not at home in the dark. Or they literally *are* home in the dark. It's eerie, this silence, although there are clues to humanity: tricycles and rakes abandoned on walkways, lights glimpsed through curtains and shades. There may be city lamps spaced along the boulevards, but the abandoned streets still feel dangerous. Teddy's own streets, where there may well be people who are truly dangerous in one way or another, feel much safer.

He's a foreigner here, off his turf; although it's also true that on his turf, he's more an observant passerby than a participant.

He has found that out in several ways, most bluntly one night when he stopped for a coffee in a twenty-four-hour restaurant. There, a hooker taking a break sized him up slowly, with some contempt, before calling out to another, "Fuckin' tourist," meaning him to hear. How could she tell? Maybe at best he is a tourist; at worst a kind of pimp, making money off those bodies, painting them and selling them. A reviewer once wrote that his work demonstrated "a gift for grittiness," and maybe that's true. He loves the lit-up stores at midnight, their dazzling sideshow of outrageously outfitted mannequins, and magazines and albums with violent and garish covers. He loves the porn shops and all-night dirty movies, too, posters taped to outside walls advertising spread-legged delights inside, nothing subtle there. Other men also pause, weighing the decision to go in: usually strange and shabby men except for the occasional real tourist, who is apt to be well-dressed but furtive. In arcades, lost kids huddle over the swift lights of space games; outside, police cars cruise by. There are waifs on some corners and drunks curled in doorways.

Sad, sure, but what a feast it all is, a smorgasbord of light and dark. He desires the sharp lines and angles of the hookers' bodies (although not the bodies themselves), limbs posed in exaggerated, surreal seductiveness, as if they've watched too many sultry movies. He has followed the line of an arm jutting at the elbow, hand balanced on an outthrust hip, and tried to catch the movement in the toss of the head, hair flying back, the defiance in that gesture when a potential customer turns down the price and drives on, looking for a better bargain, or a more attractive one. Can't beat that for frankness, although it must hurt: "You aren't worth that much." Other people find out that sort of thing in gentler ways.

He hasn't yet been able to use the babies on the streets, though, the little girls just Lizzie's age, with their kiddie stick legs and flat little bosoms, shabby and tragic and surely unloved. They cut too close. Whatever contempt he has for brick houses, he's glad after all that Lizzie's in one, and that Susannah's kept her safely back from any edge that could possibly land her out there. She'll never need to look for either love or money that way, thank God.

It's not just Susannah, though, he's had something to do with it, too. Even when Lizzie was little and staying overnight, he'd wake her up to hit the streets with him; tough kid, stumbling sometimes, blinking back sleep, but taking it all in: the noise of people shouting, horns, curses, a constant bizarre street party. The two of them have squatted beside winos in doorways, listening to the stories of the men they used to be. Hookers have sometimes been kind, pressing quarters and candies into Lizzie's hands.

Now she's thirteen, and some peculiar things are happening. Now when they go roaming at midnight, he sees men looking at her with a kind of speculation, and he keeps a tight hold on her arm. He gets odd glances, too. Apparently he's reached the age at which some men find children's bodies more appealing than grown-up ones.

God he's weary, although his head feels clearer for all this walking, watching. It's interesting, how neighborhoods change in the space of a few blocks, solid brick giving way to the truly ostentatious. Finally, Leo and Teresa's. Not quite ready to be charming or for their idea of a happy surprise, he stands on the sidewalk for a moment, looking at the lights beaming out through leaded glass far away, up a gentle slope of perfect lawn. An unrestrained stone house, elaborate double wooden doorway in the center with perfectly balanced wings on each side, deep windows straight and even as soldiers. If Teddy feels out of place, what would a poor person feel, except rage at such perfectly tasteful unfairness?

Not Leo and Teresa's fault. Leo inherited money and this place, and Teresa has adjusted to it, it's nothing to do with them, really.

It will fall as swiftly as the brick houses, and his own lofty place, and the skyscrapers, glass tumbling in sheets.

His feet scuff white gravel as he goes up the long walk. He was going to wear jeans and a T-shirt but changed to gray cords and a light blue shirt at the last minute from some unclear notion that a certain respect is owed to friends who are trying to do something kind. How much do they know about him, though? Except that he does love women. They do know that.

Leo, not lionlike at all, but dark and wiry, answers the door. And this, behind him, must be the perfect woman? Shit.

Not that *she's* shit, he doesn't mean that, she looks fine. It's just that if she turned up at some rally, or a gallery party, or on a stool beside him at a bar, he might notice a pretty little blonde thing, but hardly anyone who'd interest him. His women may not all have been dark and beautiful, but unless he's been in no mood to care, they've generally had some extraordinary feature.

"Anne's a nurse," Leo says. "You're in luck. From the way you look, I'd say a nurse is exactly what you need."

"And you," Anne says, coming close, "are an artist, I hear." The way she says the word makes him look more closely. "Did this just happen?" She gestures at his bandage.

"This morning. Eight stitches." She gives an impression of sunshine in a way, with her plain yellow dress and tiny golden earrings. He reminds himself that he prefers artificial light.

She reaches up, gently lifts the corner of his bandage. "Not bad. There might be a tiny scar, but just enough to be distinguished looking." Her fingers feel quite delicate; unusual, he imagines, in a nurse.

After all, this wound is an advantage. Teresa, hurrying in from the kitchen, throws her arms around him, stands back, her forehead crinkling with concern. "Can you have a drink, or are you all stoked up on painkillers?"

Of course he can have a drink. In the dining room Teresa seats him and Anne across from each other at the walnut table, while she and Leo sit miles apart at each end. When they're at Teddy's, they eat off plates on their knees. Here in this cavernous space there's not only this carved table, but matching carved walnut chairs, and plants placed around the walls. An ancient tapestry hangs on one wall, faded figures engaged in war or rapine, although more vaguely tonight than usual — Teresa's dimmed the lights. Is this her idea of romantic, or is there some flaw in Anne she's hoping to conceal? (Or, worse thought, some flaw in him they hope to keep from Anne?)

"So tell us about it," Teresa insists.

Anne rests her forearms on the table, leans slightly toward him. "Yes, Ted, what happened?"

How odd to hear himself called Ted. How pleasant. Sometimes it's hard to feel grown up when everyone, even his daughter, calls him Teddy.

Dinner is veal, tiny golden baked potatoes, and long, tender green beans. The food of the rich is always exceptional.

"It's nothing much, really. We were down at the American consulate this morning, protesting missile testing, you know?" Apparently, from her puzzled little frown, Anne doesn't know; or doesn't approve. "Anyway, it was okay for an hour or so, except for the rain, but then it got out of control."

"How come?"

"I'm not sure." He has thought about this, this afternoon. "For one thing, I guess, the TV cameras were there, and that can make a difference. Usually it's no big deal, and there are kind of accepted ways people behave. I mean, people go in and out and nobody bothers them and they don't bother us. Except today these two guys came along and maybe the cameras got them excited, but they pushed a couple of women to get through our line and there was a little shouting. But that's all, just a couple of people saying, 'Watch it.'

"They kept coming toward the entrance, though, which is where I was, and we all stopped moving, keeping an eye on them. Shit, they were probably just a couple of clerks or accountants trying to look tough. Anyhow, it was pretty clear they were going to try to push me, too, even though they only had to step around. So a couple of our guys moved in closer."

"Goodness." Anne's eyes widen, so he sees they are a really remarkable pale blue. "That sounds frightening."

"Not really. There wasn't time to think about it." A lie, sort of. Maybe he wasn't exactly frightened, but his body was getting ready, tensing and humming, and events were slowed down like in a dream or an accident. He could smell violence. Not exactly frightened, though, not really.

Teresa stands to collect empty plates. Another thing about the rich and good taste is that there's never quite enough of anything. Funny, that people with money must so often go hungry.

"So the American nearest me shoves his briefcase at me, just swings it up a little so a corner catches me on the thigh, real sharp and hard. Maybe the cops didn't see, it might not have looked like anything, but my arms automatically go up, defensive, because it feels like the start of something." He hears himself breathing faster and starting to talk as if it's happening right now, and his body's tightening up again, getting ready. "Somebody grabs the arm with the briefcase to keep him from swinging it around any more. I can only see the guy in front of me, but his free hand goes shooting up and catches me on the head, and he's wearing this jesus big ring that slices my skin. Next thing, I see him flat on his ass on the ground. Nobody knocked him down, I think he just got off balance, but the cops moved in and things got hairy for a few minutes."

"At least they took you to hospital." Teresa's brought out fresh fruit salad. Nothing from a can, and nothing like the chocolate cake he'd rather have. He seems to have an unusual craving for sweetness tonight.

"Yeah, but they have to do that. If I died of a head injury in a cell, they'd be responsible."

"So did they charge you?" asks Leo the lawyer.

"You bet. Assault."

Anne looks puzzled again. "What about the two Americans?"

"You mean were they charged? Hell, no, just five of us."

"What'll happen in court?" She sounds gratifyingly concerned.

He shrugs. "A fine, I expect. That's all I've ever had before. What do you think, Leo?"

"No idea. I'm corporate, remember? I haven't been near criminal law since school."

"Anyway, the point is, it wasn't fair, although I guess I should be old enough not to expect that." A mistake, mentioning age. He is, what, a decade or so older than Anne? The fact is, the skin beneath his ribs and above his belly has been developing peculiar puckerings, and the hair on his chest, not to mention his head, is getting gray.

Oh, he's been proud of his body! Women have remarked on the length of his legs and the tightness of his buttocks and the way his back curves smoothly up to solid shoulders. He has enjoyed swinging out of bed, sauntering across the room for cigarettes, knowing he looked well from behind and, returning to bed, from the front. He would pretend not to notice how he was admired.

A few months ago he met a young woman, Barbara, in a restaurant; a mere child of twenty-six. Some women are impressed to meet an artist (Anne, too, it sounds like), so he took her back to his place and his bed. He thought they'd had a pretty good time until he got up to go to the bathroom in the morning and turned to say something and was stopped in his tracks. Such an expression on her pretty, flushed face! Oh, nothing as drastic as revulsion, but something almost worse: she looked curious; as detached as a scientist spotting something under a microscope heard about but never seen before. She looked as if she were thinking, "So that's what a forty-five-year-old body looks like." (Had he mentioned his age so precisely?) "Isn't it interesting and strange, how that happens."

He's been a little prudish, self-conscious, since then.

Teresa stands. "Why don't you two go sit in the living room while Leo and I get the coffee?" This is embarrassing, how obvious she is.

They step from the antique formality of the dining room into the glaringly modern: all silver and white, pewter and platinum and cream leather. Any flaws will sure show up here in this light! Only a couple without kids could have a room like this; a couple without kids but with a cleaning woman. They've talked about getting a live-in maid, but Teresa said she'd feel guilty, watching someone work. "It's okay when it's done during the day, when I'm out, but I couldn't stand it in person." Her and Leo's lives are rampant with these delicate judgments. Is Anne a woman of their sort of substance?

The women who used to work in his apartment when it was a factory would be the women who, today, might be maids to Leos and Teresas. He does, after all, enjoy this house, enjoys sinking into this sofa beside this small, sweet-looking person. Sometimes it's hard to remember, or to be sure, which side he's on.

"I know you're a nurse, but not much else." There's a trick he knows with his eyes, an intense way of looking. "Tell me about yourself." Stupid; but she looks at him kindly.

"For one thing, I don't usually let people set me up this way. I'm sorry. I expect you feel trapped."

"Not really." He also has a boyish smile that many women find appealing. "Do you?"

"I thought I would, but it's been a nice surprise."

Messages may pass silently and indirectly and still be perfectly clear. But why make the effort for the sake of skin, company, an interesting moment or two? He thinks, really, that he suffers more from curiosity than lust. Hope, too? He always seems to have hope, although he doesn't necessarily know what it's for, beyond the next face, the next breast. Certainly it's not for permanence, he has no faith in that. Well, he wouldn't have, would he, knowing that important people can be wiped out in an instant, or that love or passion will almost certainly become — and he learned this from Susannah, years ago when he was still really a boy—boring or insistent and eventually hateful, or that the earth itself can and likely will crack beneath his feet? Adaptability, it seems to him, is the great trick of the century, and he's been fortunate to have the nimbleness required to survive.

Still, he must have hopes, or why would he bother? For that matter, he must even have hopes of peace, to turn up at demonstrations with his forty-five-year-old body again and again.

There is one other very secret, unspeakable hope: that some canvas or other will leap that terrible gap to genius. Immortality? That one's dangerously unbearable.

Anyway, one thing at a time; right now, this woman.

She tells him she works twelve-hour shifts in an emergency ward; that she's divorced after a seven-year marriage of unspecified unpleasantness; that she's thirty-six. She has a gentle, soft voice, which, on some subjects, such as her marriage, has a tinge of iron. He thinks of Susannah, but really only because Anne's not like her. Here Anne sits, small and female, special because of how she exists, not the way she demands. Susannah has gotten to wanting things her own way, and is less attractive now in ways that have nothing to do with looking older.

"I've never gone to a demonstration," Anne tells him. "Or do you call it a protest? I guess I admire it, but I couldn't ever do it. Everything just seems—" and she turns her hands toward him, palms up "—too big. Nothing really changes, you just get hurt and arrested." At best that's naive, at worst dangerously ignorant. Still, he can see that Anne's interests have probably had to be personal. She'd have to be strong to do her job, to survive a marriage, to take care of herself, as she must.

"Maybe, but we can't let them think they can get away with murder, with nobody paying attention."

She speaks as if nothing is really possible. Other countries are very far away to her, apparently, and therefore not quite real, which gives her view of world events a certain pallor. She says, "I always think you can only really try to live your own life well."

"Exactly." But he's not as annoyed as he might be.

If he were going to paint her, it might be as a sort of orchid woman, rare and delicate; although she's probably not delicate, and it's early to say how rare.

"Why are you looking at me that way?"

"I was thinking how to paint you." Usually he prefers larger breasts and hips, but there's something nice about a small body, too; a compact one, not scrawny and drawn, like his women of the streets.

Leo and Teresa, coming in with their trays, must have heard him speak of painting Anne—or they were waiting, eavesdropping, at the door. "You must see the paintings of Teddy's we own, Anne," Teresa says. She pours out coffee, Leo the liqueurs, but they wait, standing, for Teddy and Anne to get up and go with them. It's not very easy or graceful, hauling himself out of that couch.

It's probably because his works are neither decorative nor comfortable that they've hung them under track lights in a hallway leading to the sun room at the back of the house. It's a wide hall as halls go, but it's hard to step back far enough to get perspective. "Teddy," Leo explains, "has a taste for the decadent. These are part of his hooker collection. What do you think?"

Anne regards the two pieces with an expression Teddy can't decipher from her profile. Finally she turns to him. "They make me feel lonely, are they supposed to?"

Not necessarily, but maybe.

"I don't know a lot about art, so I don't know the right words, just how it makes me feel."

How tender and protective that makes him want to be! He puts his hand lightly on her shoulder, the first time he's actually touched her — how fine her bones are. "That's exactly what you're supposed to know, is how it makes you feel. Everything else is bullshit." Which of course isn't *quite* true, but it'll do.

Back in the living room, with Leo and Teresa sitting quietly, listening, and no doubt congratulating themselves, he talks about his late-night rambles through the streets, his figures of the neon darkness. He even, with an impulse toward truthfulness, confesses his place as a tourist.

"But," she says, "it sounds as if you love it, and that must make you some kind of an insider."

She uses that word love awfully easily. He's wary of it himself, scenting traps (except with Lizzie, of course, but that's different). Otherwise, say it and prepare to drown in the foreign, uncontrollable emotions of women who turn out to be strangers.

On the subject of him, though, Anne sounds wise enough.

She pays attention, and doesn't, at first acquaintance, appear to have habits that could become irritating. She doesn't twist her fingers through her hair, or pick at her fingernails, or cross her legs awkwardly, or change her voice into a little girl's, the way a stupid woman might. She's certainly not stupid, but on the other hand she's not sharp enough to cut him, causing pain. She is also, if not exactly beautiful, reasonably attractive. He imagines her nipples are like the rest of her, small. Her breasts are likely firm as oranges.

It's not late when he suggests they leave. "I'd like you to see what I'm working on now, see what you think." Leo and Teresa wave goodbye from the front doorway, their arms around each other's waists. Teddy expects that's love, the two of them, but has no idea how it came about or how they keep it going.

"Aren't they pleased with themselves?" Anne giggles. How long since he's heard a woman giggle? Another gift lost to women like Susannah, although he remembers her laughing with him when they were young.

"I'll get us a cab. You won't want to walk." She's wearing high-heeled shoes, yellow, precisely matching her dress. Her ankles are frail-looking, narrow.

It's the rituals of courtship that are tiring. He can't just say, "I'm kind of interested, let's go to bed." He must show her around his place, his work, the kitchen. "It's enormous," she says, and of course it is, since it's one big room except for the bathroom, divided only by function: old maple bed in one corner, a cluster of living room furniture, white and yellow cotton sofa, easy chair, glass tables, white ceramic lamps — he needs a lot of light in his life — and the largest space devoted to work. "You go sit down and I'll get the coffee. You've had a long day, and I bet your head hurts." She's so alert, about him and also about where things are in his kitchen. Maybe that's part of being a nurse, making these quick assessments. Or maybe it's why she's a good nurse, which he's sure she is.

His injury was possibly more exhausting than he'd realized, because he is grateful to sit, instead of what he would ordinarily do, which is stand close behind her, wrap his arms around her, kiss her hair, her neck, turn her slowly around and lead her to his bed, gently but firmly, so she can pretend, if she's that sort of woman, that it's only something happening, not something she's agreed to.

"How did you ever find this place? I've never seen anything like it." He's pleased by that; some people find it odd. Of course some people lie, too, and he doesn't know her well.

It was a vacant treasure when he found it fifteen years ago: large and high and open. When he moved in, he painted all the walls flat white and twice a year pays men with ladders and no fear of heights to clean the windows. Can he explain his appetite for light? Sometimes he can see beyond the white walls, beyond the lamps, the track lights over his work space, to what was here before, when the place was still a factory, dimly lit with small bulbs and grimy windows. Hundreds of women, at one time or another, would have sat in this space, bent over rows of sewing machines, cranking out dresses and blouses. He's even painted them, quite successfully. He suspects sometimes that if he were a greater artist, strong men would weep at his work. If he were a lesser one, they'd be sick from sentiment.

He doesn't expect Anne to understand, although she nods as if she does. Probably it doesn't especially matter.

"So," he says, stretching, shifting to a subject that's less interesting but important in its way, "when do you work next?"

"Not for three more days. I do three twelve-hour shifts and then I get four days off." So there is time, there is time. He could fall asleep right now, just lean over and put his head against her and let her take care of him.

He closes his eyes, at least, while she talks. Her days and nights, she says, are littered with drunks and victims of violence and crazy people. Weekends and full-moon nights are worst. Once a policeman and a robbery suspect were shot, and there were cops and reporters everywhere, everyone running around while she and the emergency doctor were the calm center, undertaking the actual care. He can imagine she's a fine calm center. Even her voice is soothing.

Mothers bring in tiny children with rashes or coughs or minor fevers, and Anne reassures them, but says it's annoying. "They come in for the littlest things when really, they should go to their own doctors, not use up space and money in a hospital." He finds all this comfortably, sleepily boring. "You should see the waiting room in the middle of the night, people coming in off the street to get warm or sleep. It's sad. But," and her tone gets hard, "it's awful, too, because they're dirty and if they're drunk, which they usually are, they sometimes throw up, and I know they have bugs. You should come see — they'd make a painting for you."

Usually he dislikes people suggesting he paint this and that, but that's not really what Anne's doing. She's just offering something they might see in common, that's all.

She stands and steps from piece to piece around his walls. "It's amazing, what you see." He supposes that people who deal in flesh and bones and blood might well be amazed by visions that aren't so visible.

What might she see, beyond the structure of anatomy, that he'd find interesting?

Probably not much. Probably it doesn't matter.

She tells him that five years ago, she left and briskly divorced her alcoholic husband. "I thought for a long time I could help him, or he'd learn to be happy and wouldn't need to drink any more, but that was silly. I should have known better, but you always think your own situation is unique. You never think it falls into the same patterns as other people's."

She left when he hit her. Now she shrugs and says, "There are lines that just aren't crossed." No doubt she has other lines that could be crossed accidentally and then bang, that would be the end of it. He expects she deals with pain, even her own, swiftly and efficiently, but then women are generally good at getting on. Anne would just be better than most, with all her experience of honest-to-God real, bleeding pain.

"What about you? Have you ever been married?"

"No, I've come close a couple of times, but I never made it."

These days a cautious and delicate probing of sexual pasts is part of the ritual — it may disrupt the flow of seduction, but there are such terrible diseases now. How much lovelier and more fun it used to be, diving right in! God, he used to be able to walk into a party or stand speaking at the front of a crowd and look out over it and pick out one, two, three girls, women, who appealed to him. Words rolled out and his hands would speak, his head working in the cause but the rest of his body electric, setting up sparks he could particularly aim. What a power! He can't remember it ever failing him, when he put his attention to it. Still doesn't fail him, for that matter, even though he's more cautious, and so possibly less interested — but why else is Anne here, if not because of that gift? How many rolling, passionate, exploring nights has he spent; with strangers, okay, but at the time who had to care? Poor kids now — poor Lizzie, when the time comes — who will never, if they're wise, have that terrific uplift of joy in leaping on instant desires.

He's not fond of buying safes, either, not to mention wearing them.

Also he has his credentials to establish — otherwise, at first glance what does an unmarried forty-five-year-old artist with white and yellow furniture sound like? So these days it's a matter of making himself sound virile and tender but not promiscuous; interesting, but not too interesting. He doesn't think he's quite got the hang of it all yet. Also does he imagine it, or is it possible that the mere business of wondering if it's worth it can cause failures: of electricity, of will?

"It's awkward, isn't it?" Anne looks understanding, filled with fellow feeling. "When I started dating again, it was so hard, figuring out the new rules."

She seems to have a weird knack for putting into words some things he doesn't say.

He is just turning to her, just seeing properly how full her lower lip is, turned outward, nearly pouting, and the tiny lines around her eyes — and what does she see, so close? — when the telephone rings.

Lizzie's voice. Shit, why him and why now?

She needs to come over for the night, an emergency, what

can he say? He'd like to say no, he'd like to snap, "Put your mother on the phone," and tell Susannah it's inconvenient and no time to change her mind about taking care of Lizzie. But hell, of course he can't do that. "Sure honey, come on over, no problem."

Now here's Anne, looking at him in a slightly chilly way, probably wondering who it is he calls "honey."

"That was my daughter."

"Really? I thought you said you haven't been married."

So there's nothing for it but to tell her, although it's much too soon. Anyway, nobody can expect people his age, or Anne's for that matter, to have no histories; only, Lizzie can be disconcertingly present and concrete.

He tells the bare bones. Does he communicate love? Because who would have dreamed, when Susannah drew him down into her bed long after they'd agreed it was a good place to avoid, that the result would be so ferocious? Susannah talked that night about the possibilities of love, but she said so many things, and so softly, that he thought afterward it must have been the rhythm of her words, not what she said, that was persuasive. The candles, the food, the wine, Susannah herself, all conspired to take him by surprise. Recalling it later, he thought the evening had a horrifying unreality, so that when he returned to his own place before dawn and switched on the lights, the brightness came as a shock. He thought he saw a clear and terrible error: that he must have been smothered somehow by Susannah's will, her desire. The really chilling part was that her will and her desire seemed to involve certain of his qualities and parts, but not himself.

Still, with the lights on he could see that probably nothing would come of it.

Susannah's a surprising woman, though, and more potent than he would have dreamed.

Lizzie looked like nothing at all to begin with, when he stood at the window of the hospital nursery and she was lifted up so he could see her. "You didn't tell me," he said resentfully to

Susannah, who lay in bed looking exhausted and tremendously pleased with herself.

"Tell you what?"

"How I'd feel."

She'd shrugged. "How could I know? I had no idea. How do you feel?"

He couldn't begin to tell her, any more than he can tell Anne now. But he did see she'd told him a lie, even if it was only a lie of omission. He'd been cheated, and shrewd Susannah, who can be shockingly devious about getting what she wants, knew what she was doing.

If it weren't for Lizzie, he might have concluded by now that he has no real gift for love.

One of these years, she'll be the age Susannah was when he first met her, and oh, what he'll do to any man who does to Lizzie what he did to her mother!

She even looks like Susannah: the reddish-streaked, dark wavy hair and the body that's starting to get lean, after a chubby childhood. She has his brown eyes, although there's something of Susannah's look in them. Nobody'd better hurt his daughter, they hadn't better try.

Even in that, though, he may not be necessary. Lizzie's been raised by a tougher Susannah than the one he knew. He's sometimes found Susannah a little frightening in the two decades or so since giving her up, and there's an occasional glint about Lizzie that suggests it wouldn't do to push her, either. Probably she can look after herself. Or will be able to, by the time it's necessary.

A year ago, Lizzie walked in on him and Janine. It was the middle of the afternoon, and he was only wearing jeans. He was trying to think fast of a way to keep Lizzie from coming in when Janine — accidentally or on purpose? — stepped naked from the bathroom. The girl and the woman stared at each other, and Teddy went blank with embarrassment.

"I don't suppose it hurts a twelve-year-old girl to see a naked woman," Susannah said when he called her later to explain.

"She knows what naked women look like." As if it didn't matter that Lizzie'd turned and run down the stairs without speaking; as if he hadn't seen the look on her face before she turned.

"She was upset," he insisted. "I thought you should know."

"Yeah, okay." He could almost hear her shrugging. "But really, Teddy, I imagine she knows you're no celibate. It can scarcely be news." Was there a bite in there? Was Susannah, even after so long, still in a punishing mood?

"There's a difference," he'd said stiffly, "between knowing something and seeing it."

"That's true."

He was mad at Janine, which was hardly fair; annoyed with Lizzie for coming by without calling; and furious with Susannah, who remembers everything and never lets go. With just a glance or a silence, she can remind him of how badly he once behaved, which is unkind, since all that was years ago.

Even so. She was the first woman he ever loved, back when he was young and new to that sort of thing, and she was amazingly willing. Also she's the mother of his child; although it's probably more truthful to say he's the father of her child.

No wonder Lizzie's never called him Daddy, or Dad, or even Father. That's not quite true—she did once, when she was very little, but he said, "No Lizzie, you call me Teddy, okay? That's my name." He could hardly ask her to call him Daddy now.

"She's a terrific kid," he tells Anne. "You'll like her." He has no way of knowing if that's true. He has no idea what sort of child might appeal to Anne.

"Honestly, I think I should leave now."

"No, don't. Stay and meet her. I don't want you to go." Well, he doesn't and he does. It would be easier if she weren't here when Lizzie arrives, but on the other hand he has a habit of forgetting. If she's not here when he wakes up tomorrow morning, he knows he won't be able to remember quite why he wanted to be with her.

"If you think so. If you're sure. Do you see her often?"

"Lizzie? Yeah, she stays over every few weeks. Whenever we both feel like it. I like her."

"It sounds like you love her." There she is again, using that word so easily. Of course with Lizzie, it is easy.

Lizzie knows so much. There's so much he can teach her. In a way, he feels sort of similar about Anne: that she also has potential to learn at his hands. Not quite a blank canvas filled only with possibilities, that would be insulting, but certainly there's room to draw on her. He could be excited if it weren't for his head and being so tired. And Lizzie on her way.

He probably should have offered to go and get her. It's late, dangerous for a kid to be out on her own. What the hell was Susannah thinking of? Herself as usual, no doubt. Now he's the one who gets to worry — Jesus, this city has terrible stories, some of them about young girls.

Some not. A couple of years ago, he introduced Lizzie to the Vietnamese man who ran the all-night variety store a block away. This man, Teddy told her, had survived a war in his own country, escaped with two sons on a perilous journey, undertaken a long, desperate voyage through dangerous waters in a small boat, then endured a dreadful, cramped refugee camp before he finally made it here, to this country, to this store. He left behind his wife and a daughter and was still trying to get them out of Vietnam. Things, the man said, shaking his head at Teddy and Lizzie, were very bad in his country. Things were not altogether good here, either: he'd been robbed twice, once at gunpoint and once with a knife; some people called him "gook" or "slant-eyes"; and already his sons were wanting too many things. "So far they have come," he'd said, "and so much they forget."

That fucking war again.

Other people run the store now, and Teddy has no idea what happened to the man. At the time, Lizzie wanted to know what she and Teddy could do, and Teddy tried to make it clear that it's one thing to demonstrate for a right cause and to paint lives as well as he can see them, but it's quite another to step into them with a view to fixing them. "You can make yourself responsible for things getting a whole lot worse instead of better, even if you mean well."

Maybe Lizzie was too young to understand; or probably Susannah has given her the idea that almost any difficulty can be solved, especially with words. Anyway, Lizzie must have mentioned the man to Susannah, because eventually he turned up, complete with pictures, in some piece she did on refugees. Susannah's view is, if people know about a situation, maybe they'll do something, even if it's just for one man. She might have a point, who knows? The guy's gone, anyway, possibly on to better things. He could be living happily in the suburbs with his wife and daughter and sons, another miracle performed by the mother of Teddy's child.

Even so, he does think she can be awfully shortsighted about the casual way she tosses these grenades into unsuspecting people's lives. Generally, he has tried to teach Lizzie, who is the grenade Susannah threw at him, that it's better just to pay very close attention.

Personal stuff gets so fucking complicated — look at tonight! In a way, it's simpler to get hit on the head and wrongly accused than go through an evening like this. Even the judgment of a court, however unjust, may be more merciful than the judgments of daughters or potential lovers. Maybe he should have let Anne leave and called her tomorrow, even without being able to remember her exactly.

Lizzie won't be happy about finding a strange woman here (although at least this one has her clothes on). Still, she's a pretty lucky kid if all her surprises are as mild as Anne. Whatever else he may be, Teddy's at least no Roger Moyers, teaching much harsher and more concrete lessons to his child.

FESTIVE OCCASIONS

A father-daughter banquet for a Brownie troop in Surrey, B.C., erupted into violence Thursday when two "fathers" of the same child demanded a place at her table.

When the melee was over, several chairs and a table in the church basement where the banquet was held were broken, the two men had been treated at hospital for minor injuries, several bystanders were nursing bruises, and the eight-year-old girl had gone home in tears.

Both Brian Wilkinson, 34, the girl's natural father, and Rudy Carson, 31, common-law husband of her mother, have been charged with assault and are to appear in court Monday.

Police said the battle began when Wilkinson arrived at the banquet demanding the place beside his daughter occupied by Carson.

When Carson, who had paid for the banquet ticket, refused to give up his seat, a scuffle between the two men began, police said. Nearby fathers who attempted to intervene also became involved, and several pieces of furniture were broken as the fight grew. The little girl escaped the brawl by crawling under the table.

Organizers of the banquet, where good citizenship medals were to be presented to several Brownie members and their fathers for community projects, called police and the child's mother.

Peggy Wilkinson declined later to discuss the dispute, saying only that her daughter had been "very upset and shaken."

No doubt the poor kid truly was upset and shaken, and no wonder, but what an embarrassment of paternal riches! Susannah could tell her there are worse things than having two fathers fighting for her attention. She could have none.

Of course two men intent on being good fathers would never have behaved so badly. What they must have been doing was staking out positions, marking their property with fists, although the property itself got lost in the uproar.

Susannah can hardly be too critical, though, can she, having terrified her own child tonight?

Apparently she's going to have to rework some of that piece on Ida Lovender, now that it's clearer just what Ida meant when she said a day can make all the difference. "My first husband," she'd said, laughing, "is going to die when he finds out about this."

Susannah thinks it's better if people stay alive, at least so they can feel regret or guilt. If they die, there's no hope of revenge; no hope of hope, either.

It used to amaze her, the stranger knocking on the doors of the bereaved, how often they were calm and tearless. In shock, of course. It takes different people different ways.

She really lost it for a while tonight, didn't she? Was that grief? More like rage, probably. She's wept for other men, but not like that, and only because they were gone.

Poor Lizzie. Even at the time, lost and beyond her own control, Susannah knew she had to be frightening her daughter, and if she was capable of doing that, what had ever been the point of going through so much to have her in the first place? How odd, the business of sitting outside herself, watching herself, but not being able to stop. Until finally she was too tired to go on; worn out, wrung dry — now she knows what those expressions mean.

Lizzie apparently mistook weariness for something else, calm perhaps, and dragged up questions. Well, Susannah did her best, but found herself looking at her child, for the first time, really, with dislike. Not Lizzie's fault, of course, but it was best to send her off to Teddy's.

Susannah is forty-three years old and has been amazed tonight to discover that she knows almost nothing about death. She would have imagined she knew a good deal. She supposes she didn't understand that she's only seen it secondhand, has always been a step or two removed from it.

It's not fair there's no warning any more. There used to be telegrams; people would know when they saw a delivery person coming up the walk that it had to be bad news. Now what — the telephone? Who can tell who's on the other end, and it could just as well be good news. Like today, working, when she switched on the answering machine, the clicks of people who hung up when they heard the recording could have been anyone. She remembers smiling to herself, picturing some lean, lovely, but too-shy stranger calling. It must be about time for one of those. Some longings have been building, lusts, but also more cozy desires.

Right now, tonight, would be the moment for the perfectly intuitive lover, who would hold his arms around her and stroke her hair and keep totally quiet.

She can hardly expect to have what she hasn't been able or willing to be, though, can she?

That might apply, of course, to fathers as well as lovers.

She seems to have made so many men angry, not least of them her father. Why is that? What do they want?

Still, she's enjoyed them while they've lasted. They've each offered her some love, some suffering, in various volatile combinations. They do seem, though, to end up going too far. They seem to end up displaying, like a flasher in a park, the nakedness of a need for devotion, adoration.

She wouldn't regret any one of them. It is possible that she's come to the end of the line, however. Forty-three-year-old women aren't exactly hot attractions. So gently, carelessly, she has drifted into circumstances that contain no voices deeper than her own.

This, tonight, is what being bereft must feel like: no one here to comfort her. Maybe she should have kept Lizzie home after all.

Teddy phoned today, too, but she just listened to his voice on the machine and didn't stop working. "Don't worry about the stuff on TV or whatever's in the papers, okay? Tell Lizzie it's just the usual, no big deal." Maddening man, what the hell was he talking about? Whatever, it would have to look after itself, if it was no big deal. She was busy.

Her first real encounter with death was with Teddy's parents, back when Susannah was twenty and trying to live with him in that tiny, poor apartment. Pizzas and beer, scattered books and notes, banners and posters pinned to peeling walls, the bed that never got made, where they played so joyously. They also played on the floors, in the bathtub, standing propped against walls — there can hardly have been a surface in that place untouched by their explorations of each other's bodies and the variations of how they might fit together. The four small rooms were choked with their abandon, must have been musty with the scents of lust.

They were drinking beer, smoking a joint, and cooking up midnight hot dogs when the knock came. Teddy ran to the window and came back to the kitchen pale from the sight of a cruiser below. He grabbed the remains of the nickel bag and the stub of the joint and flushed them, while she went slowly to the door. She thought of doom. She thought, "Oh, God, I'll get kicked out, I'll end up having to go home"; which seemed much worse at that moment than being arrested, charged, fined or jailed.

So many smells, though — smoke, lust, fear, and frying hot

dogs — could the cops have separated the guilty from the inno-cent? Anyway, that wasn't why they were there. They asked Teddy and Susannah to sit down, and then one said, reasonably sorrowfully and kindly, that there'd been an accident: Teddy's parents, hit head-on going home from a dance. Susannah's relief was indecent. Also short-lived. Teddy wouldn't stop trembling and talking. He trembled and talked all night about them, on and on, every tiny detail of who they were and what they'd done and what they'd wanted of him and things the three of them had done together; as if he were a little boy. She really didn't know how to comfort, but tried her best, holding him through the night, feeling guilty and also sad, although for Teddy, not for them. They were pleasant people and had been kind to her, but her connection was naturally with the living. The next day she arranged the funeral and picked out the clothes they'd be buried in and generally took over quite responsibly, saving Teddy pain. Really, she's very good in a crisis.

She still couldn't imagine, though, how he felt. She felt badly for that.

His grief went on for weeks, as he mourned them exhaust-ingly. He couldn't seem to believe what had become of them. Also, though, he inherited their house and sold it, which bought his freedom. If he'd had to be poor and struggling, would he have stayed as determined and hopeful as he has?

Of course she's actually seen death, too: on the job, back when she had a real job. The first time, a car was hit by a train and bits of the driver's body were scattered up and down the track, little lumps and humps of this and that under heavy red wool blankets with wide black stripes at the ends. She remem-bers those blankets. The cops, testing her, lifted corners, showing an arm here, a chunk of torso there, waiting to see if she'd throw up, which she wouldn't. Wasn't even inclined to, really, since she was in a hurry to get her story filed. Saved from nausea by a deadline.

One foot was off by itself, turned sideways and relaxed, as if it had decided to stay put while the rest of the body went elsewhere.

Well, maybe death, even when it's staring them in the face, isn't quite real to the young.

That sort of standing back may not be a bad thing, but it sure leaves a person unprepared.

Really, most misadventure, even tragedy, slips up quietly, almost accidentally, one thing leading to another until finally it can't be tolerated for another moment. Like Ida, in a way. There she'd sat in that dingy coffee shop, the two of them at a small gray table just a few feet from the bald fry cook, a skinny waitress juggling her early-morning customers and coffees, and there was Ida, speaking calmly and even with some humor. "My first husband," she said, "was a university English teacher, charming, good-looking, much adored by students — I expect you know the type. My two older children are from that marriage. He started beating me when I was pregnant with the second, just a slap now and then at first, then with closed fists. I got the odd black eye and a lot of bruises. Once he twisted my arm behind my back until I thought it was going to break, but mostly I wasn't badly hurt." She spoke as if this were merely history, some event from centuries ago, read in a book.

She must have learned that trick of memory better than Susannah, who for all her efforts has occasionally been jolted by some flash of history, triggered by a smell, a color, a set of objects fitting together in some familiar way. Words, expressions that someone, say her mother, may have used, a rhythm of speech. Sometimes she has heard those words and rhythms coming from her own mouth, rather frightening and disturbing.

"I didn't know what to do," Ida said. "I couldn't figure out what I was doing wrong. I suppose he felt trapped and frustrated, because we were poor, or at least we had to be careful about money. In those days, women blamed themselves, though, and of course he was such a smart man, and everybody liked him. Food seemed to set him off. We couldn't afford the things he might have liked—I don't know, truffles every night, something suitable for a man in his position." She grinned then, although she'd spoken mostly looking down, her hands turning her coffee cup around and around and her eyes fixed on the formica tabletop.

Susannah was grown up and far from home before she even heard of truffles. In her home, meals were plain, although to be sure food did, even there, have a language beyond nutrition.

"Then one night I was making spaghetti—I thought that was okay because he liked my sauce, but he came into the kitchen and you know, you get a feeling, you can feel waves coming off a person that tell you you're in danger. I kept my head down; you get sort of like an ostrich, hoping you're invisible. Anyway, he picked up the pot of boiling water and just tossed it at me. It caught me all down one side. Well, you can see where it caught me. Next thing I knew, I was waking up in hospital." She shook her head. "Incredible pain."

God yes. Susannah could almost imagine blows, but boiling water, scalded skin — she's been in burn wards, she's seen the pain. Smelled it, too.

At least Ida'd had some sense of danger when harm was about to be done to her, even if the forewarning didn't help.

"You know," she said wistfully, "I used to be pretty. I look at pictures of myself from before and I can hardly imagine how it was, being pretty. He came to visit and said how sorry he was and cried and begged me not to tell a soul. He said he'd told the hospital I'd knocked the pot over myself, although I could never see how anybody could've believed that — I'd have had to pour it over my own head. But people didn't want to know that sort of thing. I could hardly believe it myself.

"I'd seen myself in the mirror, though. Bruises go away, but this wasn't going to, however sorry he was. He was always sorry, but this time he was scared, too."

No one in Susannah's first family has ever tried to apologize, even though each member has committed some sin that was apparently unforgivable.

"It was really interesting, what happened then. I was absolutely angry, a hundred feet tall. Even lying in that hospital bed with him sitting beside me crying and pleading and me all wrapped up in those burn bandages they used then, I was a hundred feet tall." Her one riveting eye was shining like crazy, and Susannah wrote that in her notebook: "Her right eye, the good, expressive one, shines like crazy." Then she thought that while it was the right eye that was the good one, it might be the squinty, discolored left one that was expressive.

"I told him to get out. I told him I'd kill him if he came near me or the kids again, and I do believe I meant it. I got a lawyer and set him working on a divorce. Then I had to have skin grafts and physiotherapy, and that's where I met my second husband. He'd broken both legs skiing and needed physio, too. I thought if he didn't care what I looked like, he must be all right. You develop new standards in that kind of situation, and believe me, the fact he was a university teacher too cut no ice at all with me. We had the twins a year after we got married, and we've lived happily ever after, more or less. But you don't forget. I got involved in counseling and then a bunch of us started the shelter and these things expand, it's never just one thing, you see. Nobody should be so poor or trapped they have to be frightened for their lives."

Well, the story has all the usual terrible stuff, horror stories of wives and children fleeing in the night, sudden confusion and terror and poverty. At the shelter, Susannah stood for a moment with her eyes closed, sorting out the smells. Coffee, naturally, and the spiciness of frequently cleaned floors. But something less definite, too, a salty sort of scent, like the taste of tears.

When's the last time she cried, before tonight?

It turns out she's forgotten less than she hoped; as if she'd only turned off the television set for a few years, but the pictures were still in the air, waiting to be switched on again. There's her parents' home, her own old home, the place she waited and waited to get out of. A place where things matched. The furniture, drapes, lamps, and wallpaper may have been unlovely, but at least they fit together. Well, there wasn't much money; but also there wasn't much taste. Or if there was, it wasn't Susannah's. She can remember longings for teak and chrome and glass, but times change, and tastes, and teak and chrome and glass are as undesirable to her now as the florid, dark, and weighty furniture of her parents' home was to her then.

Here in her own house things do not match, although they also seem to fit together. The dining-room table is a different wood from the chairs, and the washstand is different again — oak and pine and maple muddled up together. She has venetian blinds in the kitchen, and off-white roll-ups in the dining room, and wooden shutters in the living room. In her study the windows are not covered, since nothing goes on there of a private nature, except perhaps recently with Lizzie and her clippings. Everything in this house means something: a vase and a candle holder are gifts from a former lover; a pottery cup was sent to her by an African man she had interviewed, after he went home to Nigeria; two handwoven cushions were her housewarming present years ago from Frannie. She has paintings, prints, drawings, photographs, and sketches on her walls that have appealed to her over the years, including two of Teddy's paintings from their days together, one in the living room and one upstairs in the guest room. She no longer likes all these possessions, but she is attached to them.

Lizzie is less evident than she used to be. There was a time when the house was littered with her things: a crib and a high chair, rattles and mobiles and car seats and chewable picture books. Susannah was so alone then, and so often scared — wouldn't it have been good to have had a sister or a mother to consult?

When she was a baby, did she disrupt her parents' home the way Lizzie disrupted hers? And did they stand over her crib in the night and pray for nothing to go wrong? Her mother, maybe. Her father would not have considered it his concern, unless there were some crisis.

Is that fair, or true? Everything she thought she knew about him was altered and distorted in an instant. Truly not unlike Ida and her pot of boiling water, pain and revelation merely taking different forms. When the phone rang again tonight, they'd finished dinner, the dishwasher was humming through its drying cycle in the kitchen, Lizzie was in the bathroom getting ready for bed or upstairs doing homework or reading (or clipping more newspapers, for that matter — whatever she does in her own room before she goes to sleep) — and Susannah was curled up on her blue corduroy sofa in the living room, reading the paper and feeling rather luxurious about a day that turned out to have been well spent and now was almost over. Shit.

She thought, uncurling herself and moving without hurry to take the call in her office, that it was likely Frannie, checking in to chat before flying off again the next day. Or Teddy, wanting to tell Lizzie about whatever misadventure he had called about earlier, or some friend of Lizzie's, Megan maybe. Or, of course, a lean, dark stranger with a hankering for the company of a woman precisely like Susannah. Sure.

"Susannah? Is that you?"

Jesus. Think of families, think of the devil.

"Susannah? Are you there?"

Interesting. No "Hello, Susannah, this is Elaine," or, if that were too personal, "This is your sister." No "Susannah, the first thing I want to say is I'm terribly, terribly sorry. How are you?"

Also an assumption that Susannah would know the voice. Although of course she did.

Elaine's last words to her years ago (the last ones she remembers, anyway; there may have been others, like goodbye) were hardly sisterly or endearing. Some nerve calling now.

"How could you?" Elaine had demanded then, hands on stocky hips, standing in the kitchen of their parents' house. "Of all the stupid, outrageous things you've ever done, this takes the cake. How could you just waltz in here and dump this on us? How did you think we'd explain it? What am I going to say to my sons, or anybody else? Here we are trying to be a decent family, be decent people, and you come along with this! You have *whims*, Susannah, you always have whims, and we have to live with them, but this is too much. You've done things that were wrong before, but this is downright wicked. If you don't see that, I feel sorry for you, but you're no sister of mine any more. That's it."

Susannah remembers leaning back against the yellow wooden kitchen cupboards. Who would have dreamed her practical and dutiful big sister contained such eloquence?

Who would have dreamed that she meant what she said?

A little late for phone calls now.

She slumped down in her chair against the blow, closed her eyes. "Yes, Elaine." What does she look like now? She's forty-six and may be a grandmother, but she's missed out on being an aunt.

"I have some bad news, I'm afraid." Well, Susannah already knew that, really, didn't she? There was only one reason for this sort of call, any more.

"Which one's dead?"

"Susannah!" Ah, there was the Elaine she recognized: shocked by someone else's bluntness, never her own. And assuming she could call with her news as if they'd been speaking only yesterday, as if there weren't any great gap of time and rage in there.

"All right, then. Father. He had a heart attack last night in the living room, in front of Mother. He died practically right away. I caught the last flight up from Boston when she called. So when can you get here?"

Of course it would be him. Men die before women; if she'd thought about it, she'd have known all this. How could she not have realized?

Quite a question, too: when indeed could she get there? There'd still been no apologies, or even regrets, just brusque Elaine commanding. She was like that when they were kids, too: do this, Susannah, come here, listen to that, let me show you how, you're doing it wrong.

"Are you there, Susannah? Mother wanted the funeral right away, so it's tomorrow. If you can get an early flight in the morning, I'll drive in and meet your plane, all right?"

Really? Suddenly there was a rush, when he died twenty-four hours ago? When Elaine found out last night? He was dead when Susannah was having her morning coffee, and through all the hours she struggled with that piece on Ida Lovender. He was dead while she was boiling macaroni and slicing tomatoes for dinner. While she was putting plates in the dishwasher tonight and chatting with Lizzie and clearing crumbs off the table, he was dead. So what was the hurry now?

Last night, when she wasn't doing much of anything, her mother and father were sitting in their living room, probably watching television, the heavy flowered drapes drawn, the floor lamp behind her mother's chair switched on so she could be doing something useful with her hands — darning socks? She darned socks for years after no one else did any more. Maybe there was a baseball game on television, her father used to get excited over games. Maybe there was a contentious call or a home run, and he leaped up and promptly fell down dead at her mother's feet. What a ghastly moment for the poor old woman — what would she do?

Call Elaine, of course. Even from Boston, Elaine would take over.

Jesus, she hates seeing that place again.

"Susannah? Do you want to call me back after you know what flight you'll be on?"

"I don't know," she said slowly, holding her breath against faces and moments, unwanted pictures and words. Anyway, she really didn't know. "I'll have to think about it."

She needed time: to catch her breath, or get used to her father dead. So that was that. "If nothing else, I'd have to organize things for Lizzie first."

"Lizzie? Who's . . . oh. Yes."

And Susannah, leaning forward, slammed the phone down on her sister.

Fourteen years of anger, silence, and separation, and Elaine forgot who Lizzie is? Apparently she also forgot who Susannah is.

How could he die? But what else did she expect?

And what could she have done? She made her moves, but he made none.

Shit, she's alone. How long since she's cried just for feeling sorry for herself? No lover, and she doesn't even have a father any more.

One winter when she was quite small, he made a halter for Shooter, their part collie, part Lab, and hitched him to Susannah's sled, and they went careering across snowy fields, Susannah laughing with the delight of speed and danger, her father watching cheerfully, her mother nervous, fretting. These memories are like photographs, clear and sharp but isolated.

In public school she was assigned to collect leaves, press them, fix them onto paper, and label them. Her father went with her into the woods and knew every leaf she chose (although her mother was the one who helped with the pressing and the sticking down). A garter snake unrolled from a rock and slithered into the leaves, and Susannah jumped back, but her father went after it, groping beneath the moving leaves until he came up with it wriggling in his careful big hands. Seen that way, helpless in his grip, it wasn't very frightening. She reached out and stroked it, surprised to find it dry, not damp, and quite frail, really. She held it herself for a few moments, but it didn't move. She began to think it must be too terrified, so they let it go.

Their mother tried to teach her and Elaine to bake, two little girls with smudges of flour on their faces and patches of damp dough clinging to their hands. He ate their efforts kindly.

At the station, surrounded by her baggage as they waited for the train that would take her off to university and freedom, that train she'd waited for so long, eager and impatient, she saw tears in his eyes: unexpected, touching. But she was absorbed in her own joy at the time.

The thing was, those events took place in such a silence! He didn't say, this is good, this is bad, you do this well, let me help you with that, be careful, I wish you wouldn't go, I'll miss you. So how could she have known what other words he contained?

Well, she knew when she took her news home to them that there would be upsets. Women did not deliberately set out to have babies on their own, even those few years ago. In that world, they probably still don't.

She'd forgotten, of course. She was so pleased with herself; on a roll, a woman who made miracles.

She'd quit her job, surprising herself with how good that felt. She was lining up free-lance work, not so difficult—why hadn't she tried this before? She'd had that perfectly seductive evening with Teddy, an interesting sort of pleasure, if not especially passionate; but after so long, they were kind, anyway, to each other. She'd shopped for new clothes, testing waistbands, trying on flat-heeled shoes. She stopped smoking, finding cigarettes made her feel ill. She thought the world smelled different in a way that had nothing to do with cigarettes. She stuck out her belly, trying to make it stretch, admiring her bulging profile in full-length mirrors and store windows.

Oh, she was a happy woman, going home. A bit nervous, yes, but protected by some hard, clear wall of certainty and joy, bulletproof, assault-proof.

Stupid.

But he'd encouraged her to bounce in a sled behind a dog she couldn't steer, speeding over who knew what hazards, tree stumps and rocks, and he handed her a snake so she could find out for herself it wasn't dangerous. Did he think the result would be meek? That she wasn't bold beyond sleds and snakes?

"I've decided to have a baby," she'd said. They were all sitting in the living room, and it was early evening, still light outside. "It's not an accident, and I'm not getting married. I'm wonderfully pleased, and I hope you'll love having another grandchild and—" to Elaine "—a niece or a nephew, finally." She must have been misled by distance and by her years away. Even then, she must have forgotten too much.

Well. Elaine was shocked and horrified, but Susannah figured she'd come around. Her mother, face blotched white and red, fled upstairs and wept, refusing to come down; but she'd have to come down finally, wouldn't she?

Her father, though—her father was the really interesting one. A revelation.

How well can she remember him before that moment? Only vaguely, really. Some incidents, of course, but mainly as a presence: that when he entered the house, or a room, he had the attention of all three of them, his daughters and his wife. Something she and Elaine must have learned from their mother. Just like in school, when the principal dropped into the classroom, there'd be a straightening and a self-consciousness, even by the teacher, because here was a power. Mysterious, because nobody could say why it existed, or just how it was earned, but a power. Its quality wasn't particularly relevant. It could be judging and stern, as she imagined with the principal, or benevolent, as she might have hoped with her father, but the point was the power itself.

He was not unkind, though. He didn't abuse his authority so much as take it for granted. She must have taken things for granted, too.

But at that moment he was angry, in a pale, cold way she'd never seen before. She might even have been frightened, if she hadn't been so absorbed in herself. This strange tall man loomed in front of her and called her a disgrace. He tilted on his feet toward her, towering, and said, "You're a slut. You're nothing but a common slut." She could see the pores where his beard bristles sprouted. She could smell on his breath a faint after-dinner sourness.

Jesus, what a word, though — slut! What an old-fashioned, silly, unlikely word — she almost laughed.

She was caught, however, in the instant her mouth was opening, lips widening, by the pleasure she heard in his voice. His tongue seemed to curl around the word as if he'd been longing and hoping and finally had his chance to say it. How gratified he looked, having spoken.

Did he have some love for secret dirty words? She was thirty years old at the time, and had never imagined that about him.

He became a different father at that moment; although perhaps, too, she became a different daughter from the one he thought himself familiar with.

He was taller than the rest of them, taller even than Susannah, who most resembled him — was that what gave him his authority? Truly, until he hurled that final word she didn't think of him as unloving. More likely she thought of him as solid. Did he not look after them, not always an easy matter? Maybe he didn't embrace his children, but she can't recall feeling deprived. Her mother did the embracing and got few thanks for it. It seemed she acted for him as well as for herself, in that and other matters: representing him at parent-teacher interviews, visiting sick neighbors. Just because the word love wasn't spoken, Susannah didn't imagine it was absent. She must have assumed it, and then leaped to an assumption of unconditional love. Her mistake.

Even then, she was still stupid, missing the point, presuming too much; because she never dreamed that they meant what they said. When she left that old white frame house and flew back to this home, she wept, sure, all the way to the airport, and a little on the plane. It was like a death, she thought (although now she sees it wasn't like that at all), but she didn't consider that there might be no resurrection. She couldn't believe their rules would outweigh love. Or that the word he called her wouldn't finally strike him as silly, too. Where was, if not his compassion, at least some sense of humor, irony?

She found to her surprise, however, that the silence went on and on. For some months, she expected a mellowing. She thought that her mother, at least, would weaken; her mother was the one who always weakened. On the other hand, her mother was also the one who did what she was told, which in this case was the sort of weakness that wouldn't do Susannah any good. She imagined her mother troubled and sad, but under orders not to get in touch. She rooted for just one rebellion, but there was no sign of it.

To hell with them, then.

Still, when Lizzie was born, Susannah sent birth announcement cards to her parents and Elaine, with pictures of the tiny Lizzie. This was so amazing, this miracle appearance, who could resist? She got back silence: no cards or gifts or flowers or phone calls or visits, not even a note saying, "We meant what we said."

She couldn't quite remember what they looked like. She refused to long for her mother, although she was surrounded in the hospital by women who had their mothers handy. Not to mention husbands.

Frannie visited, and Teddy, and a few people Susannah'd worked with, friends. Frannie said, "She's just beautiful." Teddy, for once, was nearly speechless. The others were a bit awkward, confused by the need to congratulate the mother of a legally fatherless child.

So there it was, and it's not as if they haven't made a family. Even Frannie, despite that laying out of rules in the beginning, often has Lizzie to stay overnight, and Susannah imagines they have confidences of their own, which is fine. Of course Frannie has had expectations of Lizzie that don't take childhood into special account. Staying over with her, Lizzie learned she could draw only in the kitchen, not the living room, but was welcome to experiment with the typewriter, eat what she pleased, and stay up until she fell asleep on the floor, for all Frannie cared. Later, telling Susannah, Lizzie would seem to imply that Frannie took her too much for granted. She also seemed to imply she was flattered by such treatment, for a change.

For that matter, visiting Teddy she's seemed flattered by his rather cavalier care.

Susannah's parents have been married for more than half a century. She has missed, among other things, their golden anniversary. Elaine would have gone up from Boston with her family to make an event of it: a party with family and neighbors and friends. Jellied and potato salads, sliced cold meats and cake. Surely that would be a day when the missing parts of their family would be on their minds?

Well, radical betrayal leads to radical surgery. Screw Elaine and her phone call, screw all those wasted words and gestures.

Still, she's been weeping again, her face is wet, and her nose is running. Here she is, wrapped in her crocheted blanket, sitting on this blue corduroy couch, knees drawn up under her chin, apparently mourning the man who taught her to be daring, however inadvertently or with whatever limitations the lesson was intended.

Does that little Brownie in Surrey adore one father and fear the other? Probably at the moment she's not very fond of either of them, but at least they come to her packaged in separate bodies.

If she'd snapped into obedience when Elaine called, what would she be doing now? Probably she'd be on a plane, headed toward that dim kitchen where they would sit, she and her mother and her sister, drinking tea and talking. What about?

Him, probably; the only subject, under the circumstances, but such different points of view! The discussion might well end in wrangling, some dispute, in bitter words (her own, no doubt) and sorrow.

Back there, people will be coming and going, bringing food and sympathy. There will be a hum of conversation and plans: schedules for funeral arrangements, small jobs to take up time. Probably the efficient Elaine will want to sort through his things, get them cleared out before she leaves. What might she find? (Lizzie, sorting Susannah's treasures, would discover correspondence from men, including Teddy, she might find distressing or astonishing. What an odd perspective for a child, to see a mother from a lover's point of view.)

Years ago, Susannah read about the death of a famous theologian who was discovered to have secretly possessed an astonishing collection of pornography. She pictured the theologian's wife opening a drawer in his desk she'd never gone into before and encountering women with their legs spread; faceless women touching themselves or being touched; women with animals; women with men with whips; women beating men with whips; women with animals; women manacled or muzzled; women being caressed or raped — a whole literature of hate. Imagine that woman, that wife, opening the private drawer of a man, her husband, whose thoughts had ostensibly been turned toward divinity, and confronting so much flesh.

Careless of him to have died.

Susannah's father was never a careless man, despite mislaying one of his daughters. Still, what might Elaine (and her mother) find among his small possessions that might be shocking, or even surprising?

And where might such a thing be tucked away, out of sight

in some private place? Where in that small house would there be a spot that might be only his? Not the long dark front hallway, too plain and empty. Perhaps the dining room, where that heavy furniture has plenty of drawers? Certainly not the yellow kitchen, her mother's territory. Nothing private in the bathroom, a simple space of narrow purposes. The living room's too spare, just small, drawerless tables, two chairs and a sofa, a television set—a room weighty with furniture and gloomy wallpaper, but no hiding places. Upstairs in the bedrooms? His own room shared with her mother, his wife, where there are closets and bedside tables and bureau drawers? Or Elaine's old bedroom, or better still Susannah's, least likely to be occupied except, perhaps, by visiting members of Elaine's family. Upstairs, up those fourteen wooden steps (which Susannah used to count, going up and down, like counting off her progress somewhere) with the brown rubber treads tacked down so no one would slip—up there could be treasures, couldn't there? Not anything of value, she doesn't mean that, but of significance.

What if he had some secret and Susannah never knew it? Or some message (a silent one, naturally, or possibly obscene). Oh, curiosity, that old lure, tightens her skin.

When she was in labor with Lizzie, she held to the thought that the pain would finally end, and of course it did. This would only be a weekend, after all. When it ended, she'd be right back here.

It's very late, almost midnight, but midnight means nothing to Teddy. Even Lizzie is likely still up, although they may be out on one of their rambles. At any rate, it's never too late to call.

It is, however, too late to disturb strangers, and for a moment she thinks she's dialed wrong when the phone is answered by someone who is neither Teddy nor Lizzie: a woman, brisk and young-sounding. "Is Lizzie there?" Susannah asks, ready to hang up.

"Yes, she is. Just a moment, please." The voice turns away and Susannah hears it saying, "Lizzie? It's for you."

From a distance, Lizzie's faint voice. "For me? Who is it?"

"I don't know, dear. Maybe your mother."

Dear? Who is this in Lizzie's life who calls her "dear," whom Susannah has never heard of?

Lots and lots of surprises today.

"Hello?"

"Hi, it's me. I'm glad you're still up. Listen, two things." She speaks briskly and calmly, to let Lizzie know she's back, more or less, to normal. "First, I'm sorry about tonight. I must have scared you, and I apologize. Second, I've decided to go home" — home? — "for the funeral tomorrow if I can get a flight. If you want to come along, you can, but don't feel you have to. We can make other arrangements, but I thought you should have a choice." Choices, she decided early, were the best she would offer a child.

"I thought you weren't going. Did you change your mind?" Lizzie sounds astonished, as well she might.

"Strange, yes, but true."

"Do I have to decide right now?"

"It'd help. I'm sorry to rush you, but I have to call the airport."

There's a pause, then, "What'll it be like?"

"Pretty dreadful, I imagine. You can probably stay with Teddy or go to Megan's if you want. I'll be back the day after tomorrow."

"How come you're going?"

"Oh, well, I guess it started to seem harder not to. I thought maybe I'd wonder about it if I didn't go." Can Lizzie understand that?

"I guess," Lizzie says slowly, "I'd wonder, too." Oh, what a smart kid. Good kid, lovely kid. Wait till they meet her and see what they've missed.

"Okay, if you're sure. I'll call you back in a few minutes. We might not be able to get seats anyway." But on an early-morning flight, no problem; so no escape. This time when she calls Teddy's, Lizzie answers. "Can you be out front at five?"

"In the morning?"

"I'm afraid so. See if Teddy has an alarm clock, but try not to wake him when you leave, okay?" Him and who else—that woman who calls Susannah's daughter "dear"?

Packing is just a matter of a few things for each of them, and it's only difficult finding clothes that might be remotely funereal. The swollenness won't wash away from her face. She needs to sleep; whatever else tomorrow, now today, may be, it will be difficult for sure. In a few hours she will see her mother and her sister for the first time in fourteen unknowable years. (And maybe a couple of nephews and a brother-in-law as well, and who knows who else?) She will also be burying her father, in the most literal way.

She isn't going to call ahead. She and Lizzie will just appear on the doorstep and then see what happens.

This may be the most terrible mistake.

Still, they are going. Not just because plans have been made, seats reserved, clocks set, but also because the thinking part's done and the action is under way—pretty much the way she went about getting Lizzie. But oh, Jesus, she had such hopes then!

She cannot imagine what will happen.

Maybe this isn't so different from the way that father in Surrey launched himself into humiliation and disaster. He maybe was sitting around home, having a beer, when he suddenly realized this was the night of the father-daughter Brownie banquet. He'd start to brood about how much he'd like to go, but then he'd remember he couldn't because her other father had bought the tickets and would be there. He might have sat for a while, getting more and more bitter and aggrieved at the unfairness, until he found himself standing up, reaching for his jacket, getting out his car keys, driving to the church hall, striding toward his daughter, demanding his place beside her. Not thinking it out, just doing it, almost as if he was watching himself.

Whereas the other father, maybe like Susannah's mother and Elaine right now, was sitting down to a banquet he might not have been looking forward to very much, sighing, perhaps, but resolved to do his dutiful best. And then to find himself the center of a brawl! Getting stubborn, his back up, because who paid for the tickets, after all?

These things happen. Maybe this is how they happen.

In families, it seems that somebody pays, or everybody does. It may not be nice, and it's probably not often fair, but at least, she supposes, it might as well be carried through to its end.

RELATIVE FATALITIES

A Thornhill man apparently despondent over the break-up of his marriage shot his estranged wife and the couple's two children Thursday before turning the gun on himself.

Police said Gordon Hamelin, 34, who recently lost his job with an accounting firm, was also the subject of an investigation by the company into missing funds.

"Apparently it all piled up on him," said police Staff Sergeant Austin Webber.

He said that according to neighbors, Hamelin arrived at the apartment of his wife, Joyce, about 7:30 a.m. The couple separated two months ago.

"The neighbors heard some shouting and the kids crying, but they thought it was an ordinary quarrel until they heard the shots," Webber said. "There were three shots about 30 seconds apart." Those bullets, Webber said, killed Joyce Hamelin and the couple's children, Richard, 11, and Lisa, 9.

"Several residents of the building called police immediately," Webber said. "It appears Hamelin was standing at the front window, and when he saw the cruisers pull up he killed himself."

All four were shot once through the head and were pronounced dead at the scene. The nightgown-clad bodies of Joyce and Lisa Hamelin were found in the kitchen, while Richard was in the hallway leading to the door of the apartment. "He must have been trying to get away or get help," Webber said.

Residents of the quiet four-storey apartment building said they didn't know Joyce Hamelin or her children well and had never noticed Gordon Hamelin around the building before.

Just for a minute, Lizzie thought that story had something to do with what was happening tonight, but she couldn't explain it and her mother didn't understand. "See?" She offered the Hamelin clipping to her mother. "Look at this."

Her mother looked at it, then, puzzled, at Lizzie. "But honey, this has nothing to do with it."

Okay, maybe not, but at least it made her mother sit up and talk, pay some attention.

"See, this guy — " her mother tapped the paper " — must have thought he owned his family, he must have thought they might as well not exist without him." She paused. "You could have a point, though, maybe it's not so different. It's all about control and power, anyway."

Lizzie didn't know what that meant.

She's been so scared tonight. Usually her mother's so *cool*. She goes tick tick tick and figures out what to do, she never falls apart. Like when Lizzie woke up a couple of years ago with an awful pain in her stomach, her mother just wrapped her in blankets, scooped her up, carried her out to the car, and drove to the hospital and in a little while Lizzie was having her appendix out, and all the time her mother was telling her not to worry, everything was taken care of, she'd be fine, and she sounded so sure that Lizzie really wasn't very scared. Her mother *never* acts like she did tonight.

What if her mother got sick all of a sudden and Lizzie was

the only one here and had to do something about it? She's never thought of things happening that way around before. Does being in charge of everything ever make her mother feel lonesome?

She couldn't get near her mother. Like her mother was behind a glass door, where she could see her but she wasn't really there. Being left alone like that is terrible—is it how her mother feels, being left? It shouldn't be. It can't be, since it's not as if she ever saw her father.

Lizzie was cleaning her teeth when the phone rang. She thought it might be Frannie, saying goodbye before she went to Vancouver tomorrow. Lizzie could hear her mother's voice at the front of the house, in her office, but not what she was saying. It didn't matter until Lizzie heard the receiver slamming down.

All she thought was, it couldn't have been Frannie. Frannie and her mother argue sometimes, but they don't fight.

Oh, where was Frannie tonight, when Lizzie needed her?

She found her mother in the living room, sitting on the couch all pale and shaking as if she was freezing. Was she sick all of a sudden? Did she eat something bad? Lizzie felt okay, so it couldn't have been dinner.

"What's wrong? What's the matter?"

Something happened to her mother's face when Lizzie said that, it crumpled and her mouth got big and her eyes screwed up and she started making an awful sound and rocking back and forth, the way she'd rock a baby except it was herself, and her face dropped and she covered it with her hands and kept on and on making that terrible noise. It was like being in a room with a strange animal, not knowing whether to reach out or run.

This was her mother, though, after all, not really a stranger or an animal. Finally Lizzie moved close and touched her, just with the point of her finger, on the shoulder, ready to jump back if she snapped. Nothing happened, so she moved her hand a little, rubbing her mother's shoulder and then putting an arm around her and holding her, only lightly because she still might need to move away fast. It didn't feel like her mother even noticed for a little while, or even as if she knew Lizzie was there or who she was. When she stopped making that sound, it was more like she was too tired out to go on than that Lizzie'd done anything.

Finally her mother's hands fell away from her face and she leaned back on the couch. Her face looked like one of Teddy's sketches, lines drawn deeply down, and Lizzie thought that must be what people mean when they say somebody looks drawn.

"I'm sorry," her mother said in a flat voice that didn't sound very sorry. "That must have scared you."

"But what's wrong?" Lizzie's own voice was kind of squeaky.

"My sister phoned. Your Aunt Elaine. She called to say my father died last night."

Lizzie couldn't think of what to say. What did it mean, her mother's father dying, her own grandfather, but she never knew him, so what could she say? All of a sudden an aunt's real, too. They're not just mystery killers or thieves or loonies, those people so awful she's not allowed to know about them.

Her mother shivered and stood and started to walk, back and forth across the room, her arms folded tight against her stomach the way they are sometimes when she's got cramps. Lizzie thought Frannie'd know what to do if she were here. She knows something about people dying.

When Lizzie went to the kitchen extension to call her, though, she only got Frannie's answering machine, and it was hard explaining. "Can you come over, Frannie? Mother's father died and she's upset." She hoped Frannie'd know what she meant by upset, and how awful it was.

Was there anybody else she could call? Probably, but not anybody her mother'd want around. Not even Teddy, even if he really has seen her at her worst.

When she went back to the living room her mother was sitting on the couch again, a blanket around her, just staring at the wall across the room. Lizzie went and got the story about the Hamelin family, but it turned out not to help.

"I could make you some tea," she offered. She had an idea, maybe from a book, that tea is good for upset people.

What did it mean to have a father die, even if you never saw him? Lizzie tried to think of Teddy dying, but it was too hard an idea, and anyway, it couldn't be the same. Also, what made her mother so mad that she smashed the phone down on her sister?

"Thanks honey, but no." Her mother rubbed both hands up and down her cheeks, like she was trying to feel them or rub something out.

"I called Frannie, but she wasn't home."

"She's probably at Alan's. It was nice of you, but I'd just as soon be alone anyway. You go to bed, why don't you? I'm okay now."

How could she be? Except she did look better, even though her hair was all hanging down and her face was white and puffy.

Lizzie couldn't go to bed wondering. It wasn't just things about her mother's family she didn't know, there were things about her mother, too, like her going crazy tonight. "How come you'd never tell me about them?"

"Who?"

That wasn't fair, her mother knew who she meant. "Your family."

"You're my family, as far as I'm concerned. You and maybe a couple of other people."

"Not before, though." Was this dangerous? Could her mother still turn on her? Lizzie watched her carefully.

"Oh, Lizzie." When she sighed like that, was she sad or mad? "Some other time, okay?" She shook herself, smiled a little. She looked as if she was trying to be nice, but it was hard. "Thanks for calling Frannie, though."

Whatever she said, she'd be glad to see Frannie, likely. It wasn't fair, not being told things, and Lizzie got braver, even though she was still scared. "So how come you're angry at them?"

Her mother got a weird sharp look, as if she'd forgotten Lizzie was there and she'd had to remind herself who Lizzie was. "What?"

"Why don't you talk to them? Why wouldn't you tell me about them?"

Oh, gosh, though, suddenly she *saw*. Why hadn't she thought of this before? Her mother says family's so important—so only a family could be more important than a family, right? "Was it because of me?"

"Shit." That sounded mean, but then her mother laughed. How come she doesn't stay one thing or another very long? "You don't give up, do you? Why didn't I raise a kid who'd do what she's told?"

Lizzie waited.

"Okay. My family didn't think I should have a child when I wasn't married. We didn't fight about you, because you didn't exist. Just the idea. Okay?"

From away deep in Lizzie's memory, the word "bastard" floated up.

"When it came to the point, they didn't love me enough."

"But how come?"

"Honey, how would I know? They were crazy. Crazed. My mother was hysterical and Elaine was furious. My father said if I went ahead I couldn't go back there, and as you know, I went ahead."

"Didn't you miss them?" Imagine never going home! What could ever happen so Lizzie couldn't go home again?

"Sure, of course I missed them. But I'd do the same again, I'd go for the future and you, not the past."

"Does your sister want to make up now?"

Her mother sighed. "Oh, most likely she just thought it was her duty to let me know. She's big on doing the right thing. Or maybe because when somebody dies, people feel they need to do *something*, so she called me."

"What are you going to do?"

"Nothing, I expect. There's lots of things I'd like to do, but nothing that'd make anybody feel better."

Lizzie felt a shiver down her back, the kind her mother says is somebody walking over her grave. What if she did something someday that her mother wouldn't forgive? "Anyway," her mother might say, all cold and hard, "Lizzie's in the past. I've got my future to think about."

"Look, Lizzie," her mother said, in that voice that means there's no more fooling around, "go and call Teddy now, please, and see if you can stay with him tonight. I'm not cross, but I wasn't kidding, I really do want to be left alone for a while."

If Lizzie'd been brave enough, she would have liked to say she shouldn't have to leave what's her home, too, after all. But it wouldn't have been smart.

Teddy wasn't exactly thrilled, either, when she called. It seemed nobody wanted her. "Tell her I'm sorry about her father," he said, but Lizzie didn't bother.

She had a million questions and when else was she going to get to ask them? But tonight, she wasn't welcome. Her mother wanted her out of the house, and Teddy didn't sound very happy she was going over to his place, and her mother's family hated just the idea of her. That's even worse than Frannie's father, who went away and didn't bother coming back or even calling. Frannie talks about him like a joke, but didn't she ever feel lost, too?

Maybe not being wanted hurt more because it got said out loud. Maybe that's why her mother never told her before. Saying something out loud makes it real, sort of.

Her mother tried to do the opposite: make things go away with words. But those people were out there, except for Lizzie's grandfather, even if nobody talked about them. Packing a night-gown and her toothbrush, Lizzie imagined three mouths: like the Cheshire cat, only with thin mean lips instead of a grin.

Her brown Teddy eyes staring back from the bathroom mirror were wide and solemn. Who else did she look like? It's like her mother tried to make the world start with herself, and Lizzie couldn't see past her.

Teddy's parents died ages ago, long before she was born. They were driving home from a dance and a drunk driver slammed into them. "My dad was a little drunk, too," Teddy told her, "but it wasn't his fault." He and Lizzie's mother were still together when it happened. "She was terrific. She's a good person to lean on when you need to, your mother."

Once, he took Lizzie out to the city's west end so she could see where he grew up. When they got there, though, he said the house was all different, that it used to be brick and now had yellow siding, and there were flowers out front where there didn't used to be, and the porch was screened in. He said he used to swing from the lowest limb of the maple tree out front when he was little. It was a quiet street with little houses. Teddy said he couldn't quite remember how it felt to live there.

Lizzie pictured those people, his parents, as slender and elegant, but maybe that was because they'd been to a dance the night they were killed. If they'd been at bingo or something like that, she might have made a different picture of them. Teddy doesn't have any photographs. He said they never even owned a camera. Maybe that's how come he learned to make pictures in his head.

She could always ask him to paint them for her, but that would just be Teddy's view, and it wouldn't help her.

He said that when they died, it was terrible, and he missed them, but also he sold their house and got some money from their insurance. Teddy never seems to care that much about money as long as he has enough, he isn't greedy, but even so, would it have made him feel better? He said it meant he could just paint, instead of having to get a job.

Will her mother get something, too, now that her father's dead, that would mean she wouldn't need to work? Lizzie guesses not, since they didn't speak. Anyway, her mother's not like Teddy, her work doesn't just come from inside her own head. She wouldn't know what to do, likely.

Lizzie doesn't know what the people in that other family did, like that dead grandfather, or what they look like or how they talk or what they say or what sort of things they like. Now she only knows one thing they didn't like.

She has hardly ever gone to Teddy's by herself this late at night. Should she have called a cab? She didn't want to bother her mother asking for the money. Her mother didn't even notice when she said goodbye and left.

The bus and subway are so familiar that usually she doesn't even think about them, but that's in daytime. The bus stop is just down at the end of her block. The bus takes her to the subway, where she goes downstairs to the southbound platform. His place is at the fifth station, and she can usually tell by the sounds of the train and the people which station she's in, without looking. Like at the second stop past hers, it gets loud because lots of people who've been shopping get on, and at the fourth one a lot of people, the ones from factories, get off. She likes watching the people, partly because she's been told to — there are purse snatchers and pickpockets, but lots worse, too — but also because it's interesting.

It feels quieter, and also more dangerous, this late at night, and she sits back in her seat so maybe nobody will notice her. If something bad happened, her mother'd feel awful, wouldn't she? Not that Lizzie wants anything bad to happen, but she imagines her mother crying and crying and feeling just terrible. Then she'd be sorry.

The idea makes her more scared, though.

When she takes the subway in the daytime, it's usually crowded with women going home from work or shopping. Sometimes they talk in other languages, so she gets to watch their faces and try to figure out what they're saying to each other. Some of them probably work in clothing factories, like the one that used to be where Teddy's place is now. Teddy talks about them like they're a picture: rows of foreign women dressed in black (although maybe they weren't) bent over sewing machines. Sometimes, the way he sees them, they sit and talk, tell stories and laugh, which might not be really how it was, either. When Teddy talks, it's like he's already seeing paintings, not like her mother, who'd talk about hard work and bad pay and being stubborn and brave. It's funny, how Lizzie can often see what they do, even though they see so differently.

To Teddy, the story about the Hamelin family would be a picture of bodies in particular places, a composition. He'd try to work out where the focus should be, with four people lying still in different rooms. Her mother would have them up and moving, she would talk about things like how the marriage ended, how scared his wife must have felt leaving, how he decided such a thing, and how the wife and her kids might have felt when he came charging into their apartment. How much they might have known about what he was going to do before he did it. Then there'd be him, waiting at the window holding the gun, his family all dead around him, watching the police cars drive up. Was he sorry by then, or surprised at what he'd done, or just scared for himself?

The difference seems to be that Teddy sees what isn't there, while her mother hears what isn't said.

Tonight the subway feels looser than in the day, as if there are different rules, or no rules. There are four teenagers older than her, two girls and two boys, at the other end of the car. They're laughing and yelling, but it doesn't look like they're paying attention to anybody but themselves. Two men, in their twenties except they've still got bad complexions, are sitting a couple of rows ahead of Lizzie, talking to each other, but low, so Lizzie can't hear. She wonders if they're anybody to be scared of. An old shabby man is riding alone, head down so she can't see if he's awake or asleep. His feet stick into the aisle, and he has ripped running shoes that are tied with string instead of laces.

At the third stop, three men get on and sit on the wide seat across from her. They're Rastafarians, she knows by the dreadlocks. They sit close together, leaning with the movements of the train. It's hard not to look at them, although she wouldn't want them to see her looking. How do they make their hair that way, and how long does it take, and how often does it all have to be undone and started over again? Are dreadlocks heavier than ordinary hair, swinging stiffly around those narrow faces? They make the men look so interesting and foreign, and beautiful, too. What would it be like, being kissed by one of those men and feeling that hair around her face?

Or what would it be like to be kissed by anybody, really kissed, she means, not little pecks at parties.

Those three have narrow hips. Dangerous eyes? Not really, just eyes she isn't used to. Where are they going, so close together like that?

Sometimes parts of her body feel warm. What if that keeps happening more and more until she can't sit still anywhere? Teddy must make women feel like this. A long time ago, he even made her mother feel warm, although that's too strange to think about very hard.

When she's out walking with Teddy late at night, the streets are so bright, all the flashing signs and store lights and streetlights and headlights. How come when she gets off the subway tonight it seems so dark? She walks the half block to Teddy's as fast as she can without running.

Right now, while Lizzie is unlocking Teddy's downstairs door, which is tucked just off the sidewalk in a space beside the big glass windows of the dress store so most people wouldn't even notice it, her mother is sitting at home all by herself. What's she thinking about? Does she feel better, now she's alone in the house? Even so, it must be awful, having a father die.

Her mother let go of at least three people, maybe more Lizzie doesn't know about, to have her. How could she do it? She must have wanted Lizzie even more than her story said.

Her mother always says how smart Lizzie is, so how come she never figured any of this out before? It seems so clear and true, now that she knows. Except why is her mother so upset? Does it really make that big a difference that he's dead now?

Teddy's even older than her mother, he's forty-five years old. Someday he's going to die, and it might not be that long from now. What would Lizzie do without him? Half her world would be gone, all the things he sees, and her world's already so little.

She would hug Teddy when he opens the door, except he's not the one who opens it. Who's this stranger smiling at her, a short-haired blonde woman in a wrinkled yellow dress and high-heeled shoes and little golden earrings? "You must be Lizzie. I'm Anne. Ted just went out to pick up a pizza, he thought we might all be hungry. He expected to be back when you got here, though."

Ted?

"I've heard a lot about you, Lizzie. I'm really pleased to meet you."

Well, Lizzie hasn't heard a thing about anyone named Anne. No wonder Teddy didn't want her over here. It seems there isn't a single person in the world right now who just wants to take care of her or who cares how she feels.

Anne takes Lizzie's sweater and hangs it on the steel peg on the back of the door, which Lizzie could perfectly well do herself. "Can I get you something? A pop while we're waiting?" Anne moves around Teddy's tiny kitchen as if she's right at home and Lizzie's just a guest.

"Ted was sorry to hear about your mother." Lizzie thinks that underneath, Anne must be nervous, to talk so much. She has no business talking about Lizzie's mother, either. "Ted and I had dinner with friends a few hours ago, but then we got hungry again, and he thought you might feel like pizza, too."

Lizzie has to say something, so she says, "Uh-huh." She turns to the living area and sits on the sofa, leaving Anne to choose between sitting beside her or across from her in the chair. Anne takes the chair and smooths her skirt with her hands, looking down as if the wrinkles are important. Good. Why should Lizzie be the only one having her feelings hurt?

When Teddy appears, they both turn to him. "Oh, good, you've met," but he's nervous, looking back and forth between them, then hurrying around getting serviettes and plates and passing out the pizza. "Did Anne tell you she's a nurse, Lizzie?"

"No." Well, what's she supposed to say? Maybe he could tell Anne that Lizzie was born in a hospital, as if then they'd have something to talk about.

It isn't usually like this when she's meeting one of his women friends. He's usually more relaxed, so it seems as if it's not very important, or as if Lizzie's the important one and the woman's there kind of accidentally. This feels different. At least with her mother, whatever men have been around, they haven't ever been more important than Lizzie. (Although it seems grief, or whatever her mother's feeling tonight, can do what love hasn't.)

Even the air here smells different. Some musky scent that has nothing to do with pizza is cutting through the usual sharpness of paints and thinners. Perfume?

"How's your mother doing?" Teddy asks. "When's the funeral?"

Oh, gosh, when? "I don't know. She didn't say anything about it."

"I suppose I should call her. She might want you to stay here a few days while she goes to it." He doesn't need to think Lizzie didn't spot that little shrug when he glanced at Anne right then, when he said that.

While Lizzie's sitting here, could her mother be planning to escape? Right now, is she flying off to that other, secret family? "She only said tonight. She said she wanted to be alone. Except I called Frannie, so maybe she's there now."

It's funny, how his face scrunches when she mentions Frannie. Maybe Lizzie's face scrunched like that when Anne answered the door instead of Teddy. It can't be the same, though, her and Anne, Frannie and Teddy, can it?

"I'll check with her anyway. You and Anne finish the pizza before it gets cold. And get acquainted."

Why bother? There's never any point; except Anne doesn't know that, of course. "So Lizzie, what grade are you in?"

"Eight."

"So you'll be going into high school this fall?"

"Uh-huh."

"Are you looking forward to it?"

"I guess so. It'll be different."

"Oh, it is, yes." Anne leans forward, looking kind and interested, but Lizzie knows people can make themselves look that way, especially when they want Teddy. "I remember when I started high school what a shock it was, being a nobody again, with everybody else older and bigger, instead of being at the top of the heap like you are in grade eight. But I expect you'll make new friends fast. I did."

Why should she want new friends when she's got perfectly good old ones?

"So what do you want to be when you grow up?"

None of her business. Still, Lizzie wishes she had something really grand to tell her, something that would make her and her nursing feel pretty small. Something that wouldn't make her laugh. "I don't know yet."

"Are you artistic like Ted?"

"I don't think so."

Finally, Teddy gets off the phone. "You were right, she just wants you to stay the night. She says she's not going anywhere. Boy," he shakes his head, "she's a tough one, isn't she? But I guess it's not our business."

Does he mean his and Lizzie's business, or his and Lizzie's and Anne's? How come Anne isn't polite enough to go away? Is she really stupid, not knowing she isn't wanted? Except Teddy must want her, and he must think that's more important than Lizzie.

"I guess," and at least Teddy's talking just to her "you've had a bad day."

"Yeah, sort of." She has to be careful and strong, so her voice doesn't shake or her lip tremble. Her mother always says, "You should only cry when you're really unhappy, never to get what you want or to make somebody feel bad. That's cheating." She didn't say what to do about crying when you really are sad, but when it might also be a way to get what you want. "Mother was upset," she says.

"She would be. It's a long time since she's seen him."

Lizzie nods. "I know."

"What do you know?" He sounds almost sharp, like her mother before.

This isn't any of Anne's business. She shouldn't be here, listening. "Just that they were mad at each other because he didn't want her to have me."

"She told you that?"

"Yeah, but I asked her. Why, isn't it true?" Of course it is, but why does he sound angry?

"The point is, her family's not your problem. You shouldn't imagine it was any of your fault, or even that it had that much to do with you. She was always running up against them. Or running away from them. Having a kid was just the last straw, so I don't want you thinking anything was your fault."

"But I asked her." Why doesn't he understand that? "That's why she sent me over here, because I made her mad, asking." Her voice has gone high and childish, and she's sorry she told him anything because now he's angry at her mother, which is dumb. Except sometimes Teddy *is* dumb.

"Okay." He pats her hand, then strokes it. "It's just, I wouldn't be much of a father, would I, if I didn't care about you being upset."

Sometimes it's hard to know what kind of father Teddy is. Even Megan's dad, who has another family now, is still her father, but Teddy's just Teddy. Maybe it's that there's no actual place where Lizzie's family has been all together, ever.

If Anne weren't here, she could just curl up on the couch, maybe with her head on Teddy's lap, and go to sleep, not have to be sharp, on her toes, watching so she doesn't miss anything or give Anne any room. Anne should know that when Lizzie's here, this is her and Teddy's place, not just Teddy's and not ever Anne's. So she starts talking about being here, telling tales in a steady voice of things they've done together. Teddy gets caught up in it, too.

"Do you remember," he says, laughing, "the night we got picked up by the cops when we were out walking because they wouldn't believe I was your father?"

Of course she remembers, but he sure didn't think it was funny then.

He turns to Anne. "It was two in the morning. They thought I was a child molester, and of course I wasn't carrying any proof I was her father. Susannah had to come and rescue me."

The night it happened, he was furious. He argued with the policeman in the car when he pulled up beside them on the street, and all the way to the police station. When they got there, he was really yelling. He told them and Lizzie told them that he was her father, but they just kept making calm-down noises. "I'm sure you are, sir," one policeman said, "but as a father, you'll appreciate that we have to check." Lizzie was maybe six or seven. She remembers sitting at a desk at the station surrounded by enormous strangers, some of them frightening, and crying because she didn't know what was happening. Teddy'd yelled about calling a lawyer and they took him someplace, so she didn't know where he was, either. "But Teddy's my *father*," she kept saying. "We always take walks."

"Just be patient," the big man across the desk said. "We'll wait and see. Are you hungry? Would you like a chocolate bar? You must be sleepy. Are you up this late very often?"

Mostly what they were waiting for was her mother, who showed up angry with everybody except Lizzie. She was mad at the police for not believing Lizzie, and at Teddy for making so much trouble. After she got calm, she said she supposed it was a good thing the police kept their eyes open for suspicious men with kids, but she stayed angry at Teddy, and since he was tired and cross, too, and maybe scared, they wound up yelling at each other right in front of everybody, and then her mother took Lizzie home with her instead of letting her stay with him.

Now Teddy tells it as a funny story. To Anne.

"You know what else?" he asks now. "I got arrested again today. It was on TV, did you see it?"

"No, we didn't watch the news. What happened? Are you in trouble?"

He looks a little hurt that she doesn't already know, but when he says what it was about, it doesn't sound very serious. He's been arrested before, after all. "Were you in jail?"

"Just for a few minutes, till I made bail. I don't think anything much will happen, I only thought if you saw it, you might have been worried."

"Is that how come you've got a bandage?" When she saw it, she hadn't even thought about him being really hurt. She figured he'd just run into something or tripped and fallen down.

"Yeah. A few stitches, but Anne says there won't be much of a scar."

Well, she'd know, wouldn't she, being a nurse. Is that why she's here, to be his nurse?

Not likely.

Never mind, whatever Teddy does, he's still a whole lot better than a lot of other fathers. He's better than Megan's father, who went off and made another family, and better than her mother's father, who must have been very cruel and now is dead. He's certainly better than Gordon Hamelin, who'd have been in jail for killing his family if he hadn't killed himself first.

Imagine Teddy charging into her mother's house, gun blazing, wiping them out!

He never would. For one thing, he hates guns. For another, he'd never be that crazy. And her mother'd be so mad he wouldn't dare. The picture makes Lizzie giggle. She'd like to give him a kiss, at least for being Teddy instead of somebody else, except love doesn't belong in front of strangers. Just like crying or hugging. Strangers should know enough to leave.

So maybe, after all, sometimes there is some point to violence. At least it must be a way to make people go away, if otherwise they won't.

HIGH FIDELITY

The renowned 80-year-old French artist Jean Martel and long-time companion Aline-Marie Giraud drew members of the elite from the worlds of international art and cultural politics Friday to a party celebrating their 40 years together.

The aging but vigorous Martel joked that he and Giraud, mother of two of his five children, neglected to have a wedding ceremony, but wanted to mark the anniversary of "the moment when we came together."

More than 300 fellow artists, friends, and representatives of cultural institutions on three continents attended the bash at the couple's Mediterranean estate.

The question of who received invitations and who did not was of consuming interest in the art world for several months, and arrivals at the iron gates of Martel's estate received the sort of attention from the media and onlookers that is normally reserved for stars at film premieres.

Martel, who abandoned surrealism in favor of a colorful style described by one critic as "a sort of demented realism," met Giraud when she was a 22-year-old model. Within a year he had left his wife and three children to live with the young woman who subsequently figured in dozens of his works.

"She has kept me alive here and here," the artist told an interviewer two days before the party, touching his heart and his head. "And also here," he added, spreading the hands that have created paintings that now sell for hundreds of thousands of dollars.

"I honor her because she has been more a wife than a wife could be," he said. "She is silent, grave, beautiful, and a good mother to my children. I am a noisy, frivolous, ugly old man, and I have not always been a good father, but she has known how to live with genius."

Giraud, still striking at 62, has also managed Martel's business affairs for the past 23 years. She spoke little during the interview, saying only that it has been "a privilege, an honor" to have spent most of her life associated with a man acknowledged to be among the greatest artists of the century.

They sure don't make women like that any more; or if they do, Teddy hasn't found them. In his experience there's always some twist, some event or demand, preventing that agreeable Giraud-style adoration. Although he has to admit he's no Jean Martel either, and that may make a difference.

What would it be like, having a silent, grave, beautiful woman paying him her full attention? Actually, it would probably be like having somebody reading over his shoulder, a vague, hovering, annoying presence.

Anyway, there's no telling what upheavals have occurred in forty years in that Martel menage. With two passionate people, even with just one passionate person, there are bound to have been quarrels, betrayals, renunciations, and appeals that didn't appear in that smooth account of forty years together.

Still, they stayed together, and that's a trick Teddy hasn't managed so far. Neither has Anne, of course, or for that matter most of the people he knows. No one is together for forty years any more. No one even expects to be. It's possible no one really wants to be.

Here's Anne, still lying sleeping beside him this morning — exhausted from Lizzie last night? — and even she, who at first glance has a softness he doesn't often see, has her rules and moments of rebellion. She has some experience in abandoning men when she's crossed.

It's cozy, watching her sleep when she's pale and ordinary but also sweetly vulnerable. Of course anybody sleeping is sweetly vulnerable, it's not just her.

She's pale in the morning light. There are creases of shadow on her eyelids. Her lips move slightly as she breathes, as if there might be words just behind them. Could she be trusted?

Once, he took devotion for granted; must have, or his disappointment wouldn't have been so brutal. He expected so much of Susannah: that she would be loyal beyond reason. Even then, when he was young, he knew it was a great quality, that kind of loyalty, and then she shattered it as permanently as she shattered glasses, aiming them at him. After all, in his way he was faithful: he had faith in her. To her, being faithful meant something else entirely.

So what would he hope for from Anne? Or anyone?

Not much. Just another run at love, maybe.

God, he'd loved those days, when he was a leader in a large and righteous cause, naive with power. Not like now, one grown-up man in a small and sometimes hopeless cause. He loved making speeches, his words lifting crowds to cheers and action. He loved knowing Susannah was out there listening, moved in other ways, slower to action, maybe, than others, more careful, his safety and well-being her main concern. He also loved knowing there were others out there, too, still to be met, still fantastic mysteries, unlike his solid, safe Susannah. He loved talking to her and the way she listened, her eyes on him, paying such attention. He loved that she let him try anything he wanted with her, finding out what the best pleasures could be. He would have thought Susannah would be his Aline-Marie Giraud.

What an innocent! He didn't know then what he later found out, first from Susannah but also from other women since: that they rebel, or get bogged down in unromantic details. They are derailed from love, or care, or even obsession, by trivial concerns. They can never grasp the difference between real affection and quick vagaries of lust, for instance: that a simple encounter elsewhere, a tiny, insignificant wandering, doesn't necessarily have anything to do with them. Their reactions, not his actions, have made his little missteps important and even sometimes cataclysmic. Beginning with Susannah years ago, they haven't understood his cry, "But it was nothing."

Women take everything so personally.

Susannah said he wore her out, and that he wore out love as well; although he noticed she had plenty of strength for yelling and heaving dishes at the end. She had quite an aim.

Maybe they can both laugh about it now, or make wry fun of it, but all that took three years of his life. Hers, too, of course. He's found it hard since to trust impressions of adoration. Women are too good at mimicry.

Strange to be lying beside a sleeping woman he hasn't made love to yet. Having Lizzie here last night was cramping, to say the least. How can Anne sleep so easily, with such deep and regular breaths—isn't that kind of insulting? Where's her excitement, that thrill of anticipation, even in her sleep? That's what must have wakened him, he thinks: suspense.

He is forty-five years old. How is he going to look to her when she wakes up and sees light on skin more aged than hers? In daylight, so much is exposed.

Forty-five — what a number! He never dreamed this time could come. Looking out from the inside, he feels like a young man uneasy about trusting anybody over thirty and filled with the rage of purity. Some days it seems everything's still possible. Then he catches his reflection in a store window or a mirror, and just for an instant he wonders, "Who the hell's that?" He never seems to learn.

What shit.

More than half his life has already been lived, and he doesn't seem to have enough memories to account for that. His memory must have huge gaps.

What the hell was Jean Martel doing when he was forty-five? Teddy should look that up. Was he already known to be a genius, one of the great artists of the century, or was he still working on his immortality, much like Teddy? Maybe Teddy needs to age even more before he can touch that secret piece of knowledge, understanding, vision, whatever it turns out to be.

It's an idea that makes him feel like aging cheese or wine.

If he ever gets to Jean Martel's age, but remains only reasonably well-known, respected, a good and interesting artist but not a great one — that will be a sorrow. Some people might be satisfied with that, but he has certain passions. Partly it's that he'd like his work to tell people he'll never meet about all kinds of things he's seen and make them feel all kinds of things they've never felt; but also, to be honest, he doesn't want to die. He hates the idea of going through all this and then just disappearing.

Not that he's had so much to go through, nothing like the ordeals of a lot of other people. But experience ought to be worth something. What he sees ought to be worth something, and how hard he tries to get it down.

On the other hand, one of these days the whole planet, including him and all his works, is going to be blown up. Roasted and deep frozen, like instant coffee. He may have trouble *feeling* that that's true, but he does believe it. He has a silly desire to hide his pieces in a bunker or a mine shaft, someplace safe, so they can be rediscovered in a century or two by whatever form any life may take. They might even be considered masterpieces then, if only because they'd be voices from an unknowable past, magical survivors.

It also drives him crazy that in his mind's eye his work is perfect. In his mind's eye, every line has a meaning that flows into the meaning of every other line, and each painting in a series shifts flawlessly into every other, until it's a whole perfect piece. And he never gets that; sometimes doesn't even come close.

Of course, maybe if he ever made a perfect work, it would be his last.

He'd like to find out, though.

Also he'd like to know if even a man like Jean Martel looks at what he does with any disappointment.

These are not matters Teddy talks about. There's too much potential in them for pity. Anyway, they're private. Hope can get wrecked, talking about it.

Jesus, he's got a woman in his bed here, what's he doing? A pretty little unknown person to entertain and occupy him. If he's lucky she'll delight him, and if he's not delighted, so what, really. What he should do is get up and pee and brush his teeth, be ready; have the jump on her.

What, as if it's some kind of contest? Well, he's never claimed to be a nice guy. Not even from the start, with Susannah, did he pretend to be that.

Watching Anne, though, it's still hard to know if it's worth beginning something when he can already imagine the end. No wonder Lizzie can be snippy and rude—why shouldn't she be, when she must know that such things never have any future?

When he came through the door last night with the pizza and saw Lizzie was already here, with Anne, he had a little hope they liked each other. From the distance of the doorway they made a happy composition: sitting at odd angles to each other, one blonde, the other dark-haired, flushed, under the lights of his apartment, surrounded by his furniture, his work, his place. But they were too relieved to see him. What they seemed to have in common was discomfort.

"I see you've met." Even to himself he sounded false and hearty. "Good. You up for pizza, Lizzie?"

"Sure."

He felt like the referee of a tennis match in some bad cartoon, switching attention and affection between them, back and forth.

Anne tried to play, but Lizzie—there were moments last night when he didn't like Lizzie very much. Even taking a tough day into account, she seemed to have some sly, unchildish purpose.

Funny to think she's old enough for sly purposes. One of these years she's going to be a grown-up, probably not an entirely nice one, although he'll love her anyway, no matter what, even if he may not always like her. She's certainly been a thoroughly loved child, even if it's really only been by him and Susannah.

Boy, Susannah's going to feel it one of these years, when Lizzie grows up and leaves home. She'll pay then for keeping Lizzie to herself. At least he's used to not having her around much—so maybe he should have paid better attention to her last night? He would have, naturally, if it hadn't been for Anne. It was her being here that really fucked things up.

For all he knows, Susannah, being Susannah, has a plan all ready, ambitions that have just been waiting, actions and goals that have been put off. She's had thirteen years with Lizzie, lots of time to think. Teddy's time has only been counted in hours here and there. It isn't fair.

Who made Susannah what she is today?

Him, maybe. Partly.

When he actually sees her these days, he can't quite imagine having loved her, but when he's just remembering the young Teddy and Susannah, a kind of tender grief comes back. Then he thinks the next time he sees her he'll give her a hug for old times' sake, but when he does see her again, she looks untouchable. Really formidable in her way.

Those are brave men who'd go out with her now.

Lizzie has some of that, maybe. She has something powerful about her, anyway, and like her mother, it's hardly appealing.

Anne tried, but what did she really think of his daughter? He would have liked to show off Lizzie, but that was pretty shitty, wasn't it? Using his daughter for seductive purposes, so if Anne fell in love with Lizzie, she'd look more kindly on Lizzie's dad? Very tacky, really bad.

Whatever he had in mind, tacky or not, had nothing to do

with how the evening went. Lizzie, it seemed to him, went to some trouble to demonstrate that she belongs here, which of course she does, but she made such a point of it, helping herself to milk from the refrigerator, telling stories, examining his paintings. "This is new, isn't it Teddy?" Obviously it was: still propped against a wall, not quite dry.

"Yeah. What do you think?"

"I like it." Then to Anne, "I always like Teddy's work, don't you?"

Anne smiled. "I certainly like what I've seen, but I haven't seen much."

"Oh, so you and Teddy haven't known each other very long?" Such a sharp, quick glance.

"No, actually we just met a few hours ago."

"At Leo and Teresa's," Teddy explained. "You remember them, Lizzie, right?"

"Sure." She nodded. "So are they your friends, too?" she asked Anne.

"I've known Teresa since we were kids, but I hadn't seen her for a long time. We ran into each other again a few months ago."

Teddy pictured Anne and Teresa as little girls together. How different they must have been, sort of like Anne and Lizzie, light and dark.

Very carefully and clearly, it seemed to him, Lizzie pointed out her own history in his place. "When I was little, Teddy made me a swing with ropes he hung from that beam over there. Only I couldn't go very high in case I knocked something over. It was neat, like a playground indoors."

Somehow Anne wound up sitting by herself in the chair facing Lizzie and Teddy on the couch. "Teddy did a painting of my tenth birthday party," Lizzie went on, "with everybody sitting around eating. Remember, Teddy? We went to a gallery later and saw it, didn't we?"

It felt as if she was making him stand beside her, facing Anne in an unfriendly way. Anne just said, "That must have been very nice. You call your father Teddy?"

"Oh, yes, I've always called him that." Lizzie managed to make her "always" sound like forever, but of course to her it was.

Anne was right, she should have left. His head hurt—maybe he'd been really injured? "Your mother," he said, to change the subject, "must be upset," and instantly felt his mistake in a tiny wince of the muscles around Anne's eyes, and a flicker of triumph from Lizzie. He shouldn't have mentioned Susannah.

"Yeah, and you know how she likes to be alone when she's upset." He didn't know any such thing, and didn't suppose Lizzie did, either, until tonight. "I called Frannie, though. She usually likes talking to Frannie." She turned to Anne. "She's my mother's best friend."

"I see." Anne nodded pleasantly.

Teddy winced a little himself at the mention of Frannie, that woman who has been whispering in Susannah's ear, and vice versa, for more than twenty years. Their confidences make him uneasy; he is unnerved by how many hours the two of them must have spent, over how many years, using how many words, discussing him. They'd be hunched over glasses of wine, or sprawled back, laughing. Why does he see them laughing? What at? He feels them dissecting his affairs, his talents — himself, really. He wouldn't even be surprised if the two of them had talked about Lizzie and his suitability for fatherhood long before he was consulted (if anyone could call that soft seduction a consultation). When he has found himself, thank God rarely, with the two of them together, he's had a vision of himself pinned down like a butterfly between them.

Would that be an image to work with, or only a cliché?

It's a gift, this habit of images, but sometimes he thinks of what to paint when he can't think of what to do.

Obviously Susannah and Frannie haven't spent their whole friendship discussing him. They must have had plenty of other things to talk about, although he can't think exactly what. Other men, he supposes, small ups and downs in their careers. Makeup, clothes, families, their little causes, child care, choice, and equal pay—whatever women like that talk about.

Lizzie and Anne were barely talking at all by then, but he could hear a number of unspoken words. From Anne: "Is this the charming, bright child you told me about?" and from Lizzie the flatter, harder: "What do you see in her? Why is she here?" So much silent judgment going on.

That's what he thought, anyway, but he's often enough made wrong assumptions, and often enough they've been about females.   Lizzie's at such a tricky age—who knows about girls at the start of adolescence? Not Teddy; although he assumed vaguely that Anne, as a woman and former girl herself, and as a nurse, should understand. Instead, he thought he could glimpse, shifting so fast maybe only an artist, anyway someone used to concentrating on lines and forms, could catch them, irritation, impatience and a kind of endurance altering Anne's expression. He thought how much her face gave away, what could be read from her mouth, or the skin around her eyes. They changed so slightly, narrowing or crinkling, and there she was, feeling something different from a second ago. That could be interesting to work with: changing moods indicated by subtle alterations of a line here, a shape there — an almost Oriental simplicity. His own eyes narrowed at the possibility.

Anne did try again to leave; she really can't be blamed. "I think I should take off now, Ted," she said when the pizza was gone and the three of them were left just looking, or not looking, at each other. The trouble was, he felt Lizzie beside him stir slightly with pleasure, and it made him stubborn.

"No, stay," he insisted, and Anne shrugged and did. Maybe she'd only wanted him to persuade her in front of his daughter. Maybe she wanted it made clear. Wouldn't that put her at the level of a thirteen-year-old, though, getting into a battle of wills with a child?

The truth was, it was all his fault. He not only let them both in and kept them both, he then couldn't think of a way to entertain them. With Lizzie, he might have played Scrabble or Trivial Pursuit or gone out for a walk. With Anne—well, with Anne his destination would have been clear. With the two of them together, they wound up watching television, the late news, guerrilla wars and politics, not much change of pace there from his living room.

What did people do during that sort of awkward evening before there was television? Listened to the radio, maybe. Or people didn't have that sort of evening before there was radio or television. Probably men in those days didn't find themselves sitting unhappily between young daughters and possible lovers.

Anne leaned forward, looking as if she was paying real attention to the program. Now, still sleeping but shifting toward wakefulness, she looks like a different woman: peaceful, pretty.

How complicated is the person behind those eyelids? How difficult is she, or how kind? He'd like her to stay sleeping, but can't wait till she wakes up.

When the phone rang again, Anne, sitting right beside it, automatically picked it up and heard for the first time the voice of Lizzie's mother. Beckoning Lizzie to the phone, Anne called her "dear."

"I'm sorry," she whispered to him, "I wasn't thinking. I shouldn't have answered it."

He shrugged. "It's okay." Although it wasn't. She had no business doing that. Perhaps she forgot where she was.

Anne and Lizzie had traded places, Lizzie sitting in Anne's chair to talk to her mother, Anne sinking beside Teddy on the couch. Actually, he drew her down there, because if Lizzie had sly messages, he had one of his own, kind of a complicated one that boiled down to, "Behave yourself. Don't be rude to my guests." What an asshole. A thirteen-year-old kid, *his* thirteen-year-old kid, and he was only thinking of himself.

When Lizzie turned away from the phone, she looked almost at the point of tears, and even her voice was tired. "Mother's changed her mind, she's trying to get us on a plane tomorrow morning. She'll be calling back in a minute." If Anne hadn't been there, he'd have stood up and hugged the poor kid.

"Why are you going? You can stay here, you know." And so she could have, although he might not have been that pleased.

"No, I'd kind of like to meet them. Anyway, it wouldn't be nice if Mother had to go by herself." And what has Susannah done, exactly, to earn that sort of concern?

Well, maybe for one thing she's hugged Lizzie with ease in front of lovers and friends.

When Susannah called back, Lizzie answered, speaking quietly for a few moments, and when she hung up, she asked for an alarm clock. Christ, five in the morning! Still, it meant that when they woke up, he and Anne would be alone.

There are times, and last night was one, when he envies proper homes with real walls and doors instead of this great open space. In the darkness, even whispers carry here, and he could hear Lizzie shifting and rolling over on the sofa, getting settled in. And listening?

"You can wear this," and he handed Anne the worn, soft top of an old pair of blue pajamas, kept for emergencies, which this seemed to be. "I'll wear the bottoms."

"No, honestly, Ted, just let me go home. This is too awkward."

So was he keeping her? Was she tied with ropes or chains, so she couldn't leave if that's what she thought she should do? "No need, we can just sleep together." He grinned. "Really sleep."

They appear to have done just that, although not quite right away. He felt, in the darkness, like a groping adolescent again, touching this and that in the face of a final no; except this time the no came from his silent daughter a few yards away. With Lizzie there — sleeping or lying awake, oblivious or hearing? — it was hard to drum up real lust anyway. Still, there was an odd sort of companionability, his arms around Anne, one of hers across his ribs — pleasant, really, in an unaccustomed way. He listened to her breathing until she was asleep.

No sleeping through the alarm, though, even if Lizzie was quick about shutting it off, or through the soft sounds of her creeping around in the dark getting dressed, going to the bathroom, being careful not to disturb and so disturbing him, and possibly Anne, that much more. Finally the door clicked shut behind her, the third step from the top creaked beneath her small weight, and she was gone. That's when he should have turned to Anne, not now when the light's so pitiless, but he must have dozed off.

He found when he woke a few minutes ago that they'd moved away from each other in the night. Their bodies had come apart entirely.

Now he does have to get up, he really needs the bathroom, and there's a taste of stale pizza in his mouth. If he's careful, he can get back to bed before she wakes up. He rolls out gently, barely running the water to brush his teeth, flushing the toilet the slow, careful way Lizzie did, as if that made a difference to the noise.

But what a brisk, bright woman Anne turns out to be. When he leaves the bathroom he finds her already in the kitchen, getting coffee, hair standing up and poking out here and there. Smiling. He tries to smile back, although it's too early, and anyway, shit, he's disappointed. Why didn't she stay in bed, luxuriating in the light until he could get back to her? Turned off, changed her mind, a tease, one of those yes-no women?

He feels wounded. He wouldn't have thought she'd have been the kind to wound him, unless he hurt her first.

Her legs are long and lean for a woman who isn't very tall. He does love fine legs.

"Sorry I woke you. I was trying to let you sleep." His voice is morning-croaky, but maybe she'll find that sexy. He kisses the back of her neck, that irresistible gesture. "Sorry about Lizzie's alarm, too."

"It's okay. She was trying to be quiet, and I went right back to sleep. She'll be tired today, though."

Well, that's nice, isn't it, that he hasn't managed to spare a thought so far this morning to Lizzie's day? She and Susannah will be high in the air by now, well on their way to that house he was in only once, for a weekend visit years and years ago. His impression, now that he's reminded of it, is of a heavy sort of darkness. What the hell was Susannah thinking of, dragging Lizzie off to those people who never even wanted to meet her? To the funeral of a grandfather she never knew? As far as he knows, Lizzie's never been to a funeral before, and this is hardly the time or place to start.

What was he thinking of himself, though? He could have taken the phone and talked Susannah out of the whole thing; at least he could have tried. He could have said, firmly, "Leave Lizzie here, she'll be fine, that's no sort of thing to do to a kid." But he didn't, did he? Too wrapped up in Anne, too peeved by his own sense of injury.

He seems to remember Lizzie's grandmother, Susannah's mother, as a tiny woman. She seemed camouflaged, as if she'd fade into her surroundings, matching the wallpaper indoors and the greens and browns of grass and trees outdoors. She didn't say a lot, although she was friendly enough. Susannah's sister — Elaine? — will be there, too, big and bossy. He sees her in a bright print dress, flowers, he thinks. Visiting that weekend on her own, husband and kids — two sons? — left behind in Chicago. No, Boston. He has some memory of her telling Susannah to do something or other, probably nothing important, but it got Susannah's back up.

Susannah's father looked him over and shook his hand. They talked about hockey. Her father made some reference to the length of Teddy's hair, and another to student layabouts who didn't know anything about a good day's work. He looked a lot like Susannah, same bones. He looked a lot *at* Susannah. He seemed fond of her but also frightened of her in a way: as if he'd lost some advantage. Because she was with Teddy? Her father spent much of the weekend in the living room watching television, or at the dinner table, concentrating on his food.

An uninteresting bunch. Teddy, bored and irritated, refused to go back for more visits, but that one did make him wonder where Susannah came from.

They became more interesting later, of course: worms who eventually turned in a particularly cruel way.

Poor Lizzie, she's so used to being loved. What's it going to be like for her, meeting people who not only haven't loved her but have sternly avoided meeting her? What kind of people are they? And here he is, Teddy the protective dad, all those good intentions, but when it comes to the point he sends her off without even thinking to the only people he's sure can hurt her.

"She'll be all right," Anne says, lightly touching his cheek. "She struck me as a pretty tough kid when it comes to looking after herself."

"How did you know what I was thinking about?" Weird. He doesn't like people being able to read his face. And what does she mean, tough? Does she mean selfish?

"You looked worried and far away, so what else?"

Nice, really. A paying-attention person. "What a clever woman you are," and he tries to say this as lightly as she touched him.

"I know."

He can see much more clearly, now that it's daylight and the three of them aren't stuck together in this room, that if he likes one of them, he doesn't have to dislike the other. That's only how it felt last night, when he was tired. "I'm sorry you had a bad time. Lizzie was upset. She wasn't herself."

"I realize that." She draws away, though, leans against the kitchen sink, looks at him seriously. She really is pretty. He really would like to be reminded what those lips feel like and to see her now that there's only the two of them here. If she'd waited in bed, he'd know by now, he'd be looking at her, touching her. Here is the thrill of curiosity, the point of these pursuits.

"To tell the truth," she says, "I think she *was* herself, at least partly, but I do understand, she'd had a rough day. I guess you know she's got your eyes; except she watches in a different way, I think."

What the hell is she talking about? He's considering nipples and thighs, and her mind is on Lizzie and eyes? Anyway, nobody gets to criticize Lizzie. He can, and Susannah can, but nobody else.

On the other hand, Anne's the one who's here, not Lizzie, and at least she's no liar. At least she isn't just making nice noises, the way some women would. "Maybe, but she has to understand she can't run people out of here. It's just that she doesn't know you, and it's probably hard for her sometimes, meeting new people."

"Does she have to meet new people very often?" Anne's still smiling, but she has a sharper look.

His own voice stiffens. "Not really." Like answering his phone, she's out of line; sounding possessive, bad enough, but prematurely possessive, which is worse.

"Sorry. Now you're mad."

"No, I'm not."

"Of course you are, and you're right, that wasn't any of my business. What I was actually wondering was if she hopes you and her mother get back together. Is that why she doesn't like it when you're with somebody else?"

What a bizarre idea! "Shit, no. We've never been together, at least not while Lizzie's been around. I don't think the thought has ever crossed her mind."

"Then maybe it's just me she didn't like. Although usually I get on okay with kids."

As if it must have been Lizzie's fault? But she's just a kid. "At least she doesn't hide things. She's pretty honest, and smart, too." It feels as if he wants to quarrel; it may be childish, but his feelings are hurt. Also he wants to find out what Anne's limits are and when she will retreat.

"I'm sure she is, but Ted, those are just qualities. What about what goes on inside her head?"

What the hell is she talking about? What is there to know besides qualities? Look at Anne herself. He might have described her, until a few minutes ago, as gentle, kind, understanding, sensitive, smart, all those good things, but underneath there are these other critical words, aimed at Lizzie. Who knows what else?

"As you say, though," she goes on, "it must be hard for her, getting used to strangers going in and out of your life."

Maybe that's not exactly backing down, but at least she's thinking of Lizzie. Better than him, and, after all, she was the one who remembered in the first place what sort of day Lizzie must be having. Time to change the subject, move on. He draws her toward him. "Well, she had no way of knowing you might be different. Why don't you stick around and we'll show her, okay?"

Jesus, what the hell did he mean by that? Honest to God, moving on is one thing, but implying some kind of future or making a promise is definitely something else. Still, he can feel her body relaxing under his fingers, he's getting there. She is attractive, even if she doesn't have the striking sort of looks that usually appeal to him.

"We could give her a little time, if you like," she says softly. "To work up a little faith."

It probably doesn't matter much what either of them means. The point is, this is the moment to take her hand and lead her to his bed, where he can pay his own kind of attention, knowing it's quite safe, since Lizzie is far away and won't come bounding in. Interesting—he hadn't realized the diverting effects of that incident with Janine, which has left him listening for that creaking step.

It turns out that Anne also is quite passionate in her small-bodied way, and agile and willing. He doesn't notice her noticing the imperfections of his body, and the little huffy sounds she makes are odd, but also flattering.

Rolling away, he reminds himself to call Leo and Teresa, to thank them.

When they fall asleep this time, they're curled together. He feels strong, and contented, and pleased with himself. With her, too, of course. Turns out her getting out of bed too soon didn't mean what he was afraid it meant. She's really something, although it's not easy, and too early anyway, to say quite what.

Strange, these accidents, even accidents arranged by friends. Who would have dreamed? A day ago he was dreading that dinner, but look at the result, a lovely naked woman with her hand resting on his thigh.

A temporary result, probably, but enough for the moment. He dozes off with a pleased picture of himself as a man of passion and of peace, politically and domestically. Rapprochements on every level seem quite possible.

He wakens to find Anne watching him the way he watched her earlier, but as far as he can see, uncritically. Not bad, waking to a sweet face, brilliant sunshine falling across the bed. What time is it?

He stretches. "You know what we should do?"

"What?"

"Wander down to the market, pick up something disgusting for dinner. How about eels? How does that strike your fancy?"

"It doesn't, unless you know a way to cook them so they look and taste like something else. I wouldn't mind changing my clothes, though. Could we go to my place?"

He'd rather not. He'd rather picture her in his life, not himself in hers, but never mind. "Sure, if you want. And the market. We'll have an outing."

Showered, dressed, and holding hands, they run down the stairs and out to the street. He supposes it's possible that the people out here don't notice them, although all this pleasure should make them stand out. What a fine, secret joy it is, to be out walking with a woman he's just made love to, and looking forward to a repeat performance. They should stand out like lights, even in a crowd.

He has an idea of painting her later: something simple, a shape framed against his window.

"I should water my plants, too." Plants? Who takes time out from passion to water plants?

She lives on the fifth floor of a high-rise, not so many blocks from his place, but once again, a different world entirely. He hates dead places like this, furniture chained down in the lobby, hotel landscapes on the walls, an elevator where people stand silent, watching the floor numbers light up, then beige corridors and matching doors. How can she stand it? A place like this is bleaker than any street corner in the city.

But when she unlocks her door and draws him inside, he might almost forget where he is. It looks like an advertisement for something, possibly taste, all clean and matching. Plants! Jesus, no wonder she had to get back to water them. Greenery hangs from ceilings and sprouts from tabletops and peeks out from pots placed artfully in open drawers. "Christ, you've got a greenhouse here."

"Too much, do you think?"

Way too much. Kind of spooky, although he doesn't say it. He might have to paint her differently now, having seen this. Instead of a tiny figure against huge glass, all distorted by the light, refined, she'll have to be some sort of jungle woman, more primitive and ferocious.

Although everything *is* contained. It isn't as if her jungle's growing free.

"You can't have pets here, but I hate living without something that's alive, so I got myself a couple of plants and then things got out of hand." At least she can laugh. Thank God she isn't serious.

In her bedroom she's jittery, like a hostess with a difficult guest, not as comfortable in her own territory as in his. Well, maybe she feels more responsible here. Or self-conscious. It is amazing, after all, and must mean something that her drapes and bedspread match and pick up precisely the silver in the wallpaper. "You must think I live in a slum, compared to this."

"Are you kidding? Your place is fascinating."

So is this.

Is it strange, that she can instantly spend all this time with him, without anything to rearrange? These must have been going to be blank hours for her, if she has nothing that needs canceling.

Or she is just what he likes, adaptable.

Maybe it's a little sudden and strange, but it occurs to him, lying on her bed and looking around her well-ordered room, that if he were arrested tomorrow and needed bail, he could call Anne. He *would* call Anne, and even if she didn't have the money right at hand, she'd go out and get it for him. Is that true? He feels pretty sure, even without any actual facts to go on, that he could depend on her. And that she'd like that.

At the market they compare vegetables and fruits, standing close, touching each other as they handle the produce. They wind up with two salmon steaks for dinner, then stop for coffee, sitting together, pointing out odd people to each other. "We can go for a walk after dinner tonight," he suggests. "It's a lot different at night."

Lizzie's the only one he usually invites, and most often he goes alone. Maybe his head's still fucking him around, a concussion, fractured skull?—but he can imagine days like this going on and on.

Except that eventually Anne has to work, and he does, too.

He almost has—not quite, but nearly close enough to reach —a sense of faith: if he began to fall, she'd hold him up. Then tie him up? If he were smart, he'd run, right now.

He must have had this sort of feeling before, men his age don't suddenly get whole new feelings, but he can't think when, or who he might have been with.

He waits on a bench, watching as she leans over a cheese display, picking out a garlic-studded cheddar, making some joke with the guy behind the counter. She looks so bright; not bright the way he means it when he says it about Lizzie, not smart, although Anne seems smart enough, but bright as in shining. Lit up.

It's important, though, to remember that events and people fade. It's nice when they endure, the way Jean Martel and Aline-Marie Giraud appear to have endured, but by and large, in Teddy's experience, radiance is a skittery, insubstantial sort of quality.

Even so, with or without any jungle effects, it would be something to try to get on canvas. When they get back, if the light is good, he'll ask her to be still and let him try to capture her that way.

HOMESICK BLUES

A Soviet sailor who jumped ship in Vancouver and sought asylum in Canada says he's changed his mind and wants to go home.

Immigration officials said Friday that Sergei Valansky, 26, has told them his defection was an "impulsive act," which he now regrets. They said his wife, a four-year-old daughter and his mother remain in the Soviet Union "and he misses them."

Valansky was a sailor on a Soviet grain ship being loaded with Canadian wheat when he slipped over the side before dawn last June 16. He made his way to a local police station where, after a struggle with language barriers, he finally made it clear he wanted refuge in Canada.

The incident led to lengthy and acrimonious discussions between Canadian and Soviet officials before it was determined that Valansky would not have to return to the ship. His fellow sailors were also reportedly angry because of the tighter restrictions imposed on them after his defection. The freighter eventually left without him.

Now, however, Canadian officials say Valansky is lonely and wants to go home. "He hasn't been able to learn much English," said immigration department spokesman Robin Shell of Vancouver, "and even if he had the right permits to get a job, he doesn't have many skills."

Valansky has been assured by Soviet officials that he will not face punishment if he returns home, said Shell. "We're not so sure of that, but it's his decision."

A Soviet embassy official said that since Valansky "is not an important person, the entire incident is minor. There is no intention to take action against him and no one is angry, except perhaps his family."

Valansky, the official said, "is a foolish and naive young man, but to be foolish and naive is not a crime. When he returns, others will learn from his experience."

The young sailor is to be flown home Tuesday.

Clearly, this isn't a bright young man. Not only impulsive, but not adept at learning a new language or skills or adjusting to a decision he surely ought to have known would be irrevocable. Foolish and naive, indeed!

Apparently he didn't realize people can't just frivolously change their minds about big decisions; doesn't understand even yet that actions have certain consequences that can't necessarily be wiped out by an expression of regret. Maybe he won't be sent to a psychiatric hospital or Siberia or any of those other well-publicized Soviet torments, but does he really think he won't be punished? Even his family — especially his family? — is angry, naturally enough. How abandoned they must have felt, how discounted and unloved, learning that their husband, father, son, preferred to take a dive from a ship and a swim through cold waters toward a strange country where he didn't know the language and had no work, to returning home to them. Does he expect to be greeted with open arms, then? Does he expect to turn up on their doorstep with, perhaps, a charming, stupid smile, and shrug and say the Soviet equivalent of, "Gosh, I'm sorry, I guess that was a pretty dumb move, wasn't it"?

Of course he'd be homesick, but shouldn't he have figured that out before he jumped ship? What on earth did he expect?

Susannah jumped ship years ago, and even though she failed to anticipate all the consequences, and even though, all right, she was homesick, homesickened for a while, at least she gave *some* thought to what she was doing. And she certainly came to realize there'd be no going back.

Although she is going back.

Sergei Valansky should have done what she did: taken a deep breath and gotten on with things. Wouldn't he have learned eventually that time and distance heal? And won't he find out now that returning only brings pain back up close and dangerous?

When the alarm went off, she wakened sharply from a dream — a banal and obvious one, sure, but that has nothing to do with how it felt. In it, she was in some room the size of an auditorium that was lushly decorated with chandeliers and plum velvet drapes, and she was facing rows of people's backs, scores of them, all strangers. She knew, although she couldn't see them, that her mother and her sister were at the front of this crowd. She needed, for some reason the dream didn't answer, to get to them, so she was pushing and shoving, trying to get around, over, through, but strong backs and sharp elbows kept her in her place. The worst part was that no one would look at her, as if she were invisible or didn't count.

If the alarm hadn't gone off, would she have finally gotten through? To which family, though? Lizzie wasn't in the dream. Where was she? Maybe she didn't exist. It seems to Susannah now that in the dream, she was a child herself.

Teddy used to laugh at her when she had nightmares of some betrayal and woke up angry with him. But dreams do carry into daylight. The people who come into them do have some responsibility.

Because of the dream, she has begun this most difficult day angry. Even in her sleep, it seems, she reacts to wounds with rage.

Poor little Lizzie comes stumbling through Teddy's downstairs door and into the car still asleep on her feet. She dozes, curled beside Susannah, all the way to the airport. What a pair they'll make, just when they need most to be on their toes!

At this hour people move sluggishly and quietly, even at the airport; none of those embraces and tears, people sadly saying goodbye or joyfully greeting each other; no unknown dramas, so interesting, usually, to watch.

She steers Lizzie to the window seat when they board the plane. Finally awake, Lizzie looks entranced by the view of what they're leaving behind.

Oh, God, what are they doing? In just a few hours, Susannah will look down on the dead face of her father. How can she do that? What will she see? His eyes, which she last saw hateful, will be closed. Maybe he'll seem harmless, but she'd still like a few words with him.

Anyway, it must be too late to turn back.

Being on a plane is almost like being nowhere at all; a pause in time, a space for shifting from the past to the future without a real present. This time, though, the future is also the past, so in a way she's traveling backward.

No, she will be a cool adult: the best defense.

Even so, she wonders what there will be to eat when they get there. Her mother always used to be baking. "Eat up," she'd say, "while it's still warm."

She tried to teach her daughters the skills she thought they'd need, but how was she supposed to know? To Susannah they seemed meager: delicate pie crusts, clean floors, and obedience to higher wills, human and divine. Likely Elaine, who was pretty good at pastry, has been adept at the rest, as well.

Susannah liked eating the food, and probably she would have been pained if the floors had been dirty. Only she didn't see herself involved. She had better (if undefined) intentions for herself. Who did she think she was?

She must have been a watchful child. She feels she must have known things, even if she could not have understood them or put them into words. She must have been aware of balances and imbalances and made certain decisions without really making them.

She can feel Susannah the child curled inside her now, the nub and kernel, plump and quiet, watching. She rather likes the kid.

It's a bit startling to shift in her seat and see Lizzie beside her, looking out the window apparently absorbed. For a minute there, she'd forgotten about Lizzie. How devastating if Lizzie turned on her one day and accused her of not providing proper nourishment. What a terrible thing if she were to say, "When I'm a mother, I'm going to bake for my kids every day. How many cookies did you ever make for me?" Well, not very many.

Susannah, who was a pretty smart child herself, has been careful to keep in mind that Lizzie is just as smart, and is also observing and assessing. It doesn't do to underestimate a child.

Is it very strange that, although the rules seemed to come from her father's world, Susannah was always angriest with her mother? Certainly it was the least dangerous course; which would make the young Susannah not just smart and watchful, but a coward and a bully to boot, wouldn't it? She could have picked on someone closer to her own size, her father, say.

What a shit she was at Lizzie's age. The sound of chewing — so damp! — at the supper table infuriated her. The way Elaine talked with her mouth full, green and brown and white bits mashing together as she spoke. The sweet and sour smell of laundry day, and then the iron hissing. The nervousness with which her mother watched her father — for what reason? He never hit her, rarely even raised his voice. Apparently he didn't need to.

What secrets did they have between the two of them, that married couple? Like a child, Susannah hasn't thought of it that way before: that she might not have known all there was to know.

Not that it's of much interest now. Too late.

If it really is too late, what the hell is she doing on this plane?

What it came down to finally was a single aim: not to live her mother's life. It took considerable concentration to become everything her mother was not and nothing that she was, but it was also a simple guide, once she had the hang of it.

Her mother obeyed a man and a set of rules there was no apparent reason to obey; Susannah would not do that. Her mother fell in with the standards of the place, which meant everything from frowning on adultery to wearing gloves to visit friends; Susannah would question, and she would wear what she wanted. "But why?" Susannah asked, mainly of her mother. "What if people love each other? Doesn't that count?" Or, "Who cares about gloves? What difference does that stuff make, if people are friends?" Her mother never appeared to understand the questions, although she could be upset that they were asked.

It's blind obedience that can still get Susannah in the gut. Those people who won't imagine or take account of other possibilities and circumstances than their own get to have such simple lives. Not that it would especially matter, they could live in whatever simple-minded way they wanted, if only they'd stay off everybody else's back; but no, there they are, ringing door-bells to peddle salvation, grubbing on TV for cash, marching around worshiping fetuses, demonstrating contempt for women and disregard for any child who's actually been born. They always look so filled with hate. And isn't that strange, when what they're supposed to do, as Susannah understands it, is to love? She does wonder what the hell they think their God is going to say when they turn up for judgment. They'd better count on *his* compassion, anyway.

Meanwhile they're pitiful, of course—flat ruled surfaces with nothing much beneath. But they are also dangerous. It's very dangerous to be so sure of truth. Maybe, then, her mother really was a good example of the enemy?

No. She was never actually wicked; just beaten. Even when Susannah was young and angry, she could see her mother was a tired woman. But if she permitted herself to pity her mother, she risked being sucked in herself.

Whose fault was that?

It must have been grim, though, living with a child like Susannah: cranky, rude, snappish, and superior.

There were months (or maybe only weeks, or days, maybe it only seemed much longer) when she barely spoke to her mother. That must have been when she was about the age Lizzie is now. What a grave resentment she cherished: as if she were trying to raise her mother in her image, instead of the other way around. Was there any love involved, either way?

Just the thought of love, present or absent, draws Susannah close to tears again. What if there really wasn't any?

When she was Lizzie's age, and older, too, she was irritable when she was wakened for school, sullen when her mother praised a good report card, ungrateful for small sacrifices, like the time her mother used her household savings to buy Susannah a graduation dress, a mauve affair of some unpleasant material that delighted Susannah at the time. How ghastly she must have looked!

"You never say what *you* want," she remembers yelling in one nasty adolescent outburst over something or other — who knows? Will her mother remember? Her mother just looked at her. Maybe she was patient, or maybe she loved her daughter anyway; she didn't say.

Susannah wanted her mother to stand up for herself, but Jesus, what if she had? She had no idea what her mother's tastes and desires might have been, and wouldn't she have been dismayed if her mother had decided to agree with her! If, say, she'd gone back to school for that education in which Susannah found her so lamentably lacking, or flounced out of the house at mealtime, announcing she was fed up with cooking night after night, year after year? The shock of such a thing! Because mothers, especially mothers like Susannah's, didn't change. How could they?

Will she be much changed now?

What on earth will she do without him? He told her what to think, how to feel, what to wear, where to live. Or so it seemed to Susannah. "Nobody's ever going to tell me what to do," she remembers promising. Of course people have: bosses, editors, naturally, but Teddy, too, in the old days. She was so pleased at leaving home that for a while she mistook that for her whole freedom, and almost fell into her mother's trap with him. She's amazed that she was once that young woman who felt flattered when he returned from some adventure and told her how good it was to have her to come back to, his solid, strong Susannah.

Other lovers since have tried for obedience, but she'd learned her lesson. Love, devotion, whatever, goes only so far.

Unlike her mother, of course, she has been able to look after herself. And her child. She must have understood quite young that not being able to do that would be a kind of slavery, however cushioned (and camouflaged) by affection.

It would be some joke, though, if she wound up strong because her mother, as she thought, was weak; so that her mother had that power, after all, to make her what she is today.

Of Susannah's two parents, her mother's the one on her mind. She's also the one who's survived.

What an odd relationship there is between time and distance, seen from up here. There are fourteen years, but only a few hundred kilometers; a few hundred kilometers, but only a very few hours. It feels much too fast.

Lizzie is leaning her head against the window, looking out at nothing but clouds. Her hair's tousled — Susannah will have to remind her to brush it when they land, she wants both of them, but especially Lizzie, looking their best. How could she imagine Lizzie might ever disappoint? That she might become, oh, worst case, a drug addict, say, a religious zealot, a fanatic defender of domestic virtues — anything guaranteed to offend Susannah.

"You know what gives me the shivers?" Susannah asked Frannie one night not long ago when they were sitting up late drinking wine.

"No, but you're obviously going to tell me."

"It's Lizzie going off to university or wherever and sitting around with her new friends complaining about me: how hard she has to battle all my unhealthy influences, but how sorry she is for me, deep down. That sort of bitter, patronizing way people talk about mothers, you know? I never realized before how disloyal and mean that is."

Frannie, though, leaned back and laughed. "You mean the way we've talked about our mothers?"

Well, yes.

The difference has to be that Lizzie's been wholly loved.

Wasn't Susannah? She's said, glibly enough, that when she was abandoned, it meant her family's love had fallen short, and so it must have. It made her angry, but right now it also hurts more than usual.

It's unwise, perhaps, to start remembering too much. This whole weekend may turn out to be urgently forgettable.

The attendant, thank heaven, bearing magazines—something mindless, please, and diverting. A little embarrassing to pick a gossip magazine, but she's a stranger on a plane—why does she care? It's as if she's already feeling judged again. Is that what she's going back to?

It's nice to see that Elizabeth Taylor has a grip on her life again, and has gotten quite thin. It must be hard to be a famous beauty getting used to aging. Admirable if it's carried off with some panache, pathetic if it's not. Still, it's hard to muster much pity for the glamorous, just as it is for the rich — really, who cares unless they kill each other off in one of those amazing family feuds they seem to lean to? At least the people in Susannah's family never contemplated murder. As far as she knows, they have merely considered each other dead.

Now, they're really dying.

Ida Lovender must feel watched all the time, even by her husband and her children. Would it be harder to be Elizabeth Taylor when she was fat, or Ida: one stared at because she was a famous woman who used to be beautiful, the other because she's an ordinary woman with an exotic disfigurement.

It's unlikely anyone would sympathize with someone like Susannah, the woman who has everything. Everything includes a certain amount of sorrow and terror at the moment, but who'd give her points for that?

Anyway, she would hate to be pitied.

She does sometimes wonder if she chose her work because she was a standing-back sort of person, or if her work has brought that out in her. God, though — what does it mean if she learned her own observing skills from living in that town?

So anyway, Liz Taylor's pulled herself together pretty well. It must be very odd to go through life with people not only staring at you, but feeling free to judge how you look and how you behave and who you might really be. Like Taylor, or Jackie Onassis, or members of the royal family. Wouldn't you maybe start looking at yourself from the outside? Eventually, you might not be able to see yourself from any other direction.

Or maybe you get used to it and just ignore it. That hardly seems possible, but then, one of the things Susannah learned in that household in that town was that knowledge is power: that letting people know things about her would give them power over her. Her dreams felt too big (and were probably too vague) to talk about.

Does Lizzie have dreams she doesn't dare speak of? Surely it's been different for her. It's important not to confuse your child with yourself.

Thank heaven Lizzie's just occasionally mysterious. Susannah couldn't bear a child as unpleasant as she was herself (although it might be only fair, a retribution).

She was forbidden to wear makeup. When she went to school in the mornings, the first thing she did was head for the girls' washroom to apply the pale pink lipstick everybody wore then, and on daring days a slash of rouge. Eyeshadow sometimes, but that was harder to clean off before she went home. She doesn't know what her father would have done if he'd seen signs of makeup.

Isn't it strange, she has no idea what his objections were. He can't have ever said.

She has always taken care to talk over decisions with Lizzie. At least if she's had to say no, Lizzie's known why.

She discovered, as a girl, a vague but pointed lust. Even then she was a person who admired bottoms; even now can call to mind the flat and promising rears of certain boys. Whatever she's done, she's never gone out with a flabby-assed man, although heaven knows her other standards haven't necessarily been so firm.

Did Elaine look at boys, men, and wonder, too? Surely sisters could have talked in whispers upstairs at night and known that sort of thing — would Elaine have liked to? At the time, she must have felt to Susannah like one of the grown-ups. For sisters, they don't seem to have known each other very well.

At night, upstairs, alone in her room, Susannah sometimes made up stories: that she was in the wrong family, and her real, extraordinary one would find her someday. Sort of the way Frannie made up a father for herself who was quite unlike the real one. Of course a kid has no way to know that the painful confusion of love and hatred is just ordinary, after all, and likely to recur in other circumstances.

Or she gave herself some terminal disease, something mysteriously unpainful and certainly not disfiguring, and pictured the regrets and sorrows—they were wild with grief and guilt, in her imagination. She thought it served them right; but why?

Susannah would almost swear that Lizzie's secrets are nothing as huge as her own were. Still her most absolute and perfect trick, Lizzie is.

Susannah read books the way Lizzie reads newspapers, devouring them for that glorious variety of other ways to live, and other places. God, that's where she thought life was, out there somewhere—any place but where she was. Sitting in Paris cafes, drinking in espresso and ideas; some city, at least, where anything could happen at any moment, any new person could turn out to be fascinating, or become a friend, where it would be possible to do anything because who would care or notice?

So she had the right idea, didn't she, even when she was Lizzie's age? She could never have had her life in the town where she grew up. Sure as hell she could never have had Lizzie.

How did she know, though? She can't remember anyone suggesting she should get away, or even could, so how come she grew up to be so sure?

She remembers counting off the years, months, days, to the

time when she would leave. It seemed forever before her real life would begin.

Although, to be truthful, she had a pretty good time waiting. She wasn't just sitting around like the maidens in those fairy stories, waiting for the prince's magic kiss.

It'll be interesting to hear what Lizzie thinks of the place. Of course it won't be the same for her, she won't have its history in her bones. Maybe Susannah ought to warn her that of all people, she will be watched today.

That would just make the kid more nervous, when she's probably worried enough. Susannah reaches over to pat her hand — reassuring which of them? She is glad Lizzie's here. If she'd come alone, she might have risked disappearing: vanishing like Alice down a rabbit hole and into a place where everything was familiar, but in absurd, peculiar ways. She could have lost her grip on what she's made of herself.

Surely she's not *that* feeble. It's still good, though, that Lizzie's here.

The sound of the engines changes and she peers past Lizzie. "We're going down, we're coming in to land." The earth circles up to meet them and it's far too soon, she isn't nearly ready, she could stay up here forever; like driving in fog, that feeling she could go on and on, but could also drop off the edge of the world at any moment.

They could have flown the long way around the globe to get here, and she still would not be ready.

"It's pretty neat," Lizzie says, "looking down from high up." She's been very quiet. Tired? How much is she fearing this and how much looking forward to it?

Susannah herself is knotted by dread and — what, hope?

The airport is bigger and busier than Susannah would have remembered. She would have expected people to move more slowly, as if they had no real urgent place to go, but either that was only her imagination or the pace has changed here. It's disorienting, to have even a small assumption turn out to be wrong, right off the bat.

She leads Lizzie briskly to the row of taxis outside the airport building, to hell with what it costs, she doesn't feel like driving. As it turns out, it was wise not to rent a car, because she sees immediately that the roads are busy and unfamiliar. The cab whips past housing developments and industries she doesn't recognize at all. It doesn't look as poor as she remembers, or as she would have thought from newspapers and TV, but this is the one part of the country from which she's cut herself off, and it's possible the poverty's been exaggerated in her memory.

It's quite tidy, but the air is different — not as clean? Cleaner?

Going the few miles from their town into this city was a big deal when she was little. They came here to shop for special things, like when she and Elaine needed new fall school clothes. Once the four of them came to a circus — so obviously they went places together and did things, her parents must have had some lighthearted aim to entertain their children. She remembers being disappointed at the shabbiness of the circus; not even the elephants, smaller than she'd imagined, could thrill her, and candy floss melted to nothing, no treat after all. What a skeptical, hard-to-please child, one who couldn't get the hang of the idea that real things, like elephants, could be astonishing. Gratified only by the unachievable?

When she was older, she also came to the city, not with her parents, but with friends, driving in to a Saturday night dance; even a concert or two, although the groups who came here were obscure, no Beatles or Stones this far from the real world she dreamed of.

She sped, in the back seat of someone's car, beside some unmemorable date, in a wild race through the darkness, frightened and excited. Thrilling to tempt death (although she couldn't have believed in death then), but unpleasant to have it in the hands of some unfamiliar friend of her date.

When she got home, her mother was waiting up. The silent reproach, the quiet fussing were irritating—what was the point? She should have known Susannah was fine.

Susannah stormed past her and slammed her bedroom door.

Well, it's a bit late to feel badly about the sort of fury she indulged in then. The causes and quality of her anger have since changed into a quite adult and reasonable rage.

One of these times, probably soon, she'll be holding her own breath while Lizzie drives off with some youth. She might even lie awake worrying. The best thing would be for Lizzie to do the driving herself.

This cab seems to be suffering from bad shocks and a disintegrating muffler system. Between the bouncing and the noise, it's hard to think. It's hard to think anyway. Certainly it's odd to be heading back, it seems irrevocably, to that house, barely recognizing anything along the way. It's only been fourteen years, so much can't have changed, can it? Did she just not see very well before?

Oh, but here's that same old chipped, weathered sign announcing the town: population, 14,000; Rotary and Kiwanis clubs; Presbyterian, Catholic, Anglican, United churches. Were there never any Jews here, never mind anyone more exotic? Perhaps they just didn't care to advertise their presence. A white-bread town, this, its people sliced out of regular loaves.

Laced with preservatives, too, it seems. Now she begins to recognize her history, because here it is. "Boy, it's small, isn't it?" Lizzie remarks.

"You're telling me."

The place, with its bare, rectangular houses, practical plots of yard, frail trees, just grips the earth with its fingernails and toenails: scarcely hanging on. She can almost smell need, some of it her own. They drive on, and the streets close in behind her.

Oh, too dramatic. Too fanciful.

Lizzie, staring out the windows, looks curious. Does she see a quaint, charming town? This might be a good time to make clear that whatever it may look like, it's neither romantic nor appealing.

Instead, "There's where my best friend in high school lived," and Susannah points out a cream-painted frame house, which now strikes her as amazingly close to the street, although it didn't at the time. "Inez Sloane. We used to go on double dates, and we'd stay over at each other's houses." That doesn't begin to say what they did: the secrets, giggling, gossip, quarrels, double dates followed by post-mortems more interesting and speculative than the dates themselves. And what they'd do when they got out of here. They read to each other from literary passages of escape and pretended they were elegant and free. They drew smoke through imagined cigarette holders, releasing it in the direction of handsome, dangerous men; and then they laughed.

"Does she still live here?"

Susannah has no idea. At some point, they lost track. "I was a bridesmaid at her wedding, and we wrote back and forth for a while, but then I guess we both got involved in other things. Our lives changed." It's hard to explain even to a bright kid like Lizzie that some friendships depend too much on circumstance to survive. "I suppose she could still be here." If she is, will she still be tiny and blonde? All those things which, in Susannah's gawky stage, she would have killed to be? By now, is Inez some pudgy, blowsy, maternal figure with her eye on supermarket sales?

What a bitch — as if Susannah's own concerns, most days, are so vital, after all.

No, really she's not so terrible a person. Really, it's only a matter of keeping up her guard.

There's the old dark brick high school, with its well-worn stone steps and the small windows that kept out both winter winds and sunshine. She and Inez walked there together almost every school day for four years. Talking! God, the dramas of boyfriends and feuds, the tiny, intricate dance of it all. She knows she got good grades, but can't quite recall her classes.

She remembers a green tartan pleated skirt fastened with an enormous pin. In her last year, miniskirts were in fashion, and her parents were appalled — another quarrel, more minor turmoil.

High schools are different now, tougher and more exaggerated. Or city ones are, anyway; perhaps not so much has changed here. Then, rebellion was sneaking beer at dances, slipping out for cigarettes at lunch. Some girls had bleached hair and wore their sweaters too tight across unrealistic chests. She remembers one, much joked about, who wore her breasts sharply pointed, tilting upward. There were good girls and there were loose girls, and Susannah kept a grip on herself. Anyway, there may have been some appealing boys with quite delightful bottoms, but none who could have kept her here.

She wasn't saving herself for marriage so much as for freedom.

Will high school be as absorbing for Lizzie? Sometimes she does seem unnaturally sturdy and adult. She might want to break free there, break loose; break her mother's heart.

God, even the stores on the main street have hardly changed. There's the old hardware store, with wheelbarrows in the window; two women's clothing stores, one showing coats, the other what look to be the same fussy pastel party dresses it might have stocked twenty years ago. A men's clothing store, and then there's the hat shop — hats! Who buys them any more, with their trim brims and jaunty little feathers? They seem as out of date as the picture of her mother still darning socks. When Susannah was a child going shopping downtown with her mother, her mother always wore a hat. Also clip-on earrings with perhaps a matching necklace. There were three levels of outfits: house dresses, going-downtown dresses, and church dresses. Maybe a fourth, too, for funerals.

Probably Elaine and her mother have just the right clothes for the funeral. Neither Susannah nor Lizzie owns anything black.

At some point, an aluminum-siding salesman seems to have struck gold here. Door to door he must have gone, turning one frame home cream, another yellow, and the next one green. It's still a *homely* town, though. She can almost taste again that sour desperation to get away.

And now — oh, shit, oh, God — the taxi's slowing, stopping, and here they are. For a moment she can't move for looking at that small, white-painted place, so innocent and ordinary, perfect camouflage for the small tragedies it has contained.

It's often startling to see how normal and unrevealing the faces of mass murderers can be. And people say, "He was always such a nice boy, so quiet and polite." Well, that's what this house is like: nice, quiet, and polite, but look what's behind it: an unforgiving father who is dead, a mother whose motherliness was not as unflawed as her cookies, and a sister whose sisterhood failed. And Susannah herself. What would she say about herself? That she learned one thing and another and then went on, from their point of view, to betray them.

It's easier to recognize on the large scale than the small; safer not to recall too sharply the Susannah who actually lived here, went up and down that walk every day, onto that green-painted concrete porch and through that wooden screen door into the little life inside. She sees that Susannah as much smaller than the grown-up one she is now, but actually that isn't true. By the time she was fourteen, she was as tall as she was ever going to get, and for a while she felt monstrous, looming over boys who took time to catch up.

Is Lizzie her permanent size now, give or take some readjustments in proportions?

If Lizzie weren't here, Susannah might run. She might lean forward and tap the driver on the shoulder and tell him just to take her back to the airport so she could fly home to the solid place she has built for herself out of the shambles of all this.

Lizzie is here, though. "Come on, then, kiddo, I guess there's no putting it off." She still doesn't know what Lizzie expects. Perhaps she should have found out.

Every crack in the walk, every shrub, each chip in the porch is so entirely familiar and utterly foreign, she's light-headed for a moment.

She really did live here. Or some version of her did.

She used to play a sort of improvised hopscotch on this walk. She hid beneath those bushes when Elaine was mad at her.

She used to walk freely through this screen door, in and out. Now, she knocks, four raps sounding hollow. Who will come? What on earth is there to say?

What a tiny woman! Smaller than Susannah, but she's been

smaller than Susannah for most of Susannah's life; but also smaller than Lizzie. An elf of a woman, a gnome. A mute elf who stares at them, her hand on the door catch, mouth open a little, eyes wide.

"Mother?" asks Susannah. Not an easy word to say.

"Mother?" This is another voice from farther back in the house. "Who is it?" The voice becomes Elaine, hurrying into the hallway until she sees and abruptly stops. "Susannah."

Well, well, the prodigal returns — what, no fatted calf?

Who are these people, anyway, these two strange women, the tiny one with an apron tied over a flower-print house dress and the plump younger one, already in black? And yet. She knows Elaine's voice. She recognizes her mother's startled eyes.

"Me, and my daughter, too," drawing Lizzie forward. "Lizzie, this is your grandmother and your Aunt Elaine. This is my daughter, Lizzie." Did that sound as triumphant as it should: that this is the point of it all, and isn't she splendid?

Elaine says, "Well." Then, "So you came after all." How flat she sounds, pointing out the obvious. No one has moved yet to ask them inside, and she and Lizzie are still standing, each with a small suitcase, outside the door. Susannah's mother is still in the doorway, her hand still on the latch. Oh, Susannah can be cool, she can wait. She can watch for some maternal glow, any warmth at all. "What kind of mother are you?" she would like to ask.

A sad and sentimental one, it seems. Or a sad and sentimental grandmother, which isn't really the same. Susannah is astonished to see that her mother, looking now at Lizzie, has started to weep; little tears, matching her little body. Her hands are trembling, too, as if they want to make some gesture but don't know what it ought to be.

Did she ever look at Susannah that way, or weep for her? Maybe, but if she did, it was much too late.

"Oh, aren't you lovely," her mother breathes. It doesn't sound very different, though, from the way she might admire a kitten or a pup.

Really, Susannah feels quite stone-hearted.

"You'd better come in, then," her mother says finally, drawing herself straighter, a little crustacean restoring herself to her shell. She wipes her hands down the sides of her dress like the old days, when she would wipe off flour from her baking to shake hands with unexpected guests.

She is old, though, much changed and lined and bent in fourteen years. She moves back from the door, out of the way, past Elaine and down the hall toward the kitchen, her room, the domain she never had to defend against anyone since no one else, even Elaine, especially cared to claim it from her.

Here is the hallway, as bare as Susannah remembered. And here she is, face to face finally with that mythical beast, a sister. "Well, then," Elaine repeats.

"It's nice to see you again," Susannah says, not because it's true, but because it's not. It is certainly interesting, though. If she'd thought about it, she might have assumed that in fourteen years Elaine would have become less recognizable. True, she's plumper, and almost entirely gray-haired, but she's still Elaine. Solid. Well, she was never the sort of person who'd take up hair dye or vicious diets or, for that matter, whimsy.

"I thought you weren't coming."

"I wasn't, but I changed my mind."

"And you brought your daughter. Will she be going to the funeral?"

What is this, Lizzie doesn't exist, isn't right here, clearly old enough to speak for herself? Susannah should never underestimate her daughter, though. "Yes," Lizzie says firmly, stepping forward, "I will."

Elaine regards her rather coolly, in Susannah's opinion, but Lizzie looks steadily back. Susannah almost laughs: Elaine doesn't know what she's got here.

Still, Susannah catches herself with an unworthy hope: that Lizzie will make a good impression; she feels like a kid, hoping for an A on a report card, praise for a well-done project. Anyway, she wouldn't want Elaine to be able to report later (to whom?) on the badly raised child of her scandalous, unmarried sister.

When Susannah was sick, Elaine used to come into her room and read stories to her. She can remember Elaine's voice in the dim light.

"Are Mark and Anthony here? And" (oh, shit, what's his name?) "your husband?"

"No, they couldn't make it. I had to come in such a hurry, Bill couldn't get away, and the boys live too far off. They're both married now, you know. I have grandchildren."

"How nice." And no, she didn't know any of that, how would she? "It's too bad they're not here, though. It would have been nice for Lizzie to meet the rest of her family." On whom, according to Elaine fourteen years ago, she would have been a bad influence, due to the wicked circumstances of her conception. "How many grandchildren?" Who cares?

"Two so far, and one on the way. Mark's in California, though, and Tony's in Florida, so we hardly ever see them."

Whereas Susannah's child is right here with her, sturdy and loyal. "That's too bad."

"Yes, it is. But families aren't what they used to be." Susannah, out of practice at interpreting her sister, can't tell if offense was intended or inadvertent. Some disarming may be needed here, a gesture of some kind, but it's certainly not going to come from Susannah. Anyway, unlike their mother, Elaine doesn't look inclined to weep, nor does she seem particularly sentimental. The way she's standing, arms folded across her chest, leaning slightly backward, doesn't hint at any wish for intimacy, either.

Is she going to let them past or not? Does she intend them to spend all day in this hall?

But here's their mother again, looking anxious now, popping her head around the corner from the kitchen. "I've put the kettle on. Are you girls coming in for tea?" Naturally she'd have some notion that sitting around with cups of tea would heal. What a belated sense of magic!

Still, she has the right idea: to sit at the kitchen table, look around, drink tea. Was Susannah ever relaxed here? At the moment she feels like a small, tough, wild animal, senses alert to menace and danger; which might of course mean missing signals of sanctuary.

It's a long time since she's heard herself referred to as a girl. No point in correcting her mother, though, and anyway, to her mother the three of them are girls, even the two who obviously are not. They are also, in a way, *her* girls, although that doesn't seem to have meant much to her. No mother-bear stuff about her, defending the litter.

Elaine turns and leads the way to the kitchen, and Susannah and Lizzie follow. How inevitable it has all become, however it turns out.

Imagine, though, the conversations and transformations that will go on in Sergei Valansky's household when he gets home! The raised voices, the explanations, the tears and recriminations, the bitterness; what are the chances of joy, relief, or love?

The point is, it will never be the same. Everyone involved will be struck by knowing that, from now on, anything can happen; a change of mind and heart will never again be out of the question. Then, of course, it will become a matter of deciding how to go on: whether that prospect is too discouraging, or heartening, after all.

FLYING TRIPS

A young stewardess who believed she was
obeying the orders of her dead parents has
been found not guilty by reason of insanity of
attempting to hijack a Caribbean-bound
charter flight last August.

Jean Morrow, 22, was ordered to a mental-
health facility for an indefinite period.

Morrow testified that she began hearing the
voices after her parents died in a boating accident three years ago. "They would tell me
what to do."

On one occasion, she said, she was told to
spill drinks over a trio of businessmen flying to
Calgary, and on another was ordered to add a
sedative to coffee she served the pilot of a
Heathrow-bound jet.

In the latter incident, the pilot collapsed as
the plane neared the Irish coast and the co-
pilot had to take over. The pilot was subsequently suspended and has launched a civil
action seeking damages against the airline,
court was told.

Morrow said she was wakened in her apartment one night last July by voices telling her to
take over a plane and divert it to Greece. She

said the voices did not indicate why that destination was specified.

She carried out the instruction, she testified,
because "I didn't have a choice, I had to do
what they said."

The off-season charter flight to Barbados
landed in Detroit after Morrow threatened the
pilot with a knife and ordered him to Greece.
She was overpowered by another flight attendant and the co-pilot.

Morrow told Judge Anthony Summers she
regrets her action, "but I had to do it. Now
they're angry with me, because I failed."

Summers said that while the incident could
have had "tragic consequences," Morrow was
obviously ill and required treatment, not
punishment.

Lizzie's always hearing voices, but that doesn't make her crazy
or dangerous, does it? Like, when she read what that stewardess
said — "Now they're angry with me, because I failed" — she
heard a sad, soft hopeless voice, she *heard* it.

She pictured Jean Morrow small, dark-haired, kind of held in
on herself, and really scared. Actually, except for the tight, scared
part, she maybe looked a lot like their own stewardess, rushing
around handing out breakfast and coffee and pillows. Flying,
that wasn't a very comfortable idea: being miles in the air, in
the hands of a crew that could be crazy.

On the ground, it's just kind of interesting.

Why did Jean Morrow hear her parents' voices, not anybody
else's? She must have missed them when they died, so maybe
she just made up a new life for them. Except, when they were
alive did they keep bugging her the way they did after they
died? Were they always telling her, do this, do that, and was
she scared to say no? Were they as mean before they died as
afterward?

She must really have wished they'd be quiet and just leave her alone.

Death feels sort of in the air this morning; like sometimes when she hears a new word and then starts hearing it again and again. If her mother died, what would Lizzie do? Who would she live with? Teddy? Frannie maybe? Staying over with Teddy is usually fun, except for last night, but what would it be like all the time? And Frannie says that if she'd wanted kids, she would have had them.

It makes sense, anyway, that wherever she lived, Lizzie would hear her mother's voice in a way. Just not the way Jean Morrow did. She'd know if she was doing something that made her mother happy, though, and maybe she'd even imagine her advice. Would that be crazy? Now that Lizzie's grandfather's dead, will her mother hear his voice?

Right now, Lizzie's having trouble hearing the voices of real people. Usually she's good at paying attention to what people are saying and even how they're sitting, leaning toward each other or away, but this is different. It feels sort of dangerous in this kitchen, even with her mother right here beside her. It feels like standing on the porch at home, watching lightning and thunder get closer and closer until the storm's right there and so scary she has to run inside.

Maybe she's just tired. She didn't get much sleep—especially because of Teddy and Anne being just across the room, and the more you try not to listen, the more you end up listening. Her grandmother and Aunt Elaine both keep glancing at her, but not the same way. Her grandmother's so little, and she maybe looks kind, but Aunt Elaine is as cool as Lizzie's mother can be, as if she's decided things without even knowing Lizzie.

The kitchen should be bright since it's got two windows facing the backyard, but somehow it feels dark. Not like at home, where the kitchen's the lightest room in the whole house and there are comfortable chairs to sit in and it's pretty, not just a place to make food.

On the plane, she couldn't imagine what it would be like here. Those people with their old, secret connections with her mother — her mother's mother, her mother's sister — the idea gave her a whirling feeling in her stomach, like a washing machine down there, and she put her hands over it to see if she could feel it from the outside. "You okay, honey?" her mother had asked. "The plane's not making you sick, is it?"

"No, I'm fine."

Her mother never gets scared on planes, but then, she's used to flying. She told Lizzie to take the window seat so she could look out better, and that was neat, a whole new view. Flying over the city, still low after takeoff, Lizzie peered down, trying to pick out her house and Teddy's place, but mostly she could only see expressways. It looked so little and crowded down there! Then all of a sudden the view was gone and there were just clouds, and sometimes big bright patches of blue, and it got sort of like what her mother said about using candles instead of lights, so everything outside, down on the ground where they came from or where they were going, was dim and far away and not real. Like they were in a whole other world.

It was really beautiful when they flew into the sunrise, a lot different from seeing it from the ground. Closer in a way, even though they weren't *that* much closer. Maybe just a better angle. Teddy might know why it was different, seeing it from up there.

When her mother picked her up outside Teddy's this morning, when it was still dark, she said, "You can still change your mind, you don't have to come." But Lizzie'd have been mad at herself all weekend if she'd gone back upstairs to Teddy. Anyway, Anne was there. She was mean with Anne last night, she feels a little bad about that, but honestly, by the next time she sees Teddy, Anne will likely be history, so what does it matter?

She'd like to make a good impression today, though. She'd like her mother to be proud of her, and anyway, it feels bad, not being liked. Anne must have thought she was really crummy. Aunt Elaine looks like she thinks that, too, but she doesn't even have a reason.

Her mother spent most of the time on the plane reading a gossip magazine, but her hands kept moving, her fingers tapping on the armrest between her and Lizzie, or on her cheek or her chin or the pages. Of course, she knew where they were going, she'd have pictures of the place ahead, and the people. Maybe her mother was scared, even without knowing about the chances of crazy voices talking to crazy stewardesses.

In a break in the clouds, Lizzie leaned her forehead against the window and saw a thin blue string of water, with narrow strips of land leading down to it. Everything was so straight, looking at it from high up. She thought the people down there must be very exact.

She was kind of disappointed when the sound of the plane engines changed, like a car switching gears, and her mother moved over to look, and said, "I guess we're coming in to land." It sure didn't take long, considering how far it was. When the plane slipped under the clouds, a city was suddenly there, a lot smaller than the one they left. Maybe if she'd known it, Lizzie would have been able to point out real houses, real places that meant something. Maybe her mother could anyway? Except her mother didn't look, just hurried them off the plane, through the airport (so small!) and out to a line of taxis. "It's gonna cost you, lady," the cab driver said. "Out of town like that."

Her mother nodded. "I know. Let's go." It made her seem as if she didn't belong, throwing money around in a way that made them different. Outsiders from the city? Even if the driver didn't already know that.

Still, she started pointing out places to Lizzie. "This highway is new," she said. "There only used to be a two-lane road." And, "Look off to your right — there weren't high buildings like that before." But they were just ordinary high-rises on the city's skyline, the kind Lizzie sees every day except not as tall as the ones she's used to. This place seemed poorer than home, it had a kind of hanging-on feeling, and once they were out in the country, the houses looked a lot shabbier than the barns. The fields were green, but even they looked faded. Do plants get worn out, too? It was kind of pretty, though.

It was hard to see that this was where her mother grew up, and then left, and then got kicked out of her family and never went back. It looked too real and ordinary, kind of small and flat, even though the road did have some hills and turns. What did her mother see, looking out the window on the other side of the cab? What if she started to feel at home? What if she forgot where her real home is?

Good thing Lizzie came.

They passed a town sign, too fast for Lizzie to read all the crests and writing on it, and the cab slowed, and the driver said, "You'll have to give me directions, lady, I don't know where the street is you want."

Her mother sat up straighter, looked around, told him where to go but also started pointing things out to Lizzie again. "That's my high school," she said, and, "There's the restaurant we used to go to after the movie on Saturday nights. My best girlfriend used to live there," and she nodded toward a little white house that was practically right on the street. Was her best friend then like Frannie? It felt really quiet here, lots of trees but not many people. Creepy, sort of—like a movie about an evil planet that fools people because it only looks like earth.

When her mother was Lizzie's age, she walked on those sidewalks and shopped in those stores and had a best friend and went on dates to the movies. Also she had a mother and a father and a sister. What was that like? What was *she* like? It seemed to Lizzie that if she stared hard enough, she should be able to see her mother the way she was, walking along the sidewalk, stopping to look in store windows. Or whatever she might have done then.

What her mother was doing now was sitting up so white and nervous she made Lizzie think of those dog whistles that are so high people can't hear them.

When the taxi finally stopped her mother didn't move for a minute, just looked out the window at the house as if she might still change her mind and turn around and go home. Lizzie looked, too. It wasn't much of a house, really, just ordinary, but there must be amazing things inside. Her family! Now Lizzie was going to see them and talk to them and touch them—they had to be real, because the house was, so it was all coming true.

She couldn't wait. Not going in now would be worse than going back upstairs to Teddy's this morning.

Her mother must have thought something like that, too, because she shook herself and took a deep breath and handed money to the driver, and then she and Lizzie were standing on the sidewalk. There was a lawn and a cement walk and a tree at the front, and a really tall tree at the back that went high over the roof. The house was white, with green trim and a porch just like Lizzie's own house, and a hedge of shrubs along the front, except neater than hers. Her mother doesn't always remember to keep theirs clipped.

When her mother was a girl, she went up and down this walk all the time, in and out of that house. Lizzie reached for her hand, because it sort of felt like a place where she might disappear, just because she wasn't dreamed of here.

They held hands all the way up the walk, until Lizzie's mother had to let go to knock. When Lizzie grows up and leaves home, will she have to knock when she goes back to visit?

When the door opened, though, things started going too fast to keep up with. There was a tiny old woman in an apron who cried, and a bigger, younger one standing back in the hallway, and everybody was talking. Shouldn't they hug each other after so long, even if they'd been mad before? But nobody touched, except Lizzie's mother, who drew her forward and said, "This is my daughter, Lizzie. Lizzie, this is your family. Your grandmother and your Aunt Elaine."

Maybe in a movie they'd all have rushed into each other's arms. What was her grandmother crying for?

Then she and her mother were inside in the hallway, and her grandmother was going farther into the house, but still glancing back at Lizzie. Lizzie's mother and Aunt Elaine talked for a minute, but then they all went in the kitchen and Lizzie's grandmother made tea. "Why don't you get Lizzie something to drink, too, Elaine?" her grandmother said, and Aunt Elaine seemed cross, although she did pour Lizzie a Pepsi from a can in the fridge.

"Thank you," Lizzie said. "Should I call you Aunt Elaine?" She wasn't sure what an aunt ought to feel like, except probably friendlier than this, but she'd have to call her something.

Aunt Elaine looked startled. "I suppose so," she said finally. "Yes, that's fine."

Lizzie turned to her grandmother — a larger range of words to choose from here. "What should I call you? Grandma?"

This time, when the question wasn't even for her, Aunt Elaine was quicker. "My boys always said Nana so they wouldn't get confused with their other grandmother." Like she thought Lizzie had a whole bunch of people in her family, so many she might get them mixed up?

"I wouldn't get confused. I don't have any other grandmothers." For some reason her mother reached out then and touched her wrist, just lightly.

"Grandma would be fine," her grandmother said, in an awfully soft voice.

Now the four of them are still sitting around the table, but it's all getting stranger and stranger. The kitchen chairs have padded plastic green plaid seats on them. Lizzie's mother is beside her, leaning forward with her elbows on the round table, and even she doesn't seem quite real, although she's realer than Aunt Elaine and Grandma, whose voices are fading in and out in Lizzie's head. Their bodies, too, like she's seeing them almost like movie people, flat on a screen. They're talking, but not to her, and she's listening, but not very well.

It's just, they don't *look* like her family. People should be able to know each other, but they could be anybody.

Is that what her mother means, that family can be anybody? It's not what Lizzie ever thought she meant.

Aunt Elaine is standing up and collecting the cups and saucers and Lizzie's glass. "We should get ready to go, I think. We're to be at the funeral home by noon."

"When's the funeral?" This is Lizzie's mother.

"One o'clock, but we have to be there at least an hour before. Mother and I were there last night, too." While Lizzie and her mother were having an ordinary dinner, and Teddy and Anne were meeting for the first time, none of them knowing what the others were doing, or where they were, probably not even thinking about each other. Lizzie's never really thought before about things going on she doesn't know about that can make things happen to her life. It's kind of creepy.

"You'd better slip upstairs, Lizzie, and get changed. I packed your blue skirt and white blouse. Maybe you could lay out my things, too, if you don't mind."

"Where should I go upstairs?"

Her mother looks startled, as if she's forgotten Lizzie doesn't know this house. Aunt Elaine says, "I suppose there's room for you both in your old room, Susannah, if you don't mind sharing the bed."

"Second on the left at the top of the stairs, then," her mother says. "I'll be up in a minute."

The banister is a really nice, smooth, dark wood. Her mother's hand must have slid up and down it hundreds and thousands of times. There should be some of that still in the wood, shouldn't there, but there isn't, it's just smooth. If she and her mother moved away from their house, would it go dead this way, as if they'd never lived there?

Is this the right room? It is the second on the left, so it must be, but Lizzie can't see her mother in it, it doesn't look like her at all. It's all pink and white: white-painted bed and small dresser, pink curtains and a plain white blind on the window. There's wallpaper even on the ceiling, pink flowers on a white background. It's pretty, and Lizzie might like it herself, at least for a while, but her mother's more a blue and gray and maroon sort of person. It's hard to believe she ever was pink.

"I like your old room," she says when her mother appears.

"Good lord, do you?"

They hurry to get dressed, because Aunt Elaine keeps calling up the stairs that it's time to leave. "Are you okay, honey?" her mother asks.

"I guess so. It's just funny here. I don't think Aunt Elaine likes me."

Her mother sighs. "It's hard to know. But your grandmother's glad to see you, and I'm glad you're here, so two out of three isn't bad."

"Are you scared?" Probably she shouldn't have asked. It's like making something real by saying it out loud. Anyway, her mother's skin goes like white paper.

"I guess I am. If nothing else, I never like not knowing what's going to happen. How about you?"

"A little, maybe." Because never mind anything else — in a few minutes she's going to see a real dead person. It's not that he'll be her grandfather, it's that he'll be dead. Her mother hugs her. She's so smart.

Aunt Elaine's rented a car, a little one, so the four of them are crowded. Lizzie and her mother climb into the back, where there's hardly any place to put their legs, and her grandmother and Aunt Elaine sit in the front. Lizzie's mother has rubbed on some of her scented skin cream, and her grandmother is wearing something that smells dry, like bath powder. Aunt Elaine must have splashed herself with something sweet, though, and it's drifting into the back seat. Lizzie feels a little sick. Beside her, her mother rolls a window down.

There isn't time to get really sick, because it's just a few minutes before they turn in beside a big gray stone building and stop in the parking lot at the back. There's a big black hearse under a kind of canopy at the side, with its back doors open, but everybody except Lizzie looks in some other direction. Aunt Elaine takes Lizzie's grandmother's arm, and Lizzie's mother takes Lizzie's hand. She seems all by herself in a way, even though most of her family's right here.

It's really amazing, how little Lizzie's grandmother is! Walking behind, Lizzie can look down at the top of her head and glimpse a pink scalp under white hair. No wonder Aunt Elaine takes her arm — that kind of tininess makes Lizzie want to make sure nothing bad happens to her, too. She's never been bigger than a grown-up before, and it feels like the wrong way around.

Inside, the funeral home is cool and dark, so it's shivery and hard to see, coming in out of hot sunshine. There are heavy, purple-red drapes that are all shut, and even though the lights are on, the lamps are like bowls, so the light goes up toward the ceiling instead of down, like nobody's supposed to see very well.

Her mother is holding Lizzie's hand too tightly, and swinging it a little, the way Lizzie and Teddy walk sometimes late at night, swinging their arms with their steps, except that's because they're having fun, and this isn't.

A dark-haired man in a dark suit is talking to Aunt Elaine and Grandma. Grandma says, "This is my other daughter, Susannah, and her daughter, Lizzie."

He shakes Lizzie's mother's hand, but not Lizzie's. Most people are like that, they treat kids as if they're not actual people. "I'm pleased to meet you," he says. "Despite the circumstances. It's good you could be here after all." Does he look at them funny before he turns back to her grandmother? "The minister's here. He'd like a few words with you before the service."

"Of course. We'll go in now." There's something about her grandmother's voice that's bigger than how she looks. Megan usually gives both her grandmothers lilac scent for their birthdays and Christmas. Lizzie's grandmother also seems like a lilac person, light and sweet but tough, too. Well, she must be tough, not to love Lizzie's mother. Maybe she looks sweet, but she can't be very nice, can she?

The minister is another man in a dark suit, except he's fatter and has gray hair. This big room he's in has rows of hard chairs and smells heavy, like Aunt Elaine, probably because of all the stiff bunches of flowers. There, of course, is her grandfather: in that shiny coffin in the center of the flowers. The coffin's made of some brownish-red wood, and it has white lining like satin, and from the doorway she can see just a little black material, too—a sleeve or a collar. Her mother's hold on her hand really hurts now, but it wouldn't be nice to pull away. Lizzie squeezes back, just lightly, to remind her mother she's here, and to complain. Her mother's grip loosens and she smiles down, with her mouth, anyway, and whispers, "It's okay, honey, hang in." It doesn't feel okay.

Lizzie's glad she came, though. Here, she and her mother are a team. She stands a little closer; just let anybody try to make her mother upset.

"So you're the other daughter," the minister says, and shakes hands with her mother, too. "I'm glad you could be here." Everybody's making such a point that they came! "Perhaps you'd like to visit with your father first, but then I'd like us all to spend a few minutes chatting about him. Just to make sure I say what you'd like me to."

"You can stay here if you'd like, Lizzie."

"No, I'll come with you."

How brave she feels! What she really wants to do is run outside into the sunshine and heat and the real flowers, not these things all stuffed together with ribbons and cards, but she's thirteen years old, and this may be the first time her mother has actually needed her.

Once, when she and her mother were in Niagara Falls, the two of them went to a wax museum, even though her mother didn't want to. It turned out it was only a little scary and not very interesting, so her mother was right, it was a waste of time. This is something like that. After being so scared about seeing a dead man, it turns out to be hard to imagine he was ever real. There isn't much about that face and those hands, which is all of him that's showing, that looks as if it was ever warm or moved.

Is this what he really looked like? When he was alive, he probably wasn't so hard and set. If he could move, though, he might look like her mother, sort of. His nose is straight like hers, and his lips have the same kind of shape. Her grandmother has a little nose and mouth and narrow shoulders, more like Aunt Elaine, even though Aunt Elaine's big. What does her mother see? She must be able to remember his voice, and his face when it moved. Lizzie can feel her mother breathing in a jaggedy kind of way, but she isn't crying, exactly.

What does it mean to be dead? Is it even nice when it happens? Lizzie remembers when she had her appendix out and they gave her the anesthetic, it was sort of pleasant and then it wasn't anything at all. Maybe people just float away like that when they die and don't mind.

Aunt Elaine and Grandma have come up beside them, so they're all standing in a row. Would he like people staring at him and thinking about him? It would be neat to know what people were really thinking about you. Except maybe it wouldn't. Do they miss him? Why are there funerals, anyway, do they make people feel better? Having to look at somebody dead like this should make them feel worse, she would think. Why can't somebody like her grandmother stay home and feel bad her own way, instead of getting all dressed up and coming here? What good are the flowers, are they supposed to make people feel better? Lizzie doesn't think she'd like being dead and stared at, herself.

Aunt Elaine says, "The minister's waiting for us, we should go and talk to him now, I think." She seems to like keeping time.

When they all get settled on chairs at the back of the room, the minister starts talking. "Now of course I knew him pretty well, and I've prepared what I think is appropriate, but I expect you each have thoughts you'd also like me to express." He looks around, but nobody says anything. "Elizabeth?" he asks her grandmother.

Is that her name? Is that where Lizzie's name came from?

"Oh dear, I don't know what to say, exactly." She seems confused. She looks at her fingers kind of twining around each other in her lap. "He was a decent man, but you already know that. And a hard worker." There are spaces between her words, as if she has trouble talking about him, but she was married to him for an awfully long time—shouldn't she have lots of things to say? If Teddy died, Lizzie's mother would have tons of words and they don't even live together. Of course, later, when it was just her and Lizzie or her and Frannie, she'd probably say funny, mean things, too, but in a way, that would be part of how she'd feel sad.

"He was a good father," Aunt Elaine says. "He knew right from wrong." Lizzie's mother gives Aunt Elaine a real sharp look, and Aunt Elaine doesn't say any more.

There's more silence and then the minister says, "And Susannah? How about you?"

"Oh dear." She sounds confused, too, just like Lizzie's grandmother! "You know I hadn't seen him for a long time, and we'd quarreled, so it's not easy for me to say." There's a pause, then, "However. I suppose I'd say he lived by his rules, so at least he wasn't a total hypocrite. It was probably a comfort for him, being so sure of himself. When we were kids he encouraged us to do things on our own, but he was surprised when he found out later how well we'd learned." Aunt Elaine and Grandma are staring at her. "I'd like to think he'd have liked to love more, or better, than he did, but he didn't let himself." She starts to cry, just a little and really quietly. Is it strange that her own words are the only ones that make her cry?

Then nobody gets to say anything more, not even Aunt Elaine, because people start showing up. Most of them are old. Lizzie's grandmother seems to know them all, and Aunt Elaine knows some of them. The four of them — her grandmother, Aunt Elaine, Lizzie's mother, and Lizzie — stand in a row just inside the doorway of the big room, and people introduce themselves to Lizzie's mother and then she introduces them to Lizzie. Some people look at them in a peering kind of way, and Lizzie moves in closer to her mother again.

This isn't really like a party, of course, because it's too serious and people talk too quietly, but it's some big deal to them. Was her grandfather important, or did they like him a lot, or is this just what funerals are like? People move past them to look at him in the coffin, and then they look at the flowers and lean over to read the cards. There's a big white-lily arrangement from Aunt Elaine, and a cross from her grandmother, made up of little white and red and purple flowers. Lizzie doesn't think there can be any from her mother and her. People probably think that's pretty bad.

When the funeral's ready to start, the four of them sit in the front row of chairs, which means there's nothing to look at but the coffin and the minister. It also means everybody else can look at them. "How come there's hardly any men here?" Lizzie whispers to her mother, partly because she wonders, but also to show that the two of them are close together and have things to say to each other.

"Probably a lot have already died," which makes sense — everybody knows women live longer than men. Aunt Elaine is looking at them crossly. She must think they should be quiet.

All the people here seem to know the same things. They say prayers together out loud, and nobody makes a mistake with the words. Music starts playing from somewhere, a tape, Lizzie guesses, an organ and a choir singing something about an old rugged cross, all sad and draggy. The minister's voice is like that, too, when he speaks, and Lizzie's attention wanders. She forgets to listen for whether he uses anything her mother said, or her grandmother or Aunt Elaine.

Then all of a sudden it's over, and Lizzie's surprised because she would have thought a service to do with death would take a lot longer. People are standing and shaking hands with each other, and some are slipping out the door, and everybody's talking louder than before. "What happens now?"

"We go to the cemetery, of course." Aunt Elaine makes it sound as if it's awful Lizzie didn't know that.

"There's another short service there," Lizzie's mother explains, "and then we go back to the house."

They leave the rented car in the parking lot and climb into a special big black car to go to the cemetery. People on the streets and sidewalks stop and look, and Lizzie imagines that even though there aren't exactly crowds, maybe this is something like how it is for royalty. She'd like to wave; not the way she would if she saw a friend, but slowly and in a dignified sort of way, like the queen.

When she's grown up and doing whatever she does to be famous, she might get a car like this, with a driver, so she has her hands free for waving. She'll sit in the back seat alone. Well, maybe her mother or Teddy could come along sometimes. Teddy especially would like it. And sometimes her husband, although mainly she'd rather be alone because after all, it'd be her car.

Another neat thing is driving through red lights, but maybe that's just for funerals, not for any black limousine.

The hearse, which is even bigger, is ahead of them. It's got the coffin, and Lizzie wonders what it's like for her grandmother, driving along behind her husband's body, going to see it buried. She's probably been to a lot of other funerals, but even so this one must feel weird. Except interesting, too, in a way, because she's really the center of attention, more than Aunt Elaine or Lizzie's mother or Lizzie or even her husband, even though it's his funeral. She's sitting up so straight her feet aren't touching the floor of the car. Does she always sit that way, feet dangling, never hitting bottom? She must feel like she doesn't weigh anything, in a way. Like she might float off.

The cemetery is rows and rows of humps in the earth and plastic flowers and short grass and tombstones. Some of them are huge, like statues in a museum, but some are flat on the ground, like a sidewalk with names and dates. The words that get said sound terrible: ashes to ashes, dust to dust. Is that possible? Lizzie can't imagine ever dying, herself. Her grandmother starts crying a little, and Aunt Elaine puts an arm around her, but her grandmother pulls away. Did anybody else notice that? Lizzie's mother, maybe.

Even so, when it's over and they go back to the car, Lizzie's grandmother and Aunt Elaine walk together, and Lizzie and her mother walk behind. In the big car, going to the funeral home to get the rented one, Aunt Elaine says, "I think that went nicely, don't you, Mother? There were quite a few people. I was surprised, weren't you, Susannah?"

"I guess. I hadn't really thought what it would be like."

Aunt Elaine sounded nice, speaking to Lizzie's mother, but now she says in a snappy way, "No, I don't suppose you would have."

"Girls," says Lizzie's grandmother, so they're quiet for a minute. What does the driver think? He must hear all kinds of things, taking people to funerals.

"It must be living in a small place," Aunt Elaine says finally. "People know each other better. And older people still have some idea of doing the right thing, although you can't say that for the younger ones any more." Nobody says anything. "I wish Mark and Anthony could have been here. It would have been hard, but they could have made the effort. That's young people for you, though."

Still nobody speaks. Lizzie's glad her mother doesn't talk about her that way, as if she isn't a very nice person. The silence isn't comfortable. "I'm young and I came," Lizzie says finally, but, oh, she didn't mean it to sound rude.

"Well, you're too young to have a choice." Aunt Elaine doesn't sound very grateful that Lizzie tried to help her out. And is anybody so young they don't have a choice? Babies, maybe.

"No, I wanted to come. If I didn't, I could have stayed with Teddy."

"And who is Teddy?"

The things these people don't know! "He's my father. He's a famous artist, and he's got an apartment downtown where he lives and does his work that used to be a dress factory, so it's all one big room. I stay with him sometimes. I stayed there last night." No need to mention somebody else did, too.

"I see." Aunt Elaine sounds like she slammed a door, so Lizzie sits far back in the seat and gets quiet. How come her mother didn't say something to Aunt Elaine then?

Once they're in the rented car again and on their way to the house, Lizzie's grandmother shakes herself as if she's coming back from a long way off and turns in her seat to smile at Lizzie. "Now you must tell me, what grade are you in?"

"I'm starting high school this fall."

"I expect you get good marks, do you?"

"Pretty good."

"She gets terrific marks," her mother says, finally speaking up. "She's a very smart kid."

"I think sometimes," Aunt Elaine says, "that it's not necessarily wise to let children think they're too clever."

"Oh, piss off, Elaine."

"Girls, please," Lizzie's grandmother says again.

What it feels like is that a lot of stuff is going on that isn't being said out loud, so Lizzie has to guess, like being on the subway trying to figure out from people's faces what words they're maybe saying.

Or it's how it feels if you're going deaf, so you don't catch some words or certain tones, and there's a kind of buzzing all the time, drowning some things out.

But mostly all this is so new and strange she can't take everything in. She can watch or she can hear, but it's awfully hard to do both at the same time.

Except she has to. This is important. This is her mother's family, and her own, too. These are people who didn't want to know her. They are strange in ways she never dreamed of when she pretended they might be murderers or thieves. That was easier to imagine than this. It's funny that it's harder, imagining something that looks just ordinary but knowing there's all kinds of *stuff* there you can't see, and trying to tell what it is. She'll have to pay better attention, that's all.

Also, whatever gets said, she'll have to try to keep the words straight so they don't get turned around in her memory or start meaning something they're not supposed to. Because she'd really hate to wind up like that poor crazy stewardess, hearing voices that get all twisted in her head.

SYMPATHY PAINS

A Vancouver man has lost his bid to be compensated for the pain he allegedly suffered after his fiancee's right leg was amputated last fall.

Tim Connors claimed he endured "real agony" in his own right leg after Sally Ferguson's was removed. Ferguson was injured when she was struck by a car whose driver was subsequently convicted of dangerous driving.

She was awarded $587,506 in a lawsuit against the driver, but Connors' claim for $100,000 in a separate suit was rejected by the court.

Two psychologists testifying on Connors' behalf said that "sympathy pains" are not uncommon when one partner in a close relationship is ill or injured. "This may occur during childbirth, when a husband may undergo pains somewhat similar to labor," Dr. Eric Handley told the court.

Connors testified he was unable to walk for two weeks because of the "excruciating" pain in his leg that started the day Ferguson underwent the amputation surgery. He could only get around on crutches for another month, he said, and still frequently gets "tingling sensations" similar to those Ferguson said she feels in the area of her missing leg.

Judge Stanley Burton, however, said awarding Connors money for his pain would "open a can of legal worms I am not prepared to deal with."

While Connors may well have been affected by his fiancee's accident, Burton said, "any injury to him was indirect, difficult to define and correctable, and neither the driver of the vehicle nor his insurance company can be held responsible."

The judge did, however, compliment the couple on the closeness of their relationship, which he called a "positive indicator" for their future.

Connors and Ferguson, whose wedding was delayed by the accident, now plan to be married next month.

Hard to believe a guy like that's for real, or that it's possible to go beyond sympathy and actually absorb somebody else's pain; be a practitioner, if Connors can be believed, of a sort of faith hurting.

He sounds a little nuts, of course. Wouldn't it drive him crazy, being pounded by other people's pain? Except it's only one other person, really, it's not like people who pick up radio signals in the fillings of their teeth, who must get deafened by music and words.

What does the fiancee have to say about this, though? Well, she still plans to marry him, so that's one answer. Even so, his pain couldn't have been much help to her. It might even have been annoying, having him moaning about how much his leg hurt when hers was actually gone. He could be the sort of guy who hangs around uselessly while somebody else is changing a tire or trimming a hedge or washing the dishes. He might just be the sort of guy who can't stand to be alone.

"How are you feeling?" he might ask, but with a view to stealing her condition.

Tim Connors would probably also be hanging around uselessly watching Anne pull together breakfast. Teddy, watching her himself, likes a great many things about her, not least of them the way she looks right now in his blue bathrobe, hair rumpled, even her flesh somehow out of order. He likes knowing she's different, a little unfocused, because of passion. But what else?

He loves how smooth her skin is, and how adaptable her body. He feels almost like a boy again, the young man he used to be, strong and powerful and filled with the juices of discovery. He's startled, glancing down, by the view of his chest, where hair that used to be dark is now mainly gray.

He has to be in court in a couple of hours. Anne's going to work. They still have some time together, though, and he takes his feet off the coffee table as she carries over a tray loaded with plates and food and cutlery and coffee. It looks heavy, but being a nurse, she is strong. "This is a feast," he says, and it is, too: scrambled eggs, cheese from the market, the coffee maker with the plunger, which he uses only for special occasions.

"I figured we needed to build up our strength." That coy little smile is irritating — is that mean, or is it just that he's not good in the morning?

The eggs have dill in them — she has a touch with small, special things like that. She has even gone so far as to make taking care her profession. Tasting the eggs he feels suddenly, tenderly, unworthy of her.

"You might want to skip the garlic cheese," she suggests. "It's okay just for us, but we do have to go out in the world."

They have hardly been out in the world all weekend. They have rolled around in his bed and eaten and slept, and she hasn't minded that his favorite cheese is garlic. Would she ever mind? She does shower more than he considers necessary, and she brought over her own particular scented shampoo from her place, and she uses perfume automatically. She paints her fingernails and toenails. Might his garlic and her perfume eventually conflict?

She's pushing down the plunger on the coffee maker, bending over it so that he sees the tendons in her narrow wrists, the slight lifting of her shoulders. Suddenly he remembers the first —the only—animal he ever killed, when he was a boy and his father was teaching him manly pursuits and took him into the country with a gun. God, he hasn't thought about that for years! They crept across a snowy field and into what his father called "the bush," although it was just a little bunch of trees. His father clutched Teddy's arm and pointed. "There." A rabbit, perfectly still except for an upturned, twitching nose and the slight ruffling of white fur in the breeze. "Hurry," and Teddy, obedient child, pulled the trigger. He was no marksman, but it was his luck, good, as his father saw it, to hit the damn thing. So much blood! And steam rising—he turned away to throw up. Partly it was disgust, but there was also an awful desolation. That may even have been the moment he became opposed to death.

What was there about Anne just now that reminded him of that? She certainly doesn't look either quivery or dead, but there is something about her that's like that rabbit. Perhaps that he could shoot her down, if he wanted to.

He still can't figure out what it is about her that appeals to him, growing on him like a vine — a pretty picture, a vine-covered building, but finally the walls get wrecked. He thinks he's read that somewhere.

Oh, what a paranoid asshole he is. Probably.

She has been, in the past few days, bright and kind and passionate at different times, and she's also been content to sit quietly and read or watch television and be there when he glances up. Naturally she must have flaws, but the strange thing is that neither they nor her qualities seem to have much to do with this urge, desire, longing—demand—to burrow right into her, curl up safe.

Today will be their first separation. "See you tonight," he says downstairs on the street, heading for the courthouse.

"Good luck," and she reaches up to kiss him, just lightly because they're in public now, there are people around. He finds, when he turns to look back, to see if she stands out in the morning crowd, that she's looking back also, at him. Is she content, or wondering what the hell she's done, spending a weekend with that old man?

Pleasures don't end right away, there are aftershocks to a weekend like this: rushes of warmth from a particular moment, a movement, touch, a picture of flesh, light falling across a body, the slapping, sweating sounds of passion, lust, love — whatever he'd call it. The *luxury* of skin and desire. It makes his own skin rosy.

He braces himself to climb the steps of the courthouse, that great gray building, marbled floors, dark wooden panels. This is not a building of justice, it's a building of intimidation, and it stinks of fear. It says, "We know you are a guilty human being. You may not be guilty of what caused you to be here, and we may or may not figure that out, but you are certainly guilty of something and deserve to be punished."

It *is* frightening. Great high, looming ceilings, a queer echo to footsteps. Men in suits and men in jeans, women with briefcases and women with bare legs and dirty hair. Not much in between. In the courtroom, he resents having to look up: like a petitioner before a sovereign, centuries ago. A cheap, intimidating trick; and who says the runty gray-haired guy in the glasses up there gets to tell Teddy anything?

He does, though. The rosy remembrance of pleasure and the fear combine to leave Teddy defenseless and surprised, so he has trouble believing this judge, peering down at him through judicial steel-framed half-glasses, looking stern and saying utterly unexpected words. "I see you have quite a record here. It seems to me your activities indicate a degree of escalation that warrants some attention, and I believe it's time for you to understand that this is not the sort of offense a court will take lightly." The judge hitches himself forward and frowns. "There's a considerable and dangerous difference, you know, between spray painting a wall and assault. Seven days. And I recommend that in future, you act your age and confine yourself to more peaceful pursuits."

Seven days! Teddy stares, his mouth fallen open in astonishment.

What the hell does the old asshole think Teddy was pursuing, if not peace? What does he mean, "act your age"? At what point, exactly, should he have outgrown outrage, stopped putting his body on the line? Jesus Christ!

He figured he'd be found guilty—after all, why would a judge believe him over the cops and the guys from the consulate? But jail? Seven days? Well, five really, since weekends don't count and anyway, nobody serves a full sentence.

What would it feel like to hear himself sentenced to ten, twenty, thirty years? Even one year, or two. Seven days are puny, laughable to a guy getting a sentence like that. Of course, a guy like that might not be surprised, he'd know what he was guilty of. Teddy's just furious at the injustice. Scared, too. This isn't the same at all as spending a few hours waiting for bail. What he finds when he gets there is that this is days and nights in a small gray room behind a barred metal door. It has an open toilet and two bunks — oh, God, will they put somebody else in here with him? If he's lucky, one of the others from the demonstration will be found guilty, too, and be sent to join him. If he's less lucky, he might get a drunk or a vagrant. If he's really unlucky, it'll be some menacing thug, jailed for some truly dangerous crime (assault?) who will look at Teddy with contempt, or worse, with interest.

Surely they wouldn't mix the weak and the dangerous, would they? Teddy's never thought of himself as weak before, but he also hasn't been in this sort of spot before.

Nobody even knows he's here — well, the judge knows, and the cops and guards, but nobody who cares about him. Is he allowed to call anybody? Anne? She must be smart enough to figure out eventually what's happened, but not before she's worked her shift and gone back to his place. How long would she wait before she realized?

He really doesn't know her well enough to tell.

He doesn't have a toothbrush here. Nothing.

If there were reporters in the courtroom, Lizzie, who reads everything, might see it in tomorrow's paper, but that's tomorrow, and she and Susannah may not even be back in town.

Teddy mostly knows about jails from what he's seen in movies. Now that he's actually here, that hardly seems enough. In movies, prisoners slash metal cups along the bars to get attention. He doesn't even have a metal cup. Or a prisoner goes to the door, grasps the bars, and shouts. That he can try. "Hey!"

"Hey what, asshole?" Jesus Christ, the guy's right beside him, except in the next cell where he can't be seen. Still, even if the words weren't exactly warm, the voice was more or less neutral; or bored.

"How do I get their attention so I can let somebody know where I am? I didn't expect to be here."

"Who did? Try talking nice to the guy that brings lunch, maybe he'll do you a favor. What're you in for?"

Again from films, Teddy has understood this isn't a proper or safe question to ask in jail, but maybe that's wrong. "Assault. Except I didn't do it. How about you?"

"None of your fucking business."

Shit. But at least he's in this cell, not that one. He retreats to the bottom bunk, lies down, and promptly sits up again. Then he climbs to the top bunk. It's best to hold the high ground.

Lunch is coming, apparently—all kinds of banging, clattering, slamming sounds. The guard bringing Teddy's looks around, looks up. "What the hell are you doing up there?"

"More comfortable. Better view." But he isn't fooling anybody; the guard looks as if he sees right into Teddy's terror.

Vaulting down, landing a little heavily, Teddy says, "Listen. Can I make a call? Nobody knows I'm here. I didn't even bring a toothbrush."

"Not very smart, are you? Pretty sure of yourself."

"I wasn't guilty. I thought the judge might take that into

account, but since I was wrong, can I make a call?" He thinks that sounded good: articulate and with just the right touch of injured defiance.

"No, you can't, but I can. The thing is, will I?"

What does he want then, standing here with his amused, beady eyes and thin lips: what a portrait he'd be; or a caricature. "Try saying please."

Son of a bitch. It'd be simple if he wanted money, that would only be greed. This is meaner, though. It's about power, showing power. Even so, "Please," Teddy says.

"Right." Now the guard is brisk and satisfied. "Gimme a name and a number and a couple of things you want, and I might get around to it later."

Teddy gives him Anne's name and number and a list: toothpaste, toothbrush, pajamas ("Skip it, we provide nighties"), a razor ("Are you kidding?"), and clean underwear. Left alone with his lunch, he feels subdued. Well, that's exactly what he is, isn't it — subdued, panicked into pleading. God, that awful helpless sound when he said "please." For the sake of a toothbrush and a touch from the outside, he's caved in from the start.

He's no criminal. He's a prisoner of politics. He wouldn't have dreamed he'd be a coward, though. Here he is, a forty-five-year-old white North American man, frightened by five days in quite a comfortable cell, really, where he's just been served a ham and lettuce sandwich, a cup of canned soup, and bitter coffee. In other countries, people are doomed to damp cellars, beatings, and slaughter. His balls are free of electrodes, even if they're not, at the moment, quite what they might be. His eyes aren't black and his lips aren't split and he doesn't actually hurt anywhere, except in his pride. He won't have to recant any words as a condition of release. So what's the big deal?

All right, then. From now on, he'll be tough; no matter who gets thrown in here with him. Maybe he just won't mention he's an artist, or that he was arrested at a peace demonstration. He can frown and say he's been convicted of assault and imply, maybe by standing in a certain way or speaking in a certain tone, that assault is not an unfamiliar act.

He could eat that "please." Now he'd stare down that guard, hands on his hips, feet apart, and tell him, "Fuck you, I don't need a thing from you. You can take your 'please' and shove it up your ass."

Too bad it's too late.

It'll be nice to see Anne. He wishes they hadn't taken his watch.

It can't be more than five or six hours since he was watching her make his breakfast. Now he thinks he must have been as nearly happy and content at that moment as it's possible to be, and even though he didn't know a lot about her, he assumed there was plenty of time to find out. What a miracle, especially for a man like him who's not likely to be bowled over.

He misses her. If he were home now, concentrating on his work, would he also be missing her?

Five days isn't much, but it's also an awfully long time. Do jails have exercise yards, or is that only penitentiaries? Maybe they figure it's okay for people to sit in one dull place for a few days, contemplating their sins or crimes.

If there's nothing to see, people must make up their own visions. At least he's used to doing that.

What leaps to mind, however, is fire: a prisoner, more adept than Teddy at smuggling, bringing in matches or a lighter, a drunk setting his bedding ablaze out of boredom. It's been known to happen, that sort of thing.

There'd be some flames, and maybe he'd be able to see their reflection leaping on walls, but with bedding there'd mainly be smoke, thick and gray, billowing down the corridor. Even if the fire itself were contained, that smoke could be lethal. He'd try to hold his breath and hold it and hold it, turning pale and pink and finally purple, until he had to let it go in a great helpless rush. With the next breath he'd draw in that first lungful of burning, choking smoke, and that would be the end of it. Men wearing masks would be spraying water and unlocking cells, but these things happen too fast. He could easily die waiting.

The most terrible part of this is helplessness. Being locked in.

He hates being locked into anything, but this cell is especially literal.

If there were a fire, and if he died so horribly, who would pay attention? Well, he's not entirely unimportant, his passing and its circumstances would be noticed by the newspapers, which might say that a relatively respected artist, sentenced to a week in jail for a not-very-serious assault on two Americans during a peace demonstration, was one of the inadvertent victims. Briefly he might be a minor martyr, and his paintings might bear higher price tags. Even after such a short acquaintance, Anne would be sad. She'd go to his funeral with Leo and Teresa, possibly buy a new black dress with a little black hat to cover her shiny bright hair. She'd feel a loss, but would she see his last moments, that's the question. Would she know the awfulness of dying like that, head spinning, no air?

He suspects she might picture the result, instead: what he would look like, having put up that battle for breath. She will have seen the bodies of people who died that way, and anyway, she probably pictures results better than she pictures causes.

Still, she would mourn. So would some others. Peace International might use the occasion of his funeral to make a point. Susannah would be sorry, partly because of Lizzie, but also on her own behalf. They may not be what they once were to each other, but he's pretty sure his absence would leave a gap.

All those people, though, would be grieving for something more to do with themselves than for him and his suffering.

Lizzie, now: Lizzie's the imaginer, good at envisioning circumstances to fit around a few facts. He bets she'd want a detailed portrait of what happened; she'd see just about what he's picturing, and with a similar anguish. She might feel as trapped by her imagination as he does in this cell. And she would miss Teddy himself, not just him in her life. From his point of view, her grief would likely be the purest.

God, he'll drive himself crazy if he keeps this up. If he doesn't pull himself together, it's going to feel like five years in here, not five days.

Maybe he should be grateful for slowly moving time. The trouble is slowly moving *empty* time.

There must be more useful, less horrifying images than fire here, if he looks around and pays attention. This could turn out to be a good experience, if he stays calm about it. He wishes he'd thought to ask Anne, through the guard, to bring a sketch pad and charcoal. He probably isn't allowed pencils or pens or brushes, but it should be obvious that he couldn't do much damage to himself or anybody else with a stump of charcoal.

Maybe Anne will look at his list and think, "This isn't much, what else might he like?" Shit, she'd probably bring food or a magazine, no idea what's important. Why should she know what's important? Well, she just should.

So now he's resentful and critical of a woman to whom he said, just this weekend, this morning, "I love you, too"? Love does seem to make him wary and cruel.

Jesus, he really said that, what did he think he was doing? There are jails and there are jails, and this one almost feels comfortable and safe, compared with that one.

The guard comes back, he's unlocking the cell and he's not alone. "I got hold of your girl. You shoulda told me that number was a hospital, I had trouble tracking her down."

"Sorry. But thanks."

Sorry? Thanks? What happened to "so what" or "fuck off"?

"You got a roommate." Tall, thin, gray-faced, maybe a decade older than Teddy and, best of all, wearing a suit. Not that Teddy usually has much use for men in suits, but standards are different in here. A man in a suit probably isn't a burglar or a mugger, and if he's a murderer, it'd be a case of domestic, not random violence. Most probably it's some white-collar crime: fraud or corporate pilfering.

Interesting, seeing somebody as scared as Teddy was a few hours ago. Does Teddy in his beige pants and T-shirt look as menacing to this suited-up guy as some leather-jacketed thug would have looked to Teddy?

Unkind to make him suffer too long. Like a host with an ill-at-ease guest, Teddy reaches out to shake hands, introducing himself.

"Gil Avery." Speaking, the man gives away his flaw, or perhaps his crime, in a sour blast of booze fumes. His hands fly over his face. "Oh, Christ, I hit somebody." What, with his fists? With a club or a car? Now he's crying in great, heaving sobs, a maudlin drunk, for Christ's sake. The smell, which until now has been mainly just musty with a sharpish overlay of disinfectant and a dash of sweat that's probably Teddy's becomes truly unpleasant. It's not just the booze, there's also a really nasty stench of fear and disbelief.

"Sit down," Teddy orders. "Pull yourself together." What is he, a baby-sitter? This isn't why men go to jail, to cry.

Instead of moving toward the bunk, Avery simply slides to the floor and slumps against the wall. He makes an interesting composition, a little bald, a little gray, thin except for the minor below-the-belt paunch some thin men get. His arms are crossed awkwardly against his chest, one leg stretched out straight, the other crooked at the knee. There are delicate shadings from the lights from the corridor and the ceiling of the cell. Teddy sees elongations and spiderish lines.

He's thinking he could really get absorbed in this, and he wishes Anne would bring something soon to work with, when Avery leans slightly sideways and very quietly throws up on the floor, catching the sleeve of his suit. Oh, shit. Teddy, furious now, strides to the door, grips the bars and yells, "Hey, get in here! This guy's sick."

They must think he means Avery's having something serious, like a heart attack, because two guards come at a clip. Then their faces wrinkle because it's nothing so clean, and they go away briefly, coming back with a mop, pail, dustpan, broom, and the same absorbent dry stuff Teddy remembers from public school, that sharp smell after some kid threw up.

"What's he here for, anyway?"

"Drunk driving."

"So he's just in till he sobers up?"

"Nope. He put a woman in hospital and nearly got her kid,

so he'll be here longer than that." Now Avery's slumped over and is making small snorting sounds.

Nothing clean, then, nothing like scooping a little money that didn't belong to him. Some guy like this wiped out Teddy's life when he was young.

Well, not his actual life, but his history. Watching Avery, that feeling comes back, the pain that made his head feel too small, as if it was going to explode with all the sorrow it couldn't hold. Never to see his mother again, or his father, those people with all their hopes on him, truly never again — he couldn't get hold of the idea that something could suddenly be never. It must have been grief, but the word was tiny.

Thank God for Susannah. They were together in that dingy apartment when the cops came to the door; dear Susannah, whom he loved at the time, although he hated the place, too small for two and too dark to get much proper work done. His mind wasn't on working, though, in those days; or his heart was diverted from it. It was late at night when the cops came and, he supposed, left, and Susannah stayed awake with him and held him and rocked him and listened to him. Then she took care of practical matters, like the funeral arrangements. She even picked out the clothes his parents would wear in their coffins, even though the coffins were closed. In theory, he's always thought coffins should be closed, but in fact, he missed saying goodbye. He would, after all, have liked to see them.

She told him what they were wearing. She ordered flowers and talked to the minister. She is horrendously strong sometimes.

She made him eat, and she lay down beside him, holding his head on her shoulder, letting him hold himself against her to borrow her warmth. He was so cold! He thought he must have been very stupid before, not to understand that they could change utterly and be dead, that they wouldn't always be the same people, apparently more or less pleased with themselves and with him. He couldn't get over that.

Later, he felt at a disadvantage. Susannah'd seen him lose his head. Also he owed her for those days she spent listening and cradling. He used to catch himself thinking that if her parents died, he'd be able to return the favor, but they didn't die, and he never got the chance, and now that her father is dead, it's too late; Teddy's comfort is no longer of interest to her.

He should have paid more attention then to the kind of strength she had. It seems to be something she went right on practising until she was so strong all by herself that she left him. There were signs, if he'd noticed, but he was misled by her willingness to let him be. Give or take a few tears — but she always gave in, she always accepted, until she didn't any more. What a surprise!

Now, right here in this small gray room with him, is another murderous, behind-the-wheel bastard. Who now has good reason to be scared of Teddy.

Anger feels fine, though, pleasingly powerful. "It's always better to be the lovee than the lover," Teddy told Leo once, consoling him in a bar after some quarrel with Teresa. It was supposed to be a joke, but he meant it, too. It's also better to be the feared one than the frightened.

So out there somewhere, some woman's in hospital because of this asshole. All of a sudden her life's inside out, although at least she's alive.

Teddy should have learned something when his parents' accident happened. He ought to have learned the importance of proper goodbyes. When Lizzie's alarm went off the other night he should have gotten up and given her a hug, because she was flying off with her mother and who knew what might happen? And Anne this morning—he ought to have looked more closely, kissing her goodbye.

Time has started to move a little more quickly now. Almost one day down, and only four to go. Dinner is roast beef, peas, mashed potatoes, custard, and more coffee, and Avery stirs, probably prompted by the smell of food, and finally opens his eyes. There is a progression of expressions—could Teddy catch them? — of confusion, disbelief, then horror. "God," and he moans, touching his head, "what's that smell?"

"You. You threw up. So far you've been a real pleasure to know."

Avery looks at the stain on the sleeve of his suit. "I gotta change. How do I get some clothes around here?"

"How would I know?"

"This isn't happening," Avery mutters. "It can't be real." When he looks at Teddy, does he see hate? "I'll go to jail, won't I?"

"You're *in* jail, asshole."

"Oh, Jesus, I remember, I hit a woman. She was just there all of a sudden, I don't know where she came from. God, the sound!" He looks as if he may throw up again, and Teddy glances away, just in case. The guy doesn't seem able to get over what he's done; or he can't get over the effect it's had.

"You'd have seen her if you hadn't been pissed."

"No, she came out of nowhere, I swear. Anyway I wasn't drunk."

"Bullshit. You're still drunk."

Avery straightens. He looks belligerent now; not used to being contradicted? Probably a boss in some office, throwing his weight around, bullying small fry. "What's it to you?"

Teddy leans forward, trying to look dangerous. "Nothing much, except you're a liar and you barfed in my cell and you stink. That's about all."

"Ah, shit." Sullenly, Avery pulls his tray over, but he doesn't get far with the meal before he gives up, closes his eyes, leans against the wall. Teddy's eyes narrow, seeing forms Avery might take on canvas. Something may come of this week, after all. Anyway, if he has to be here, he might as well make some use of it.

Still, he leaps up with pleasure when the guard comes back and says he's got a visitor. Thank God for Anne, here to remind him there really is an outside world, with time and events that move on normally in a way he can already hardly imagine.

It turns out he and Avery both have visitors, although Avery doesn't look too excited. Along the corridor they go, a guard behind them, to a metal door leading into another gray room, this one much larger than a cell, with orange plastic chairs arranged around cheap fake-wood tables. This isn't like prison movies, either, no row of cubicles and mesh and glass, no phones linking visitors and prisoners, just a plain, institutional room. And here's Anne, looking nervous, but fresh! That's the thing, that freshness she carries around with her. She keeps reminding him of flowers: this time a daisy. Jesus, he's going to have to stop seeing flowers, sentimental crap.

A plump gray-haired woman is standing beside her. She peels off in the direction of Avery. "Gil Avery, you *fool*." Furious, hardly the meek mate Teddy would have assumed for him. "How could you be so stupid?" Teddy sinks his face into Anne's hair, which this morning smelled slightly of shampoo and now smells of disinfectant — a whole outside world of scent.

This must be why men try to escape from prison, this hunger to be comforted. "Are you all right?" she asks, and her voice sounds to him like music, like a piano playing gentle jazz — and this after only a day! What a thirst for the female voice must build during a long sentence!

Depending on the voice, of course. Avery's wife is still scolding, and maybe she was also magic once, to him at least.

"I'm fine," Teddy says, and he is, now. Really Anne's the one who needs comforting, she looks so concerned, and it's up to him to be brave. "It's nothing terrible. Only five days." But saying that he can already feel, in advance, how loneliness is going to weigh on him when she's gone.

"I brought the things you asked for. Did you know they'd search the bag, though? Like they thought I'd be bringing in a file or a gun or something?" She's chattering too brightly, her voice is too high, but he's found out for himself that this place can make anybody nervous. "Toothbrush, underwear, change of clothes—they said no razor, I'm sorry." What else would she have found, going through his drawers and cabinets in search of the things he wanted? Anything he would have preferred to keep to himself? Old letters or photos or notes to himself that would tell her things she has no right to know? He can't actually think of anything, but still it's an invasion of sorts, even if she was only getting what he wanted.

"I brought a few other things, too, that you didn't ask for." She's stepped back, must have felt some change in how he was holding her. "I thought you might like them. They weren't going to let me bring them, but I talked them into it."

Oh, how he has misjudged her, what resources of comprehension she has, after all. Because, unzipping the small beige travel bag, Teddy finds, right on top, a sketch pad and a package of charcoal. He keeps looking for flaws and not finding them.

He feels himself watching the two of them together, seeing a perfect picture, just as pictures are always perfect in his head. "What a terrific woman you are," and his voice is low with gratitude.

She grins. "Close, anyway. I do my best."

She does, she clearly, obviously, does do her best, and isn't it a wonder? "You're so close to perfect," he hears himself saying, "I think I'd like you around all the time. Let's get married when I get out."

No. He didn't say that. But there's an echo of the words out in the air, so he must have. Jesus, though, she'll know they were just a gesture, for effect, not for real, of course she will.

Her face is bright, pink-tinged, and she reaches up, smiling, to touch his cheek. "Ask me again when you're out of here and back to normal." The words are lighthearted, and he feels faintly, perversely hurt. Does she have doubts about him? Who does she think she is, treating him lightly?

"Oh, Ted." She takes his hands and swings them as if she's keeping time to some song. "You should see your face! You look so offended, but you know if I'd said yes, you'd be petrified. You'd be trying to think of a way to tell me you were only kidding. Which you were."

How does she know? Would it be terrific or eerie, being with a woman who knows him?

"What makes you so sure? Maybe I meant it."

"We'll see." She has a secret-looking smile. He doesn't seem to have her gift for reading faces.

Saved by the guard, who steps forward and calls out, "Time's up." What an earful he must get during these visits. Or maybe he's bored by other people's conversations and tunes them out.

The Averys are still murmuring angrily at each other. It must take some nerve, Teddy thinks, for Avery to be mad under the circumstances.

"I'll be back tomorrow," Anne promises.

"Thanks. I'll look forward to it." God, he will, too. Walking back down the corridor, hearing the door clank shut behind him, he tries to make his hand remember how soft her hair is.

Now he takes the bottom bunk. At least it's good to know that on any scale of guilt, Avery is a worse, more careless, weaker man than he.

Avery seems able to sleep, though. Or he's passed out. Anyway, lying on his back, hands clasped behind his head, Teddy stares at an unshifting sag in the mattress above.

He's still amazed by circumstances. He's really here, isn't he, sharing this small dark space with that unlikable man? This morning he woke up with Anne, a cheerful free man, and tonight he is lying on a spare narrow bed, covered by a rough gray blanket, a prisoner. Just a few days ago he woke up with a full day planned — demonstration, work, and a dinner with friends — and ended it with a headache, the surprising Anne, and Lizzie asleep across the room. On the face of it events appear to have gone wrong, capped by that blurted proposition tonight.

When he finally sleeps, he dreams of bars and wakes up unsurprised.

There is breakfast, there is lunch, and there is dinner. There are the voices of men, slurred or angry or commanding. Teddy is accustomed, on the streets, to the mixed choir of men and women, and in his own place to music or silence. He is not used to three full meals a day. Avery disappears the second afternoon for a court appearance, but is returned before dinner, bail refused. Apparently there is some chance the woman he hit might still die, which would change the charges against him. He's worried now, and looks irritated that Teddy's doing push-ups and running on the spot in their cell, working off the meals. Perhaps he's also used to silence? Or control?

Teddy sits cross-legged on his bunk, back against the wall, sketch pad on his lap, trying to capture the shape and light in Avery's angular form: the starkness of a tall man bent into whatever his regrets or fears may be, and the shadows altering the barren shapes in their cell. Still, there's only so much to be done with charcoal, just hints, like making notes. The real work is attention, burning images into memory so they can be properly transformed when he gets free. It's interesting, how good this feels; a queer sort of freedom, but there is something relaxing about this kind of helplessness. No phone calls here, no rallies, or plans to make or paintings to show — not even any conversations, since he doesn't care to talk to Avery, just wants to use his body.

It's hard to sustain hatred. To regard someone with this sort of intensity creates a kind of closeness, even if Avery isn't aware of it, and if he were, it'd probably only make him nervous. It's not that Avery gets chatty or friendly, or that Teddy is forgiving; just that the lines he's drawing are Avery's lines. Maybe it's something similar to what happened with that guy Tim Connors and his fiancee's leg? Of course, that must have been even more intense, since love was presumably involved, as well as concentration.

Interesting that Avery isn't angry about being kept here. He seems, sober, like the kind of man who's used to his comforts and feels he deserves them; not the sort who's good at deprivation. Also, unlike Teddy, he has nothing to occupy himself with except food, rest, and thought. What does he think about during all the vacant hours? Possibly he feels safer here with Teddy than at home with his furious wife. Or maybe it really doesn't matter to him where he is while he absorbs the nature of disruption and change. When he does speak, though, it's about his own changes, not those of the woman he hit. He doesn't seem interested in the nature of responsibility, either, and never says, "God, I'll never drink again," or, "How will I ever make it up to her?" What he does say, more to himself than to Teddy, is, "I don't believe this," and, "I can't believe this happened."

After every meal, Teddy spends some time exercising. Otherwise he'll leave here bloated, and his body has enough flaws without adding weight to them. He enjoys having three meals a day, and finds himself looking forward to them. They're events, after all, something that happens. The exercising feels good, too. Maybe when he gets out he'll keep it up. Maybe those saggings in his flesh can still be beaten smooth again.

When he gets out, he also plans much larger canvases: great explosions of color, as well as the new stark grays he's learning here, the terrible white and black outlines of unfreedom of one sort and another. Can he make people touch and smell and taste Gil Avery and this place, as well as merely see? He has a picture of people stepping out of their lives right into his work.

That dream: of some work so magnificent, so illuminating, that even he will look at it and think, there, that's it. That's the most I've ever wanted, the thing I aimed for. Finally, a piece of work. God, wouldn't that be something!

Anne comes each evening, bringing some treat: more sketch pads, and even a joke: a homemade muffin with a tiny charm inside, a set of handcuffs. Well, he has to laugh, and in these circumstances laughter is quite a gift.

They don't discuss what he said the first night. Anne looks tired from work. It's probably hard, putting in a long day and then coming here. She says, "It's amazing, but you look better every day."

"I'm getting a lot of work done." He touches her hair. "And I'm looking forward to getting out. That makes me happy."

The fluorescent lights in the visitors' room are very harsh. They show up the tiny creases under Anne's eyes and around her mouth where makeup sticks like dots of drying plasticine. She almost looks more naked this way than she did in his bed.

What does he know about her, anyway? That she drinks Scotch on the rocks—unusual, because most women don't like Scotch, in his experience. That she's stubborn, and that when they stand beside each other, the top of her head comes to just below his shoulders. That she doesn't like lies and has tiny ankles but very strong legs. That if he ever hit her, she'd leave him instantly.

He wouldn't dream of hitting her; hasn't struck another human being, despite this sentence for assault, since he and Susannah were breaking up, and who could blame him? She *wanted* so much, she was enraging beyond words. Anyway, she hit back. And anyway, he didn't hurt her. He can't imagine hitting Anne. Of course, when he met Susannah, he couldn't have imagined hitting her, either.

It's probably hard at his age, anyway, to be either frightened or passionate enough for violence.

He hates walking back along that corridor to his cell after a visit from Anne. There is no darker moment, that bottom-of-the-pit, bone-deep loneliness.

Is it just a matter of being here? Is he usually too busy to notice if he's lonely? What exactly is it that sends him out of his perfectly bright and warm apartment in the middle of the night and into the streets, looking for life in its various and peculiar shapes? Is he hunting or escaping?

In here, there's too much time to think about stuff that really doesn't matter. It's his life, after all, what he does; it adds up. What comes out of those nights and these days is work.

He supposes what he said to Anne the first night he was here will have to be talked about when he gets out, it's not the kind of thing that can be brushed aside undiscussed. It could get too important, take on far more meaning than he intended. Anyway, Anne's too frank—look at the way she talked about Lizzie the morning Lizzie left. She doesn't seem to let much go unspoken; not a mysterious woman. She even seems almost unshadowed, although perhaps that's mysterious itself. Would Tim Connors know? Could Tim Connors and Anne read each other's minds and never need to say a word?

Too dull. Where'd be the excitement, the anticipation of fresh, unexpected events? Teddy would rather be Teddy. Or Ted. Anyway, a middle-aged man, an artist, an angry campaigner for peace—whatever, a man with all kinds of chances still for new discoveries. That's really not bad for someone his age, although he's only forty-five after all, and in plenty of ways that's still quite young. There's no reason at all as far as he can see, today at any rate, that just about anything can't still happen.

FAMILY FEUDS

Two elderly brothers who hadn't seen each other since the Second World War were reunited last night at Toronto's Pearson International Airport.

Marco Palestrini, 78, and his brother, Emilio, 75, were separated by the war and their politics and lost touch completely when Emilio immigrated to Canada in 1946.

According to Emilio's grandson, Tony Jamieson, the brothers were on opposing sides in the war, Marco joining the Italian army and Emilio a group of anti-Fascist partisans.

While the brothers embraced tentatively at the airport, Jamieson, 28, explained that the two men remained estranged until six years ago, when he visited Italy and contacted members of his great-uncle's family.

"We all wanted them to get in touch with each other again," he said. "It seemed wrong to have this feud going on and on, especially so long after the war and when they're not young any more."

An exchange of letters and telephone calls followed, "and there's been a sort of reconciliation we're hoping will continue," said Jamieson.

Members of Emilio's family in Canada, several of whom were on hand for the reunion, contributed toward the fare for Marco's flight and the six-week stay that is planned.

"We are old," said a beaming Emilio, his arm around his older brother's shoulder, "and maybe those things from before don't matter so much any more. Maybe we are different men now and can be brothers, like when we were children."

Speaking through an interpreter, Marco said only that he was pleased to see his brother, meet new relatives and visit Canada for the first time.

It sure doesn't sound like a promising start to a reunion, does it? Marco's six-week visit, Susannah suspects, is going to seem awfully long before it's done.

She imagines relief at the airport when it's time for the brothers to say goodbye. She'd also bet the experience will teach the younger members of the family a thing or two about the perils of interference, however benevolently intended; although she could be wrong, it could turn out that a forgiving strain runs through both men and that, after all, it no longer matters so much that one was a Fascist many years ago and the other whatever the opposite of Fascist was called at the time. It might be her own outlook on family forgiveness that is askew.

Lizzie's wearing a blue skirt, white blouse, Susannah her light blue silk dress with the small white dots, demure little collar and ruffles at the wrists, the best she could come up with for the occasion. Elaine and their mother are in black, of course. "You look very nice," Elaine says, but Susannah detects disapproval. She thinks.

What strange, unreal places funeral homes are! But then, what a strange and unreal circumstance, the four of them here, preparing to look down on a dead familiar face. Maybe funeral homes have artificial air and artificial light to keep grief and panic at some artificial level also. Even the undertaker is false: unctuous, falsely sympathetic (his sympathy must be a lie, or at least an exaggeration, because how could it be true, funeral after funeral, year after year?). Susannah has an urge to violence: to brush him aside, or knock him down, or yell at him and strike him, make him vanish; make him appreciate the extent of his falsity.

She can hardly blame him that her father's dead, though, can she? It's hardly his fault.

Some words, if not ones she means, are being spoken, and hands are shaken. She keeps standing, holding on to Lizzie. She can't stop her eyes, her attention, from shifting toward the end of the long, darkened room, where the coffin lies, surrounded by a pool of silence, separation. There he is. What would she say to him?

Maybe just push Lizzie forward and say, "See?"

Now there's no avoiding it. Still holding Lizzie's hand, she walks across the room, toward her father's face.

Jesus, is that him?

Of course it is. It's only that he looks so young; or if not quite young, not much older than she is. She might be looking at herself. Oh, there are differences: his eyebrows are thicker — that must be why his frowns could feel like blows — but there's her narrow nose, the mouth in a narrow line. This is his face when she was a child, the way he looked during her best memories of him. Those hands folded on his chest once held out a garter snake toward her. The voice that called her a terrible name came much later and was much older than this man.

What a mystery he is! This morning, sitting at her old place at the kitchen table (rubbing her fingers with an odd sense of comfort over the ridges on the edge made by the small destructive child she was, who carved into the wood with a fork), she heard how he ended, but not how he'd been. Susannah, the cool grown-up who makes her living asking questions of strangers, had leaned forward, resting her elbows on that scarred table and asked her mother, "How are you? All right?" Knowing the methods of begging questions.

"Oh, yes, I expect so. It's a shock, but there's been so much to do I can't feel it's really sunk in. Only, I've had trouble sleeping. When I shut my eyes, I keep seeing what happened."

And what was that? "Were you alone?"

Her mother nodded. "He said he wasn't feeling well after dinner, but he thought it was just heartburn and gas, although we only had stew and dumplings. He had trouble that way, but you know your father, it was like pulling teeth to get him to a doctor."

Now, of course, his lips are sealed, no teeth in sight.

"He just took an antacid tablet and went to the living room to watch TV. He had on one of those police shows I don't like, so I was reading a magazine, not paying much attention." Susannah didn't remember her mother ever being still long enough to read, but no doubt she's had more time in recent years. "It was an article on day care, and I remember thinking what a dreadful thing it is, dropping your children off with strangers to raise." Her hand flew up to her mouth. "Oh, I didn't think. You'll have had to do that, I suppose." Not that she didn't mean the words, just that if she'd thought, she wouldn't have said them.

"It's okay, Lizzie and I won't take it personally." But Susannah could feel that her smile had an edge to it, she could feel a brittleness around her lips.

His lips, too, are straight. All those familiar angles from her own mirror, in fact, are here, except he has no softening curves that she can see.

"Yes. Well, I was just thinking that when I heard this awful sound." She sounded herself, Susannah thought, almost unaffected. She also seemed to have more words than she ever used to. "It was like a gurgling, and when I looked, he was holding his shoulder for some reason. Why would that be, do you know?" She didn't wait for an answer. "Then he went all rigid and fell back, and his hand dropped away from his shoulder, and his head rolled a bit sideways, and by the time I got to him, he was gone. Or," she added thoughtfully, "I think he was. I always meant to take one of those courses about how to revive people, but I never got around to it. I suppose I might have saved him, if I'd known how."

That didn't seem to be said with great regret or particular guilt. She seemed to be merely stating a fact. "I didn't know what to do, so of course I called Elaine and she just took over and called everyone. The ambulance and Alice Willett. Alice came right over and then Elaine got here and now you're here. With Lizzie. We're all together now."

With one notable exception.

It was a while before anyone thought to call Susannah, wasn't it? Something of an afterthought, apparently, not someone who sprang to mind at a family crisis.

She would have liked to ask her mother, "When did you learn to speak? Before he died or only since?" And what about him, did he change, too?

What would he say now if he could see her standing here looking down at him, her daughter's hand clutched in hers? What would he say to that, his slut of a daughter with that bastard, her child?

She really cannot hear his voice at all. "He looks so peaceful," people say on these occasions, but peaceful isn't quite the word. Empty, maybe. Or clear. She could read anything into that face, but she'd read it with no help from him.

She reaches out, touches the back of her hand to his cheek, but he doesn't feel warmer or colder than he ever did.

Did it hurt much, in those moments when he was gripping his shoulder, making that sound? What was he thinking, right then? Or was it too late, or too intense, for thought?

When the minister, another false gray man, asks them for words they would like to hear said about him, she can only think of words she might have liked to say to him. If she can't hear his voice now, though, he also can't hear hers. There really is such a thing as an incurable conclusion, and that's so tragic she finally cries, first time today.

As other people begin to arrive, she keeps seeing the backs of her mother and Elaine as they move in front of her and Lizzie;

like that dream, except there's nobody standing between them. Where have all these people come from, though, with their watchful faces? She is careful to look unreadable and firm. At the graveside, the usual words are spoken—ashes to ashes, dust to dust. It doesn't seem like much, not a fair conclusion to a life, but that's a childish thought, something the grown-up Susannah ought to know.

She keeps her own home in her mind like a charm, and can't wait to get back. Still, she can't imagine waking up any morning from now on without seeing this place and knowing her father is dead.

Lizzie looks like him, too. She hadn't really thought of that. She'd thought Lizzie looked like her, with a little Teddy thrown in for variety.

Too late, too late. Nothing has ever been so truly too late before. She can hardly imagine it.

And then Elaine picks and picks on the drive home. Is that her sorrow, her form of grief, or is it just Elaine?

There are too many people at the house, almost like a party. Susannah's mother sinks into her soft chair in the living room, and people approach her to talk. Some people laugh. Susannah and Elaine lead Lizzie to the kitchen, where they put on the coffee and get the trays of sandwiches and cake out of the refrigerator. What Susannah would like most is silence and solitude right now, but there's that crowd waiting to be fed. And entertained?

The next best thing would be a drink. "I don't suppose—" she turns to Elaine "—there'd be anything like alcohol around, would there?"

"In this house?" Then Elaine grins — imagine, she grins! "I brought a mickey of rye, though. If you'll hold the fort a minute, I'll slip upstairs and get it. That's why I bought the Pepsi." So that's why she was reluctant to share it with Lizzie?

"You clever old thing." Susannah laughs, then notices the puzzlement on Lizzie's face. Well, it is puzzling, isn't it? "Here, honey, take these sandwiches around, okay? Elaine and I'll bring in the coffee in a minute."

By the time she and Elaine have poured their drinks, cam- ouflaging them in teacups, and reached the living room, which is every bit as gloomy as Susannah remembered, poor Lizzie has been trapped. An unpleasant little tableau around Susan- nah's mother's chair, with Alice Willett on the scent. That'll teach Susannah to let down her guard, assume benevolence. "I don't suppose you ever met your grandfather at all," Alice is saying to Lizzie.

"No. I've never been here before."

"Such a shame," turning toward Susannah's mother, "these upheavals. You've been so brave about it, although I expect it's just as well they came. Some things are simply right, aren't they, no matter what? Of course, Susannah was always the stubborn one, wasn't she? She always liked her own way."

And why not?

"What a thing to do!" Alice goes on.

Enough. "What's that, Mrs. Willett?" Susannah asks, step- ping forward, holding the teacup close and casting her voice dangerously low. She thinks Lizzie regards her with some relief.

"Susannah! I didn't see you." Alice has the grace to blush, at least.

"Apparently not. I see you've met my daughter. She's being such a help today. I'm so grateful to have a terrific kid, especially when daughters don't always turn out as you'd hope, do they?" She looks at Alice blandly. "How's Lily, by the way?"

"Oh, she's in Calgary."

"Mrs. Willett's daughter and I were in school together, Lizzie." She turns back to Alice. "I understand she hasn't married?"

"No. No, she hasn't, but she has a wonderful job and a great many friends. I flew out to visit her last summer and had a lovely time." Elaine has come up and is listening now, too; maybe drawn by something in Alice's rushing voice.

Oh, Susannah should leave it there. If she doesn't, she'll feel awful. However. "Actually, I ran into a friend of hers in Toronto this spring. It was interesting, hearing all about her." A little extra push of breath on the *all*. "Do say hello to her for me when you talk to her again."

Alice nods, then says to Lizzie's grandmother, "I'll speak with you later. I'll just see now if anyone needs anything."

"What was all that about?" Elaine asks when she's gone.

"Just something I happen to know about Lily."

"Tell me."

"You girls be nice," their mother says. "She's been a good friend. She came over the moment she heard about your father and stayed until Elaine got here."

"Whisper it then," and Elaine leans in close. A moment of sisterly mischief?

Not really. "It's nothing bad, it's only that Lily's living with her lover, who happens to be a woman."

"Oh, my." Elaine steps back, no longer mischievous.

"That wasn't nice, Susannah," her mother says.

"No, you're right, it wasn't. I notice, though, you're quick to her defense, but you weren't too swift to mine or Lizzie's. Don't you think that's interesting?" How cool she can be. How satisfying.

"Alice has always been around when I needed her. She may be difficult sometimes, but I can always count on her."

"Really? Well, you might have been able to count on me, too, if you'd been different fourteen years ago. There was nothing to stop you from calling, you know."

"Oh, but you know your father."

"And you wouldn't ever have done anything without his permission."

Their voices, or her own voice anyway, must have been lifting because Lizzie's elbow nudges her and Elaine says quietly, "If we have to discuss this, let's wait till half the town isn't here."

"Ah, yes, Elaine, you're quite right, as usual." Susannah straightens, casts her most brilliant smile around the room and sees that it's quite true: people are watching. But they turn away — ashamed of being caught? She makes sure, doing a tour of the room with Lizzie, that she speaks to every person, and she introduces Lizzie, forcing them to speak.

It's the closest she can come, she supposes, to gripping her father by the lapels of that black suit and shaking him alive.

When everyone's finally left, though, she does feel bad. She did treat Lily poorly, a cheap shot using her as ammunition. Really, besides Lily Willett's mother, who cares who Lily Willett sleeps with?

As for Susannah's mother — those loving looks at Lizzie don't come to anything with her, apparently. And interesting that Alice's aim was avoiding embarrassment, not defending her daughter. What happens to these women, anyway?

Her old room, where she goes to change into gray slacks, yellow blouse, is beginning to feel familiar again, but it came as an awful shock before. "Is it still the same?" she asked her mother earlier, as they sat around the kitchen table.

"Your room? I guess so. I don't think we ever redid it."

This uncertainty about just what Susannah's room was like was surely the least of her mother's sins, so how to account for that moment of pain?

Her room was light, made for a little girl as little girls were assumed to be at the time, all pink and white, with a floral cotton skirt, stitched by her mother, over the legs of the vanity — not a bit like Susannah, even then. When she first stood in the doorway of this room today she could almost have cried for the ill-fitting child who lived in it. She must have wondered, that child, what was wrong with her, not with it.

All this now feels like reading a book or seeing a movie she hasn't read or seen for years. The characters are vaguely familiar, and she can remember where she was at the time, but there are gaps and unfamiliarities and surprises.

Twelve hours ago, she and Lizzie were on their way to the airport. She doesn't think she can have had any idea before, the distance and time that can be traveled within a mere twelve hours.

Running downstairs to the kitchen, the thump of her feet on the rubberized treads is so familiar she might be Lizzie's age. Or better, eighteen and racing out the door toward her own real life. God, she *remembers* that: running downstairs. What did she think would happen when she was finally out that door and down that walk, away?

Probably nothing as ordinary or as fine as what has happened.

She can't head away this time, though; instead she slides to a stop at the bottom of the stairs and turns to the kitchen where Elaine and Lizzie are at the sink doing dishes. "Where's Mother?"

"Having a nap in the living room."

Susannah takes the tea towel from Lizzie and nudges her aside with her hip. "Why don't you take off for a while? You haven't had any kind of break today. There's a park down at the end of the block — it's still there, isn't it, Elaine?"

"Oh, yes." Elaine answers absently, intent on plates, one thing at a time.

They used to play baseball, boys against girls, in that park. And tag, and marbles, and skipping. Now it probably has slides, a wading pool, a climbing structure, maybe a proper ball diamond and tennis courts for grown-ups; not so many secret places any more, less room to imagine. "Don't get lost," she calls out to Lizzie. What a motherly thing to say, not like her.

The kitchen wallpaper is new since she was last here: yellow again, though, with little green sprigs that are probably supposed to be leaves. Picking it out, her mother would have called it cheery. The cupboards that used to be yellow are now painted white, matching the fridge and stove. There's a modern double sink in place of the old stained porcelain one, and the linoleum, a deeper yellow than the wallpaper, looks different, too. What on earth possessed them to get linoleum, though, instead of one of those shiny floor coverings that never need waxing or polishing? There's no dishwasher, no food processor, not even a blender in sight, none of those work-saving tools her parents might have regarded as temptations to sloth.

For some reason the room smells to her of muffins. It's amazing, how much she remembers; how close to the surface the old yellow cupboards must have been. The difficulty is not details, but the big picture.

Here they are, she and her sister, side by side at the sink, just the two of them, as if they'd never gone anywhere. The skin on Elaine's arms looks too red — a blood-pressure problem?

How can they speak to each other? Where is the line to be found between punishment and love? Or even truth and respect?

"Gee, it's strange being here. It feels like home in a way, but it doesn't. I must be tired."

"Well, you haven't been here for a long time. I expect it would feel strange." There are several tones Elaine could have used for those words; it's nice she chose an almost neutral one.

Even so, this is like some story about a heroine picking her way in darkness across rocks at the top of a cliff, for some purpose like saving someone, or for her own escape. At any rate a delicate mission, maneuver, and oh, she is tired, and not nearly clearheaded enough. "I suppose you get here a lot?"

"Not really. Every three or four months. The flying gets expensive, and I don't have time to drive, especially alone, and Bill doesn't like coming. The boys haven't been here for ages. They always say there's nothing to do, and I suppose they're right. Anyway, now they're so far away."

Have they found the place unwelcoming? Susannah would have pictured Elaine's sons doted on, adored by their grandparents. If she'd pictured anything. "That's too bad. Did Mother and Dad visit you?"

"Oh, you know Dad, he wouldn't fly and he'd never have driven. I've asked Mother down on her own, but she wouldn't hear of it. I don't know what she'll do now, without him. As a matter of fact, now that you're here, I think we should discuss it."

What's to discuss? What are they supposed to do about their mother's life? If she wanted one, she should have made one long ago.

"The long haul's going to be hard for her," Elaine goes on, and no doubt she does have more experience than Susannah with long hauls.

This flushed plump woman with the reddened hands and the hair curling from dishwater steam once said, "You have whims, Susannah," and, "You're not my sister any more, that's it." But they are sisters. Otherwise why on earth would they be standing here doing the dishes together after their father's funeral? If they hadn't been born into the same family, they certainly would have never met. Elaine was three when Susannah was born — did she want to injure the newcomer, the disrupter?

When this woman was young and Susannah was sick (flu? mumps? measles?) Elaine hauled one of those heavy wooden dining-room chairs upstairs and placed it beside Susannah's bed and read to her adventure after adventure of Buster Bear's Twins, Old Granny Fox, Danny Meadow Mouse, Chatterer the Red Squirrel. How patient she was, and kind!

"Remember when you cut my hair?"

"Oh, lord, don't remind me." But she's smiling, isn't she? Remember, though, "You're not my sister any more, that's it."

Susannah's hair went gloriously uncut until she was seven, when Elaine undertook one day to shorten it, keeping at the job, standing back occasionally, eyes narrowed, until Susannah had only a couple of rough-cut inches left. Their mother was furious with both of them, which wasn't fair, since Susannah was the ugly, heartbroken one, and Elaine was more frightened than sorry.

When Susannah was twelve and Elaine fifteen, Elaine used her face for experiments with makeup, painting it with different shades of lipstick and dashing rouge across the cheekbones as if Susannah were a doll. Then of course they had to wash it off before either of their parents saw. So yes, they did have some secrets together, didn't they?

"How do you like being a grandmother? Is it fun?" Susannah may be a grandmother herself someday; Elaine is always the first to reach these places of ordinary life.

"It might be if I ever saw them, but they're so far away. We try to visit Mark and Tony for about a week each, every year, but it's hardly enough." Poor Elaine, who put all her eggs in a family basket, now sounds dismayed that they've cracked. "What about you? What have you been doing?" How polite they are being, how restrained; like meeting an old lover at a party, brightly ignoring disastrous events.

"For the past fourteen years, you mean?" But Susannah tries

• 196 •

to say this lightly, still feeling her way. "Let's see. I quit my job before Lizzie was born, and I've been free-lancing ever since. I own our house, I've talked to a lot of people and written a lot of stories, I've made some friends and lost some, and there've been a lot of movies and parties and plays and books along the way. I've raised my kid. It doesn't sound very interesting, I guess, but I think we've done okay."

"Sometimes," Elaine says softly, wiping her dishcloth around and around a dinner plate, "I've been jealous of you. It made me mad sometimes that you could always do what you wanted, and I guess, to tell the truth, it still does. I've always thought you get off so lightly all the time."

So much for party chat. Susannah's mouth falls open. "It's hardly getting off lightly, Elaine, to be kicked out of your family."

"Kicked out! You did that to yourself, nobody did it to you. Isn't that just like you, though — never taking the responsibility, so it ends up that you're the one who gets to be free."

Well, well. What a chasm of misunderstanding — God, she could do some damage to Elaine's self-satisfied, self-sacrificing face. What a comfort that would be, letting go, letting loose. She has to do something with her hands, so instead tries putting an arm around Elaine. "I didn't know you felt like that," she says, as mildly as she can manage, although a trace of violence escapes in a quiver of the voice.

Elaine snaps, "Don't feel sorry for me," and begins scrubbing at already clean cutlery, her face tight and angry. So much for sisterly conspiracies over covert drinks.

"I don't feel sorry for you. I just think it's incredibly arrogant for you to decide you've had a tough time and I haven't, or that your tough time is my fault somehow."

"It's what I think. I prefer to be frank." Susannah should have known better than to touch her.

What an odd, stunted family, though, that not only has no kind words, but also no gestures. Their estrangement can hardly be just a matter of a few moments of fury years ago, then. There must be a strong and continuing thread of separation that reaches beyond memory. Estrangement as a bond—now there's a piece of family absurdity.

Lizzie, who has always been embraced, must be out of place here, too.

What was it Susannah wanted—something foolish to do with restoration, salvage? Stupid—there's only rubble here, it seems, no floors or walls left on which to build a restoration, or materials that can be salvaged.

Still, there is always curiosity of sorts; even real longings? And anyway, she's come this far. Where is the trick here, or the key?

She can't say, "I love you, Elaine," since that wouldn't be true, or even, "I like you," because she doesn't know Elaine well enough to tell if that would be true, either, and doubts that it would be. What there should be is some word she doesn't know, and which may not even exist, that signifies the mixed longings of the members of a family for each other. It would have to imply a kind of ferocity and passion, but not necessarily fondness or similarity or even respect. It could not be a word that requires or assumes love.

She says, fairly mildly, "It seems to me you have a funny view of my life, Elaine."

"I don't have any view of your life. I have no idea what you get up to."

"That's hardly my fault, is it? I'm the one who should be angry, not you."

"Me angry? Why would you think that?"

"For one thing, look at your hands." Which are clenched on the edge of the sink, white-knuckled fists.

Elaine, glancing down, seems surprised, unfurls her hands and holds them toward Susannah, but hardly in peace. "You're spoiled. You've always thought you could get away with anything. You come charging in here at the last minute, and you have the nerve to bring your daughter, when you know perfectly well people were already upset enough."

"My goodness, a minute ago you were envying my freedom, and now I'm just spoiled?"

"Oh, don't get clever with me, don't try to twist words around. You always used to do that to make me feel stupid, but it won't work any more." Did she? She doesn't remember using words as a weapon, but maybe she did make Elaine feel smaller or not as bright or no match for her little sister, who knows? Maybe everything Elaine's saying is true in its way; just not the way Susannah remembers.

And isn't it interesting that Elaine's the one who's given way to shouting? There must be something huge she wants to say, but what she does say is, "Think about Mother—her husband dies in front of her, and there's the shock and all the arrangements, and then you turn up with a granddaughter she's never met, and you're rude to her friends, and she has to cope with what people are saying. She's the one who has to live here, you know. You may be pretty fancy, off in your own life, but you're no picture of glamor here, Susannah, and your daughter's no charming little free spirit, either."

Susannah raises her eyebrows, looks questioning. "Really? It seems to me Mother's rather taken to Lizzie. She may be upset, but it doesn't seem to be about meeting her grandchild."

"Right now, maybe, but you'll go flying off tomorrow and she still has to face people, and that's not going to be any fun for her, let me tell you."

"Elaine! Susannah!" Such a sharp, crackling voice, and here's their mother in the doorway, wrapped in an old yellow cotton dressing gown, her silver hair spiking up here and there like some of the kids Lizzie goes to school with.

"Oh, dear, did we wake you?" Elaine is instantly solicitous.

"You'd have wakened the dead." For an instant she looks horrified by what she's said. Or horrified that they really might have wakened the dead? "Where's Lizzie?"

"I sent her off to the park. I thought she'd had enough."

"Thank goodness. Terrible if she'd heard the two of you. Surely you could get through the day of your father's funeral without fighting." How did the frail, startled old woman who opened the door to them earlier turn into this snapping person with her hands on her hips? If they were little kids, which is what she has made them sound like, they might be abashed, ashamed. They might even cry, if they were young and their mother spoke to them in that tone of voice. When they were young, their mother never spoke in that tone of voice. Something has come over her, and it almost seems like the spirit of their father.

"Sorry," Susannah says like a child. "I'm sorry we disturbed you."

"It doesn't matter." Her flourish finished, she sounds old and tired again. "Everything disturbs me at the moment. It's very queer."

"What is?"

"Oh, things like how much will be different without your father."

"You'll miss him," Elaine suggests, rather flatly in Susannah's view; as if it's bound to be true.

"Oh, yes, so many years. Still, he died well, I think. He would have preferred going quickly like that. I worried about it so long, how I'd look after him if he got so he couldn't get around, and now I don't have to. I wish I'd known."

What, that he would die fast? So she wouldn't have wasted time thinking about it? "Do you think he wondered how he'd look after you if it was the other way around?"

"Heavens, I don't suppose so. I don't think he'd have known how." But how placidly she says this—something to be assumed, apparently, of the man she lived with for half a century. What can it have been like, believing that if she broke a hip or got sick, he'd be no help?

"He was such a big man," her mother continues. "Tall. I couldn't see how I'd manage. Still, that's not the way it turned out, is it? I spent all that time worrying about the wrong things." An odd point of view, but she probably doesn't hear how she sounds. Susannah has interviewed people as innocent as this.

"I didn't think about all the other differences, either. Not having to get up early to make his tea and toast first thing. And I suppose I'll be able to read myself to sleep now."

"You mean you couldn't?"

"He didn't like a light on when he was trying to sleep."

"Good grief."

"Well, maybe, Susannah, but you never married, you don't know all the little things that make living together easier."

Not true, Susannah does know: it's precisely the details that get people down. She wouldn't dream of letting someone make her turn out her bedside light; except for Lizzie, of course, when she was a newborn sleeping in Susannah's room. Then she was careful not to disturb, but that was out of loving, not bullied fear.

"What if you'd said no?" This really is the question, isn't it: what is so terrifying about simple refusal? It is also the question that lies in the heart of her mother's betrayal. "What if you'd told him to get his own breakfast, and learn to sleep with a light on? What could he have done?"

Her mother frowns. "I suppose nothing, but it was easier to go along and after all, it wasn't important or hard, they were just little things he liked."

Like hell.

"Now I guess I'll have to get into new habits." Suddenly she looks up, stares at her daughters in open panic. "What am I going to do? I don't know what to do. I don't even know how much money there is, or where it is."

Are there really still women like this? And her mother one of them? "Why not? You mean you never talked about money?"

"Oh, he wouldn't have liked that, talking about what would happen when he was gone, he wouldn't like that at all. I'm not even sure he realized he *would* go sometime. I think he must have been awfully surprised." How quickly her moods shift; how serene she sounds now, speaking of her husband's terminal surprise. A bit of a shocker herself, she's turning out to be.

"Still, he always looked after me before, he always gave me what I needed and he wasn't mean. I'm sure I'll be fine." She doesn't miss the way Susannah's head shakes. "I know what you're thinking, Susannah, and it's all very well, but it's a matter of getting along. You don't understand."

No, she certainly does not. Her mother may have been caught

in a particular time and place with a particular man, but there have always been brave women, and why couldn't she have been one of those? Except she had two children and no great skills. To have done differently, she would have had to be a lot braver than Susannah has ever had to be. There should be a way of saying that, without implying forgiveness or forgetfulness.

"Never mind, Mother," Elaine says. "Susannah and I will go through everything in the morning. We'll find out exactly where you stand, don't worry about it." She turns to Susannah. "You'll have time, won't you? When do you leave?"

"We have a flight late tomorrow afternoon. You?"

"Tomorrow night."

Again their mother's hands flutter in distress, and she cries, "Oh! Don't talk about leaving. What will I do all alone?"

"You have lots of friends," Elaine says briskly. "The main thing is to keep busy."

If their mother has lots of friends, that's another change. She had acquaintances, of course, but no friend like Frannie—unless she's found one in the past decade and a half, which is perfectly possible. It's a long time, after all. What a desolate picture, though: this tiny old woman going back into this house after waving goodbye to Elaine. Alone for the very first time.

"Yes, of course, you're right, I'll be fine." Their mother is wiping her hands down her dress again; smoothing, always smoothing.

The front door slams and Lizzie skids into the kitchen. All three women erase their expressions, look up at her blandly. Susannah asks, "Did you find the park okay?"

"Yeah, but there wasn't much to do. Did I miss dinner?" A foreigner in this place, where dinner is called supper.

"No. We're just having funeral leftovers."

Whatever Elaine says, it was no mistake to bring Lizzie. Her grandmother can't keep her eyes off her, and keeps reaching out to touch her shoulder or her hair. Interesting, though, that she doesn't touch Susannah. Lizzie talks to her so easily; but then, they have no history.

"You should go to bed, I think, Lizzie," Susannah says finally, explaining to the others, "She was up at five this morning." Her mother is drooping as well, and the two of them, the oldest and the youngest, walk upstairs together with their arms around each other: a pretty picture, but Susannah is wary of her mother's affection. It wouldn't be wise for Lizzie to put too much stock in something that's likely only sentiment.

"Lord, I'm beat, too," Elaine says. "How about one last drink?" Well, why not? Another opportunity to watch the minuet and tango of her sister's moods.

In the living room, Elaine slumps in the dark brown easy chair that was always their mother's, rubbing her glass back and forth across her forehead. Easing what pain? Poor Elaine, after all. "I'm sorry you had to do so much on your own," Susannah says.

"I had help. Neighbors. People like to be helpful." She sips her rye, sets it down with a click and looks hard at Susannah. "Why did you hang up on me?"

"Good God. Because you didn't know Lizzie's name! All that upheaval and all these years and you didn't even remember her name!"

"Oh, Susannah, of course I did, it's just when I called, it went right out of my mind, with everything else to think about."

Did Susannah, asking earlier about Elaine's family, not momentarily forget her husband's name? "I'm sorry, then. I misunderstood." Anything else?

Still, in the scheme of this family, Lizzie's name must be more important than Elaine's husband's; so after all, she isn't sorry.

She sits forward in her matching dark brown chair — her father's, she realizes, the one he stood up from the other night and fell over from. Time here is getting short. "I want to know some things, Elaine. About what happened when I was gone. Didn't anybody ever want to get in touch? Wasn't anybody sorry, or even curious? Didn't any of you care?"

Elaine sighs — is she too tired to tackle this, or does she find the subject dull? "I don't know. Bill and I talked about you sometimes, and I guess I wondered, but I knew you'd be managing, being you. I suppose I was angry for a while, but after that, well, it gets harder to do anything if something's gone on and on. Maybe Mother would have liked to talk about you, but even that felt — forbidden. You know what Dad was like." Why do people keep insisting Susannah must have known this and that about him?

"Why was that, Elaine? Why did everybody care so much what he said?"

"*I* don't know, Susannah. You did, too, though." That's true, isn't it? After all, when he told her to leave, she left.

The point at the moment, however, is that Elaine has been speaking as if none of this was especially important, as if she'd only committed some minor transgression like forgetting it was her turn to do the dishes, nothing like turning her back on a sister who might (or might not) have been in need, or just lonely, anything. "It was unforgivable." Susannah says flatly. "The whole thing, all of you. Can't you imagine?" If not, she can't possibly explain. What a colossal ignorance, failure of feeling, if Elaine truly does have no idea.

"I don't know what you want from me, Susannah." And really, Elaine does look blank and helpless, her palms turned upward, shoulders caught in a shrug. "It's been so long."

"Yes, hasn't it? Well then," and her own drink slams down on the table beside her, "good night." She's out of the chair, out of the room, and climbing the stairs before Elaine can speak; if there were anything else Elaine might want to say.

Elaine said once, "You're no sister of mine any more, that's it." Well, she's no sister of Susannah's, either. These knives cut both ways.

Oh, but it's awfully lonely — she would have thought she had learned not to be lonely. Undressing quietly in the dark beside the bed where Lizzie's already asleep, and easing herself under the covers, she can suddenly hear her father's voice. Singing. She was very little, sitting on his knee, and he was jigging her up and down, singing, "Oh, Susannah, don't you cry for me, for I'm bound for Alabama with a banjo on my knee." Just those lines. The second one was nonsense to her, but how delightful to have her own song sung to her.

She's wakened in sunshine by a shifting beside her in the bed. Where the hell is she? For a wild instant she's stricken with the thought that she's still a kid, still trapped in this room, and nothing she thought she has done and become has happened at all.

Lizzie's face, though, is real. Also this is a new day, and sleep and light bring back a sanity that sometimes gets lost in darkness.

Downstairs on the back porch with Lizzie, sipping the blessed first coffee of the day and talking peacefully with her child, she feels balanced and in control. She is a grown-up woman after all, with a life of her own, and a home of her own, to which she will return today. She can already imagine ways of describing this weekend to Frannie that will make them both roar with laughter. Tears will come to their eyes, especially, no doubt, her own.

There is even something—pleasant?—about sitting out here with Lizzie, then Elaine, and finally her mother; an amazing circumstance, really, and quite fine as long as they're silent and cautious. Some things have happened, and she and Elaine and their mother have taken some small steps, however backward and sideways, and however bound and somewhat painful their feet remain. They aren't ever likely to be free, but that's hardly a reasonable aim anyway. For the moment Susannah is nearly contented; as if sunshine spreads benevolence as well as light.

Except Elaine can't let anything be for long. "We'd better get going, Susannah, if we're going to sort out Father's things before you leave."

What an unexpected old bird their mother is. Not interested, she says, in sentimental relics of the man. "Just give it away or throw it out."

Standing in the doorway of her parents' bedroom, Susannah considers how spare and unfrilled it is, and how narrow its prospects likely are. For more than fifty years, her parents lay together in that white-painted metal bed, with its white cotton sheets (flannelette in winter) and the worn, light blue chenille bedspread. No fancy designer sheets for them, no exotic materials. Her mother used to iron the sheets and pillow cases — does she still? In the past few nights, has she learned to stretch out, fling her arms across the width of the mattress, now that it's all hers? More likely she clings to her own side and wakes up to the sight of the barren space where the matching body ought to be but isn't any more. How much difference is there that way between a husband dying and a lover leaving? And when a lover leaves, there's a sort of self-induced pain, yes, a stone lying somewhere just below the heart, but there's also a tiny, secret fluttering of pleasure because he's gone, and who knows what may happen next?

There does seem to be a sort of unexpected ripeness about her mother, something tart.

Elaine, surging past Susannah, opens the closet door. How carefully they've been ignoring last night's words and any possibility of going on from them. Which is fine, for the moment, with Susannah. She feels like Elaine, only able to do, see, deal with one thing at a time. "Gee, this may not take long after all. He doesn't seem to have had much."

He was buried in his black suit. A brown one and a navy one are still hanging there, along with several pairs of worn khaki work pants and four flannel shirts in various plaids. Three cardigans, which ought to have been folded, not hung up, because now they've got points in the shoulders from the hangers. A cluster of ties draped over a nail on the inside of the closet door, and two pairs of black shoes and two pairs of brown on the floor, along with his red plaid bedroom slippers.

Elaine is examining trousers. "Really, I don't think these are worth giving away. Except for the suits, they're only fit for throwing out." He was a tall man, Susannah knew that and anyway was reminded of it yesterday, but even so the length of the trousers is unexpected.

Pockets are where people put things: little scraps of paper with significant notations. Susannah does it herself. "Here," and she reaches out abruptly as Elaine starts going through pockets, "let me do that." And then, after all, she feels like a child, embarrassed by her own disappointment when a piece of paper turns out to be a shopping list for a hardware store: half a dozen inch-and-three-quarters screws, a package of two-inch nails, windshield washer fluid. But look at the handwriting: straight, clear, and firm. He always pressed down too hard with a pencil; not one of the tools he used comfortably.

"We can give away the shirts, though." Elaine has moved on to a closet shelf and a pile of neatly folded, blazingly clean shirts —all washed here, never taken to the cleaner's. He used to take starch in the collars and cuffs. Susannah remembers her mother struggling away, ironing his clothes on the wooden board set up in the kitchen in the evenings. Of course, she ironed Susannah's and Elaine's clothes, too, and they thought no more of it than their father did.

She pulls one of the flannel work shirts off its hanger. It's amazingly soft, from being so much worn and laundered, and she folds it in her arms for a moment, just to feel. But the smell! Not precisely dirty, not in this house, but a sharpish old-man scent that links her father to those men on park benches who sit leaning over, elbows on knees, staring at the ground — *old* men, whether they're really old or not, the kind who smell as if they've already started to decay without even being dead yet.

"What's the matter?"

"Smell this." Susannah holds out the shirt to Elaine.

"What about it? Do you think it's musty? We could hang it out on the line to air."

"No, never mind. It's fine." Susannah feels foolish: making too much, likely, out of nothing.

"The slippers will have to go."

Elaine's right, they're worn out, worn to the shape of his feet, the right one jutting to one side where he maybe had a corn, and both of them run down badly at the heels. His slippers used to wait just inside the front door, and first thing when he came in, he'd kick off his boots and put them on. Perhaps in recent years he's worn his slippers all the time?

If someone went through Susannah's house, they'd find out

all sorts of things about her: her history, her tastes, even some of her events. Why isn't this room like that? Where are the drawers filled with mementoes; why aren't there letters, say, from her parents' courtship, or oddments that struck them as important during fifty years of marriage? No wonder her mother doesn't want anything; there's nothing to keep.

Fifty years! How can that be done? The longest Susannah's lived with anybody (except for this family, and Lizzie, of course) is a couple of years. Even Teddy only lasted three, and that was when she was young. How do people get used to each other enough to survive, in this way or any other?

She looks avidly at the bedside tables: her mother's as well as her father's. She'd like to find out their secrets, now that she's here. It's not very satisfactory to have to wait until somebody dies, but she can hardly search her mother's table in front of Elaine. She might not be so scrupulous on her own.

Such odd debris in the small table on her father's side of the bed, though — what does it say? A jackknife, old and bone-handled, an assortment of paper clips (and why would he have had a knife, and what use would he have ever had for paper clips?), a small desk calendar from a local garage, dating back two years, with a picture of a golden mongrel. In the second drawer down, envelopes and a pad of writing paper, but no pen or pencil. Who would he have written to, anyway? She doesn't recall ever seeing him write a letter, and perhaps he never did; the package of envelopes is unopened.

Maybe he meant to. Maybe he woke in the middle of the night here and composed letters in his head, words he would have liked to say to one person or another; possibly to her. Abusive notes to a renegade daughter, or letters of contrition and forgiveness? In daylight, he would have come to his senses. So many ideas that seem quite brilliant and tempting in the middle of the night are so much gibberish at dawn.

She slips the jackknife into the pocket of her slacks and empties the rest into a box, discarding only the calendar in the trash.

Elaine, always a little ahead, is examining the bureau. "I guess he had the top two drawers and she had the bottom two." So in this as in other matters, their mother would have had to do the bending.

They tip his underwear, unexamined, into the trash. His socks, however, all rolled neatly in fresh pairs of brown and blue and black, are perfectly impersonal and could very well be used by some chilly-footed poor man. There are also two stacks of white handkerchiefs, each with his initials stitched in a corner. Surely monogrammed cloth handkerchiefs must be a luxury, in a household where anything extra at all is apparently forbidden? More likely they're just leftovers from pre-tissue days.

Elaine is holding out a small brown box containing two sets of gold-colored cuff links, one plain and square, the other etched with a diamond design. "Would you mind if I took these for the boys?"

"Sure, go ahead." How guilty she feels, though, for slipping the jackknife into her pocket without asking. Why did she want it, anyway?

Lizzie might like it, but really it appeals to Susannah: the streaked, smooth whiteness of the bone handle.

The bureau drawers are lined with the dry and yellow pages of old newspapers. "I'll take these, though," and she pulls them out, folding them carefully. "For Lizzie. She likes newspapers." Elaine looks puzzled by a mother who salvages old newsprint for her child when she could have had cuff links.

Are they finished? Is this it? "How could they have lived here so long and had so little?"

"Well, they never had much money. Not to throw around."

"Even so, people *have* things. At my house, stuff just accumulates." She is struck by an unhappy thought. "You don't mean they were poor, do you?"

Elaine shrugs. "Not really, but they've always been careful." She is briskly gathering up the two boxes of clothes to be given away, leaving the trash bags to Susannah. "Do you know what we haven't found, though? A will or a bankbook or anything else to do with money. I'm sure it's not here. There must be something downstairs."

So: still some opportunities for discovery, some secrets not uncovered yet?

When they get back to the porch, Lizzie has a box of photographs on her lap but is looking bored, and their mother appears to be dozing. "Oh, neat," Lizzie says, taking the old pages from Susannah and settling back to read words that were news before she was born.

Elaine, leaning over her, picks up one of the photos. "Remember this, Susannah?"

It's missing a corner and is cracked in several places, but there are the four of them, at a beach somewhere. They are standing on stones, and their expressions are stony as well. Susannah would have been, what, about eight? "God, look at our faces! Didn't anybody tell us to smile for the camera? Where were we, anyway?"

"I'm not sure where this was exactly," and Elaine taps a finger on the pebbles in the picture, "but we were driving all around the coast for some reason. It was probably only about a week, but it felt like forever to me. Mainly I remember sitting in the back seat trying to keep you from pinching me."

"Really? Was I that bad?"

"You were awful. Pinch pinch pinch — nothing would stop you. I tried looking out the window, reading, I even told Mother, but she just said I was older so I should be nice and try to keep you entertained. I was so glad to get home, you wouldn't believe."

Now, thirty-odd years later, they can smile with some shared recollection of unhappiness, although not necessarily the same unhappiness. "I'm sorry. I didn't know I was such a rotten kid." Now she can put her arm around her sister like an apologetic child, and this time Elaine doesn't pull away.

These two women here are the only people in the world who have known Susannah her whole life. If she doesn't count that fourteen-year gap.

But she does.

"Mother?" Elaine is shaking her gently, and she opens her eyes, looking at them as if she'd merely blinked, not slept.

"We've finished upstairs, but we haven't found anything to do with money. Do you know where else we could look? There should be a bankbook, at least."

Their mother frowns. "I know there's a big brown envelope in the middle drawer of the dining-room buffet. I suppose it might be business things. I can't think of anywhere else he kept things of his own."

"I'll get it." Elaine hustles back indoors; she does like to be busy. Susannah settles into a chair beside her mother and stretches her legs into the sunshine.

"You mean he kept stuff and you never looked to see what it was?"

"Well, no. He put it there, it was his." Maybe to her that's obvious, but Susannah would have gone through it in a flash. Either she's the only unethical person here or the only one who understands about community property.

Elaine is back with the envelope. "Is this what you meant?"

"I guess so, if it was in the dining room."

It isn't even sealed! Susannah marvels at her father's trust. He must have known his wife very well to have such faith in her sturdiness of character, or her timidity, or, most amazing, her lack of curiosity. She must have had many opportunities and temptations, coming across it in the course of tidying and dusting, but if she is to be believed, and of course she is, she never even peeked. There is something a little creepy about it, though, private and taboo — Susannah is reminded of the nastiness in that dead theologian's files.

Tipping it over the table, Elaine pours out of it a bankbook, two legal-sized white envelopes, two business cards and another white envelope, a smaller one. She opens the bankbook and leafs to its final page, raises her eyebrows and passes it to her mother, who breathes, "Oh." Then, "How could we have had so much?" Susannah reaches for it. The balance is nine thousand three hundred and six dollars and twenty-seven cents. "When I scrimped and scrimped."

Here they've been, with hardly ever a new coat of paint on the walls, hardly ever a new appliance, never a trip, and here he's been piling up pennies. Not enough to live on, but so much that could have bought small things to make their lives easier. Now let her mother say, "He always looked after me before."

"I suppose," Susannah says, "if you scrimp hard enough, this is what you get." Did she intend to sound cruel?

"Anyway, it'll be a nice cushion for you." Elaine seems to have inherited their mother's habit of trying to smooth. "It's not a bad thing to have this kind of money to fall back on."

Does Elaine rely for money on the grace of her husband? After all, Susannah knows as little about her sister as Elaine does about her. What sort of house does she live in—too large, now that her sons have grown and gone? Does she have gardens, the way their mother did? Do she and Bill sit silently, with separate thoughts, in the evenings, or do they pull chairs together and bend over games like Scrabble? Not Scrabble, no; double solitaire or euchre with two dummy hands? Does Elaine ever cry?

Well, does Susannah, often? Perhaps they're not so unlike, except in direction.

"This seems to be the insurance policy on the house." Elaine has moved on to the legal-sized envelopes. "Nothing to worry about at the moment. This one is his life insurance. Where does it say what it's worth?" She flips through the pages, steps over to Susannah. "Is this right? Seventy thousand dollars, is that it?"

It seems to be. It appears that their mother now has a house and a total, with one thing and another, of seventy-nine thousand and some dollars. Would she have ever found that out for herself?

The business cards belong to an insurance agent and a lawyer. "If there's a will, the lawyer must have it," Elaine says. "It isn't here, anyway. You should call these men tomorrow, Mother. Or I can call them from home, if you'd rather."

"You do it, please. Or Susannah. I don't know how to go about these things."

She presumes, then, that Susannah has rejoined the family? Is available to phone lawyers and tackle other errands? This seems premature, and anyway, if Susannah were going to do her mother any favors, she'd rather teach her to do these things herself.

Elaine, however, seems cheered by her own efficiency and prospects of action. "You don't have a thing to worry about, Mother. You're not rich by any means, but with your old-age pension, you ought to be quite comfortable." It seems to Susannah somewhat sweeping to suggest their mother has nothing to worry about. She has living alone to worry about. Things like learning to sleep in, or nodding off with the light on.

What did Elaine think about their father? Or feel? She hasn't slumped or slowed down the whole time Susannah's been here. Perhaps she really does believe, as she advised their mother, that keeping busy is the main thing.

They haven't been paying attention to Lizzie, drawn back quietly into her chair, the old newsprint in front of her a sort of defense or a camouflage. Susannah, glancing her way, thinks suddenly of her father sitting in his living room holding a newspaper in front of him while his family, his wife and two daughters, went on with their lives around him in peace or turmoil. Staying clear. There are many ways of looking at events, though. Maybe he felt left out? Maybe that made him angry.

But who were the grown-ups in this house? "Why didn't you know about the money, Mother? You could have asked, you could have found out for yourself. You could have stood up for yourself." She doesn't mean about money only. "It's not as if you were helpless."

"Susannah!" Elaine is aghast.

"Susannah, what? She's not brainless, you know. She wasn't exactly chained to a post." Hearing in her own voice the girl again, attacking and complaining.

"You don't understand." The voice is so quiet they both turn to look at her. "You hardly visited, Elaine, and Susannah, you just walked out that door and that was it, we never heard a word from you again. You never even let me know if I had a grandchild, or if it was a boy or a girl. I was here on my own. So don't tell me how I should have managed. I managed, and that's enough."

"But that's not true." Susannah is astonished.

"What's not true?"

"I did send you an announcement of Lizzie's birth. One to you two and another to Elaine." She turns to her sister. "Didn't I?"

"I suppose so. I got one, anyway."

"Then," asks their mother, "why didn't you mention it?"

"I thought nobody was supposed to talk about Susannah. You never did."

"It must have gone somewhere," Susannah says softly. "He must have gotten it and never told you. Like that money, stashing it away." She sees him opening the card, all secretive and silent, keeping it to himself.

Even Lizzie has put down her paper and is watching.

"I don't know," Elaine says unhappily, "but I guess we know now what he did with it. Look at this." She draws a card from the small white envelope, hands it to Susannah.

And here she is, the baby Lizzie, eyes squeezed shut, little firm chin even then, sprouts of dark hair, wrapped in a pink and white striped hospital nursery blanket. From this distance maybe not a particularly distinguished baby after all. But Lizzie. How alone the two of them were!

"Lizzie Sarah," the card says. Lizzie, partly for Susannah's mother Elizabeth, but that was too soft and meek, and Susannah, desiring a sharp little kid, picked a sharper-sounding name. And Sarah because it seemed equivalently gentle. "Six pounds, eight ounces," it continues on the next line, and then the date of the birth. At the bottom, a handwritten note: "Please be pleased. I am. She's beautiful. Love, Susannah." She does not remember writing that, but here it is: "Love, Susannah."

She hands the card to her mother, who stares and stares at it. Watching her is like watching a photograph being developed in a darkroom, the faintest of outlines turning firm and even harsh around the edges. When she looks up, it appears that the entirely unfamiliar expression now carved on her features is something quite different from anger: real rage.

A little late, surely, for that? Hardly to the point now, is it?

She must be inexperienced with fury. It looks hot, flaring across the tiny, trembling body.

Hot words, too; fierce words that fill the lines of a crumpled old face into remarkable smoothness. It does sound as if she means them.

Although there's no way now to test that; not any more.

Out there somewhere are the Palestrini brothers, in the first weekend of their reunion. How are they spending it? Are they keeping busy, talking, sitting silent — maybe Marco has just slept, recovering from jet lag. Will they find forgiveness possible at all?

Why did they agree to put themselves through this in the first place? Were they forced into it by their families, or did they, too, have hopes?

It would be interesting to talk to them in six weeks, when their visit ends. Susannah would have lots of questions, but the main one might be to ask the two old men, who must have enormous experience between them, if wartime fascism has turned out to be a harder or easier hurdle to get over than less political betrayals.

FREE FALLS

Three members of the world-renowned Haldini trapeze troupe plunged to their deaths Saturday afternoon in a big-top performance in Miami.

Natalia Haldini, 16, and two of her brothers Franco, 20, and Giovanni, 18, plummeted more than 20 meters in front of a sparse audience of horrified children and their parents.

Investigators said later that Natalia and Franco were each gripping one of the ankles of Giovanni, who was suspended from a trapeze swing. When a rope broke, the jolt caused Giovanni to lose his hold and all three fell.

Seven members of the troupe have now died in the past five years in performance-related incidents. Franco Haldini Sr., patriarch of the clan since the death of the troupe's founding father, Sergio, six years ago, insisted that the three latest deaths, all of them his children, will not spell the end of the family's high-flying career.

"We are circus," he told reporters Saturday night. "We know no other life." His oldest son, however, is reportedly training in Italy to be a lawyer, and a 10-year-old daughter has never performed with the rest of the family.

Old Franco sounds to Lizzie like an awfully stupid man. Members of his family, his own children, keep tumbling to their deaths, and he doesn't even care? How come he can't think of something else to do? Does he think "we know no other life" is an excuse?

Also, think about this: his children died in the afternoon, and he was talking to reporters just a few hours later, as if nothing very important had happened at all. He didn't even say something nice about them. If he were her father, she'd hate him. Don't the people in his family who are still alive hate him?

If Lizzie died in some way that got reporters' attention, her mother would absolutely kill them. Her mother says she can never understand why people talk to reporters when their families die. Lizzie supposes her grandfather wasn't important enough and his death wasn't weird enough to bring any reporters around. In a way, if Lizzie died it would be kind of neat if her mother did talk about her to them. It must be hard, if you die and only a few people know you were even alive.

Those trapeze people, they must have done that trick hundreds and thousands of times. They'd have to know every time that this could be the last one, because even if you practice and practice something like that, it doesn't likely get much less dangerous. What would that feel like? Would you be a really good person, just in case it happened, or a bad one, just so you got to try everything? The thing that's really hard to imagine is taking it for granted, flying through the air as if you might die or might not.

Once, her mother did a story about people who died and came back to life. Imagine if somebody you loved died—you'd hope and hope for that, like it was just a mistake. These people really did die, the doctors said, even though it was just for a few seconds, mainly — their hearts stopped, and even their brains. And then they came back, just like that. Most of them said, when her mother talked to them, that they'd been so happy dead, and it was beautiful, like a big golden room. One said he was mad for a while about coming back. The one her mother talked about most, though, was the man who hardly noticed.

She said she asked him, "Do you feel as if you have a second chance? Coming back, knowing what you know, is there something now you particularly want to do or accomplish?" She said he didn't seem to know what she was talking about. She said he told her no, unless she meant that he'd been looking forward to retiring, and that he'd always wanted the time to play a lot of golf, and now he had it, and that was what he was doing. "Isn't that amazing?" her mother said. "He has this incredible experience, a second chance, a fresh run at things, and he plays golf!"

Maybe he didn't tell her mother the truth, though. Maybe he kept the important things to himself. Maybe he still wakes up every morning and looks at himself in the mirror and thinks, "My God, here I am." Or something like that.

She wonders what her grandfather saw when he died. And he really died, too. Do people get a choice, is there a second when they stand in the middle, looking back and forth and making up their minds which way to go? It would have to look pretty great up ahead, wouldn't it, not to decide to come back to life.

Of course, if you die like those people on the trapeze, there probably isn't a choice. They'd be all smashed up.

If Lizzie got hurt like that, dying in front of her mother in some big awful way, her mother wouldn't just go *on* like that Haldini man. She wouldn't just say, well, this is the way things have always been, and even if it turned out bad for Lizzie, that's no reason to stop. No way. But then, it's hard to see how such a thing could happen with them, since her mother only likes some kinds of danger, and they're not really dangerous.

Right now her mother's upstairs with Aunt Elaine, and Lizzie's out here on the back porch with her grandmother. Except her grandmother's asleep, so Lizzie's on her own. She stares at her sleeping grandmother, pretending she's dead and it's like yesterday, looking down at a dead person's face. Only not really, because even sleeping her grandmother's face moves, it has an expression, it's not all wiped off like a blackboard, like her grandfather was.

Nobody seems to be talking much about him. It would be awful to just disappear like that out of everybody's mind.

Lizzie wishes she could nap as easily as her grandmother does, because she's really tired. She's so tired all her inside parts, like her veins, feel as if they're humming like wires, keeping her awake. How come her grandmother doesn't feel that way, too, too excited to sleep? But then, Lizzie will be in her own bed tonight, and maybe her mother will let her stay home from school tomorrow to catch up on her rest. Maybe old people can't store up sleep that way.

Maybe it was being in a strange bed, or sharing it, but Lizzie woke up really early this morning, before everybody. The sunshine was just starting to creep across the bed, making her knees warm and lighting up all the pink and white. When she grows up and gets married, she'll have to share a bed, too, but probably people get used to it. She'll want a different kind of bed than that strange, uncomfortable one, though, something more solid. A couple of times she woke up in the night to find herself rolled into the center, lying against her mother, because the mattress was too soft and Lizzie too light to keep her place on her own side.

It's the exact same bed her mother slept in when she was a girl. Lizzie looked around the room this morning, trying to see what her mother saw then, trying to tell what it would feel like to wake up belonging here, knowing that when she went downstairs she'd be having breakfast with a father and a mother and a sister, and then going to that school her mother pointed out on the way into town yesterday. Meeting her best friend on the way, like Lizzie meets Megan.

It was hard, though, too strange to think of her mother as a whole different person, with these pieces of her life that had nothing to do with Lizzie. Sometimes it seems to Lizzie that she can imagine strangers better than people she knows.

When she sighed, just a little louder than she needed to, it worked because her mother rolled onto her back and made a little sound like a groan. Then she flung her arm out sideways so it almost hit Lizzie, and all of a sudden her eyes went wide open and she sat straight up, looking around and then at Lizzie. It was kind of neat, watching her figure out she was in her old room but didn't live here any more, and that Lizzie was beside her. Then she lay back as if she was still tired, so maybe she was remembering about her father's funeral or what she had to do today.

"You been awake long?" Lizzie always likes her mother's morning voice. It's low and kind of slow, not fast the way it gets once she's wide awake.

"A little while."

"Any idea what time it is?"

"No, but I think it's still early. I don't think anybody's up yet."

"How'd you sleep?"

"Okay, I guess. Except the mattress is kind of soft."

"I know. I used to like that, sinking in, being cozy. God, I could stay here all day." She stretched her arms above her head and yawned. "Do you think we could sneak downstairs without disturbing anybody? We could sit out on the back porch for a while, just us."

"Should we get dressed?"

"Probably, but let's not."

It was nice, the two of them creeping out of bed and out the door and along the hall and downstairs to the kitchen, where Lizzie's mother got the percolator going and Lizzie helped herself to orange juice. "If you have to go to the bathroom, go ahead," her mother said, "but don't flush."

"I can wait."

It was a whole different place outside. Bright and soft, and not nervous, like it felt inside. There were four wicker chairs set out around a green plastic table, but the chairs weren't like the wicker ones Frannie has at her place, they weren't white, and they didn't have bright flowery cushions. These were old and brown, with high arms and thin seats, and the pillows were faded, and the wicker, when they sat down, creaked loudly. There were patches of ground right by the porch and away at the far end of the yard where it looked like there used to be gardens. In the early sunlight, the lawn was a bright green, except for right under the big pine tree, where it was dark, almost blue.

"I used to play out here sometimes when it rained," her mother said. "Elaine would play house and I'd be her kid, or I'd be the father and the dolls would be the kids. But that was when I was just little. When I got old enough, I mostly went to the park, the one you went to yesterday."

"How come?" This yard was bigger even than theirs at home, so why go to a park?

"Probably mostly because there were other kids there. And it was okay to be noisy. I don't think it was here, my parents didn't like a lot of racketing around. Also, though, in the park I could have my own life. I mean, nobody could just look out a window and see what I was doing."

"So what were you doing?"

Her mother shrugged. "Nothing much. Hanging out. We made up games, we even made up plays for ourselves. We'd be Cinderella and the stepsisters, or Sleeping Beauty, that kind of thing. I always liked being the wicked stepmother or the witch. Everybody else wanted to be Sleeping Beauty, but I always thought that part was kind of pale and dull."

Lizzie'd never really thought of that before; but then, she's never had much to do with fairy tales. Stories that depend on magic or spells seem like cheating.

"You know," her mother continued, kind of dreamily, "sometimes at home I've sat in the kitchen watching you out in the yard with Megan or whoever and it's been so great just seeing you there. I wonder if my mother ever missed that?" It was strange, this view of her mother as a child who hid things from her family and would rather play a witch. "I suppose when you grow up and have kids, if you do, you'll look at my mistakes, though, and think of ways of doing better."

That sounded like something she was just saying, but it felt like a question. "Oh, I don't know," Lizzie said. Really, she had no idea how she'd raise kids, or even if she wanted any. She might rather be like Teddy or Frannie: only having kids around sometimes, just for fun.

Lizzie was just going to ask, "What was it like, having a sister?" when Aunt Elaine appeared, signaled first by footsteps tapping across the kitchen floor, then her voice at the screen door. "There you are, you two—I wondered where you got to. I went in to wake you up and there was just an empty bed." So for once they beat her to something; but why was she going to wake them up, why wouldn't she have let them sleep? Also the bed wasn't made. Lizzie bet Aunt Elaine grumbled and made it herself.

If she was going to make up an aunt, it would have been somebody nicer and more fun, somebody more like Frannie. At least Frannie likes her.

"How long have you been up?"

"Not long," Lizzie's mother said. "There's coffee—get yourself a cup and join us." She sounded polite, and not even as if she was trying hard to be polite. There were a lot of things Lizzie wanted to know about sisters.

"In a few minutes. I'm not dressed yet."

"Neither are we. Let's just relax while we can."

Aunt Elaine hesitated, then said, "Oh, well, I suppose. Just for a few minutes."

That feeling of Lizzie and her mother sitting out here together at the start of the day, just like they start most of their days except slower and in a different place, changed when Aunt Elaine sat down. It felt jumpy and scrambled, like a bad TV signal. When Grandma came, everybody in Lizzie's family would be here, except for Teddy and Frannie. It was weird having almost twice as many people in her family as there were yesterday morning. It was also weird, not knowing what was going on. Like sometimes when her mother and Teddy talk about things from when they were together, and their voices and how they look are like secrets.

"Isn't Mother up yet?" Lizzie's mother asked.

"I haven't heard her, but I didn't check. I expect she's worn out."

"You must be, too."

"I suppose, but then, I like being busy. Now I don't know quite what to do with myself, until we can get started on Father's things. I don't like time that's empty this way."

Aunt Elaine said that as if she was proud of it, but wasn't it a strange way to see time, as empty? It felt to Lizzie as if there was always something going on, even if it was only in her head; but maybe that didn't count with Aunt Elaine.

"Never mind, there'll be plenty to do very soon."

"Yes." Aunt Elaine sighed. "But you know, I'm starting to dread going through his things. It's not very nice, when he was such a private man."

"But that's what makes it interesting, don't you think?" Her mother flushed. "I guess that doesn't sound very nice, but from my point of view—what did I know about him? He was such a mystery to me; or at least he turned into one, and now's my last chance to find out about him."

"I don't see what was a mystery about him." Aunt Elaine sounded stiff and sniffy.

"Ah, but he didn't call you a slut, did he? He didn't turn into somebody you didn't know right in front of you."

Gosh, did he? Lizzie wasn't sure exactly what a slut was, except it wasn't a nice thing to call somebody. Imagine if your own father called you names! Some people's parents do — Megan's mother got mad and called her stupid once, when she forgot to turn the oven on for dinner one day when she got home from school and her mother was out, and Megan was really upset. Neither Lizzie's mother nor Teddy would ever do something like that, and if they did, it would hurt so much she wouldn't be able to stand it.

"Besides," her mother said, "I've missed a lot of years. I guess I'd like to find out anything I can." She gave a little laugh that didn't sound very nice. "Better late than never, I suppose."

"Susannah!"

It sounded to Lizzie as if people weren't supposed to say things out loud here. Maybe that's why they got so upset, even her mother, when words really were said.

The thing was, her mother seemed to be doing it too, here. "Lizzie, why don't you run inside now and use the bathroom before there's a lineup. Then when your grandmother comes down, you can keep her company while we sort through things upstairs." Every time really interesting words started getting said, Lizzie got sent away. Last night, too, when she got sent to the park. That isn't what happens at home, but then a lot of things, even her mother, are different here.

She could have cried, almost, she wanted to go home so badly, back to where she knew her mother and there weren't all these *feelings*. She wanted to be sitting in the living room and have her mother walk past her and touch her hair. She wanted them to be sitting around watching TV together, or be getting ready for bed and have her mother tuck her in, like a little kid. And this was just the start of the day. It'd be forever before she was back in her own blue room, and even then it might not be the same, because she'd know different things than she did before.

At home, she'd just be waking up, most likely, and there'd be a whole surprising day ahead. Well, it was surprising here, too, but not the same way. She stood and looked at herself in the bathroom mirror for a couple of minutes. The mirror was old and wavery, so her nose was kind of off center, and her eyes farther apart than they really were, and wider than usual, as if she'd been startled. She was almost as pale as Megan, but maybe that was mainly being tired.

Out in the hall, she met her grandmother just coming out of her bedroom. Even though her grandmother stayed in bed the longest, she still looked sleepy. She was tiny before, but now she looked caved in.

"You're up early, dear."

"We've been awake for a while. Mother and Aunt Elaine are out on the back porch."

"Oh, my. Are they getting along all right?"

How could Lizzie know? "I guess so. They were talking when I left."

"Good. I really don't feel up to any bickering today."

"Are you sick? Didn't you sleep very well?"

"Oh, yes, I slept like a log. I just can't seem to wake up." She sounded amazed, as if she'd never slept like a log before, or had a morning when she didn't wake up bright. "I suppose they're waiting to go through his things?"

"They were talking about it." In a way. Her grandmother looked so *sweet*; Lizzie could have just leaned over and hugged her, except she was also so small, and what if Lizzie hugged too hard and knocked her down or broke some bones? Anyway, people can look one way and be another, which was actually kind of frightening when you thought about it.

Lizzie was wrong about Aunt Elaine making the bed. The covers were still muddled, so Lizzie pulled them up and smoothed them and shook out the pillows so all the hollows disappeared from where she and her mother had slept. She wished she had more clothes than the jeans and T-shirt she wore on the plane and to the park, but she guessed she couldn't be repulsive yet, anyway, because even Aunt Elaine looked glad to see her when she got back downstairs. As if Lizzie was something happening, not just a person, or as if she was supposed to do something entertaining. What, turn cartwheels, or tell a poem, or sing? Tell a story, say the one about the Haldinis and their father? Better not.

"Come sit beside me, Lizzie," and her grandmother patted the only empty chair. It was funny, nobody was actually saying anything, but it felt as if they were all connected in different ways. Like one of those yarn games she had when she was little, where a small change in how she turned the threads turned the pattern into something new. "Can you see where the gardens used to be, Lizzie?" her grandmother asked. "I had flower beds here by the porch and vegetables back at the fence. I remember going through seed catalogues in the winter, and planning out where everything should go and how it would look—I did love those gardens!" She sounded nearly happy.

"How come you don't have them now?"

"Oh, it got beyond me. I still like to do window boxes, and

I plant a few things, but the gardens got to be too much work. Still, I always go through the catalogues every winter. I think about what I'd have if I could manage."

Aunt Elaine leaned forward. "You know, the whole place is a lot for you to keep up. Have you thought what you'll do with it?" Lizzie saw her mother glance crossly at Aunt Elaine.

"No, I haven't. I suppose I'll just wait and see." Her grandmother didn't sound very interested.

"You know, you'd get a good price if you sold. You should think about doing that and moving into a seniors' apartment, the kind where you'd have your own place, but there'd be other people around if you needed them. You'd have company, and it wouldn't be nearly as much work." *There* was the difference between how Lizzie's mother talks and how Aunt Elaine does: Aunt Elaine says things as if they're for sure. Lizzie's mother would have said something like, "What would you think, Mother, about selling the house and trying an apartment? Would you feel safer or freer or not so lonely?"

Grandma didn't miss much, though, she's pretty sharp for somebody old. She sat up straight and her voice got harder, the way it did a couple of times yesterday, and she said, "I don't want to make any big decisions right away. It's better to wait and see, I think. Anyway, as far as the house goes, I can't see why it'd be more work now. In fact, it should be less. I'm starting to wonder, though, how much money there is, and where it is." Didn't she miss him, just for being him?

"Well, then," said Lizzie's mother as she stood, "we'll get started on the sorting and find out. Coming, Elaine?"

"There are boxes in the cellar," Grandma said, "and garbage bags in the drawer to the left of the kitchen sink."

Aunt Elaine said, "What should we be sure to keep, Mother? What do you especially want to have?"

"Oh, nothing I can think of." Her little lined hand, curled like a claw, waved in the air. "You and Susannah take what you want and throw the rest out. Or give it away. The church has a mission box."

"Surely not, Mother! There must be keepsakes you'd like to have."

"Really, Elaine, he didn't keep things himself." When Lizzie's mother and Aunt Elaine were back indoors, Lizzie and her grandmother just sat quiet for a few minutes; except it was a nice silence, not uncomfortable the way it can be with Aunt Elaine. Then her grandmother sighed. "Makes you wonder, doesn't it? They're so different, but stubborn, both of them. They must have got that from their father."

Lizzie's chance. "What was it like when my mother lived here?"

"What do you mean, dear, what was it like? It's just the same now as it always was." Did she think Lizzie meant the house or the yard?

"What was my mother like? When she was my age, and when she was grown up, before—" before what, exactly? "—I was born."

Her grandmother was quiet so long Lizzie started to think she wasn't going to answer. "Well," she said finally, "she was always a surprise."

"You mean having me?"

"Yes, that, but other things, too. Leaving here, going so far away, not doing what people expected. She was always contrary, and there was no talking to her, once she'd made up her mind. I do believe that's what got her father so cross, that she wouldn't listen." That didn't sound like criticism, for some reason. It almost sounded as if Grandma was proud. Also it sounded like the mother Lizzie knows at home.

"Did she and Aunt Elaine get along?"

"More or less. In their way. When they were children, Elaine spent a lot of time with your mother, playing with her, and I remember her reading to Susannah sometimes. She was very good to Susannah. I guess they started going different ways in their teens—those are years when the age difference gets important. Do you mind being an only child, Lizzie?"

Lizzie was off balance for a minute; she wanted to ask questions, not so much answer them. "Sometimes, I guess. I used to wish I had a little sister, just to have somebody to play with. But mostly it's okay."

"Yes, I suppose people get used to whatever they have. I suppose we all have to, one way or another." Oh, but then why do people keep trying for things they don't have?

"Elaine's like her father, you know. Neither of them was ever very forgiving when other people didn't do what they said." She leaned toward Lizzie and smiled like she was saying things she shouldn't. "You know what I think the secret is?" Lizzie shook her head. "I think people like that get disappointed a lot, and that makes them angry, and after a while they've been disappointed so much they're angry almost all the time." That didn't sound funny, but there was a little twitch again at the corner of her grandmother's mouth. "But I don't suppose you know what I mean. I hope you don't."

"Why?"

"Well, it wasn't very nice." Her grandmother was now grinning so recklessly that if it wasn't so early, and Lizzie didn't know better, she'd have thought Grandma'd been drinking. Just a nip out of a bottle hidden in the kitchen, something like that. When Grandma looked that way, Lizzie saw for the first time how she and her mother and her grandmother might be related, in the way her lips curved up and that sort of glitter in her eyes.

"It's okay, Grandma." Lizzie grinned back. "I'm only a kid. I don't always understand what people say."

"I must say, I'm relieved to hear that. We used to think only children grew up too fast, and there should always be at least two. Although that wouldn't have been wise, in your mother's situation."

Why not? What's two, or ten for that matter, when there's already one?

"If you don't have sisters and brothers, I expect you have friends, do you?"

"Oh, sure. I have a best friend, Megan, and we hang out with other kids. Movies and stuff like that. And I go places with Teddy, too, like art galleries." It didn't seem smart to tell about their late-night walks through the streets, or the demonstrations.

Grandma might not understand. "I like reading, too." And if Grandma could say things she shouldn't, maybe Lizzie could too. "I make up things sometimes, you know."

"What do you mean? What kind of things?"

"When I read a story, sometimes I make up more than it says. Like what the people are like, or how things happen. I sort of make stories bigger, I guess."

Her grandmother nodded. Did she really know what Lizzie meant? "Did you make up things about us?"

In a way, but nothing she could tell her grandmother, who might not realize how little Lizzie knew, and that what she imagined was that they might be either criminals or crazy. "It's hard," she said carefully, "when I couldn't really picture what it was like here."

"Would you like to see pictures?" Her grandmother got bright and interested-looking. "There's an old chocolate box in the top drawer of the dining-room buffet that has all sorts of pictures in it. If you want to get it out, I can show you your mother when she was little." Of course, photographs—all parents aren't like Teddy's, most of them have cameras. There'd be a whole past there.

She'd got the box from the drawer where Grandma said it was, and was carrying it with both hands to the back porch, when she met Aunt Elaine on her way to the basement for more boxes. "What's that you have there?" As if it was any of her business.

"Old pictures. Grandma and I are going to look at them." Whatever was bugging Aunt Elaine, it was a lot clearer when there were just the two of them.

Lizzie just looked straight at Aunt Elaine until Aunt Elaine shrugged and turned and muttered, "Good grief. At least try not to upset your grandmother with them. They're not a good idea." But her voice trailed off as she went down the basement steps, and the words, floating back up, didn't have any bite.

Lizzie set the box down in front of her grandmother on the green plastic table. The cover had pictures of chocolates cut in half, each with a different center: orange and lemon, nuts and caramel, a cherry with white cream oozing out around it. All that sweetness—but remember Pandora's box: it was tempting, too, but look what came out.

Except pictures aren't the same as words. Pictures stay still, and words fit together to make something, a whole story.

The photos were all jumbled and loose. They were all in black and white, too, so they must have been old. Her grandmother looked at them and said, "Heavens, we haven't taken any for years."

"Do you still have a camera?"

"I'm not sure. I suppose it must be somewhere." Considering she lived here, Grandma didn't seem to know where a lot of things were.

Lizzie thought if she could find the camera, she could take a picture of them together before they left. Then later, her grand-mother could sit here and take it out and look at it, and maybe that would make her happy.

A man was standing in front of an old car—except probably it wasn't old when the picture was taken—wearing a suit, look-ing too warm, and not smiling. "Is this my grandfather?" She hardly knew what to call a man who was her grandmother's husband and her mother's father, a man she'd never met. Maybe Aunt Elaine was right, maybe it wasn't a good idea to look at these. It might upset her grandmother to see this man again, especially when he was younger and they were all together and even happy, maybe.

Her grandmother nodded. "You saw him yesterday. Don't you recognize him?" Well, but yesterday was different. He was old then, and dead.

In another picture he was with her mother and Aunt Elaine. They were easy to tell apart, because Lizzie's mother was smaller and younger. She was smiling up in a shy sort of way, and her hair was short and all curly. Aunt Elaine was staring at the camera, kind of pop-eyed. Their father had his hands on their shoulders. Aunt Elaine was maybe about Lizzie's age now, so her mother would only be ten. Lizzie looked and looked at her, but couldn't see anything to make her think she might have a Lizzie in mind for when she grew up.

Grandma probably took that picture, but somebody else must have been around to take the one of all four of them. They were standing at a railing, except the background was out of focus so she couldn't see what the railing was around. Something outdoors, anyway, like a church, because there were shapes of shrubs and stones behind. Lizzie's grandfather was standing behind Aunt Elaine, and Grandma was behind Lizzie's mother, and Lizzie's mother and Aunt Elaine were just little, maybe five and eight. They didn't look anything like they do now, either of them. They were all standing really straight, and nobody was smiling.

At home there are pictures of Lizzie and her mother — her mother holding Lizzie high over her head, when Lizzie was a tiny baby; or Lizzie at three, sitting on a lawn chair between her mother's legs, her mother looking down at the top of her head with such a look on her face — love? wonder? — that it always makes Lizzie shiver when she sees it.

These pictures, though, made her feel a bit like crying. They made her want to hug that little girl and take her away from those people.

Except in a way, that's what she did, right?

"How come nobody smiles? How come everybody's so stiff?"

"Oh, I expect we were trying to be dignified."

Here was one, though. "Is this you?" A small and slender woman in a dark-patterned dress to below her knees, and white high-heeled shoes, holding a baby wrapped in white lace, and another child with its arms around her thigh. The woman looked really pretty, and gentle and happy.

Grandma's eyes filled up—they didn't even fill up yesterday, at the funeral. "Your mother's christening." Then she smiled again a little. "I think she was sleeping when that was taken, but once we got to the church she certainly woke up. Howled like a banshee through the whole thing. I guess we should have known right off the bat that nothing would go smoothly with Susannah." She still didn't sound angry or disapproving, though. If she wasn't angry at Lizzie's mother, and if she didn't disapprove of her, how come she could let her go? And if she loved that little baby in the christening dress, wouldn't she have loved Lizzie, too? How could she stand to miss all that?

It might have been neat to have a grandmother. It's kind of late to start now, even if there is something interesting and sharp about her. It'd be too bad to get fond of her, though, and then have her decide not to care all over again.

There's a ton of questions Lizzie would have liked to ask while the two of them were alone together, but it was hard to find the words. Anyway, it might not be a very good time. This was just a tiny old woman, after all, not somebody strong, and a lot had already happened to her in the past few days.

It was funny, though, that nobody here seemed to take very good care of each other. How come it didn't break Grandma's heart not to see her daughter for years and years? Grandma seemed nice, but how could she have let that happen?

Maybe that's why Lizzie's mother could give them up, too: she knew they didn't care enough, and she wanted somebody who would. It would hurt so much, knowing that!

It was a funny feeling, being sorry for her mother.

In the pictures, that man, her grandfather, was always pushing down on his daughters' shoulders. They got away, though, or he pushed them. Could Lizzie ever do something so awful her mother would do that to her? No. Even if she took drugs or stole things or turned into one of those girls she sees on the streets when she goes walking with Teddy, her mother would hang on to her.

It's kind of discouraging now that her grandmother is sleeping, her head nodding toward her chest and her mouth a little open.

Her mother and Aunt Elaine come thumping downstairs, though, carrying boxes and bags of things, which they set down in the hallway. Lizzie's mother brings her a present, a bunch of yellowed newspaper pages — a treat from years before Lizzie was even born! She starts to search for some item from history, something she's studied in school as if it was old, but in this paper, it'd be new.

She sees there was fighting in different countries then, and people held up banks, and one guy's body was pulled out of a river after he'd gone through the ice. Some of the places are different, and the people, too, but there doesn't seem to be anything really new, nothing she hasn't read before. That's sort of disappointing.

From behind the paper, though, she can listen to them talking without them noticing she's here; it's mostly about money at first, so not very interesting. But then the voices change, and when Lizzie lowers the paper to look, she sees that. Grandma's holding a baby picture — a familiar one, Lizzie herself, they have one at home, too. Aunt Elaine looks upset and confused — the first time Lizzie's seen her not sure. Lizzie's mother looks a way Lizzie hasn't seen before, either. Naked, kind of. Her face is just kind of hanging open, like she wants something so badly she can't cover it up. Grandma's the real shock, though. She's scary. Her hands are shaking, and so is her voice, and her face — the lines are almost gone. She looks like a whole different person.

These are wild women, underneath their faces. Violent, murderous. Is Lizzie, too? Is this the kind of thing that runs in families?

Maybe it's just because she hasn't met hers before, but the whole idea of families feels strange now. Full of mysteries and secrets and odd feelings that aren't explained. Like those Haldinis, holding on to each other's ankles and wrists, depending on each other's strength and balance. Except even after that failed and they let go of each other, there must still have been a last chance. Even when they were all plunging to the ground, there was maybe a second when they could have caught each other and grabbed a rope and saved themselves. There must have been plenty of ropes around. A lot of this looks like luck and bad luck.

Pretty soon now, she and her mother will be leaving for home — calling a cab, riding to the airport, waiting for the plane, taking off, landing, riding home at the other end. Unlocking the door. Safe at last.

Now that everybody's been together, will they all go back to ignoring each other? But you can't go back to not knowing something once you've found it out. You just can't ever do that.

The grown-up women have gone silent. They don't seem to know what to do, like they're frozen right where they are. It seems to be up to Lizzie again. She tries to say something hopeful to her grandmother so that look will go away. Then she says, "If you tell me where the camera might be, Grandma, I could try to find it. I could take a picture."

That would be okay, wouldn't it? At least if they were all together in a picture, they'd be able to look at it. Maybe she couldn't say it in words, but it feels sort of like it's not so much holding on to each other as getting a grip in the first place. Not quite like the Haldinis, because even though Grandma just said something awful, nobody's actually fallen out of the sky. There aren't any broken bones or bloodstains, and nobody's going to die who hasn't already died.

Things don't so much happen here as *feel* as if they're happening. So much stuff gets said without being said out loud. Only the really little and the huge things have gotten turned into words, and there's no telling ahead of time who's going to say something unexpected next. Look at Grandma, after all, the littlest person in the place, who just said the biggest words, in the most awful voice, that Lizzie's ever heard.

LUCKY DRAWS

A tearful 34-year-old single mother of two has become the country's newest multimillionaire, winning $5.8 million in the provincial lottery.

Sandra Cooper of Toronto, who was waiting, clutching her winning ticket, when the lottery offices opened, said she watched the televised draw alone in her living room and couldn't believe she'd won.

"I just sat there all by myself and cried," she told reporters. "I couldn't sleep, and this morning I got the kids off to school and came right here to find out if it was true."

Lottery officials, who reassured her that she is now a wealthy woman, accompanied her to a nearby bank where she deposited all but $500.

The divorced Cooper and her children, 11-year-old Andrew and nine-year-old Andrea, now live in public housing. "The first thing I'm going to do is find us a place of our own," she told a news conference, during which she broke into tears several times.

Cooper said she hasn't decided what other changes the money will bring, "but I know it means my kids have any future they want now.

I'll give some away, but I'm going to make sure what they need comes first."

The petite redhead said she's still shocked by the abrupt change in her circumstances. "You wish and wish for things to be different, but after a while you stop believing they ever will be." The only chance for change, she said, lay in the single lottery ticket she has bought each week since her divorce three years ago.

"To be so poor one day that you have to keep track of how much change you have in your purse, and then the next day to have so much money you can't imagine it — it feels like a fairy tale, like a fairy godmother came along. It's hard to believe it happened, and it's hard to believe it can't all be taken away again."

Cooper said the win probably marks the end of her lottery-ticket purchases. "Now we have so much, I wouldn't want to be greedy in case I lost it. What it really means, I guess, is that we get to start over."

Teddy knows exactly what she means. He is flooded with good fortune himself at the moment, positively awash with luck. When he read that story, he thought how nice it was that somebody who probably deserved it had won a pile in the lottery. He was also interested in her notion that greed could cause it all to be lost again — it sounded like some lesson she'd learned in childhood, from a fairy tale. What thrilled him, though, was the amazing hope that must lie behind those words, "We get to start over," and the pictures Sandra Cooper must have of what her life can be now.

Him too, he has pictures of a new life. His are populated with new people, fresh rituals, more crowded and cozy surroundings, changing habits, all still to be discovered and learned. His pictures aren't precise — well, realism isn't his style — but they do contain movements and shapes that will be new to him. Quite a future, and entirely amazing that just two weeks ago it wasn't even dreamed of.

It's true that at the moment he's in a tough spot, facing Susannah and Lizzie, and on their turf; Susannah's living room, all closed in and smothered by the softness of colors and textures she surrounds herself with. A temporary obstacle, but he needs to keep his wits about him. Like Sandra Cooper, he is aware of the whims and vagaries of fortune; or, if there were such things, fairy godmothers. Because of astonishment and also possibly dread, he is finding the room a little airless, making it hard to breathe.

His daughter's face, staring at him, is unreadable. Susannah looks ready to leap. He has, he thinks, since being freed from jail, become more alert to what's unseen.

Searching for a word that would suit what occurred to him with freedom, he came upon "acute." Like having sight restored after a period of blindness, or hearing after being deaf, he has been seeing such brightness and hearing such sounds! He had such longings for those five days — and then to step outside, walk down the steps to the sidewalk and into sound and space and all those colors, the explosion of honking cars, bright dresses and sweaters, and people moving, moving, with nothing like walls in the way. Even the gray grittiness of the air was glorious. He had all the room in the world to move in, walking home.

Anne was at work, but had been to his place before him, leaving bouquets of flowers on his tables, great happy splashes of color. A banner hung across the entry to the kitchen, facing the door, read "Welcome home" in red, celebratory paint. On his pillow he found a note in her curly, careful handwriting: "I've missed you. Can I come by at midnight and get all caught up?" He liked that "all caught up," with its multiple possible meanings. There was more, though, much more: the enormity of the room itself, the spaciousness and variety and choice of sitting here, lying there, looking at this, touching that; making himself a drink and having a long and scalding shower. And, hours later, burying himself in Anne: all of this nearly the precise fulfilment of his longings during five days of deprivation; the first miracle.

Today, now, is something else: an unhappy circumstance but obviously a duty. A loving duty, he'd hurry to add—there's no question he loves Lizzie, that doesn't change. It's hard to explain so she'll understand, but his strength today is the strength of ten. People adjust, after all. Lizzie will, given time. Susannah, too, although that's hardly so important.

The wonder couldn't last, anyway, not in its first pure rush; that's only normal. Even a young man couldn't maintain that soaring, glistening, shifting perfection, that feeling of being filled so tight and far he could barely contain himself. Joy. Well, love, kind of.

He isn't totally certain of that. Wise Anne has pointed out, however, that certainty may not be necessary or even possible. Once she said it, he felt a little foolish not to have realized it before, a man with his experience. For a guy who's seen himself floating free and happy at the edge, he must have devoted a lot of time to looking for safety on various canvases and mattresses.

There are so many things he could now teach a small figure in his image!

That's not disloyal. Lizzie's a smart kid, she'll understand, although it may take a while, and she has her ways of making him uncomfortable. Like now, just staring at him, not talking, not helping. This isn't easy.

It's hard to talk calmly, as if what he's saying really is true: that it doesn't have to make much difference to her. Like a convert to some new cult, he longs to evangelize instead, drawing Lizzie and even Susannah into his joy, preaching these discoveries. It's not easy to keep in mind that some pleasures can be neither understood nor shared, and also that, of all people, these must be the least sympathetic.

Compassion is called for—even pity? His benevolence must be large, because this will come as a shock to these two. They have fallen behind in news of each other—he, for instance, has no idea what happened with Susannah's family, and Lizzie has had no way of knowing what's happened with Anne since that unfortunate night they met. Sometime he'll get around to asking, probably Lizzie, what went on back east, but not today. Today is his, for his news.

Susannah's house always smells good: a bowl of dried this and that beside the sofa is some mix of sweet and bitter scents that comes out sharp and insistent, but unexpectedly pleasing. Lizzie's face is shining like a pearl, almost opaque in the light. Susannah is more like a rock.

Even his work has changed since his release. He can almost believe the week in jail has begun to touch his visions, and he has had occasional tremors that hint at something greater; even great. Does he dare?

Is he wrong?

Oh, these poor people, he's leaving them behind. Well, not Lizzie, but Susannah—Susannah looks very far away now, such a dot on his horizon that he can barely make her out here in her own living room. And as he keeps saying, Lizzie will grow accustomed, she will grow. She'll have to. Anyway, Anne's a good person, after all.

Her goodness was not only in the bouquets and the banner and the note, but in herself, after they'd been to bed and she'd showered, and fed him, and he was just beginning to think it was time for her to leave, so he could get on with his life. His work, at least: he had all those stored-up images from jail. To be truthful, though, he wanted her to leave because he was afraid of what they'd say once they began to talk. He might not have admitted that then, but he will now. His vision is much clearer now.

Her vision is unnervingly clear, he has learned.

"We should talk," she said, and oh, here it came, as she handed him a cup of coffee in the evening of his second day of freedom. He remembered again that rabbit he'd shot, but this time, too, couldn't quite think why, since she still wasn't looking particularly bunnylike.

"What about?" Eyebrows raised, all deceptive innocence.

He'd annoyed her, he could tell by the click of her mug on the coffee table and the sharp lines on her forehead. Good then; they could quarrel, probably the safest outcome.

"Ted," she said in a tone he recognized, although he couldn't quite place it — another childhood leftover, this time a recollection of his mother? Or some other, later female, Susannah, perhaps, or even Lizzie? (Although any of them would have said "Teddy" in a crisp sort of way, never "Ted.") Or it could have been that voice in his own head when he's nursing a drink late at night that says impatiently, "Pull yourself together," or words to that effect. He hadn't noticed before that that could be a female voice, and not necessarily his own.

"Don't screw around, Ted, you know what I'm talking about. All I want to say is, you don't need to think I took you seriously, I know you didn't mean it, and I won't be suing you for breach of promise. So relax, okay?"

He shrugged as expansively as he could manage. "I'm relaxed, aren't you?" He failed to be crafty, though, and sounded merely foolish. "Oh, look, I'm sorry. I'm an asshole."

"Yes, you are sometimes." She grinned. "Not all the time, though. Sometimes you're really quite nice."

Jesus, there was a sad thought — nice? "But not enough to marry? You're turning me down?"

He'd done it again. What made him say these things? It wasn't as if he was even really saying them: they just came out.

"I'm not turning you down, I'm saying you never asked. I mean, if you were the sort of man who said that kind of thing on the spur of the moment and after just a few days, and meant it, you'd have been married years ago and we wouldn't ever have met."

"If I were that sort of man, I'd have been married and divorced years ago and we'd still have met. With a little help from Leo and Teresa." Whom he really did have to call, as soon as he figured out whether to thank them or blame them.

"Didn't you ever want to?" She sounded curious, but in an almost impersonal way, as if it were no great concern of hers.

He wasn't sure he liked that. He thought she might show more interest.

"What, get married? I guess I've come close a couple of times, but something always happens. Things change. Feelings. Something I'd think was great to start with would just get irritating. At least it always happened before I got married, thank God. Saved all the mess of when it happens after."

That made her laugh — what was so funny? What he said might not have been some huge admission, but it was still a leap of confidence. She could hurt him if she wanted to, which made laughter quite a weapon. "What's funny?"

"Oh, Ted, you are. Listen. You've lived here, what, fifteen years?"

"About that."

"And you've known ever since you were a kid what you wanted to be, that you'd try to be an artist?"

Try? Was that a shot? "Yeah." He was sulky.

"And your daughter's thirteen now, and you love her, you like having her around?"

"Sure." He hoped they weren't going to talk about Lizzie, though. That would move them from unsteady to dangerous ground. "What's your point?"

"Well, look. My life isn't exactly filled with change, but in the past ten years I've moved apartments four times, and switched jobs three times, although I admit I've always been a nurse. And I've lived through a marriage and dumped a husband. So it seems to me, if we're talking about change, I might know more about it than you do."

Okay, maybe, but that wasn't his point. "Love," he said. "Love changes." He hesitated about using the word, but couldn't think of another one. "It's frail stuff."

"Sure it changes. The thing is, you hope it doesn't. I assume it will and hope for the best. You think it's frail, but I think it's pretty tough. In my experience, anyway. Maybe yours is frail on purpose."

One way of putting it; possibly a reasonably true one. The

odd thing was, those could all have been cruel words, but she didn't seem to have intended them that way, and he wasn't particularly hurt.

She was laughing at him again. "You know, Ted, you're the strangest man. Transparent in a way, like looking at an X ray. I can see every move you make. You come close and then you pull away, back and forth like a dance."

She looked at him as if she really could see inside him, then tossed back her drink and stood. What an abrupt, decisive woman! "I'm going home. I have to work tomorrow, and I think you need time to yourself." He wouldn't argue with that.

Still, when the door closed quietly behind her—he wouldn't have blamed her if she'd slammed it, and might even have been pleased—and the third step down from the top made its small creak, he suddenly thought, "I don't like this," and almost leaped after her, to bring her back.

If she'd stayed, what? They'd have gone back to bed. Finally they'd have fallen asleep, and there'd have been the sound of her breathing, the feeling of her hand on his chest or his shoulder, a warm thigh beside his own. That would have been nice. In the morning, she would still have had to leave, and he would still have had the day to himself to work. By the time she got back, he'd have had a full, productive day, and time to get dinner ready. He could have gone out to pick up more Scotch. She could have looked at whatever he'd accomplished, and told him about hospital events, possibly dramatic ones. Even dull ones might be interesting.

She might not have felt like joining him on a midnight prowl, but that didn't need to stop him. She could go to sleep and he'd know she was there; like leaving lights on for when he got back.

Was he such an idiot? It seemed that what he'd been after was some kind of magic, telepathic woman who would vanish at a hint and reappear the instant he might consider longing for her. What fantasies he still had!

He may still be making a fool of himself, he may still be wrong, but so what? He's forty-five years old, and has had, in the past few days, a shot like adrenaline of—what? Anticipation.

Fear, too. He's never been so frightened; not even the day of a big show opening, a really important one.

Honest to God, he can't tell what's different about her. Maybe nothing. Maybe just that she appeared at a particular moment. He's almost sure that in another time or place, he would have taken no notice of her.

Honest to God, it doesn't seem to matter. He doesn't feel like himself.

Susannah, a lot less alert about him than Anne — although naturally she would be, she doesn't love him — was offhand when he called earlier to see if he could come over and talk to her and Lizzie; as if it could hardly be anything important, but she'd try to fit him in and keep Lizzie from bounding out to do something more entertaining. Well, surprise, Susannah: he's making himself a new life. He could almost feel sorry for her, stuck in her old one.

What a cold woman, though, just watching him—so different from Anne's warm gaze. He'd like to think she might envy him, or wish for fresh chances herself, or simply miss him, but who can tell?

He mustn't get rattled. A vision of Anne helps: not the naked, passionate one, that's too distracting, but the small one in the yellow dress, with the calm voice and the terribly clear eye.

This should open a new world to Lizzie, he hopes she realizes that. She may not see it right away, but this could turn out to be her lucky day, too, just like his, or Sandra Cooper's. Right now, though, she's making him a little impatient. He does think that sometimes she might consider somebody besides herself.

Except she's still a kid. His kid, too. Must be the Susannah in her that can make her so difficult, sometimes, to face.

To Lizzie, he looks so serious and truthful, sitting on the couch across the room from her, his elbows on his knees, hands holding onto each other, talking on and on, explaining and explaining; making bigger and bigger ripples in the silence with his words.

How come grown-ups get to do things like this to kids, just deciding things and never asking? Like refugees or foster kids— they must wonder all the time what's going to happen to them next. How do people say, "I love you, goodbye," anyway?

Is that what Teddy's saying? Or, meaner and worse, "I love Anne, goodbye." Not much choice for Lizzie.

"It doesn't mean anything much has to change as far as you're concerned," he's saying again. He's already said this several times, in different words. "It's only that Anne'll be around more."

Honestly, Lizzie's never thought of him and her mother as a couple, but this breaks them apart completely. Where does that leave her? She has a horrible black rush of such a hatred she could kill Anne. No, she couldn't really, not kill exactly, now that she knows what those words sound like when they're truly meant.

How can he say it won't make any difference? He wants things to happen, but only good things. He's actually a little stupid that way.

"Anyway," he's saying, "for the time being she's only moving in, and we'll see where it goes from there. I just wanted to let you know so you could start getting to know her better. You'll need time to get used to it, everybody does. I'll need time myself," and he smiles in that way that's supposed to be like, who could be mad at somebody who smiles like that?

Then his face gets all smoothed out like peanut butter. "The other thing is, Anne's thirty-six and she might like to have a kid one day soon. So if we do okay living together, we might get married and try to have one. I figured—" and there's that smile again "— you'd be a terrific big sister." Lizzie allows herself a quick flash of scorn, enough for him to catch sight of but not enough to get mad about.

"So," he reaches his hands toward her, "what do you think? You've been so quiet—you're such a good listener, Lizzie."

He's so silly, thinking she doesn't know he's just being flattering to get her to be nice. Does he think she's a baby? He probably wants her to say something like, "That's terrific, Teddy, I'm really happy for you," because that'd make him think everything's okay and he doesn't have to worry. He only wants to be sure he can feel good.

She shrugs. "No big deal. Anne's going to move in with you and you might get married and have a kid, that's all. Why should I care?" What a lie — but she can be sly, at least about Anne.

"But I want to know how you feel about it."

"Why? What difference does it make?"

"Lizzie," her mother warns, but she's not really cross.

"It makes a difference," and he sounds almost mad, "because you're my daughter, and I care what you think."

So she's supposed to be like that minister at the graveyard, burying her grandfather, saying words that would be like a blessing. She asks, instead, "Would you change your mind if I said I hated it?"

"Well, no, that's not what I meant." He looks flustered. "But if you hated it, we could talk about whatever was worrying you, and maybe I could clear it up. It's just, I figure that now you know Anne's going to be around, you'll feel freer to like her. I think you will, when you give her a chance."

Not if; when.

"Then if we do get around to having a kid, you could baby-sit and spend time together. You'd have a brother or a sister, and you could teach him things. Or her."

So a daughter comes second, he'd like a boy, somebody different from her. "I don't know," she says carefully, "I don't think I'm very interested in baby-sitting. In general." Right now she'd be interested in running upstairs to her room to cry, but then he'd only come after her and talk and talk some more, and that'd just make everything worse. Besides, she'd have to think about why she wants to cry. It might be for him leaving her, but she'd have to be sure it wasn't just to get her own way or to make him feel bad.

Anyway, she's made him angry, and that's something. He

stands and says, real sharp, "You think about it." Then, "Anne and I want you to come to dinner Friday night. To celebrate and get better acquainted."

Think fast. "Oh, that's too bad," she says as lightly as she can, "I already have plans for Friday night. And" (quickly) "all this weekend. Maybe some other time."

"Maybe some other time" is what her mother usually says, getting out of an invitation to do something with somebody she doesn't particularly like.

"Definitely some other time, then." His voice has gone hard, but he's still trying to be patient. "You'll find it works out. Anne's a very nice woman, you know."

Probably, but so what? Her mother and Frannie laugh sometimes about what a dumb kind of praise it is, just calling somebody nice.

Now they're all heading to the front door to let him out. "I'll talk to you soon, Susannah. Figure out a time for dinner, that sort of thing."

Her mother laughs, a queer sound. "Why, am I invited?"

She's made him blush — oh, lovely! "Well, I meant Lizzie. I'm not sure . . . "

"It's okay, Teddy, I was just teasing. It's the shock of hearing the word marriage on your lips. But sure, let us know your schedule. And of course you'll keep us up to date about any wedding plans. Or pregnancies. I'll want to send gifts, of course."

He leaves too fast. Lizzie, standing in the doorway with her mother, thinks he gives too much away. Her mother can still get him on the run.

"Poor Teddy," her mother says. "We were mean."

So was he.

What a lot of terrible words Lizzie's heard in the past couple of weeks! How come grown-ups don't stay the same? Why don't they know they're too old for this stuff?

Some awful words are more awful than others, though. If she had to decide, she'd have to say her grandmother's words were worse than Teddy's, even if they didn't exactly change Lizzie's life, not like his.

What Grandma said into the silence, all strange and cold and flat, was, "I could kill him. I could just kill him for this."

It sounded like she would have, too. That tiny old person, with the smile that made her eyes go squinty and the hands that kept touching Lizzie, and if he'd been there and alive again, she would have killed him. People have too many parts to them, too many sides that don't show. What else? And who else, her mother?

It was when they were all sitting around the table on the back porch, watching Grandma hold Lizzie's birth-announcement card, some strange baby wrapped in a pink and white blanket. It didn't seem possible that was really her, or that she was ever so little and blank. But it sure meant something to her grandmother.

Even Aunt Elaine didn't have anything to say. She just looked upset and scared.

Lizzie's mother looked amazed, watching Grandma like she wondered what was going to happen next, and like she wanted to stop it, whatever it was, but didn't know how.

Finally Lizzie was the one who moved, because if nothing happens and nothing happens, words just stay in the air sounding worse and worse. She reached out and touched her grandmother's arm and said the first thing she could think of. "Never mind, Grandma. You can come and see us now. We'd have a good time."

Would they? She kind of liked her grandmother, maybe because her grandmother seemed to like her, but you probably couldn't depend on somebody who'd do what she did to Lizzie's mother. Anyway, it might be scary. Lizzie's fancy from before, that this family might contain murderers, hasn't turned out so wrong after all.

At least her grandmother's body started to relax, slowly, until she slumped back and put the card down on the table. "That would be nice, dear, yes. I'd like that." Her voice was a little shaky, but she looked okay again.

Lizzie found the camera. The pictures probably won't turn out because the only film she could find was really old, but it got them all together on the doorstep. When they were leaving,

Lizzie's mother leaned over and kissed Grandma on the forehead and said, "I'm sorry you've had such a terrible time." She probably didn't just mean the funeral.

"Oh, well, you know," Grandma sighed and rested her hand on Lizzie's shoulder, "I always try to remember how fortunate I am compared to so many other people. I like to keep in mind how much worse things could have been." Lizzie's mother frowned, but it sounded right to Lizzie.

Saying goodbye was sad. It wasn't like there were happy endings, although Lizzie's used to stories that don't have happy endings. Grandma and Aunt Elaine looked kind of lonesome, standing on the front porch waving goodbye as Lizzie and her mother drove off in the taxi, waving back.

Her mother must know plenty of things about people in families saying goodbye.

What does her mother think about what Teddy's doing? Maybe it's weird for her, too, even though they haven't really done anything together since they were young, except for making Lizzie.

Now there's only her and her mother. Back in the living room, they kind of collapse beside each other on the couch, where Teddy'd sat.

"The night you were at Teddy's and I called and a woman answered the phone, was that Anne?"

"Yeah."

"I remember she called you dear. I wondered who she was and how come you hadn't mentioned her. What's she like?"

"But that's just it, I don't know! I only met her that once. She and Teddy'd just met, so how could it happen so fast?"

"I don't know, honey. It doesn't sound like him, for sure."

"She's *ordinary*." Is that what hurts most, that he wants something ordinary? So he's less interesting himself? "She paints her fingernails. Her toenails, too. He's had lots of girlfriends, but this never happened."

Maybe she's mostly upset because she's so surprised. She's wondered before if her mother might keep somebody around someday, but never Teddy.

Her mother sighs. "I don't know, but he's right about one thing, you're going to have to do your best to get along. Who knows, maybe it'll turn out fine. You might like having a sister or a brother, you know."

A couple of weeks ago, seeing her mother and Aunt Elaine together, she was curious about that, at least. Now it just feels sad. If Teddy and Anne do live together forever and have a baby, Teddy'll be with it all the time. He'll be able to play with it whenever he wants, and sing to it and feed it lunch, tell it stories, teach it words. He might start taking it for walks, even, so it'd meet all her people. He'd make drawings and paintings of its birthday parties, he'd *be* there for its birthday parties. Maybe he'd even be there for its birth. It would be his kid as much as Anne's; not like Lizzie, made because of only one of them.

"Did you ever want another baby?"

"Not for a minute. You were just what I wanted, and besides, no offense, Lizzie, but having a kid is hard work, and there were times I wasn't sure we'd both make it. I even cried sometimes when you were a baby, I was so scared and there wasn't anything I could do about it."

This is a picture she hasn't shown Lizzie before, and it's not a very nice one.

"But mostly that was when you were a little baby and I was so tired I could hardly stand it. I was all alone, although that was my own fault—or rather, my choice. And then, you know, I'd go in to check on you when you were sleeping and just fall in love all over again." She smiles. "You were so pink, and at least part of the time, you smelled wonderful."

It's great to be just what somebody wanted, except for it weighing so much.

Her mother puts an arm around her, which makes Lizzie want to cry. It's weird, how often she's felt like that lately. Because of different things at Grandma's house, not just here—all sorts of stuff. Her mother's different, too. She touches more often, and she feels softer, sort of the way she sometimes is when she's happy with a man.

"Would you ever get married?"

"Oh, gee, Lizzie, I doubt it. I don't think I'd be very good at it. I know how things don't last."

"But they can, can't they? I mean, some people stay married." This is important. Lizzie intends to get married herself.

"Sure, of course. But sometimes that's only because one person tries harder than the other one. I'm not so good any more at giving more than I get back, I guess. Anyway, Lizzie, the only person I'm sure I'll always love, no matter what, is you. You make me feel safe." She kind of shakes herself, as if she was getting too far away. And what does she mean? Lizzie can't think of anything she does to make her mother safe. "Listen, honey. There are men out there somewhere who used to be the first thing I thought about in the morning and the last thing when I was going to sleep. Teddy, too, years ago. I had dreams about them, and my heart jumped when the phone rang, or the doorbell. But now, with some of them I have to think hard to even remember their names, and I don't think about most of them from one year to another. So none of that lasted, for one reason and another. You, though, you're with me for good." Her mother's voice trembles a little there, and it almost sounds as if she feels like crying, too. Like at her father's funeral, when what she said broke her down when nothing else did?

"The point is, anyway, I like things too much my own way."

"Teddy does, too."

"I know, but he usually *gets* his own way. I think he assumes that's how it should be. It's Anne who'll have to do the adjusting if any of this works out, I expect, not Teddy."

It's true. Lizzie saw for herself today that he came here to say what he was going to do, not ask her what she thought. He made up his mind and then just said she'd get used to it, and he's likely right, because what choice does she have?

Maybe if Anne wants him, she doesn't have much choice, either. Maybe it's only who wants what more.

Or who loves who more?

Except that would mean Teddy loves less, wouldn't it? Or

just differently. Maybe love just means something different to him, and part of it is getting his own way.

Like the nights Lizzie'd be sleeping over at his place and he'd wake her up to go out on one of his long walks—it wasn't that she didn't want to go, but more that he took it for granted she would. Sleepy or not, off they went, and it always turned out to be fun. She's met all kinds of people she wouldn't have without him, and heard stories that are never in the newspapers or on TV.

"Anyway," her mother says, "don't borrow trouble. None of this may happen. You know Teddy."

But how come grown-ups, even her mother, try to take feelings and make them reasonable? How come they think words can turn one thing into something else?

Her mother's voice goes soft. "I know it's a hard idea to get used to, Lizzie. It'll take some time. Likely you're partly feeling grief over losing somebody important, but you're not losing him, you know. Teddy's your father, the way I'm your mother. No other kid could change that."

Is that what this is, grief? Something like what Grandma felt when her husband died, before she was so angry? Did Lizzie's mother or Aunt Elaine feel like this about their father? It doesn't *look* the same to Lizzie.

"Lizzie, think of all the things you and Teddy have done! Even if he and Anne do have a kid, do you think she'll let him wake up a four-year-old for long walks at midnight? Do you think," she says, laughing, "he'd ever get arrested, the way he was with you?" So that story is funny now to her mother, same as Teddy. Maybe all kinds of things turn into jokes after a while. Maybe when Lizzie's twenty or so, even this will make her laugh.

"Anyway, honey, all the changes that come along can't just be yours. Other people change too, you know. Even me, sometimes. I'm maybe not as bold as Teddy, but I do think I'm still brave."

That sounds hard. A warning? Her mother decided to have Lizzie, after all, and there's no real reason she might not decide to do something else just as big and sudden.

Lizzie can see herself, grown up, coming home for a visit and finding a For Sale sign on the lawn, her mother's bags all packed and her ready for some other kind of life—maybe flying all over the place, like Frannie, only landing now and then to do a laundry, see a friend, pack up again. Her mother might find a place she likes better than this one, somewhere completely different—a dry African village springs to mind for some reason. Her mother might come back with an armload of carvings and pottery and possibly a black man: carrying her new world around with her.

Or Lizzie could do any of that herself.

Looking past her mother through the open doorway into the office, she can see all those clippings, hundreds and hundreds of them. Her mother explained a long time ago about news: that it's really all about change. Things that stay the same are hardly ever news. A lot of times it happens by accident, but sometimes on purpose. That's what her mother did, changing everything by making Lizzie. The other part is that people can't always stop things from happening; like Lizzie can't stop Teddy.

Her mother's trick is better.

The office is an awful mess. Why did she bring all that stuff downstairs anyway? Well, maybe she had some questions, but it was ages ago and now all she remembers is pulling a box of clippings out of her closet and starting to go through them and then having the idea to move them. Partly she was in a bad mood, maybe, but also she just wanted her mother to notice, even though they've never been a secret.

How come her mother still hasn't asked about them? Isn't she interested?

Her mother isn't perfect, either. She doesn't always listen or pay attention, and sometimes she has her mind on other things, like work or men, or things Lizzie doesn't know about. Just taking for granted, like Teddy, that Lizzie will understand, or at least get used to it. Her mother's grumpy first thing in the morning, and she isn't very tidy, and she can't cook very well, and she doesn't care, either. Of course if she cared about things like that, she'd be mad at Lizzie, making such a mess.

She loves Lizzie, though. Wouldn't it be terrible, not to be loved? Some kids aren't; even her mother maybe wasn't. Does she get lonesome, or is she scared of getting lonesome? Is that a reason she had Lizzie in the first place? Maybe she had more love than she needed or had places for.

Maybe it would be neat, having a sister; like her mother and Aunt Elaine, only not so mean to each other.

Stories she reads are going to be more complicated now. Like, even if it's hard to imagine, Lizzie might have to wonder what was going on besides awfulness when that girl drowned her baby in a toilet. Where is she now? Sometimes it's hard to think up futures for people.

There's her own story, too. Teddy might have had a bigger part than she's ever thought, because didn't he say yes? He could have said no. He's said yes with Anne, after all. So is Lizzie less of a miracle than she thought, or more of one?

Maybe all the stories, even her own, are sort of like what Teddy says about his work. It starts with a picture in his head, and then he makes a sketch, and then he puts down paint on a canvas, and finally, after a lot of work, there's something that just hangs there all by itself that might not be what he had in mind when he started at all. What hangs on a wall is the ending, but nobody ever sees where it gets started, in his head.

"Oh, Lizzie," her mother says, "don't look so worried. I know it's tough, but we should try to be happy for him, if he's getting what he wants." Sure, that's easy, like a drippy birthday card. It's not even the point any more.

Lizzie feels almost grown up when she stands, looking down at her mother but sort of distantly. "I think I'll clear out that stuff in your office. I guess it's in your way."

"Well, it is, but a lot of it's interesting, too. Can I help?" Her mother stands up. Maybe she means to be helpful and nice, or she's making sure Lizzie doesn't feel left all alone, or she's curious. Or all those things. Things aren't just one way or another any more.

"Sure. Except it might take quite a while."

"That's okay, we have time. Are you throwing them out?"

"I don't know. Maybe some of them." She doesn't think so, though. That would be like throwing out years and years, and anyway, she might forget, if they weren't around. If people can even forget other people, they can probably forget stories really easily.

Lizzie feels older than she did when she got up this morning, and ages older than she did a couple of weeks ago, before she and her mother went east. Except this isn't quite like her vision was of growing up. It should feel bigger, like a huge flash of knowing.

There are all sorts of things she can ask her mother, as they go through the clippings. Even if Lizzie's getting old, her mother's a lot older. She must know some hidden stuff that will come up, like about the awful and really strange and different ways that families, and love, turn out. Also, though, it might not just be asking her mother questions. There are things Lizzie could tell her, too, that might amaze her.

Maybe somewhere in all those stories, there's even a clue to what great thing she'll be when she grows up. Whatever it is, it'll be better than bowing on a stage, or waving from the back seat of a limousine, like the queen. It'll still be something grand; it'll also probably be more complicated than she expected, and maybe harder, too.

There are a lot of stories, anyway; and there are magic moments when people know things, after all. Like her mother knowing she wanted Lizzie and then setting out to have her. Lizzie has her mother's hair, and nose, and mouth, and there's no reason she won't also have an instant just like that when she'll be absolutely sure.

One thing at a time, concentrate on one thing at a time: the highlights in Lizzie's hair, like Susannah's used to be before the red tinges started coming in gray; the prickly bumps on her arms, gooseflesh that won't go away, even though the house is warm; the brushing paper sound of Lizzie separating clippings. An unknown father dies, a mother proves amazing, an old lover will marry—so what? It's just events, nothing much to do with her.

So why is she angry? Why does she want to hug Lizzie so tight the poor kid's ribs might break? Changes hurl themselves at her like rocks, grazing her head, thudding into her heart. None of them to do with her, so how come she's so battered?

Lizzie must be, too, although for different reasons and in different ways. There are times, though, when Susannah'd almost rather not have to be a mother; when she'd rather be mothered herself.

Small chance of that.

Lizzie likely has the right idea, going through the clippings. It may well be helpful to take another look at some of those abrupt and violent changes. Susannah's mother is right: worse things do happen to other people. Worse things happen to refugees, to children and women who are beaten, to families who are starving, to men who go to war—worse things happen to practically everybody, really.

Who would have dreamed this of Teddy? Not Susannah, never.

The point is, and it feels like a nasty sharp point, this slices the legs from under her past. If he can do this so unexpectedly, she can't have ever known him. She must have just assumed, and if she was so wrong, her own history is lost, plowed under at the hands of someone else.

Maybe he was even the wrong choice for Lizzie's father. He does, after all, turn out to have dull longings, and perhaps ordinary fears as well.

This is stupid. Once she lived with a lean and eloquent young man with a talent for stirring feelings of one kind and another. He stirred hers, real enough, and the results were real enough. A beautiful and wild young man, and a childlike, hopeful older one, fired by his various beliefs, mainly, as it turns out, in himself.

God, it was easier to picture him as a grandfather than as a husband. Husband! What does that mean — something like a shepherd, to do with gathering and holding; garnering and keeping safe — can that be Teddy? A quarter of a century after they formed the perfectly balanced pair, one sturdy and solid, one rootless and uproarious, he's the one settling for solid sturdiness?

Well, maybe that's it, though, that quarter of a century. He may be frightened in his way, too.

If he's scared, what hope for her?

She might, of course, become rootless and uproarious.

Anyway, he's stolen something, and she's as betrayed as she was years ago. She could almost smash glasses again (except for knowing she'd have to sweep up the mess).

Of course she didn't have to believe him then, when he told her what a haven she was for him. He might have only wanted her to be what he wanted. It's also quite possible she returned the favor, turning him into someone else as well.

Circles and circles — no wonder nothing lasts. People end up biting not only each other's tails, but their own.

Still, in the end, after the shock and the queer pain (because she would have thought herself more immune to him), there is, after all, a tickle of triumph: that he's the one who must have lost courage, lost faith; while she, whatever her failures and hesitations may be, is no quitter. She may also have lapses of courage and faith, but she wasn't kidding, talking to Lizzie: she does believe that she's still brave.

Or Lizzie may be wrong, this Anne may not be so ordinary. Lizzie has her own reasons for fury.

Poor kid — she puts her hand briefly on her daughter's head — Lizzie, sitting cross-legged on the floor in front of her, is sifting stories, handing them over now and then, although Susannah's having trouble reading the words. She's gotten used to the clippings themselves, though, and imagines missing them when they're gone.

What a kid, after all. How gracefully she behaved, meeting that new family whose grown-up members (including Susannah) did not always match that grace. Who taught her to be quiet when being quiet was a very good idea, and how to touch people when they most needed touching? She remembers now, although she may not have noticed at the time, that Lizzie stuck close at the funeral, and felt, standing at Susannah's elbow, unusually stern. Since they've been back, Susannah's been feeling fairly protective herself, and loving in a way that's almost as purely sensuous as when Lizzie was a baby. Like her mother, Susannah's barely been able to keep her hands off the child. Soon other people are going to feel that way about her; possibly they do already. A pretty young girl with small beginning breasts and a kind of sweet wisdom is going to appeal to boys, and then men, who will make efforts to embrace her. Lizzie's going to have a lot of pleasure. She'll also have a lot of pain, which Susannah won't be able to prevent.

Even today, when it came at the hands of Lizzie's own father, she wasn't able to prevent it. As Teddy talked, Lizzie's face was so sorrowful — Susannah could have torn out his tongue for that.

Lizzie is looking up, handing her another clipping, this one a quickie police story — a girl, young woman, who drowned her newborn infant in a toilet. Good grief, what does Lizzie want to know about that? It's terrible and pitiful — what else is there to say?

These are very complicated matters, to do with explosive emotions. Children do know about explosive emotions, though, even to Lizzie they won't be foreign turf. It's a question of shock, and the individual capacity for control. These are all tragic tales of one kind and another.

What is it Lizzie knows, and what is it that she wants to know? Susannah can't always answer questions, she isn't always going to be enough to satisfy. That may account for her own flares of irritation, which have oddly died down since they've been back. She and Lizzie seem to be, in a way, on a new footing: more equitable, more equal.

This is interesting: Susannah fretted about changing circumstances as Lizzie grows up, but apparently she hasn't taken into account changing feelings. There are grounds for hope, ways of being quite pleased about that.

Also since they've been back, Susannah has reworked her piece on Ida Lovender, a superior version this time, containing at least some of the astonishment at what truly can happen in an instant: a life bowled over. She can imagine Ida liking it, or at any rate believing it says something true about her.

Maybe she should do it yet again, knowing what she's learned today from Teddy? But then, she could write it over and over forever if she was going to wait until she was finished with surprises. Anyway, she turned it in this morning to *Aura*, where, as expected, Bobbi had a fit about the photographs. Frannie and Alan are coming to dinner tonight. Lizzie's going out to a movie with Megan and a couple of boys. Small events here and there.

Until Teddy came along, it was a pretty good day.

She was wrong before, thinking she would not wake up any morning from now on without remembering she no longer has a father. It hasn't been every morning at all, by any means.

Unexpectedly, however, her mother has been much on her mind. Or perhaps not so unexpectedly, given that abrupt passion. What words!

"I'm so angry," her mother had said, staring at that card with Lizzie's newborn face. And then, "I could kill him. I could kill him for this."

Jesus. They all just sat there. It sounded utterly true, and there was sure no easy comfort for it, no slick words to make it go away.

There were some things Susannah wished for from her mother, but she must not have wanted to touch the heart of the matter, or get so close to the bone.

Well, she never dreamed where the heart and the bone might lie, did she?

She almost felt pity for him; even that pathetic kind of love of the strong for the weak, in the face of this unexpectedly extreme old woman.

Probably he never imagined his wife's potential for venom, violence. How tough she must be in her way, quite different from Susannah's.

Even so, her rage came a bit late, didn't it? Fourteen years ago would have been a better time, not when he was dead, when her mother was safe.

Was that envelope his idea of a message, or was it a legacy? When he took out his bankbook, did he draw out that envelope, too, and look at his baby granddaughter? Did he wonder how she was turning out, or how she and Susannah were getting along, or what he might be missing? Did he regret what he'd done, mourn his stubbornness, or did he gloat over this piece of secret knowledge? Did he ever wish he hadn't kept it secret, long to show it to his wife and talk with her about them, having to hold back, realizing too much time had passed and it was too late?

Perhaps he looked at it to renew his outrage.

Or perhaps he viewed it all fondly, sentimentally, as his last gift to his wife: a healthy bank account, an adequate life insurance policy, and a grandchild she didn't know. A kind of compensation for his death. Oh, surprise!

That seemed unlikely; too benevolent a point of view. Still, what did she know? These people, even the dead one, were unpredictably beyond her.

It was Lizzie, who had been silent, who came to the rescue, reaching out to touch her grandmother. Did she understand what was happening, all those passions that both had to do with her and had nothing at all to do with her? She must have been frightened, but she touched her grandmother anyway and said, "You could come and see us, Grandma. We'd have a good time."

The effect was a faith healer's: her grandmother's features shifting, lines altering, fury draining, replaced by that softness again.

Lizzie does have eerie moments of wisdom.

Elaine, on the other hand, does not. Nor, unlike Susannah, was she speechless. "I feel badly," she said. "He's gone. We can't know."

So what? Susannah thought they knew all they were ever likely to and all they needed to.

"Lizzie's right, Mother," Elaine went on, brightly now, "you *will* be able to travel. Isn't that nice?" How brave of her, and how stupid, to patronize that terrifying woman. "You can come and see me, too, and even visit your great-grandchildren."

"I expect that would be nice, yes. And you, too, Susannah, couldn't I, just like Lizzie said."

What, drop in as if it had only been her husband who'd held her back, as if she and Susannah didn't have a few things of their own to clear up? What made her mother think she could just step into the middle of events after that long, meek absence?

For that matter, how could Susannah fit her, even for a few days, into her life with Lizzie? Susannah has lived most of her years in this house as a motherless woman, or at least as one without a past, or with a past she made for herself. She could see her and Lizzie running through their morning routines, in their usual rush, waiting for the bathroom, brushing past her mother. What on earth would they do together?

Still. There might be some satisfaction in showing her mother this balanced and comfortable house, pointing out the life she has created out of nothing her mother ever gave her.

An exaggeration. A lie, really. But there is a kind of revenge here, and surely that's not so terrible?

Anyway, it was Lizzie who invited her.

If her mother visited, what could they possibly say? There's a fourteen-year gap in there, so perhaps they could discuss what her mother's been up to all that time. That might take a couple of sentences, or a minute or two. Susannah would be in no mood to tell her mother much about herself, or what she'd been doing, she was pretty sure of that. It wouldn't be any of her mother's business. Anyway, her mother would likely disapprove, and look where that disapproval can end!

Oh, there were some questions, though. It might be something, sitting up at night after Lizzie'd gone to bed, discussing this and that: what her mother was like as a girl, and as a young woman getting married. What she'd seen in Susannah's father, and what she'd hoped for. How she felt about her children, what she thought, if she ever did (but she must have) about her own life. What went through her mind in those fourteen years.

How speaking that sentence changed her — because surely it must have. Susannah pictured soft lighting, herself with a glass of wine, her mother most likely with a cup of tea, two grown-ups talking because being a daughter no longer came naturally, and her mother hadn't earned her motherhood. Susannah might learn about ideas and events she hadn't seen at the time, blinded by childhood and possibly childishness. Her father, too; he might have left some redeeming message in words only her mother could now relate.

It was a question of curiosity, really. "I'd like it if you came. So would Lizzie."

"Well, we can talk about it sometime. It's a long way, though, and I've never flown."

Then why the hell did she bring it up? No wonder Susannah's father made all the decisions!

Lizzie took a picture of the three grown women, standing gingerly beside each other on the front step. What sort of expressions did she catch, pressing down the shutter release? Susannah kissed her mother lightly goodbye, and touched Elaine's arm. It didn't feel like a permanent farewell, but then, it hadn't felt permanent before, either.

If Alan weren't coming along tonight, she'd be able to talk to Frannie about all this. As it turns out, she doesn't think she'll want them to laugh about it right away.

With Alan here, though, they won't be so free. Men tend not to understand the ways she and Frannie talk, they're too easily offended, and take everything too literally and personally.

A man, for instance, wouldn't be amused by the jokes they'll make (but not tonight) about Teddy and his plans. Alan would think her cruel and hard, and wouldn't dream of why she felt that way. Frannie will know and laugh anyway. All sharp-edged, sharp-tongued, she keeps Susannah on her toes.

Possibly those were her father's problems: that he was easily offended, took everything personally, and was much too literal. She supposes he'll have to stay mainly a mystery, that man for whom it was like pulling teeth to get him to a doctor, who knew the names of all kinds of leaves, whose instructions were so quiet she apparently misheard. Now that he's dead, it's easier to think of him with more astonishment than judgment. And possibly more mercy, in a way. At least recalling the father of her childhood she has found a few kind words, although she still has none for the grown-up one.

Some friend (who?) years ago, with a passing interest in such things, once read Susannah's palm. "Your head line goes on forever," she said, "but your heart line peters out in the oddest way." Susannah snatched her hand back. How embarrassing, to have no heart; to be *caught* having no heart. It's not true, though, it's only that her head is strong. She hears her mother saying (to whom?), "Susannah's such a headstrong girl."

After Frannie and Alan leave tonight, she might phone her mother, make sure that she's okay.

One thing about Teddy's plans: she won't be free just to call him up any more. She only has called him, really, over matters to do with Lizzie, but still there was something about knowing he was there, all these years.

Well, no more. No doubt Anne wouldn't like it; and Susannah can see that she wouldn't, either. Hearing the phone picked up at the other end, she'd be too sharply reminded of that new and unfamiliar domestic life of Teddy's. Nothing she could picture.

Lizzie's right, these are interesting clippings — such tales of turmoil! Unhappy, mainly, but that's why they're news. There are other, happier stories, but they don't usually get written down, and the ones that do are less gripping and unlikely to be saved.

So many possibilities!

When Lizzie leaves, Susannah will have twenty, thirty years worth of things to try before the next change comes. She hasn't the faintest idea what they'll be. Even considering fresh chances, people, adventures, requires a kind of thinking she hasn't used for, oh, fourteen years or so. Still, she has several years to picture herself in new ways.

It could be quite exciting: a sort of hobby, imaginary futures.

In the meantime there are other exciting events: Lizzie going out and coming in, her features changing, and her body. Problems ahead, no doubt—will she be defiant some months, rebellious? Get pregnant, messing up her future? Drop out of school? Really, not very likely. A kid who keeps an old clipping about a girl who drowns her newborn baby isn't likely to have one herself, is she?

Susannah will learn new things and anticipate familiar ones. Getting out of bed for that first coffee of the day, heading out to meet strangers, watching her hips change shape and her hair get spikier as it comes in more gray. Would it be relaxing just to let herself get matronly? She could take up good works, like Ida Lovender, in an unsentimental way, or go back to school to learn new things, or take off traveling, cultivating the obscure and undiscovered. None of this is very likely. If she had gifts for either goodness or discovery, she'd have noticed them by now.

Something, however, out of all the many, many possibilities, will make itself known. Something always has. And it's not only her family that can be any damn thing she wants it to be.

Here's that familiar clipping about the two old sisters, caught beneath collapsing walls. She points it out to Lizzie, who picks it up to read. They'll never get the room cleaned up at this rate, but there's a ton of time for this and that.

She does have plans for when she's old; she and Frannie have a fancy: to share a house, probably this one (although Susannah has wondered if they expect the ability to share, not noticeably strong in either of them, to develop naturally along with wrinkles). They do each have some horror of dying alone, bodies undiscovered, perhaps, for days, so there's that kind of self-interest involved; but other things, too.

"You can be crippled," Frannie has said, giggling, "and I'll be stone deaf. I'll push you around in your wheelchair and you can hit me with your cane when you see a car coming or when the doorbell rings. Symbiotic, see? You'll keep the bedroom downstairs because you won't be able to climb, and we'll put in a bathroom upstairs for me, okay?"

So here they'll be, two oldish women, disabled (in this vision) only in reasonably painless and compensatory ways, looking after each other as well as they can, being as kind as they are able about each other's frailties and oddities. Arguing, of course, and even feuding on occasion, but also joking and watching television and pointing out bits to each other from newspapers and books, and looking forward to Lizzie's visits home. By then they'll surely have given up men (or been given up) and they'll probably talk a lot about the past. Well, there'll be a lot of past to talk about by then. They'll make coffee for each other in the mornings, and tea and popcorn in the evenings. Occasionally they'll have friends for dinner, or guide each other out to restaurants. Some (which?) members of their tiny respective families may visit for a few days at a time, but mainly it'll be Frannie and Susannah, just the two of them.

It'll be great when Lizzie comes visiting with her friends, lovers, husbands, children — all her own life and plans, which Susannah imagines will be grand ones. She and Frannie will look forward to those visits, entertaining themselves with plans for food and outings and conversations. They'll talk loudly, and also in whispers, and presumably with laughter.

For a few hours each time, Lizzie will have to break away to go see Teddy and his other family.

Anyway, that picture of her and Frannie is quite pleasing, by and large, and complete with flaws, which gives it that important touch of realism. Just two companionable, familiar women, sisters of sorts, taking care as best they can.

Of course they'll have to be careful not to get ingrown and dull, or timid. They'll pursue many interests, although probably those interests will be, necessarily, the sedentary sort. They will also maintain some kind of order. Not being poor, they'll have a cleaning woman — no, better, a delicious young man with golden skin and a lovely tight ass — to come in and keep the place in shape. Make sure they don't end up burying themselves, like those other sisters, beneath whatever obsessions they may have by then.

For the moment at least, it sounds pretty good.

Lizzie is passing along another clipping, asking something. "Say again, honey?"

The story is something to do with a crazy stewardess, a hijacking. "I said, do you think she really heard her parents' voices, or did she make that up?"

Susannah scans the story quickly. "Oh, I think she heard them, all right. But either way, poor woman."

All histories, after all, must be partly true and partly false. There may be facts, but there are also misinterpretations and expectations and missed opportunities, all that excess that gets steamed away in memory, leaving behind a hard, indissoluble residue.

Not quite indissoluble, perhaps. She does seem to have tears in her eyes — and why not? They may be sentimental, but they're also for hard-edged loss. And they are a kind of mourning for her future, all those losses and joys that are both foreseeable and unknown.

It seems to her that Lizzie regards her in a pleased and grateful way — just for a moment of paying attention, a sentence, or for hardly visible tears? — before turning back to her stories.

How silly, all this drama, in a way. Life goes on (the sort of thing her mother would say). It goes on until it just doesn't any more.

It does seem to be a matter of the small things: an emphasis on the rich, sad, terrible, joyful, and irretrievable details, all the stories and voices and moments of touch. They may have separate wonders of their own, but they do also add up finally to a few enormous things. Like death, like love.

All extremely curious.